SURRENDERING TO THE HIGHLANDER

"If I kiss you," he whispered.

"I know and I don't care."

And no longer did Crevan. *Right and wrong be damned,* he thought as he placed a hand on the back of her neck and laid a kiss on her mouth that was so soft, so beautiful, they both trembled. Slowly, he parted her lips and drew her in to him, seeking all the passion that she had to offer. Her body pressed against him, snuggling against his chest. A deep groan of satisfaction escaped his throat.

He pulled her even tighter against his torso, straddling her legs over his powerful thighs as he untied the laces to her gown. Raelynd bit her lip upon the onslaught of wet desire and a small whimper escaped her lips. The growing need to touch and be touched by him was one unlike she had ever known.

And in that moment, Raelynd knew he was the only man she would ever give herself to. . . .

Books by Michele Sinclair

THE HIGHLANDER'S BRIDE

TO WED A HIGHLANDER

DESIRING THE HIGHLANDER

THE CHRISTMAS KNIGHT

TEMPTING THE HIGHLANDER

HIGHLAND HUNGER
(with Hannah Howell and Jackie Ivie)

Published by Kensington Publishing Corporation

Tempting The Highlander

❧ THE MCTIERNAYS ❧

Michele Sinclair

ZEBRA BOOKS
KENSINGTON PUBLISHING CORP.

http://www.kensingtonbooks.com

ZEBRA BOOKS are published by

Kensington Publishing Corp.
119 West 40th Street
New York, NY 10018

All Kensington titles, imprints, and distributed lines are available at special quantity discounts for bulk purchases for sales promotion, premiums, fund-raising, educational, or institutional use.

Special book excerpts or customized printings can also be created to fit specific needs. For details, write or phone the office of the Kensington Special Sales Manager: Attn. Special Sales Department. Kensington Publishing Corp., 119 West 40th Street, New York, NY 10018. Phone: 1-800-221-2647.

Zebra and the Z logo Reg. U.S. Pat. & TM Off.

ISBN-13: 978-1-4201-0856-9
ISBN-10: 1-4201-0856-5

First Printing: September 2011
10 9 8 7 6 5 4 3 2 1

Printed in the United States of America

To my dear friend Carrie,
who was there for me

I thank you from the bottom of my soul

Prologue

1310, Caireoch Castle

Raelynd silently both cursed and thanked the large crowd in the Great Hall that made her escape difficult, but possible. Ironically, they all had come to watch and cheer for her as she chose one of the men her father had carefully selected to be her groom. She had stayed long enough to confirm her father's assertion that all were fine-looking men and they were undoubtedly able soldiers, but not a one was interested in her. And why should they be? They did not know her nor she them. Greed had motivated their supposed interest in her, craving appetites to become the next Laird Schellden. Fortunately, her sister had finally come to her rescue. Mistaken identity was a taxing consequence of being a twin, but tonight, it allowed her presence to be seamlessly replaced at the head table without anyone aware.

Making her way out the Hall's back entrance, which led to the buttery and the kitchens, she was seen and recognized by many servants, but they knew to remain silent. To them, her popping up unexpectedly in places where nobles normally would not venture was no different than any other night. Raelynd and her sister often caused mischief using their physical similarities to relieve their boredom. And with an overly indulgent father and their mother dying when they were only twelve, there was no one to intervene and teach them otherwise.

Sticking her head out the kitchen door, Raelynd quickly scanned the small bailey and let go a long sigh. There were a few soldiers and clansmen mulling around but they numbered less than a dozen. By the way they were staggering, they were on the verge of passing out and would be unable to remember anything. Straight ahead held the entrance of the one place in the castle that might serve as a potential refuge.

With a grimace, Raelynd lifted up the hem of her bliaut and dashed across the courtyard to the closer of the castle's two large round towers. Darting inside and out of sight, she leaned back against the cool stones and closed her eyes. "Courage, Lyndee," she said aloud, reminding herself that this was the one place no one would look for her. Taking a large gulp of air, Raelynd forced her reluctant limbs up the narrow, winding, four flights of stairs until she reached the top.

Pressing her hand against the heavy wooden planks that led to the outside, she paused, debating which was worse—the cramped damp space of the tower staircase or the high view that came with open air. Making a decision, she carefully pushed open the door and poked her head outside. The night breeze whipped through the battlements, freeing a lock of her tawny-colored hair and flicking it across her eyes. Raelynd tucked it back behind her ear and then hugged herself, reconsidering her plan.

"Where is she?" came a muffled grumpy bellow from somewhere in the Great Hall as the music and clapping suddenly ceased.

Raelynd bit her bottom lip at the sound of her father's stinging question she knew was directed at her sister. But Meriel was the expert at handling her father. The sounds of the Hall's doors repeatedly opening and closing as people went in and out could mean many things, but Raelynd knew her father had ordered his soldiers to look for her. And once found, she would be forced to return to the festivities and her supposed destiny. Why couldn't her father understand that neither she nor her sister was interested in marriage?

More shouts. Taking a deep breath, Raelynd stepped out onto the tower floor and shuffled as close to the battlement's edge as she dared, balancing her fear of falling with her need to see. Glancing around a crenel, she verified the accuracy of her guess. Soldiers were emerging from the Great Hall, several of whom she recognized as being eager, potential groomsmen. Groaning, she squeezed her eyes shut and rested against the uneven stones, wishing she was as good at deflecting her father's plans as her sister was. In very few areas would Raelynd ever consider Meriel stronger than her, but when it came to handling their father, her sister was the expert, easily ignoring anything she did not find desirable.

After a minute, the shouts died and Raelynd reopened her eyes. Her heart came to an immediate and abrupt stop. She was not alone. As she should have guessed, someone was on duty manning the tower.

A male figure was across from her, hidden within the shadows and leaning against a precipice, looking up at the stars. Based on his bulky silhouette, the man resembled the type of suitor her father had selected to woo her. Debating how she could sneak back down before being seen, the dark figure shifted and returned Raelynd's unavoidable stare. She blinked. Now that he wasn't bending over, she could discern his real height. Whoever he was, he was enormous.

The shadows hid all but a few physical details. His gaze, however, pierced the darkness. His eyes were examining her, and Raelynd felt suddenly exposed. It was as if he had the ability to peer down into her soul, her true self, and was deciding if she were indeed worthy.

A crisp, angry shout from below caught his attention and the momentary bond was severed. His chin jutted toward the opening in the battlements. "Your suitors are looking f-for you." The voice was deep, silky, and unfamiliar.

"Are you going to tell them where I am?" Raelynd asked, and hugged herself even tighter.

"As that w-would bring them here, I had not planned on it." The mocking tone made it clear he was serious in his desire to be alone, but also that he was not upset with her presence. Raelynd released the breath she had been holding and ordered herself to relax.

"May I ask something that might be considered overly bold?"

Her question brought forth a deep laugh, not loud enough for anyone in the courtyard to hear, but of ample volume to convey that he knew of her—what she called daring, but her father deemed audacious—personality. "If you'd like."

Raelynd took a half step forward. "Are you one of them?" she asked, gesturing down to the growing number of men searching the grounds below. "My suitors, I mean."

"And if I w-was?"

Raelynd cocked her head and peered into the shimmering eyes that had held hers so easily just a few minutes ago. Almost immediately she recognized her question as foolish. If he were a suitor, he would not be escaping the crowd, but participating in it. So what was he doing up here? Perhaps he, too, was evading someone. "Are you already married then?"

Crevan choked. "No," he blurted out. Every soldier who spent any time training with Laird Schellden knew of his beloved twin daughters, so Crevan had assumed Raelynd had also been aware of who he was. But he was wrong, for if she did, she would have never asked him that particular question.

"Why? Do you not wish to be?"

The inquiry Raelynd posed was sincere, but far from new. His sister-in-law had been verbally dancing around the concept of his getting married for the last couple of years. He could hear Laurel now. "Your elder brothers have found wedded bliss, do you not wish for the same thing? Come now, Crevan, you are young, but if you are ever to marry you must at least begin to look. You are not even pretending to try."

Truth was, he did want the deep love his brothers had discovered. They had not only found passion, but an unwavering friend. But that type of relationship was never likely to be his. If he ever did marry, it would not be from emotional compulsion. "Perhaps someday," he finally answered.

"Not me," Raelynd huffed, moving just a fraction farther away from the tower's side.

Crevan suppressed a chuckle. Taking over guard duty for a few hours was turning out to be far more interesting than he had planned. "Is that w-why you are here? To hide?"

Raelynd nodded. "No one will ever look for me up here. I do not like heights and this is one of the places Father refuses to light the torches."

Crevan leaned back, finding himself surprisingly at ease with the boldest of Laird Schellden's twin daughters. "Light only alerts those on the ground how many are on guard and w-w-where, but I w-will light them if you w-wish."

Raelynd's jaw tightened. "Did you not hear what I said?" she snapped, fighting to keep her voice soft. "I want to *hide*, not announce my whereabouts." She did not actually add the words "you fool" but her thoughts were reflected in her expression, clear for all to see.

Crevan shrugged, unperturbed. "I shall leave you then."

Raelynd waved a hand to stop him, just as he suspected she would. "No, wait. I, um—" She paused, desperately searching for a reason to keep him from leaving her alone while up so high. "What were you doing . . . before I interrupted?"

He appraised the young girl before him. At sixteen, people thought Raelynd Schellden, with her dark gold hair and green and amber flecked eyes, a beauty and Crevan agreed that she would someday become one. For him, however, it was her indomitable spirit that made her attractive. Luckily, her youth also made him immune. "Looking at the stars," he finally answered.

"The stars?" Raelynd repeated as she scrunched her brows and looked up at the night sky. She had seen them many times, but stargazing? She had never understood the appeal. "Why?"

"It helps to clear my thoughts," he replied, wishing that tonight it had worked. Unfortunately, he had not found the peace and solace the heavenly objects usually brought.

The evening's party had originally been planned to observe Schellden's twin daughters turning sixteen, but over the past few days it had evolved into more than just a birthday celebration. His eldest brother, Conor McTiernay, had returned victorious from battle, helping King Robert's forces ward off a second invasion led by England's newest earl, Piers Gaveston. And Rae Schellden, the McTiernay clan's closest neighbor and ally, had practically demanded the privilege of welcoming Conor home.

All night Crevan had heard the praise for his fraternal twin brother, Craig, and how well he had managed the clan affairs while their eldest brother was fighting in Perth. It mattered little that the responsibility should have been given to both Craig *and* Crevan, since both had an equal claim to the right of temporary chieftain. Yet, it was Craig who Conor had, without any discussion, placed in charge. And why shouldn't he have selected Craig? Unlike himself, Craig could talk without a stammer. He could easily address the masses. And yet, no one knew that Craig would have mishandled the responsibility if Crevan had not been in the background, listening, advising, and basically directing all the work and decisions.

On the battleground, his brother was fearless and resolute, but when it came to the livelihoods of his fellow clansmen, Craig was continually hesitant to the point of inaction, fearing an incorrect or harmful decision. So Crevan had managed the clan covertly. Not until Conor's return had he realized just how much he had enjoyed the position of leadership. But with three capable elder brothers and the unspoken title as fourth son going to his twin, the likelihood of his inheriting the McTiernay lairdship was extremely slim. And with his speech impediment, Crevan was under no illusions about any chances of wooing a noblewoman and marrying into such a title.

"Never let anyone determine your f-future, my lady."

Raelynd huffed and crossed her arms. "I don't intend to. Not my father, not anyone. I bet you find that shocking."

Crevan took in a deep breath and sighed. "I f-find that I am jealous."

She stared at him and determined that he was serious. "Why? You are a man. Can you not determine your own fate? You do not look so old to me."

Crevan grinned. He hoped not. He was only twenty. "I

was reminded tonight that my f-fate was written f-for me long ago."

"Sounds like it is not a happy one."

Crevan pushed back against the stones behind him and then dusted the dirt off his hands using his plaid. "It is not a gloomy one," he countered nonchalantly.

"Well, I want happiness. Nothing else."

"Then I suggest you f-find w-what w-will give you that happiness and never let anyone s-w-way you from your course."

Raelynd watched the group of her would-be suitors regather and then disperse once again with new instructions. Soon, her father would order the entire castle to be searched, which would eventually include where she was hiding. "My father believes my happiness entails marriage."

"He wants an heir."

Raelynd's head snapped back to glare at him. "That's not cause to marry. I mean would you pledge yourself for life to one person for such a reason?" she demanded.

"It depended. For myself? No. For my clan . . . ? Perhaps."

Raelynd paused. She had thought she had been talking to one of her father's soldiers, but it suddenly occurred to her that the mysterious stargazer might not even belong to the Schellden clan. Stepping forward, she asked, "Who are you?"

Crevan smiled and inched deeper into the shadows. "Just a man who enjoys looking at the heavens."

Raelynd eyed his clothes but could not make out the colors of his plaid. Her father had invited only one other clan tonight, the McTiernays, who had gathered in part to celebrate their latest success. Could this be one of the famous McTiernay brothers? He was definitely not Conor, the clan chieftain, whom she knew she had left below. The next two older brothers were married and no longer lived in the area, but it was possible she was visiting with one of the McTiernay twins. They had come years before, for training, but they had kept their distance and had successfully avoided her and her sister. A fact that had rankled both of them enormously, even to this day.

Against prudence, Raelynd decided not to leave and instead, pointed to the night sky. "Tell me about them."

Crevan suspected that she had figured out his identity. The little he had witnessed of her from afar, Raelynd Schellden was quite intelligent, she just lacked the maturity attained through life experience. "See that one, the bright one?" he asked, moving in behind her and pointing upward so that she could follow the direction of his finger. "It never leaves the sky and it alw-ways lies to the north."

Raelynd nodded, enjoying the sound of his voice. It was strong and soft and made her feel like she was in a bubble, protected from the world's criticisms and expectations. She had never been kissed, nor could she ever remember wanting to be. She had no idea what to expect from an embrace, but if she were to ever learn, a McTiernay was going to be the one to teach her.

"Tell me more, would you?" she pleaded, not wanting the moment to end. But it was too late. Before he could answer, a shout from below revealed that someone had spotted her.

Crevan stepped back. "Your hair gave you away. Best you go down before you get into trouble."

Raelynd turned and moved toward the floor opening. She stumbled and Crevan instinctively grabbed her elbow to steady her, stepping just outside the shadows enough for her to see his eyes.

They were a spell-weaving color of blue. Like brilliant sapphires.

Raelynd knew then that her instinct had been right.

He *was* a McTiernay. One of the twins was rumored to be reserved and rarely seen. The other could supposedly woo a woman with his gaze. And this one, with a single touch and look, had turned her body into liquid and lit her skin on fire. Here stood Craig McTiernay, known to be the most charming of all the McTiernay brothers.

Footsteps climbing the staircase echoed through the opening and Raelynd knew she had to leave. Not only was she about to be found, but she was about to do something foolish. Breaking the connection, she darted around him and quickly descended the tower steps without another word, but not without a promise.

Someday, she vowed to herself, *I will find you again, Craig McTiernay, and when I do, you will be the first to kiss me.* Until then, other men could keep their distance.

Chapter 1

1315, early fall

Raelynd studied her target one last time and bolstered her resolve, remembering her sister's fateful questions nearly two months ago. *Really? Only one time?* Meriel's shock had been genuine. It, however, paled compared to Raelynd's own upon discovering the level of knowledge her supposedly shy and timid sister had of men. *You really should try it, Lyndee. It passes the time and if he knows what he's doing, it can be pleasurable and . . .* Raelynd had stopped listening. Pleasurable? Kissing! The one time she had endured the diversion, it had not been by choice and it had been far from pleasant, let alone enjoyable. She could imagine only one man who might prove to be the exception.

Five years ago, she had encountered him by chance and only for a few minutes, not realizing it would be four more years before she would have another opportunity. But earlier this year he and his brother had agreed to spend several months helping her father train new recruits in an effort to recuperate from some severe losses in battle. Unfortunately, the opportunities she had been hoping for arose with the wrong brother.

Crevan had spent much of the summer months in the training fields, but altogether too often, he found reasons to be closer to Caireoch Castle, regularly retreating in the Great Hall where she preferred to direct servants and give out instructions. The man had found an endless number of things to fault her with, and never failed to lecture her in the most irritating, overbearing, and condescending way. His brother Craig was the opposite. Though she had tried time and again to stumble across his company in a seemingly accidental way, the man had somehow kept his distance, preferring to eat and sleep outside with the men or accepting shelter and hospitality from one of the married soldiers.

Today, Raelynd was determined for that to change. Not only was she tired of waiting and impatient to learn the secrets her sister possessed, Craig was planning to leave next morning.

Harvest had arrived and with it the McTiernays' assistance to her father ended. Tomorrow both brothers would be gone. That made the timing perfect to test Meriel's proclamation. Based on his notorious stance against committed relationships, she was sure Craig would have no sudden intentions of proposing even if Meriel was correct and the kiss was found to be enjoyable by both of them. Besides, everyone knew the McTiernay brothers were good at everything—good fighters, excellent strategists, and undeniably good looking, so they had to be experienced with women. So, if she was going to do the unthinkable and kiss a man, it was going to be with one of the most desirable men available.

Swallowing, Raelynd moved until she was noticeably in front of the crowd and prayed her idea would work. Infatuated young soldiers had chased after her since she could remember and she was an expert at getting them to keep their distance. Trying to get their attention, however, was something altogether foreign.

Craig could feel the strain in his shoulders as he pushed even farther to lean back. He gave a final twist and then threw, letting the spear slide through his fingertips just a moment too late, shortening its arc and intended distance. *"Mo Chreach,"* he muttered under his breath as he saw it fall just short of Hamish's pike.

He held up a hand to the cheering crowd who had come to witness the impromptu games Laird Schellden was holding to celebrate this year's bountiful harvest. Walking up to the long pike, Craig yanked it out of the ground with frustration. Just as he had been releasing his grip, a distinct head of semidark blond hair knelt down to pick something up, practically begging his eyes to stare at her cleavage.

Winding up for a second throw, Craig paused, twisted, and again the same figure dressed in bright blue moved into his line of sight. Her pale hand was dabbing a small white cloth along perfect breasts, as if to cool them from the nonexistent heat. If he didn't know better, he would guess Raelynd Schellden intended for him to miss. Hesitating for just another moment, Craig threw the heavy weapon into the air, this time uncaring of its distance.

As expected, the spear fell significantly short of its target. The crowd snickered and Craig knew it paled to the torment he would undoubtedly receive from his brothers for blundering an event he should have easily won. But he didn't care. Brotherly harassment was a small sacrifice to discover if Lady Schellden's lips were as soft and welcoming as they had looked from a distance. Even better, there would be no expectations afterward.

Everyone knew how the Schellden twins felt about marriage—completely disinterested. They were independent spirits who refused to be pinned down. At twenty-six years of age, Craig not only understood the feeling, but admired it. Freedom was one of life's gifts he was not ready to give up. Not even for a blond beauty.

Ignoring the cackles, Craig headed away from the fields and the boisterous crowd toward the nearly vacated castle grounds. As he suspected, a wisp of blue turned and followed him as he walked by. He smiled. He had not misunderstood.

Not more than ten steps inside Caireoch's nearly abandoned bailey, Craig deftly swiveled behind a wagon and grabbed Raelynd's wrist as he ducked into the shadows. He peered into her hazel eyes, verifying his assumptions were still accurate. Curiosity, anticipation, and willingness shined back at him.

"Kiss me, Craig McTiernay," Raelynd whispered.

"Aye, Raelynd. I intend to."

Raelynd pulled back slightly at the mention of her given name. "Call me Lyndee."

Craig chuckled. He remembered hearing her father grumble something about her trying to change her name. Fact was her parents had believed they would never have children. To be blessed with twins had been a miracle. Knowing a son would never follow, Raelynd had been named for her father, Rae Schellden. Thankfully, she looked nothing like him. Pretty, with long dark gold hair and a willowy frame like her mother, she possessed only her father's sparkling green and gold flecked eyes that dared anyone to stop her from seeking what she wanted in life. And Raelynd had decided she wanted him. Luckily, his time in service to her father had ended that morning, freeing him to enjoy the invitation.

"I think I'll just kiss you instead," he softly murmured into her ear.

As his heated breath caressed her ear, Raelynd felt a shiver run down her spine. *This,* she thought, *this is what I have been waiting for*.

His fingers closed around the back of her head and he leisurely brought his mouth down to hers. Raelynd's breath caught in her throat. His lips were warm, soft and surprisingly agreeable. Perhaps Meriel was right.

Raelynd felt his lips move against her own and she mirrored the action, waiting for the burst of emotion that was supposed to accompany the experience.

Nothing.

Inwardly she sighed with disappointment. At least it wasn't completely unpleasant.

Craig's arms were strong and large and rather than making her feel confined and pinned in, they were somewhat comforting. Perhaps Meriel was right. It wasn't such a bad way to pass the time.

Then his mouth released hers so he could move down and nibble at her bottom lip. It occurred to her that Craig might actually want her to open her mouth. Just before a wave of panic hit her, someone nearby shouted across the bailey. Cool air immediately replaced the spot where Craig's lips had been.

He peered around the back of the wagon and said, "Come on. I know somewhere that should provide us several hours of privacy."

Before Raelynd could either agree or disagree, her hand was clasped in his and she was scurrying behind him, keeping out of sight until they reached the stables.

Before anyone saw them together, he had opened and
closed the doors, closeting them inside.

Just as Craig had predicted, the stables were empty.
"How did you know no one would be here?"

Craig grinned. "The race," he replied.

Like all the McTiernays, he had thick dark brown hair,
which he wore too short to tie back but long enough to
reveal the natural wave it possessed. His eyes were a rich
blue that twinkled when he was happy. Large and strong,
he was incredibly good looking.

Raelynd scuffed one foot on the ground, trying not to
act nervous. Everyone was at the race. Even the stable
masters and their young helpers had left to assist with the
horses and their owners. Her black mare was practically
the only horse left in the stables. "I wanted to ride in it."

"The race? You?"

She nodded.

"Um, I've seen your sister ride. Not a good idea."

Raelynd suppressed a huff. At least Craig had not said
that she was a girl and therefore unable to possess the necessary skills to ride. "I am not my sister. Meriel doesn't
like to ride. She thinks it's dirty and uncomfortable."

Unexpectedly Craig grabbed her waist and twirled her
around in the air. "She's right."

Just as Raelynd was about to argue, he let go, plopping
her onto a bed of clean hay. He fell down beside her and
pulled her body close to his and resumed kissing her lips.
He began to deepen the kiss and this time she resisted.

"It's all right. I promise I won't let it go too far, Lyndee.
I am not about to do anything that will force us into something we both don't want."

Raelynd ordered her body to relax. She had wanted to
kiss Craig and she was finally able to more than achieve
that goal. Unfortunately, it was not until now that she

realized she really did not know how. "I'm glad about that. I just—" But before she could finish, several pieces of hay fell down onto her face and into her mouth, causing her to sputter. Looking up, she saw her nemesis staring down at her.

"Either get busy or be quiet," came the velvety command.

Crevan McTiernay! Of all the people, it *would* have to be him, here, in the stables, spying on them. For the past couple of months, whenever she had sought out Craig, she would find Crevan instead. It seemed that he practically lived in the Great Hall for he was always there whenever she came in, ready to scold, correct, and patronize whenever and however possible. Even at night, he would come to dinner and spend hours debating her skills in running the castle until all others had left the room. The themes to his speeches were all the same—that she had great potential, but it was a shame that she chose not to use it.

Well, right now, here in the stables, kissing Craig, was the one time she absolutely did not want his opinion. She already knew she was lousy at the pastime, but it was also the one thing she had done Crevan had yet to insult. And that was only because it was the single area of her life of which he had no knowledge . . . and never would.

Raelynd removed a piece of straw from her hair and glared up at him. "Why? Are we interrupting your endeavors to practice wrestling?" she taunted, referencing Crevan's poor performance in the sport earlier that day during the games.

"Be careful, *Raelynd*."

That was the last insult. Only this morning, he had been telling her that her attempt to get everyone to call her Lyndee was juvenile and he refused to participate in it. She had argued that her given name was too masculine. Ignoring her logic altogether, he had told her to resign her scheming for his brother and go pretend to be Lady of Caireoch by scolding some undeserving servant.

"Why should I be careful?" she goaded.

"Because it was me for whom he failed that particular wrestling match," came an altogether too familiar feminine voice.

"Meriel!" Raelynd shouted, jumping to her feet to peer over the stable wall. She ignored Craig, who was now leaning back on the hay listening and enjoying himself as the argument unfolded. It was rare to hear Crevan talk, let alone raise his voice and quarrel. And practically unheard of for his brother to do so with a woman.

"What?" Meriel asked ingenuously as she stared up innocently, blinking her eyes. Her face was identical to Raelynd's, so much so that if they wanted to they could change roles and deceive almost everyone. But at any normal given moment, their personalities were so unique and equally strong, they were unmistakably distinct individuals. "We were doing nothing you weren't planning on doing."

A chuckle from behind Raelynd filled the air as Craig's voice floated upward. "Well, you must not have been having as much fun as we were just starting to have; otherwise, you would have been too busy to interrupt us. You a little out of practice there, brother?"

Arching a triumphant eyebrow, Raelynd crossed her arms and grinned at Crevan. He returned the mischievous smile and bestowed a low bow. During which, he seized a large amount of straw in his hand, stood up, and with one adroit move, threw it in her direction.

Raelynd squealed and Craig, also getting a face full of hay, joined her as she dashed around the stall to return the favor. Seconds later, the four of them were racing around the stables as wads of straw went flying through the air. Anger was replaced by laughter as all four tossed and shoved hay onto and into any opening presented. Crevan was a mess. Raelynd was a disaster, and neither could remember having a better time in recent memory.

Rae Schellden stared down at the nearly empty courtyard, his hazel eyes focused on the closed stable doors. He stroked his short white beard, which matched the rest of his—at one time black—hair. The last of the games were taking place now out in the fields and the horse race would begin at any moment if it had not already started. He should be out there, encouraging the participants and celebrating with the victors, but he had a serious problem. One that he had been struggling to resolve until just a few minutes ago when the solution fell into his lap.

"I got another message from the king."

Conor, the only other person in the Great Hall, said nothing. The eldest of the McTiernays and laird to their formidable clan, he was Schellden's greatest ally and in many ways, a close friend despite their age difference. Conor was intelligent, decisive, and rarely offered advice without thought and some basis of reasoning. As a result, Rae trusted the young laird's counsel.

"My nephew, Cyric, is on his way north and will be here either tomorrow or the day after."

"You have little time then," Conor finally said, impassively stating facts they both knew.

"Then you agree with my plan."

Conor pulled out a chair and sat down with a noncommittal shrug. "I find it hard to comment. You are meddling in people's lives."

Schellden shook his head, but continued his gaze at the stable doors. "Not meddling."

"Influencing then."

"But for a good purpose."

Conor shifted in his chair and stretched out his legs. "Only if it all turns out as you hope."

Schellden finally turned around to lock eyes with the one man who knew the details of the plan and the reasons behind them. "But do you think it is possible?"

"Possible?" Conor repeated, crossing his arms behind his head. "Aye, your plan is *possible*. But is it probable? You are one of the best strategists I know, Schellden, but this is no battlefield. We are talking about people and two of them are my brothers. Both happen to be quite perceptive to being manipulated."

"And your wife?"

Conor threw his head back and laughed. "Aye, Laurel could be a challenge. I have no idea how she will respond to this plan of yours but I know that she *will* react in some unpredictable way."

"But will she cooperate?"

Conor stopped laughing as his face took on a look of total incredulity. "Cooperate. No. But I doubt she will be able to keep herself from participating. Best not to tell her anything. If I explain your plan and she thinks you are right, she will most likely support your cause. If she thinks you are wrong, then . . . well . . . But your biggest problem isn't Laurel. It's my brothers."

Schellden looked back at the stables. All four were still in there and if the couples were engaged in what they had been doing when he spied them sneaking inside, he had hope. Never did he believe he would wish his daughters to be caught in such a shameful way, but in truth, it made things easier. Especially, as Schellden knew deep down neither Craig nor Crevan would ever do anything to compromise the two people he loved most in the world. "Do you think your brothers will do as I ask?"

Conor pulled back his legs and leaned forward so that his elbows were on his knees. He clasped his hands. "I cannot say," he answered, his tone turning serious. "I will not interfere with your plans, old friend, for I know you only seek the best welfare for all involved as well as the future for your clan and these Highlands, but do not ask me to be a part of your schemes. I cannot. My brothers have been men for some time. They can make up their own minds and both you *and they* will have to live with the consequences of today's decisions."

Schellden grimaced and after one last look, he walked over to the table, picked up his mug and downed the last of his ale. "That I know all too well. But it has to be done. In the end, the choice to act will remain theirs," he said with assurance.

Conor raised a single brow. "Does that claim include your daughters?"

Schellden's jaw tightened. "I have protected them too much, as evidenced last month when both turned down the last marriage proposal so publicly and in such a way not a man in two hundred miles would ask for their hand in the next ten years."

"I think that was their goal."

Schellden banged his empty mug on the table. "MacDougal's boy was nice!"

Conor shook his head. "A good soldier perhaps, but admit it, even you found him boring." Then, realizing that he was transgressing from a listening friend to an advising one, he threw up his hands in the air and resettled himself against the back of the chair. "But what do I know? When it comes to a sword, I'll have an opinion, but not regarding relationships or people. I'll leave that to you and my wife."

"Well, then I best confront them immediately. Your

brothers could have given me no better opportunity than the one I have now." Schellden waited for a second and seeing that Conor had no intentions of rising and coming with him, Schellden marched to the exit and grabbed the handle. Just before he opened the door, he paused and said, "I know your position on the matter, but can I expect you to be here when I return?"

An enormous grin took over Conor's face. "Aye. Wouldn't miss this for anything."

Schellden examined the four bodies sprawled in the hay of one of the larger stalls. None of them had heard his entry, enabling him to watch the singular commotion without notice. A giggling Raelynd was dancing all around Craig as both were attempting to tackle the other, while his other daughter, Meriel, rolled around in the hay with Crevan engaged in a similar leisure interest. He had expected them to be actively engaged—had even hoped to find them with lips locked—but a hay fight? That was something he had not anticipated. Worse, the *lack* of impropriety was going to make his plan all the more difficult to execute.

Raelynd swung around Craig, who unceremoniously tossed her onto a mound of hay before flopping down beside her. She was about to stand up and attack again, when she froze. "Papa," she spurted, spitting out a piece of straw. "What are you doing here?"

Schellden crossed his arms and stared down at Raelynd and then Meriel, hoping his expression conveyed severe unhappiness. His daughters' eyes darted everywhere but his gaze. Both McTiernays, now aware of his presence, did not feel similar shame and rose to their feet, looking at him with a bemused mixture of feigned innocence.

Craig and Crevan McTiernay had trained under

Schellden as young men several years ago. They had fought with him and his late commander last year at Bannockburn, the hard-won battle that resulted in deep losses. Earlier in the year, the brothers had agreed to assist him in guiding and training new recruits until a new commander could be decided upon.

Fraternal twins, Craig and Crevan McTiernay possessed similar features, but in personality they were unmistakable individuals. An exceptional soldier, Craig's booming and decisive voice grabbed the men's attention and held it. Soldiers listened to him, respected him, and followed his lead without question. But off the field, his wit, quick mind, and merry disposition typically made him the entertainment for any gathering.

Though just as commanding on the battlefield, Crevan interacted with those around him quite differently. Possessing an introspective personality, most believed his quiet demeanor due to his halted speech. But after years of knowing him, Schellden knew such assumptions were shortsighted and unwise. Crevan had accepted who he was long ago and his style of command did not reflect insecurity, but thought, consideration, and firm resolve. With one exception—Raelynd.

With her, Crevan was discomposed . . . though he never let anyone see it. Raelynd was his opposite. She was vivacious and strong minded, but she too often walked without aim. That is unless angered by Crevan. Then she possessed unusual focus and determination.

Schellden finally captured the mortified gazes of his daughters. "Both of you return to your rooms until I call for you."

Then, without pause, he turned to face Crevan and Craig. Two pairs of bright blue eyes returned his stare without qualm. Both men knew they had been caught in a potentially compromising situation, and yet neither spoke a word of apology. The McTiernay brothers were known throughout the Highlands for their ability to outthink their opponents and for their incredible obstinacy.

I can be stubborn too, Schellden reasoned to himself. *I have to be.*

After looking both men in their eyes, Schellden inhaled deeply and said, "Follow me. We have things to discuss."

Crevan glanced at his brother, who mirrored his grimace, and then pivoted to follow Schellden out of the stables and across the bailey. With each step, Crevan replayed the actions of the last half hour against what he knew of his neighbor.

Rae Schellden loved his daughters. Too much in many ways, and Crevan had told him so on several occasions when Schellden refused to address Raelynd's officious conduct with the servants. She and her sister were the man's most precious gifts and since his wife passed away nine years ago, he had become even more protective and indulgent. The close bond between their two clans would have mattered little to Schellden if either Crevan or Craig had done anything wrong, but both women were still innocent and that was clear. Whatever Schellden had in mind, Crevan had no compulsion to capitulate based on what happened in the stables.

Schellden shoved his hands against the large doors of the Great Hall and they swung open. The place was empty with one exception. Crevan nodded at his eldest brother, who was sitting relaxed in a chair across the room. Schellden moved to the chair next to Conor, but stopped before sitting. Crevan and Craig followed him inside, but did not join him at the table.

Schellden's jaw tightened with resolve. "When you leave this room, I intend to announce a double engagement. Raelynd will join with Craig and Crevan is to be with Meriel."

Crevan said nothing. Schellden was laird of one of the most powerful clans in the Highlands and he was accustomed to getting what he wanted. Countless times Crevan had seen him masterfully wield people, bending them to his decisions. Today, however, would not be one of those times. Not on the topic of marriage. The last thing he or his brother would be when they left Schellden lands in the morning was engaged—to anyone.

Crevan glanced at Conor, who just shrugged his shoulders and said, "You are both grown men. You can make your own decisions and need no input or approval from me."

Shifting his gaze from his brother to Schellden, Crevan asked, "W-w-what is the true motivation behind this impromptu marriage decree? W-w-why do both your daughters need to suddenly be engaged and to us?"

Schellden's hazel eyes soberly returned the royal blue stare and with a serious tone that reeked of foreboding, replied, "Cyric is due to arrive tomorrow and he is not coming for a visit."

Crevan held the stare and after several seconds, exhaled the deep breath he had been holding. "So King Robert w-w-was being sincere last summer."

Craig swung around to glare at his brother. "Just what happened last summer and *who is Cyric*?"

"Cyric is my nephew," Schellden explained calmly, and yet the weight of his words conveyed that Cyric was much more than a nephew—he was a burden. "My only nephew and King Robert intends for him to be the next Schellden laird upon my death."

"But why?" Craig asked, mystified. "Why would the king desire an outsider to oversee one of his largest and wealthiest clans?"

"Because the Schellden army is just that—large and critical to the king's future needs. *And* he doesn't consider Cyric an outsider. Though he was raised by his mother in the Lowlands, he is my brother's son and therefore a Schellden and a Highlander by birth. The king thought it time to ensure the unity of this clan, and he is achieving that end with the only male heir. And in that, he is right."

Crevan moved over to the table and leaned back against its edge. "Remember Ian Lainge?" He directed the reminder to Craig, whose face suddenly transformed with understanding.

Just before the Battle of Bannockburn, Ian, laird of one of the larger Lainge clans and armies, died unexpectedly with no presumptive male heir. His three daughters had quickly married into other clans for reasons of security and the Lainge lands ended up being divided amongst their new husbands. The split killed the strength, numbers, and leadership of the once strong and deadly Lainge army.

With Schellden's twin daughters unmarried and no definitive heir, the Schellden clan was similarly vulnerable. All knew Robert I's desire to free Ireland from English rule, which meant more battles lay ahead. And while the king had not yet called upon the McTiernay or Schellden clans for support, it would eventually happen and the new ruler expected all of his clans and their armies to remain strong. That included securing their futures. And since neither Raelynd nor Meriel had found a man worthy for marriage, the king had selected one for them. Their cousin.

"Cyric is not the solution," Crevan replied quietly. He had met the man briefly while visiting court after the successful spurning of the English from Scotland's soil. Looking at him, no one could doubt that Cyric had Schellden blood in his veins, but his height and build were the only Highlander traits he possessed.

Schellden sighed and nodded in agreement. His younger brother, Abhainn, had left years ago to fight for Scotland's freedom and soon afterward had met and fallen in love with a wealthy Lowland noblewoman. But his desire to follow Robert I on his campaigns caused Abhainn to be absent during much of his son's childhood. Upon his return, Abhainn had found the lad weak and pampered due to excessive coddling by his mother. Shamed, Abhainn had avoided his son, only exacerbating the boy's sensitive temperament—something Schellden had personally witnessed. "I have met Cyric briefly on several occasions, and while he is not unintelligent, he is soft."

"The w-word you w-want is pathetic," Crevan mumbled under his breath, remembering his one encounter with the man. Robert I had gathered members of key clans together and Cyric had been included. Many Highlanders had wondered why since Cyric had never taken a step onto a battlefield. Crevan had the misfortune of sitting near him and had endured several hours of hearing the man complain and whine about everything from his uncomfortable, cramped accommodations to the coolness of the weather. The idea of such a useless person becoming his neighbor sent a shiver down Crevan's spine.

Schellden grimaced, neither agreeing nor disagreeing with Crevan's assessment. "Cyric intends to marry one of my daughters. All know that whoever marries Raelynd will be the next Schellden laird, but if she refuses and Cyric instead marries Meriel, he will have an excellent argument for inheriting my title, even if Raelynd eventually does wed."

"Neither of them seems very w-w-worried about the possibility," Crevan surmised. "I assume that is because they don't know about Cyric's impending arrival."

"Why not?" Craig barked as he threw his hands up in the air and began to pace in frustration.

"I don't expect either w-w-would react w-well to the idea of being f-forced into marriage . . . or an engagement," Crevan answered, making it clear that he fully understood what Schellden was intimating.

"Aye, they wouldn't," Schellden confirmed. "But if they were both engaged to a very powerful ally, then no one—not even the king—would interfere."

Craig stopped his pacing and looked Schellden in the eye. "An engagement would change nothing if marriage did not follow. Even if Cyric were so easily fooled, upon learning the truth, the man would return and seek his rights."

"True, unless by the time the engagement was called off, Cyric was found to be unworthy of becoming a Highland laird," Schellden countered, returning Craig's stare. "King Robert is trying to ensure the longevity of this clan, not its ruin. If I can disgrace Cyric as a leader, he would not be able to return and reclaim his inheritance when he learned the marriages did not take place."

Crevan crossed his arms, but continued to lean up against the table. "You w-w-want time."

"Aye. Just a few weeks. Something only you and Craig are in a position to give me."

Craig shook his head. "No one would believe it!"

"In that you are right," Schellden agreed, "if Raelynd and Meriel remained *here*. All at Caireoch know them both too well. But if they left this afternoon, with you, under the guise of seeking Laurel's help to prepare for their wedding, no one outside us four would know the truth. Once I prove my nephew's incompetence, I promise to seek more appropriate suitors to address Robert's concern."

Craig grumbled skepticism under his breath and resumed his pacing.

"They w-w-won't cooperate. Raelynd especially," Crevan said evenly as he watched his brother march back and forth furiously, feeling the same agitation but holding it in. For years, Crevan had practiced emotional control and though people often thought him remote, even dull, it enabled him to think clearly in times of great stress. And right now, he needed to consider all the sides and ramifications to Rae Schellden's request.

If he and Craig were to agree to such a plan, Crevan could imagine the reaction of his clan, and one sister-in-law in particular. Disbelief. Unless they were convincing and steadfast in their claims, rumors would spread back to Cyric, who would most likely demand his rights given by Robert I.

"They *will* cooperate," Schellden refuted. "And they will do so *without knowing why*. I have indulged my daughters for years and as a result, they are fiercely independent. They are also inexperienced and don't understand that they cannot just say no to the king. And they would try. The only solution is for them to leave, with you, and they won't if they know the truth about Cyric."

Normally, Crevan would never entertain such a request, but the risk of Cyric as the next Schellden chieftain could be disastrous for not just Rae's people, but that of many western Highland clans. Alliances would not easily transfer over to someone who had never lived in the Highlands nor followed their ways—even if Highland blood did run in Cyric's veins. Still, Crevan was not about to sacrifice his life and future by actually marrying.

Meriel was beautiful and sweet and while he was attracted to her on a superficial level, Crevan could never see himself desiring her beyond a few kisses. And falling in love with her—with anyone—was not something he could envision happening. The love he had seen between his parents and that his elder brothers had for their wives had never once afflicted him on any level. Craig had been smitten several times, but Crevan had never sparked with anyone. He doubted he could.

"Just f-for a f-few weeks," Crevan said.

Schellden nodded. "A month at most."

Craig must have been thinking similarly. "I won't get married, Schellden," he stated, and there was no mistaking the seriousness behind his words.

"Of course not!" Schellden snapped. "I'm not asking you to! You four just need to pretend to be engaged for a month and then devise a reason to abruptly end it. I'm asking for time, not a life promise, not even a handfast."

"And if things don't go according to plan? What if Cyric *is* found to be capable?" Craig challenged.

"Then he will marry Raelynd, or Meriel if he prefers. And you will have a foreigner as a partner and ally."

Craig returned Rae's glare, his jaw rigid. "Just so you understand that is preferable to marriage."

Crevan glanced at Conor, who had refused to engage in the conversation. His eldest brother's posture was relaxed as he sat outstretched in the chair with his hands cupped behind his head. But his knuckles were white. Something more was not being said, but what it was Crevan could not fathom and asking would be pointless.

"W-w-we w-will do as you ask, but in a month, the f-farce is over. Raelynd and Meriel come home and our role is done," Crevan stated for both himself and his brother, who he knew would lean on him for the final decision.

Craig nodded and added, pointing at Schellden, "But you will have to deal with Laurel when she discovers the sham."

Conor shifted in the chair at the mention of his wife. Everyone present knew Laurel would not be pleased to learn that two women's lives were being manipulated.

"I will take care of Lady McTiernay as well as the king," Schellden assured them.

Crevan pushed himself off the table and stood upright. "O-o-ne last thing. If it becomes necessary, I w-w-will tell them about Cyric."

Schellden's face deadened and a coldness took over his expression. Very few challenged him on a decision. "*Only* if necessary."

Crevan nodded and glanced at Conor, who was studying Schellden incredulously. Again, it felt as if a secret lay between the two beyond what had been discussed. Crevan knew he had been carefully guided to make his current decision. Rae Schellden was a master at covertly directing circumstances and people to achieve his goals, but not until today had Crevan become one of Schellden's prey. The man had been honest with his reasons for wanting a false engagement, but Crevan suspected there was more. Much more.

Unfortunately, after knowing the laird for several years, Crevan knew those reasons would not become apparent until Schellden wanted them to be.

Chapter 2

Cyric Schellden winced as another thornbush scraped his leg and bit back a curse as the warm blood trickled down the cold skin of his calf. He disliked the bitter mountain wind and the perpetual dampness that seemed only to grow as their small group proceeded north. Most of his life, he had spent in the Lowlands near and around Ayr. Until now, the farthest he had ever ventured north was Strathaven. That trip had also been miserable and cold and had ended any compulsion to travel north again. Only a missive from the king offering Cyric a chance to gain the one coveted thing that had eluded him throughout his life could have persuaded him otherwise.

One of the two Highlanders traveling with him waved a finger at the small gash on Cyric's leg. "Do you need to stop?" he asked without any effort to hide his mockery.

Cyric fought back a haughty snicker and said through gritted teeth, "I do not."

He knew both men held little respect for him. Few Highlanders did and Cyric was fully aware as to why. He was a Highlander by blood but disagreed with many of their customs, preferring the comfort his upbringing had allowed. Cold was not something to be endured but averted with solid walls, a roof, and a decent fire. Pain was not to be sought but avoided. The few times he had encountered any northern clansmen had only confirmed that his father's people had little in common with him and this trip was proving to be no different.

"How much farther?" Cyric inquired, and then quickly prepared himself for the scorn he knew the question would bring.

The first time he had asked the distance to Schellden lands his face must have conveyed every emotion he was feeling about the length of their journey, and none of them were good. He was unused to traveling such distances and in uncomfortable conditions, so he thought it natural to stop often and address minor injuries or just rest from being on horseback for so many hours at a time. The two Highlanders who were assigned to be his guides had made clear their opinions—all derisive. If they had been people of importance, their stinging judgments might have carried some influence, but as they were merely soldiers, Cyric held their estimation of little value.

"We could have been there today," answered the taller and darker haired of the two guides.

Glimpsing the man's accompanying sneer, Cyric once again wished the escorts traveling with him belonged to the Schellden clan. Then they would be forced to respect him. And it was attaining that very elusive quality that had compelled Cyric to agree to travel north. It certainly was not the desire to be a laird, even if the Schellden clan was as large and powerful as it was purported to be. He had spent enough time in the company of his maternal grandfather to know just how burdensome the position was with petty decisions. But when Robert I's message came with the possibility of becoming chieftain of his very own family

line, Cyric had quickly agreed. It might be the one way—
the only way—to get his father to acknowledge him as a man.

"You didn't answer my question," Cyric finally countered.

The younger of the two men was about to unleash an insulting Gaelic retort when his comrade kicked him in the shin with a warning. Then with the same dead expression the leader had maintained during the length of their trip, he turned to Cyric and said, "Tomorrow. By midafternoon if you are able to wake up and leave *early*." He nudged his horse's hind flanks and was soon out of speaking distance. To Cyric's relief, his friend immediately followed.

Cyric didn't even know their names. He had asked once and the response he received had been less than friendly. What neither man realized was that while Cyric rarely spoke in Gaelic, he did understand it. His mother was the daughter of a laird from a wealthy clan and as her only son, he had access to the best instruction his grandfather could offer, which included languages. And since his father was a Highlander, Gaelic was one of those he had been forced to endure learning.

Cyric had planned to apply his education in other ways. His father's unique relationship with Robert I as well as Cyric's close proximity to the king had provided Cyric with many opportunities to mingle and interact with nobles and leaders and listen to their problems. The intricacies of diplomacy and the politics around such decisions fascinated him. Nothing was more exciting than mediating between warring parties, whether they be neighbors, clans, or even family. But the moment he agreed to ride north all dreams of pursuing such a career had come to an abrupt end.

A half hour after the sun had set, the leader of their three-person group pointed at a small clearing, indicating where they were stopping for the night. Cyric grimaced.

Another cold night on the ground. In the past hour, he had seen at least three cottages. He suspected any one of them could have housed them for an evening, but neither Highlander had indicated any interest in imposing on someone for even a hot meal.

Knowing better than to argue, Cyric slid off his horse, bent over to stretch his hamstrings and then stood back up, rubbing his lower back. His only comfort was knowing that this would be the last night he would have to spend outside and with men who held him with little regard. By tomorrow evening, he would be in a position of power and his father would finally have to acknowledge him as a man.

While his father had never actually disclaimed him, Cyric knew, even when he was young, that he was a disappointment. For years, he had pretended otherwise, telling himself that while his father was away, he spoke with pride about his son to his friends. And as soon as his mother had let him, Cyric had trained and practiced with the sword, studying with some of the Lowland's finest personal trainers. As a result, he took great satisfaction in being considered a master by his peers. Unfortunately, they did not include his father.

At nineteen, Cyric learned that Robert I had journeyed back to Ayr to recapture his childhood home. Turnberry Castle had been the very place where Cyric's parents met and where his father had become lifelong friends with the Earl of Carrick and the future king of Scotland. Hearing of the battle being waged, Cyric had left, against his mother's wishes, to join the fight. But he had arrived too late. Robert I had achieved success and had driven the English away once again.

The look his father had given him when he galloped in, sword drawn, onto the celebratory scene was one Cyric would never forget. A look of deep shame—as if he had arrived late on purpose. As if he was a coward coming to reap the rewards of someone else's bravery. Never again did Cyric attempt to join a fight or a battle. And yet the one thing he desired above all others was the opportunity to replace that searing memory. The next time his father stared at him it would be with pride.

Two weeks ago, that opportunity had finally arrived and even though it meant traveling in cold weather, being uncomfortable, and marrying some god-awful Highland girl, Cyric vowed to himself that he would be the next Schellden laird. He would oversee one of the most powerful clans in the western Highlands.

And in doing so, he would at long last gain the admiration of his father.

Chapter 3

Crevan followed his brother outside so they could talk privately in the courtyard. Normally the bailey teemed with activity, but today only a few people were mulling about handling responsibilities that could not be dismissed or delayed to watch the games.

Craig shielded his eyes and looked up at the sky to see where the sun was. "What now?"

"W-we f-find the w-women and prepare to leave."

"That's what I was afraid you were going to say. I'm still not too sure why we agreed to this," Craig growled, not expecting a response. Then seeing a squat, rotund woman exiting the kitchens, he called out, "You! Can you point me in the direction where I might find Ladies Meriel and Raelynd Schellden?"

A slight brow raised and her red chubby cheeks plumped up with a mischievous smile. "Aye, I expects you do. I suppose I can tell ye both since I hears ye are to be married." Then with a chubby finger, she pointed at the keep adjacent to the gatehouse. "Third floor," she added before waddling off, but just before she was out of earshot, she began to laugh. No malice was in its tone, but it sent the same sense of foreboding Crevan had been feeling since he saw Schellden standing over him in the stables less than an hour ago.

"How did she know?" Craig whispered in disbelief. "How *could* she know? *We* just agreed."

Crevan gestured at the kitchens from which the woman had come. It and the buttery were adjacent to the Great Hall. "Schellden is w-wasting no time."

"*Mo Chreach!*" Craig muttered, and started to march toward the entrance to the keep the woman had indicated. "Nothing is worth this."

Crevan took the lead climbing up the staircase. They had encountered no one in the keep, but based on the well-used mat outside the door to the third floor bedchambers, that fact was far from typical.

After giving the thick wooden door a single knock, he realized he had no idea how he was going to impart their father's news to either female. Rae Schellden should be the one delivering such tidings, not them. Bolstering himself, Crevan knocked again, this time much stronger.

"Come in, Ula!" Meriel sang out from the other side.

Craig banged the door with his foot and it swung open. A spacious room occupying at least half of the keep's third floor came into view. Crevan stepped around Craig and immediately understood what shocked his brother into stillness. The shared bedchamber proved that both women might be identical in appearance, but possessed very different personalities. How they could live amicably sharing the same space was inconceivable.

On one side, the room was tidy, well managed, and while not sparse, not overly decorated. The other side was a disaster, with material strewn everywhere and multiple chests all wide open with a mixture of gowns and undergarments tumbling out. Contraptions of varying size and shape blocked the few potential paths winding through the chaos.

Sitting on the floor in the middle of the mess was a surprised Meriel. "So, did you explain everything then?" Her and Raelynd's eyes flew to Craig as he usually was the vocal one during social gatherings.

Craig crossed his arms and tucked his hands into his armpits. "Well . . . we, um, we . . . did meet with your father. . . ."

Raelynd stepped forward, her brows furrowing as her green and gold flecked eyes bored into Craig. Crevan knew her mind was whirling, for it was how she looked when working on a problem. This time, she did not like the conclusions to which she was arriving. "And?"

Crevan observed Craig gulp and for a brief moment he felt for his twin brother. The most outgoing of the entire McTiernay family, Craig was quite comfortable being the center of attention, but that was in times of merriment. Like the rest of his brothers, Craig preferred using a sword to handle confrontations. Under the pressure of two pairs of hazel eyes, Craig took a deep breath and blurted, "We four are engaged. At least for the next month. And since Crevan and I are going home today, you both are coming with us. So ready yourselves to leave within two hours." Craig glanced over his shoulder. "Did I forget anything?"

Crevan shrugged his shoulders. The explanation was brief and would be poorly received, but it did impart the basic message. He hooked his thumb on his belt as he studied the horror Meriel had made of her room. "Pack only o-o-one bag."

Stunned by the news, Meriel sat unmoving. Raelynd, however, was only temporarily robbed of her voice. "*Forget* anything?" she yelled at Craig. "How about 'no'! Because that is *my* answer. Absolutely not! And since that is something obviously neither of you *men* could manage to say, I will deliver the news to my father myself!"

Crevan's arm snuck out just in time to catch Raelynd from leaving the room. As usual, he had stood by quietly, letting Craig take the lead with the situation, but his brother had only spent a fraction of the time in the Great Hall Crevan had and therefore knew little about Raelynd's fiery temper. Her willful moods were well known throughout the castle along with their eventual success. She managed the responsibilities of the Lady of the Castle not through leadership, but through petulance. For most everyone, it had become easier to just agree. Someone who was familiar with Raelynd's outbursts had to intercede and make clear what was and what was not going to happen over the next month.

Though Raelynd was Craig's supposed intended, Crevan had no problem intervening if necessary. For the next month, Lady Raelynd was going to live at the McTiernay Castle with him and his family, and he was not about to endure—let alone make others suffer—any of her childish tirades.

"No, you will not," he gritted out.

Raelynd tugged her arm to try and gain her freedom, but Crevan just squeezed harder until she looked at him and realized he had no intentions of letting her leave. "F-for the next month, you w-will abstain f-from tantrums and *you,*" he said, glancing over his shoulder at Meriel with his grip still on Raelynd's arm, "w-w-will learn how to put things w-where they belong. F-for the f-first time, your f-father is asking you both to put the clan's interests ahead of your own."

Meriel's jaw went slack. Between Crevan's cutting remarks and his ability to halt Raelynd's outburst—something no one had ever been able to do or dared enough to try—she was in a full state of shock. Raelynd, on the other hand, was far from stunned. She had heard every word and issued Crevan a withering glance that had no effect. "The *clan*?" she bellowed. "The *clan* isn't getting married. Why us?"

Assured that she knew the futility of trying to leave and find her father, Crevan let her arm go. "A far from surprising question coming from you," he accused, ignoring the others in the room. As it always did when he was speaking to just Raelynd, his stuttering disappeared, though he had yet to realize it. "I tell you that your clan is in trouble and needs your support and you act like a little girl and think only of yourself. And as to why you, that we have pledged not to say, mostly because your father does not trust how *you* would react."

The room became instantly silent. Raelynd stood rigid as if Crevan had physically slapped her. Meriel, feeling the need to rally to her sister's aid, jumped to her feet and appealed to Craig. "How can you let him say that to her? How do you expect us to act when you come into our bedchambers and tell us that we are to be wed in a month to men who clearly look on the idea of marriage to us with disdain?"

The sincere entreaty compelled Craig to speak. "But we *aren't* to be married, just engaged," he said softly. "Just for the next month, all are to think the four of us are pursuing marital bliss. Then, when your father has handled a situation he has here, we can tell everyone that we have decided not to go through with the plans and part as friends. So you see? There is nothing to be upset about."

Meriel refused to be so easily persuaded. She looked down at all of her precious materials, tools, and threads. She did not think it possible to live without them for such a long period of time. "But why can we not stay here?"

"At McTiernay Castle my sister-in-law Laurel will be able to help you prepare for the wedding."

"But why?" Meriel pressed. "If there is not going to be a wedding, then why do we have to prepare for one?"

Craig rolled his eyes in frustration. Crevan was once again forced to answer. He calmly leaned against the door frame, which belied his turbulent emotional state, and said, "If you do not, then no o-o-one will believe that w-we are to be married. And you cannot prepare *here,*" he quickly added before she could ask, "because too many here on your f-father's land know you and w-w-would guess the truth."

Meriel stared at Crevan with disgust. "You better find a way to end this marriage because in a month's time you are the last person I will ever wed." A few hours ago both had thought the other to be attractive enough to kiss. Now, each wondered how they were going to muster up the will to pretend to feel something for the other.

Craig, in an effort to decrease the growing tension, laughed and said, "Believe me, Meriel, Crevan and I are even less interested in the idea. Not to you, necessarily," he said, quickly adding, "but to anyone. In a month, if all goes to plan, all four of us will still be wonderfully, delightfully unwed."

Raelynd continued to stare at Crevan, who matched her cold look with one of his own. She arched a brow and argued, "If Father just needs us to be away without causing any questions, why not just say we are going with you for a visit . . . why *marriage*?"

Crevan threw his hands up in the air. "She's your f-f-future bride. You handle her," he mumbled.

Craig, flummoxed as to how to answer Raelynd's simple question, spurted, "You don't need to understand. All you need to do is pack and be ready to leave in two hours."

Crevan knew Raelynd was about to erupt once again. Rather than enduring multiple waves of anger, he decided to give her the rest of the bad news immediately so she could expel all her rage at one time. "Call your maid to help you pack, but know this—she w-w-will not be coming w-with you."

Both women gasped. "But traveling without Father or a chaperone would be highly improper!" Meriel squealed.

"Aye, but the decision stands," Crevan affirmed, and turned to leave. Before he reached the door, he locked eyes with Raelynd. She glanced at her normally unflappable sister, who was becoming increasingly more tense and knew it was in part because of her. Shifting her eyes back to Crevan, she took a step closer and touched his arm.

Crevan stared down into her troubled hazel pools, pleading with him to find another way, to end the farce and her sister's anxiety. It was a selfless act he had not expected. "Trust me," he whispered. "What we four have been asked to do is important, not to just your future, but that of your clan and the Highlanders around you. Your father has an unusual situation that he must take care of and to do so, both of you need to be away for a month. A wedding is the only way he can explain your departure when he has never allowed it before."

Raelynd held his gaze, and after a moment, nodded, but Crevan knew it was not capitulation he received. It was a promise. Raelynd was no doubt silently vowing to get a full explanation of what was behind her father's sudden situation. She wanted to know what was serious enough to convince both McTiernay brothers to agree to the insane idea of marriage.

Craig walked to the door and pulled it back open. "One month," Raelynd said aloud, gaining his attention but still staring at Crevan. "That is all the time you have to end this farce, because if you think I am being difficult now, you haven't seen anything yet."

Crevan began to follow his brother out the door. Just before he left, he turned and gave Raelynd a wink, completely disarming her in a way for which she was not prepared.

"I cannot believe the laird—*your father*—is doing this," Rowena said, sinking down onto Raelynd's bed. With thick reddish brown hair and matching brown eyes, the only thing that kept her from being a true beauty like her twin distant cousins was the smattering of freckles sprinkled over her nose and cheeks. Still, she was undeniably attractive and was the recipient of a constant stream of suitors. Without Meriel and Raelynd nearby to provide interference and constant emotional support, she did not know what she was going to do.

Raelynd went to her chest but before she bent down to open it, she pointed at her friend and said, "You promise to say nothing? No one can know that we are really not to be married."

"I already promised you I wouldn't. I just don't understand why."

Across the room, Meriel sank down onto her favorite chest of odds and ends and said miserably, "Neither do we."

Grabbing a green bliaut, Raelynd placed it beside the rose one on her bed and dithered on if she could bring both with her. She had already selected three other gowns, including the blue one she had put on for travel. One was a deep purple everyday gown and the other was a more elaborate gold one, but the third selection was proving to be more difficult.

"If you cannot decide, I will take it in one of my chests," Meriel offered.

Raelynd, who had been ignoring her sister's sniffles and moans, glanced to the other side of the room and realized exactly what her sister was planning. "Meriel! You cannot take a chest! How will they bring it?"

"*That* is not my problem. And I am not bringing *one* chest. I'm bringing them all."

Raelynd sighed. "I highly doubt it, but I look forward to hearing you try."

A loud thud echoed in the hallway. Raelynd went to see what had made the noise. Swinging the door open, two simple, six-sided, flat-lidded traveling chests that were propped up against the door fell down, nearly crushing her toes. *No doubt placed there by the high and mighty Crevan McTiernay,* she sarcastically thought, and then chided herself. For the silent comment had once again brought to mind the large dark-haired Highlander with snapping blue eyes. An image she did not wish to mentally conjure ever again.

Raelynd hauled one of the chests inside and plopped it on her bed, recalling the seriousness of Crevan's stance, words, and tone of voice. She had no choice but to do what he ordered and explanations as to why were not coming forthwith—yet. She had always needed to understand the decisions that happened around her, and instinctively sought to manage or at least influence them. But after her mother's death, the need to control all things in her life had only grown. Today was the first time she could remember since that horrible day of feeling so powerless.

Only one moment had given her hope. Just before they left, when Crevan had asked her to trust him and she had nodded—he had nodded back. It had not just been a gesture of acknowledgment, but one of gratitude. It was then she had realized that whatever was going on most likely had nothing to do with what happened in the stables or saving their honor, but something—if possible—far more important. When Crevan had mentioned the welfare of the clan, he had not been overplaying the situation to gain her and Meriel's compliance. He had been honest.

Meriel dropped the item she was holding and stared mystified at her sister. "Why are you no longer angry?"

Raelynd was unsure how to respond. She couldn't say, "Crevan winked at me." It made no sense. But there it was. Crevan *had* winked at her and in that moment, the preoccupation of her thoughts changed from anger to curiosity.

Crevan McTiernay, a man known for not communicating, had said more with a simple nod and wink than any other man could have—even his brother.

Men considered her a decoration, something to be desired, and in truth, Raelynd had let them. For months, Crevan had been urging her to be more, but today he had demanded she rise beyond herself. And when she finally did—even though it was just a small head nod—he had acknowledged it. Raelynd never would have guessed his small recognition could make her feel so good. But it did. And she hoped to get that same burst of warmth again by quickly packing as requested.

"I am still angry, but I am not in the mood to be lectured again because I packed too much," Raelynd finally answered, pointing at the second travel case leaning against the door.

Meriel wrinkled her nose and ignored the small carrier. "Well, Crevan can scold me as much as he wants, but I don't care. I have never packed before and don't intend to leave anything important behind."

Raelynd grimaced. Problem was, Meriel was correct. Their father had always shielded them as children, and if possible, became even more protective after their mother's untimely death. Consequently, neither had ever left Schellden lands. When they were younger, they had pleaded to see

more of the Highlands, but with the English's constant—
and often successful—attempts to seize Scottish lands and
homes, their father had been adamantly against the idea.
Now, with the taste of freedom less than two hours away,
Raelynd could feel her nerves start to take hold.

"You think everything you own is important."

Meriel threw a wad of colored thread into the nearest
trunk. "That is because it is. You never know when you
might need something."

"You could pack more in a chest if you would fold your
dresses," Raelynd advised as she watched her sister move
to sit on top of the lid to get it closed.

"No need," Meriel replied as she clicked the lever to
keep it closed. Then with more gravity, said, "I wonder
what is going on with Father. Whatever it is, it has to be
serious. I guess he trusts the McTiernays even more than
I realized."

Deciding on the black-and-gold-trimmed gown, Raelynd folded the garment and grabbed the matching rib-
bons for her hair. "Much more," she agreed, placing the
items in the carrier. Hearing an annoying scraping sound
behind her, Raelynd turned around and gasped.

Meriel had decided to forgo using the smaller chests
and had dragged her large oak trunk next to her bed, into
which she was dumping everything that she had already
packed. Raelynd stared in silence as her sister calmly and
chaotically tossed items into the large container. She knew
she should not have been so surprised. If anyone knew the
truth about her twin sister's penchant for hoarding things
it was her.

Meriel, whom the world saw as a sweet docile creature, was obsessed with weaving and stitching. She enjoyed anything involving a needle and very few could
match her skill. Raelynd never tried. It was a tedious craft

and required dedication to countless boring hours and cramped fingers. Then again, one only had to see Meriel's masterpieces to know that her sister was a talented artist with whom very few could be compared.

Raelynd strolled over to the large trunk, looking at the yarns, needles, and various items haphazardly thrown together. "Good Lord, Meriel. This mess is like your side of the room, cluttered, unkempt, and a complete disaster. It also contains not a stitch of anything personal, such as clothes or a hairbrush," she added as she started rummaging around, pulling out what she deemed unnecessary items.

"Leave my stuff alone, Lyndee," Meriel ordered, and closed the lid, uncaring that she almost pinched the fingers of her nosy sister.

Raelynd straightened and walked haughtily back to her side of the room. "Do you plan on personally dragging that chest to the McTiernay Castle? For I am fairly certain neither brother intends on hauling *that* heavy object with them."

Meriel, realizing her sister spoke the truth, looked to Rowena for support. "I cannot simply leave everything behind!" she wailed.

Rowena, still shocked by the news, replied, "I don't understand how you can be more concerned with leaving behind your precious tapestries than the prospect of marrying someone you don't want to."

"But we *aren't* getting married and if I leave something important behind, *that* will cause me to be miserable," Meriel fretted. "Making us pack in such a short time frame is unfair and unreasonable."

Rowena nodded, agreeing with her cousin's sentiments. Seeing that Raelynd was nearly complete with her packing, she said, "Unless we assist Meriel, she will never be ready to leave."

Raelynd put her hand up to halt her cousin from going

to help her sister. "And just why is that *our* problem?" she asked. "Meriel's situation is not of your making nor of mine. So why should we be the ones to fix it?"

Pasting on a large grin, Raelynd went and sat on a pillowed bench underneath one of the three large windows that let an abundance of light into the room, regardless of the time of day. She unlatched the window and tilted it open, pleased to see Crevan and Craig below talking with one of the stable hands. "Oh, Crevan!" she yelled sweetly, and waited for him to look up. She smiled at his look of annoyance. "Meriel is having difficulty packing and since she is *your* intended . . . it is *your* problem." Hearing his grunt of frustration, she gave him a coy wink and closed the window.

Below Crevan raked his hand through his thick hair and rhetorically asked his brother, "Is this w-what w-we are to expect f-for the next month?"

Craig shrugged. "You might as well go up and find out what Raelynd was talking about if we are going to leave on time. I don't think she was jesting."

Crevan scowled and pivoted toward the keep. *No,* he thought to himself, *Raelynd was not one to make idle threats*. Craig had best watch himself with her.

Entering the room, he immediately spied Meriel sitting in the middle of a mess on the floor looking far from packed. Crevan sucked in his breath and redoubled his vow. Laird Schellden—friend and ally or not—had better find a way to discredit his nephew quickly, because if he didn't, Crevan suspected he would be tempted to hand deliver Cyric his new bride.

But just whom he chose to hand over—Meriel or Raelynd—changed with each passing minute.

Chapter 4

Crevan swung a leg over his horse and sat waiting as the rest of the group mounted and prepared to leave. Three others were coming with them, his eldest brother, Conor, and two McTiernay soldiers who had participated in the games. That made their group totaling seven—two of which were so accustomed to being constantly indulged that the normally easy day and a half ride was going to be anything but quick and painless. And Schellden's departing words only confirmed the hunch.

"You will be fine. Craig and Crevan will see to your safety," Schellden repeated for the fifth time. No one who had ever fought with the man would dream that the fierce warrior could also be an overanxious father. Even Crevan had difficulty believing it, but then never had Raelynd or Meriel ever been out of their father's protection.

Knowing Schellden was emotionally vulnerable to his daughter's pleas of staying at Caireoch Castle, Crevan waited for Meriel to tear up and Raelynd to begin her pleading, but neither woman acted as he would have thought. They simply said their good-byes and pasted on friendly smiles.

Meriel's horse shifted abruptly under her unsteady hand

and Craig reached out to halt the animal's movement. "You seem to have recovered from your packing ordeal," he whispered with a hint of tease.

She flashed him a genuine smile and then waited for Raelynd to finish hugging all she could of the small crowd that had gathered around them. "Good-bye, everyone!" Raelynd shouted out. "We'll be back in a month, but not as we are now . . . as happy, delightful brides!" she added with an overabundance of cheer.

Crevan studied Raelynd's smile, trying to hide one of his own. Her mirth was genuine. She was practically sparkling with hidden enjoyment as she darted from person to person. The secret behind her pleasure he could not fathom, but whatever it was, Raelynd was getting enormous delight from it. Her whole life she had been coddled but that had not suppressed her independent spirit. Though he would never admit it aloud to anyone, her determination was the one aspect of her indomitable character he considered admirable. Of course, that was when he was not completely annoyed by it.

"Congratulations!" a deep voice chimed.

Crevan turned around just in time to see one of Schellden's guards clap Craig on the back. "I hear in a month's time, you will become the next in line to be our chieftain. No longer will it be just us soldiers looking to you for guidance, but a whole clan!"

Crevan watched as the blood drained out of his brother's face and suspected his own cheeks mirrored the same pasty color. The idea of marriage was not something either of them relished, but Crevan's cause for sudden paleness was for a far different, far less honorable reason—envy.

Commanding soldiers was interesting, even challenging, but nothing compared to leading a clan. Such opportunities were few and Crevan knew his chances of permanently holding such responsibility hovered around none. But for the next month, there would be many more comments about Craig's becoming the next Schellden laird. And though in truth Craig was no closer to becoming a chieftain than he, just hearing the congratulatory words was jolting.

Meriel urged her horse to follow her sister's out of the only home she had ever known. A frisson of fear ran up her spine and it reminded her of Craig's strange reaction to the warm wishes he had received just before leaving. True fear had momentarily registered on his face—something she had not thought possible. Others who had witnessed him suddenly go ashen assumed his reaction to be about his impending marriage. Meriel, however, suspected something else was behind the reaction. Craig had been congratulated several other times that afternoon and not once had the idea of marriage caused him discomfort. No, something else spawned Craig's sudden uneasiness and with nothing better to do, Meriel allowed her mind to be preoccupied with the reasons why.

Like any woman with decent eyesight, Meriel had enjoyed the intermittent glimpses of the McTiernay brothers working to rebuild and train the Schellden army along with a handful of other commanders. Not only were Craig and Crevan exceptionally good looking, they had a confidence that truly captivated one's attention. It almost bordered on arrogance, but not quite. Their self-assurance was not born from an overactive ego, but from experience. Until today, Meriel could not recall ever seeing a moment of doubt coming from either of them.

Craig especially.

Like her sister, Raelynd, he had always seemed comfortable as a leader with all the men's eyes on him, but if Meriel had to name the look on Craig's face this afternoon, she would have called it panic. But why?

After considerable effort, Meriel finally convinced her argumentative horse to move closer to her sister. "Lyndee, did you see Craig turn ashen back before we left?"

"No," Raelynd answered with complete honesty. Her attention had been solely focused on his aggravating brother Crevan. She had been so interested in trying to shock him with her amenable behavior that she could not remember even looking at Craig. Fact was, she hadn't even really thought about him until Meriel said something.

"How could you have missed it? He is your betrothed!"

Raelynd rolled her eyes and suppressed the need to remind Meriel that she was not, nor would she ever be, betrothed to Craig. "Tell me, then. Just what was my future husband's expression upon leaving?" Raelynd bid, knowing she had made her point upon hearing her sister's huff.

"Well, I don't think Craig wants to become a laird," Meriel announced quietly so that no one else could hear.

Raelynd furrowed her brow and glanced at her sister. "That is ridiculous. Every soldier wants to lead, and every commander longs for the opportunity to become laird. And *most* lairds would relish the idea of leading an army the size of Father's."

Meriel twitched her mouth and mumbled, "I'm not sure that Craig is like 'every' man."

Raelynd shrugged her shoulders, unconcerned. "It doesn't matter whether he is or isn't as the marriage is not going to take place."

"You are not understanding what I am saying, Lyndee," Meriel protested.

Raelynd turned to stare pointedly at her sister. "I understand perfectly. You do not think Craig wants to be a laird.

I disagree. All men desire power. Especially someone like Craig McTiernay. More than that, it doesn't matter who is right—you or I—as all of this is just a pretense for something that will never happen."

Meriel realized her discovery was of little importance to her sister and probably never would be. Still, the quandary continued to needle Meriel, for Lyndee was right. Most men did desire power, so why didn't Craig?

Yanking on her horse's reins severely, the gentle mount whinnied but slowed, allowing Meriel to eventually fall back alongside Craig, who chose to ride in the rear of the small group.

Craig watched as Meriel struggled with her mount, causing pain to both rider and animal. He wondered how a child of Rae Schellden could be so awkward on a horse. Didn't her father ever teach her how to ride? But even as he asked himself the question, he knew the answer. Schellden, hard and demanding on his men, was dangerously soft when it came to his daughters. The answer was simple. Raelynd had wanted to learn to ride where as Meriel had declined.

"The more you fight the horse, the harder Merry will be to handle," Craig said gently. "Ease your grip. She won't run away."

Meriel issued him a slight smile and then cautiously did as he instructed. Merry, feeling free from the constant pressure of the bit, threw her head up and down several times, but Meriel, with Craig right beside her whispering reassurance, continued to relax her grasp. After a few seconds, Merry calmed and for the first time Meriel did not feel like she was going to fall. "I can't believe that *not* holding on actually makes me feel more in control!" she laughed.

Craig grinned, surprised by Meriel's easy nature, which was so very different than her sister's. Until the hay fight earlier that day, he had believed Meriel to be inordinately shy. But he had been mistaken. She was not timid, just mellow. Her personality did not seek to be noticed, but preferred to relax and let others receive attention.

Now that she was able to focus on something besides not falling, Meriel considered how to broach her question. She finally opted to just ask openly what she had observed. "Which was the random thought that bothered you so much just before we left? The idea of being a laird or the thought of becoming a *Schellden* laird?"

Craig twisted his mouth and forced his hand to loosen its grip on the reins. It was clear that his earlier attempt of outward indifference had failed. Discovering he had revealed his inner turmoil made him feel exposed and he wondered just how many other people witnessed his distress. "Neither," came his terse reply, "especially since neither possibility is in my future."

Normally, Meriel would have been tempted to argue, but the stiffness in Craig's frame she had witnessed back at her father's castle suddenly reappeared. All McTiernays were enormous and Craig was no different. A body of his size and bulk abruptly becoming rigid prompted her to address the underlying uneasiness behind his sudden quiet reserve. "I do not believe anyone else saw your discomfort," she guessed, hoping to lessen the tension growing within him. "And I won't tell anyone. It's your business. I am only surprised. Everyone knows you McTiernays are great leaders. I heard my father speaking favorably of your command over his soldiers several times." She paused and waited for him to respond. When he didn't, she could not resist asking him again, "So why don't you want to be laird?"

Craig forced his face to remain blank. It was the second time Meriel had asked that question and he knew continued denial would not change what she already suspected to be true. "I had the chance to be laird once. For a month five years ago. I discovered then that such a tedious responsibility was not something I would ever desire."

"Why is that a bad thing?"

Craig had never really thought about it. Everyone just assumed he would jump at the chance to become laird. And truth was, if the opportunity did arise, he probably would. McTiernay honor would demand it and he would never shame his brothers or clan, but it wasn't until he had the responsibility temporarily thrust upon him did he realize just how glad he was that such a possibility was remote. For if it had not been for Crevan, quietly sitting by, assisting with the variety of odd questions and tedious decisions that seemed unending, he might have gone mad. Craig knew then that there was a vast difference between commanding a group of soldiers and that of being a laird, and he was one McTiernay who preferred to lead only warriors. But never did he intend for anyone else to know.

And yet one person had discovered his secret. Or at least suspected it. He glanced over at Meriel. How could an overly pampered daughter read his inner thoughts? The idea that she could was more than unsettling.

"I ask you to tell no one, not even my brother."

"Crevan? He doesn't know?"

Craig shook his head. "The possibility never came up before," he replied, but he knew that even if it had he would still have said nothing. No matter how uncomfortable the idea of leading clansmen was to him, it had to be even more alarming to his brother. "Crevan's the quiet type. He prefers to be in the background, which is . . . unfortunate."

"How?"

"When I stood in for Conor and acted as laird for our

clan it was actually Crevan who came up with most of the solutions to the problems that arose."

"Then why not let Crevan pretend to be the next Schellden chieftain?"

"I won't even pretend to do that to my brother. That awful month, he may have come up with the ideas, but not once did he ever step forward or handle the situation personally. He does not like . . . speaking to people."

"So? It's not like he would really become—" Craig's jaw went rock hard and Meriel let her voice trail off as understanding dawned on her. She had known for years how men made her sister uncomfortable and had done all in her power to thwart their attention from Raelynd toward her. And similarly, Raelynd had protected her from the onerous duties of running a castle. Realizing Craig felt a similar protective bond toward Crevan, she sighed, voicing her thoughts aloud. "I guess it is good then that it doesn't matter."

Craig visibly relaxed at the reminder, for while lairdship was a title he never wanted, Crevan had to desire it less. If it ever became necessary, Craig would take the position himself rather than force his brother into a life of misery. But Craig was secretly glad that the likelihood of such a situation was somewhere between not likely and never. "Never tell him," he pleaded quietly, but the force behind the softly spoken words was close to an order.

Meriel was surprised by the absolute seriousness behind the semirequest, but then upon reflection she realized that there were several small aspects of her own personality she kept completely private—even from Raelynd. And she suspected her sister did the same. Being identical twins, they had been forced to share much in their life. Some things needed to remain their own. "You have my word. I will say nothing, not even to my own sister."

"Thank you," Craig breathed with audible relief.

And in that moment an unforeseen connection formed between them, erected from a shared secret. She was not attracted to Craig physically as she sometimes found herself with other men. Oh, he was good looking, some might even think him extremely handsome, but Craig appealed to her in a way she would not have thought possible. He was the first Highland soldier with whom she actually felt comfortable just talking. Craig conveyed a calmness she had not expected after months of only observing the assertive aspects of his personality. She suspected he allowed only a few ever to see this side of him and she was quietly pleased that he allowed her to be one of them.

"You are far different than I believed," she stated, giving voice to her thoughts. "Whenever I saw you before, you were on duty barking orders or in the Hall with the men joking, being the center of attention."

Craig shrugged, not denying her assessment. "Speaking isn't hard. It's this—one-on-one conversation—that's difficult. All that other stuff just makes real talking easier to avoid."

"I know what you mean. I do not banter like you, but in my own way I also avoid conversations. And yet, with you, I find talking to be near effortless."

Craig chuckled in agreement and glanced to his right. Meriel looked identical to her sister. Their outward beauty was obvious to anyone who saw them, but never had he thought to appreciate Meriel beyond her appearance.

He liked women, always had, believing them to be capable of strength, bravery, and intelligence. He just never had found those admirable qualities in a female with whom he wanted to spend a significant amount of time. If he ever did decide to get married, he hoped it would be with someone with whom he could carry on a conversation. Something very similar to the one he was having with Meriel. It was unexpected and he wasn't quite ready to give it up. Not yet. And he sought for something else to say. "Now it is my turn to ask a question. Why is it you cannot ride while your sister does so with ease?"

"Aren't I as good as my sister?" Meriel replied with undisguised mirth. "I will point out that we have been riding for nearly two hours and not only am I still on top of my horse, the animal is still aimed in the right direction. Both are miracles."

Craig broke out into laughter, catching the attention of all but Raelynd and Crevan, who were riding up ahead, either unable to hear his boisterous cackles or uncaring.

"Make another comment about my riding and I will publicly challenge you to a weaving contest—as in *tapestries*." The comment ended Craig's laughter and caused him to look at her with a crooked brow. "Riding to me is how weaving would be to you. Unnecessary, un-natural, and exceedingly painful."

Craig rolled his eyes and said playfully, "I concede!" Then leaning closer, he whispered, "If you're in too much pain tonight, find me and I will give you something to help."

Embarrassed, Meriel swallowed and said, "I think it is time I rejoin my sister."

Craig pointed in front of them. "You're too late."

He was right. She was too late for Raelynd was urging her horse up alongside Crevan.

"I wonder what she wants to say to him," Meriel whispered, opting to stay with Craig.

Craig grimaced. "Whatever it is, it cannot be good," he answered, mirroring Meriel's thoughts.

* * *

Raelynd listened to her sister and her supposed-groom-to-be converse. She couldn't make out most of the words, but the tone and Meriel's periodic laughter indicated they enjoyed each other's company. *Good,* Raelynd thought. *Hopefully you will engage his company often during the next month.* Craig was nice enough but Raelynd had wanted to spend time with him with only one purpose in mind—a kiss. And he had given her that. If it had not been for this ludicrous demand of her father's, she and Craig would have parted company and on friendly terms. Instead, she was stuck with him—*and* his meddlesome brother—for another month.

Unlike Craig, whom fate had kept from her these past few months, his brother had been constantly around the castle, and as a result, she knew exactly what to expect from him for the next few weeks. Reproof.

Raelynd glared at Crevan's back some more, wishing he could feel the sharp point of the evil stares she was giving him. She had been at it since they had started out in the hopes that he would look back and witness her scowls firsthand, but true to his contrary character, Crevan never snuck one peek. The man either somehow knew what she was doing or couldn't care less.

A reckless rabbit leaped in front of the group and Crevan instinctively tugged his reins to the right to keep his horse from rearing. The muscles in his back rippled with each quick movement as he gave commands to his mount. Like his brothers, Crevan was large, both in height and general physique, and possessed the McTiernay rich dark hair and bright blue eyes. But there the similarities ended. Something about how he held himself differentiated Crevan from not just his brothers but from every other man. He exuded a calm authority over those he engaged— a power Raelynd had always coveted but never mastered.

Nothing the man did was big. He never spoke loudly or asserted himself in a flamboyant manner. His brother Craig tended to play that role, which was probably why he had been the one who had captured her attention during the past few months. But this afternoon the driving force behind much of the departing activities had not been Craig—but his brother.

Crevan had been the one to enforce understanding of their current predicament and secure a reluctant agreement from her and her sister to become betrothed . . . at least for now. And it was he who had confronted Meriel about her luggage and placated her feelings by making only minor concessions, something close to a miracle. For Raelynd could not remember Meriel ever yielding to anyone about something she felt passionate. Crevan had also been the one to address questions coming from the servants. As Raelynd considered the events of the afternoon, she realized he had been behind most of today's decisions. And though she would never admit it aloud, Raelynd admired him.

Her father usually barked orders and her whole life she had done the same. Whenever pushed, she pushed back. Craig admired her independent style, but not Crevan. He was repulsed by it and for some reason, his disapproval bothered her. Enormously.

Resigning to her initial impulse, Raelynd signaled her horse to move alongside Crevan's. For the first time since they departed, he took his eyes off where they were headed and glanced at her. His blue eyes quickly darted over her form and then shifted to the back end of her horse where four overstuffed bags were attached to her mount's flanks. Only two of the bags were the additional ones he agreed Meriel could bring. A single eyebrow rose.

"Say nothing," Raelynd warned him, and then added under her breath, "She begged me."

Crevan shot her a disarming half grin. It had been hard not to turn around while hearing Meriel ride only a few feet behind him. The woman was a nightmare on a horse. When she was in his peripheral view, he got a headache. But Raelynd was elegant and graceful, moving as one with the animal. "So, if Meriel was the one who was determined to bring two more bags, why are they not hooked to her saddle?"

Raelynd let go a short huff. "You know why."

A rare grin transformed his normally hard face into one that was almost attractive. "You ride well. Why did your father not teach your sister?"

Raelynd blinked. A smile and now a compliment? Both were rare and to her recollection, the first Crevan had ever bestowed upon her. "How did you know my father taught me?"

Crevan jutted his chin toward her grip. "You hold the reins as he does."

Raelynd looked down. "Oh," she replied, and then feeling the compulsory need to protect her sister, continued, "Meriel *can* ride—"

"What she is doing is *not* riding," Crevan countered. "She merely sits astride a large animal and if Craig wasn't helping her, she would have fallen off by now."

Raelynd could not deny Crevan's criticism, for it was true. That and more. "It is just that she never really learned how to ride. When we were young and Father offered us lessons, she always became quite impossible and refused to participate."

"Raelynd, impossible does not describe your sister," Crevan grumbled, and Raelynd knew he was referring to his earlier confrontation with Meriel. Both individuals proved that not only were they equally stubborn, but also that while it was a rare thing for either of them to raise their voices, they were more than capable. But in the end, Crevan had definitively won, if not the argument, the outcome. All of Meriel's trunks had remained behind.

Raelynd sighed, conceding. "I don't know why she does not like horses. I find them peaceful. After my mother's death, I would sneak out and ride to get away from everyone hovering over me, pretending like nothing had changed."

Her voice trailed and suddenly, the headstrong woman who so cavalierly caused chaos in her home disappeared. Left behind was someone he had always suspected lurked underneath, but until today had never witnessed.

Crevan stole another peek at Raelynd, noticing her regal frame as she rode expertly along the rocky path. She was a natural horsewoman and watching her ride only confirmed what he already knew—Raelynd looked nothing like her sister.

Meriel was soft and sweet and had an aura of innocence around her. It had pulled at the protective side of his nature. Raelynd, on the other hand, was all fire and spirit. For months, he had watched her manage the Schellden household. On the surface life in and around the castle ran smoothly—for like riding, Raelynd naturally understood what needed to be done. Underneath, however, was turbulence. She just did not know how to inspire people and as a result, both she and those around her became frustrated, creating unnecessary tension.

On a handful of occasions, he had tried to advise her, but each time, Raelynd had spurned his input. Yet today, she had proven there was much more to her than what appeared and that she had promise of being a great Lady of the Castle. He doubted she herself even knew the depth of her true potential. A potential he should care nothing about.

To the world, he and Meriel were a couple. And yet, it was not Meriel he had been thinking of the past few hours.

"Have you and your sister always shared a room?"

Raelynd nodded. "Always."

"Unbelievable," Crevan mumbled. If he and Craig were ever forced to share a room, blood would be spilled in less than a week. Curious, he asked, "How can you live with someone so different than you?"

Raelynd shuddered at the idea of sleeping alone. The concept had never occurred to her, but now that he had mentioned it, she wondered if he thought her immature for doing so. "Which are you? The messy or the clean one?"

Crevan glanced sideways and gave her a playful grimace indicating that she should know. "I'm the one who doesn't appear half naked and weaponless when the laird decides to do a battle drill in the middle of the night."

Raelynd laughed aloud at the memory of Craig hopping half undressed out into the courtyard. Of course Crevan was the orderly one. Everything he did was completely under control; consequently, she had assumed that everything about him was methodical . . . and well, boring. Never would she have guessed him to possess this droll personality he was showing her. Moreover, she would never have believed she could find Crevan McTiernay even remotely attractive. But she did.

Silence permeated the air and Raelynd sought to fill it to continue having a reason to ride beside him. "Why do you insist on calling me Raelynd?"

The question startled Crevan. "Because that is your name," he answered honestly.

"Everyone else calls me Lyndee."

"Not your father," Crevan argued.

Raelynd frowned. She was christened after her father and as such, she always thought her name sounded masculine. "I prefer Lyndee."

Crevan disagreed. Fact was he liked Raelynd. The name was unique and strong and had a fiery sound to it that reminded him of her father. And yet it was also soft and feminine, and anyone taking even a brief look at Raelynd knew one thing—she was very much a woman. One of the prettiest the Highlands had ever produced. *And also one of the most difficult,* he reminded himself. "Maybe, but Raelynd suits you better."

Raelynd rode in silence waiting for him to continue his thought, but as usual, Crevan gave no indication he ever intended to expound on his simple response. The man's terse communication style was completely aggravating. Gritting her teeth, she demanded an explanation. "And just why does it suit me better?"

Crevan shrugged. "It just does."

She bristled beside him. "You're impossible. Can you say more than three words about anything?"

"When necessary," he answered, wondering why Raelynd would allow herself to get so agitated over something as unimportant as a short answer. "Why are you angry?" He sensed the tension rise in her further and before she could speak, asked her again, "Seriously, why do you allow my answers, short or long, to bother you?"

Raelynd blinked and the need to defend herself began to ebb as she considered what he was asking. Why did his short replies bother her? Partly because she wanted a full explanation, to truly understand his position and why he believed the way he did, but in part the reason was much deeper. Short answers made her feel insignificant, unworthy of more.

Being an identical twin, no one—not even their father—could tell her and Meriel apart if she and her sister really tried. Only their mother could differentiate who was who when they were growing up and since she had passed away, both Raelynd and Meriel had switched roles whenever a whim struck them. But when they wanted to appear as individuals, it had been Meriel who always stood out. Raelynd took care of the castle, but it was a responsibility that lacked praise or even appreciation. Meriel, on the other hand, consistently received both for her skills with a needle.

The question hovered unanswered and Crevan could feel the tension in Raelynd as she continued to mull inwardly. They were like two wary cats dancing around each other, using abrasiveness as a cloak for their intense awareness of the other. Something he had never felt with another person, and certainly not with a woman.

Raelynd was evolving into an enigma and part of him wanted to learn more, but the situation demanded he stay away. Instinct told him that spending any amount of time with Raelynd would make creating the illusion of wedded bliss with Meriel only that much harder. He debated whether he should move his mount forward to end their conversation.

"What's the matter?" Raelynd asked, interrupting his thoughts.

"Nothing," Crevan lied.

Ignoring the fib, Raelynd furrowed her brow in puzzlement. "Well, something is bothering you. You have that same look you have during Father's parties, as if you are building some kind of wall between yourself and those around you."

Crevan bristled. That she could read him so easily rankled and caused him to respond both harshly and defensively. "You are a spoiled young girl and know nothing of men, and certainly nothing of me."

The insult struck hard and Raelynd lashed out, aiming to hurt him as he had hurt her. "I may be just a *girl* to you, but most men see me as a woman. And while your fellow soldiers may consider you a worthy Highlander, you are far from what a woman desires in a man."

His knuckles whitened and a bolt of triumph flashed

through her. Then she caught his darkening blue gaze for just a brief second and in that moment witnessed a flicker of pain. She had hit her mark, but the satisfaction from doing so had vanished. She had been countering his reference to her young age, but Crevan had interpreted her words differently.

Raelynd tightened her reins and her horse slowed, causing her to fall behind. She wished she could take the insult back, rephrase it, and make it clear that his halted speech had been the farthest thing from her mind. But saying anything now would only come off as pity.

How could she declare that he was more of a man than any other she had ever met and make him believe it? Especially when she had just claimed no woman could even desire him?

Chapter 5

Cyric gnawed on the leg of an animal someone had hunted down and cooked for the evening meal. It was the same fare they had been eating since they had left Perth and he looked forward to the decent meal waiting for him at his uncle's.

The men beside him were chatting in Gaelic and their conversation was all about home—a nearby clan he remembered hearing his father mentioning with respect. They were impatient to arrive and see their loved ones, but mostly they were eager to relieve themselves of their duty toward protecting him. Hearing such scorn, a violent coughing attack overtook him, almost causing him to reveal his understanding of Gaelic. But he quickly got it under control and was able to keep quiet that he had heard every word. Still, it galled him to know that they believed themselves as not just guides, but guardians. Defending himself was one area in which Cyric felt supremely confident. But that was not something his traveling companions needed to know. Rule one in negotiation—keep as much information as you can to yourself.

Still, their conversation about home did make him

ponder on Caireoch Castle, the heart of the Schellden clan and what was to become his new home.

In his youth, he asked any Highlander who came to visit about Caireoch Castle, but no one had ever been there. Some though had heard of it and relayed that it was a castle to make Scotland proud or that it was fitting for a Highlander. When Cyric had asked his father about the place where he grew up, his father just snorted and glared at him as if he was asking for greedy purposes. The one time his father had actually answered the question, Cyric received only a short, terse "Caireoch is not for those who want to be coddled." His uncle had offered even less of a description, issuing Cyric only a challenge to ride north and see for himself.

For years, Cyric had envisioned the Schellden lands as rich green farmland that stretched over rolling hills with a grand fortress at its heart. Scotland did not possess the large number of castles of England or Wales, but over the past century, many of the wealthier clans had erected strongholds, and Cyric understood his clan to be among the largest and wealthiest clans of the Highlands.

Desperate for conversation, Cyric decided to once again reach out to his temporary comrades. "The meat is delicious. What is it?" he asked in Scot, the language of the Lowlanders and those who lived in the northern parts of England.

"Cum do theanga ablaich gun fheum."

Cyric blinked at the insult and fought his rising rage. The few times he had tried to engage either soldier, they had replied honestly—just in Gaelic. Tonight, however, answering his question in what they believed to be an unintelligible tongue no longer satisfied their dislike. He was now an idiot ordered to be silent.

Cyric glanced at his horse grazing on the other side of

the camp, spying the silver glint reflecting the small fire's glow. It would be easy to go, pull the sword out of the scabbard, and teach both men a lesson, but he refrained. Physical confrontation should never be a first reaction to a situation, whether it be a man or clan. Such response was that of emotion, not logic, and therefore doomed to eventual failure. Fighting should not be avoided, when necessary, but only used when peaceful solutions were not possible. It was a basic tenet of his father's and why he was one of the king's most trusted advisors.

And Cyric knew his father would not consider ignorance—such as these two men's belief in his limited knowledge of their language—as justification to fight. If anything, his father would call it cowardly.

Swallowing his pride, Cyric took another large bite of meat and reminded himself of his plan. Assured victory might not include respect from his two companions, but it would of the bigger prize—the Schellden clan. He would apply the same diplomatic skills that served him so well in the Lowlands with his new clansmen. And in return, they would accept him—if not admire him—as their next leader.

First, he would secure a position of authority through marriage to one of his cousins. Based on experience, this would be the easiest to execute. Women had always fawned over him, expressing their attraction to one of his many masculine features. Like his father, he inherited the Schellden black hair, size, and etched facial structure, but his golden eyes came from his mother. Of course, his grandfather's wealth and position helped, but he was losing neither taking over for his uncle.

Cyric threw the meatless bone into the fire and pondered how he would choose between his two cousins, if both wanted to be his wife equally. He knew them to be identical so appearance would not be the deciding factor. This left only personality and he intended to choose the one most accommodating to his needs. Too many times he had witnessed the combative nature of a woman with her husband and he had no desire to be constantly embroiled in one battle or another with his wife.

On the other hand, Cyric hoped his cousins would not be entirely submissive either. In truth, what he desired most was to find someone he enjoyed being with and who felt the same about him. He would care for her and she would see him as her hero. He had yet to play such a role for anyone, but hoped he would be such a man to his wife.

The second step in his plan centered on securing respect from his clansmen. This he intended to quickly achieve by assuming the responsibilities of commanding his uncle's elite guard. Such a position would enable him to demonstrate his aptitude for leadership as well as his skills with various weapons. By this time, he would have if not all, at least the majority of the clan's respect, enabling him to execute the final step of his ingenious plan—working with his uncle in making clan decisions and eventually assuming them altogether.

Within three months—maybe even two, his father would have to acknowledge him as a man and finally look at him as a son he respected and not as a disappointment.

How hard could it be?

Chapter 6

Conor dropped his rolled plaid onto the log farthest from the fire, wondering how his brothers could endure the oppressive heat. The campsite was a familiar one often used by Schellden's clansmen or his own when traveling between lands. The open space nestled between the trees was important when needing protection from the often-times bitter Highland winds, but tonight's breeze was light and did nothing to counter the unusually warm, humid air.

He glanced at the divided group. Craig and Meriel had not stopped chatting since they had begun earlier that afternoon. Conor could not recall his younger gregarious brother ever acting so relaxed in the company of a woman. Craig chased women. He enjoyed them and was vigilant in avoiding anything more. Nothing that might be misconstrued as a relationship, or even worse, a commitment. Meriel appeared to be the exception.

Conor sat down with a definitive thump, disrupting the garrulous couple as the action caused the log they were using as a seat to shift unexpectedly. Realizing she and Craig were the only two conversing, Meriel reluctantly moved to sit by Crevan and joined the silence.

Conor grunted. The sudden quiet became uncomfortable even to him and he contemplated escaping to the bluff with Hamish, Loman, and the horses. The air would be foul, but a good deal cooler. And while Schellden had not out-right asked for him to play the role of chaperone, Conor knew the man had hoped he would. But with these four it was completely unnecessary. Besides, the situation was not one of his making and certainly not his responsibility. More than that—it was doomed.

Both couples were behaving more like strangers with their intendeds than anticipated lovers and if they did not figure out how to better act the part, word would quickly spread doubting the veracity of their engagements. His wife was certainly going to challenge their claims of sudden love. And if they kept the truth silent as Schellden wished, Laurel was not going to be easy to live with for the next month.

Just thinking about what her reaction would be caused Conor to have second thoughts. He had firmly refused to help Schellden with his scheme, but somehow the crafty old man had used Conor's inaction to his advantage. By *not* getting involved, Conor had remained silent when Schellden slyly transferred the problem of the women to the McTiernay home. When his brothers had looked to him for advice, he had remained mum. And now, for the next month, he—not Schellden—was going to be running interference between the lie and the truth.

And yet, Conor could not fault his friend.

One only had to sit in the two couples' presence for a few minutes to know Schellden had been right to remove his daughters as quickly as possible from the discerning eyes of their clan. Crevan sat beside Meriel; opposite them were Craig and Raelynd. And the silence among the four was deafening.

People think Laurel and I are loud, he thought. Admittedly their fights would catch the attention of those nearby, and sometimes one only had to be in the vicinity of the castle to hear them, but he would not change a thing. Not only was every argument thoroughly worth it by the time they finished making up, giving voice to their frustrations was far better than this quiet angst building between his brothers and their supposed future brides.

While Conor loathed to admit it and hated even more the turmoil it was likely to bring, the four of them had only one hope—Laurel. The sudden realization made Conor nearly double over with laughter. *Oh, Schellden, you are the cunning one,* he said to himself, wiping away the tears that had started to form. Just as Schellden had known Conor would refuse to meddle in the lives of his brothers, the old man was relying on Laurel's inability to sit back and not interfere.

By sending his daughters to McTiernay Castle, Schellden had issued a silent, but clear challenge. Not to Conor, but to his wife. And the one thing Laurel never did was back down from a challenge. Conor just hoped Schellden fully appreciated what could happen in the next month. Laurel was a natural schemer who tended to plot on her terms— no one else's. Life was about to get very interesting.

Conor caught the scathing look Crevan was sending his way, but it only served for further amusement. His younger brother rarely revealed his emotional reaction to what was going on around him, acting more like a chunk of ice than a man with feelings. It was good to see Crevan experience something so deeply that he could not hide it within. It was just too bad that it was anger, and not something more fulfilling.

Crevan finally gave up his silent beams of frustrations

and stood up abruptly. "Keep your w-w-wits, Craig, f-for our brother here is no longer in control of himself."

Conor took a deep breath and smiled. "Going somewhere?"

"Aye, to the bluff, and you're not invited."

Conor shrugged in mock resignation. "Since I had already intended to go there and keep Hamish company, you are going to need to find another way to cool off."

Anger spewed from Crevan's eyes, but he said nothing before pivoting and heading toward the river, the opposite direction of the bluff.

Before Crevan totally disappeared into the dark shadows of the trees, Raelynd sprang to her feet. "I . . . I . . . I need to . . . well, you know," she said, uncaring that she was obviously lying as she hurried to follow Crevan.

Conor sat there staring into the darkness for several seconds before turning to look at Craig and Meriel, who were also stunned, with mouths gaping open. "Wasn't that *your* betrothed following *her* betrothed?" Conor asked.

Craig raised an eyebrow, clearly mystified by the question as the answer was obvious. "Aye."

Conor looked back to where both figures had disappeared and then returned his gaze to Meriel. "I . . . I thought Crevan and Raelynd did not like each other."

Meriel's green eyes were large and hesitant. "They don't," she at last affirmed, before biting her bottom lip.

Conor grabbed his bedroll and rose to his feet. "The four of you are giving me a headache. I'm going to the bluff where it is cool and, hopefully, dull."

Meriel blinked. "But you can't leave us alone—"

Before she could finish, Conor stomped off toward the bluff, ignoring her. Based on what he had seen, there was no safer place for the virtues of Schellden's daughters than with his twin brothers.

Besides, the four of them knew what was in their immediate future if they did not behave—a *real* wedding.

Crevan trudged through the foliage toward the sound of the rushing river, hoping the cool waters would calm the inner turmoil that had been twisting inside him since that afternoon. It was rare for him to allow his emotions to circle out of control, and that he had only heightened his frustration.

Breaking free of the line of trees, he continued across the rocky shore that became a riverbed during the spring floods, as the mountain snows melted. After a fairly dry summer, the shoreline had receded but the river remained wide and deep enough for a swim. Crevan was just about to free his leather belt and drop his plaid when he heard the crunching of footsteps behind him. He did not need to turn around to know who it was. Raelynd.

Crevan knew her probing eyes were on him, just like they had been all night—green-and-gold-flecked pools, unapologetic, but also ashamed. Neither sentiment gave him any peace. If anything, they just vexed him even more. And the fact that she continued to be able to trouble his thoughts only compounded the tension running unrestrained throughout his body.

His whole life people had made snide comments about him, whether it be his stilted speech or his calm, somewhat aloof demeanor. To some, these flaws made him less of a McTiernay than his brothers. But he had always been able to dismiss their comments. So why would a simple retaliatory statement from a self-indulgent girl wearing a woman's body needle him so?

Raelynd had always been an enigma, and today was not the first time they had engaged in verbal combat. But never before had what she said or did affected him. He had known her for years and not once in all that time had she given him pause. Raelynd had grown to be quite beautiful, but she was often self-indulgent and therefore, quite easy to ignore.

Until today.

First in her bedchambers when he asked her to trust him and then again later that afternoon. When she had looked at him, she had not just quickly glanced his way, but truly had taken the time to see what others had not, discerning the truth behind his indifferent demeanor. In that instant, his mind had been consumed. No one had ever looked at him like that. It was not with lust or even sexual desire, but her eyes had held something different and far more powerful.

She had peered beyond the surface, deep to the elements of him that he intentionally kept well hidden, allowing no one to see. But somehow she had perceived the truth of him, and what Raelynd saw, she did not like. No matter how hard he tried to dismiss her comments—her assessment of him as a man bothered him. A lot.

Dreading being the object of her sympathy, Crevan finally said just loud enough for her to hear, "Leave, Raelynd. I cannot ease your guilt." Then he prepared himself for a weak denial or even an apology. But neither came.

After several seconds, a soft, but anger-filled insult hit him full force. "*Tolla-thon*. I feel neither compassion nor remorse. I knew we were both still upset and I thought . . ." Her voice trailed off. Seconds of silence followed and he could hear her turn around, but just before she left to return to the campsite, she said, "Never mind. I should have known it would be useless."

Crevan stood motionless, looking out at the ripples in the moonlit water as he heard her departing footsteps. He knew he should finish stripping and dive into the water, but clearing his thoughts and regaining his composure was no longer a priority. The woman was not going to have the last word, not when it was he who had been wronged!

Retying his belt, he turned from the riverbed, squared his jaw and headed back to camp, plotting their next encounter. First, he intended to rebuke her attitude in general with Conor, Craig, and her sister as witnesses and then take issue with the shallowness of her judgments. Whenever she would attempt a defense, he would cut her off, ending her desire to ever confront him again.

Inwardly applauding his scheme, Crevan emerged into the clearing and came to a sudden halt. With the exception of Raelynd, who was hastily grabbing the plaid Craig had laid out for her, no one was in sight.

Spying his befuddled expression, Raelynd scoffed and then walked as far as she could from the slowly dying fire before dropping her things back onto the ground. "I am beginning to think the famed McTiernay ability to handle and respond to any situation highly overrated."

Crevan mentally replayed her statement at least twice and it still made no sense. "What are you talking about?" he asked, not caring to hide his frustration.

"You," Raelynd said, waving her arm at the empty clearing. "Our being alone obviously was not part of your plan on how this argument was to take place."

Crevan could feel his eyebrows pucker and his jaw go rigid at the accuracy of her statement. "Explain."

Raelynd openly returned his glare just before she smugly bent over to spread her blanket out. When done, she looked up and saw the perplexed look of anger in his face. She had actually guessed right. He *had* planned this fight.

Raelynd smothered a self-congratulatory smile. "You understood me. What I want to know is, when you were preparing your side of the quarrel, did you also figure out how you were going to apologize to me?"

Crevan opened his mouth to silence her question with a biting, belittling remark, but before he could utter a word, he digested her comments and his own reaction.

Never in his life had he actively argued with anyone. Such hostile interactions were nonsensical wastes of energy. He may have disagreed, even debated, but he had been on the verge of launching an actual verbal *fight*. Worse! He had been looking forward to it. Damn her! He had been visualizing how it would unfold, who would say what and how he would receive her remorse . . . but just like everything else with Raelynd, plans were worthless.

A mental war began to rage within Crevan. One side, the calm, indifferent piece of him, wanted to walk away, leave and avoid such confrontations. The other side, the one that was winning, could not leave until he had some explanation as to why Raelynd was so furious with *him* when it should be the other way around.

"Why should I apologize to *you*?"

Marching across the clearing, Raelynd came up to him and stood so close that she had to crane her head to look him in the eye. "How . . . how can you think so little of me?" she finally managed to get out.

The anger Crevan had heard before was still very much there in Raelynd's voice, but standing so close, he could see considerable pain reflecting in her eyes. He did not know how, but he had hurt her deeply. "What are you talking about?" Crevan asked as he flashed back to that afternoon, searching for what he said or did. "Was it when I called you spoiled?"

Raelynd bristled. His assessment was undeniable, but it was also not exactly her fault. Her father had indulged her and her sister with the goal of ensuring their happiness.

She had never known another way of life. But while she might be spoiled, she was not cruel. And she was not shallow. And knowing that Crevan thought her to be both—hurt enormously.

Unable to suppress her thoughts and feelings any longer, Raelynd began to pour out all she had been thinking. "It's not what *you* said, it was what you thought *I* said that angers me so. How *dare* you think I was referring to your speech. At first, I did feel guilty knowing what you thought I had meant, but then I realized it was *you* who should be feeling bad, not me. I had done nothing wrong! I only spoke the truth! You *aren't* what a woman wants. Do you know how many flaws you have that irritate women?" she asked rhetorically. "Many. But how you talk, which by the way I don't even notice most of the time, is not one of them."

Emotionally drained, Raelynd realized she had already said more than she had intended. Turning, she headed back to her blanket. No longer did the idea of going to sleep sound unappealing. She wanted nothing more than to lie down and wake up to discover the whole day had been just a horrible nightmare. But just before she reached her plaid, Crevan caught her arm in a firm grip that forced her to turn back around.

"How I talk really doesn't bother you?"

Raelynd's brows came together in confusion. "No. It never has. Besides, only when you're around a group of people does it ever slow down."

As the truth of her words sank in, Crevan gradually released his grasp. His whole life he had stuttered. And Raelynd was wrong, he stammered not just in front of crowds, but with everyone—everyone except her. When alone with Raelynd, he spoke normally.

Raelynd was just about to try again to lie down, when

Crevan stopped her once more. "Then if it is not how I speak, what flaws are you talking about?"

The question came out of his mouth before he had thought it through. Other people's opinions had always been just that—their opinions. Crevan was well aware of both his strengths and weaknesses and held himself accountable to the ones he could change. What others thought of him was meaningless . . . until now.

Raelynd stared up at him. She knew Crevan had flaws for he was constantly irritating her, but her mind had gone completely blank. "You have . . . well . . . too many for me to narrow them down."

"You are impossible," Crevan muttered, his blue eyes growing dark and unfathomable.

"No, you are," she spat back as several of his faults came to mind that had just seconds ago escaped her. Stubbornness was one, but most of all was his autocratic way of telling her how to improve herself. Unfortunately, she had lost the opportunity.

"How so?"

"You refuse to tell me why we had to leave our home under the pretense of marriage."

Raelynd waited for a few seconds and was not surprised to hear only silence. Kneeling down onto her blanket, she began to flick off the specks of dirt and leaves that had floated onto the material. She could feel tears beginning to form and to keep him from noticing her rapidly weakening emotional state, Raelynd pointed at Meriel's rumpled plaid, which had a multitude of scattered items dumped on it. "I suggest you spend more time preparing to deal with that. My sister may be prettier and nicer, but when it comes to order, she is an immovable force of chaos. I may be troublesome, but for at least the next month, you are going to have to deal with Meriel's shortcomings, not mine."

Crevan watched as Raelynd stood back up to walk over and pick up one of her sister's overly stuffed bags full of scraps of material to use as a pillow. The accuracy of her comments about Meriel's cleanliness was worrisome, but it was Raelynd's inflection that held his attention.

He moved to stand in her path as she returned to her blanket, but instead of trying to walk around, Raelynd stopped in front of him. She once again craned her head and looked up. Her eyes were large and wide and searching his own just as intensely. Gone was her anger. Instead, hurt and longing swam in the deep green pools.

Crevan was unable to move, wondering if he was just seeing what he wished for or if Raelynd truly did desire him. He wanted to tell her that her sister was indeed very pretty, but it was she who had the capacity of being far more attractive. Raelynd possessed the qualities men desired the most. She was strong, independent, and all of a sudden, everything that made him a man demanded for him to pull her into his arms and show her how he really felt.

Just as Crevan was about to grasp her shoulders, a loud crack echoed across the clearing. Someone had stepped on a branch. Crevan abruptly stepped back and headed to where his own plaid was laid out, but it was too late.

Meriel reached out and clutched Craig's arm just as they breached the surrounding forest. They had gone to the horses to retrieve one of her bags and both had been so engaged in conversation, they had forgotten about their siblings. Seeing Crevan and Raelynd together and the seriousness of their expressions, it was clear the animosity between the two had only grown.

Craig, coming to the same conclusion as Meriel, whispered, "I have never seen anyone make my brother lose his temper faster or more often than your sister."

"Then get ready," Meriel whispered back. "I have a feeling that whatever is going on, there is more to come."

Feeling the bright morning sun on his face, Crevan stretched and forced his eyes to open and immediately looked to the far side of the campsite. Raelynd was still unconscious, lying on her side with her back to him, just as she had been when he last spied a look at her before finally going to sleep. A noise caught his attention and he glanced the other way to see Craig and Meriel both up and packing their things.

He was never the last to awake. Just the opposite, Crevan was usually the first to rise and begin the day, especially when traveling. It was yet another way he and his twin brother differed. Craig could enjoy festivities that went late into the night whereas Crevan was typically one of the first to retire. Last night and this morning, however, the reverse was true. Crevan listened for what seemed like hours to Craig's light snores while his mind refused to let go of all that had happened, analyzing it from every angle over and over again. Being slow to rise this morning should have been expected.

After finishing tying up her things, Meriel walked over to Raelynd and nudged her with her foot. Startled, Raelynd jumped to her feet and gave her sister a scowl. Crevan wondered if Raelynd had also been similarly plagued with restless sleep. Immediately, he dismissed the idea, remembering how quickly slumber had found her.

Based on when they left yesterday and the pace they were traveling, McTiernay Castle would not be in sight until tomorrow morning. That left a lot of riding and

Crevan refused to spend another day and night absorbed with thoughts of Raelynd Schellden. They were pointless as they brought only discomfort, and not peace.

He rose and went to relieve himself and when he returned, Raelynd was nearly done preparing to leave, already having brushed and replaited her hair. He thought about acknowledging her haste, but singling her out to offer praise for accomplishing something everyone was doing bordered on nonsensical. So instead, he quickly rolled his plaid, packed his things and then sat down to eat the cold meat the cooks had packed for their trip.

Meriel finally broke the silence. She looked at Craig and then realizing she should be directing her questions to her supposed husband-to-be, asked Crevan, "When will we get there? Craig thinks tomorrow morning."

Crevan, not in the mood to make small talk, shrugged his shoulders. "Depends on how often and how long w-w-we have to stop."

Craig shot him an annoyed look and then tried to compensate for his brother's brusque manners by issuing Meriel a big toothy grin. "Hope you and Raelynd like bread," he teased her, "for unless we want to extend this excursion by hunting and cooking the noon meal, after this meat is gone, bread is all we will be having until dinner."

Meriel inhaled deeply and faked a shudder. "Bread is just fine. Nothing to lengthen this trip. Right, Lyndee?"

Raelynd glanced at Crevan and her hazel eyes held his blue gaze. What she was thinking he could not fathom for her expression held no emotion. But it was unlike her to be so reluctant to share her opinion. "Aye," she finally stated. "Anything to get this month over quicker."

Crevan stood up and said to her, as if no one else were around, "Then we best leave."

* * *

The morning sun disappeared behind thickening clouds and after lunch, rain looked more and more likely. If it was only his brothers traveling, Crevan knew they would just continue riding late into the night and through the weather until they reached McTiernay Castle and shelter. And if it was only Raelynd, he would consider suggesting it, since they were now on the outskirts of McTiernay lands. Despite the miserable ride, she would be happier to have their journey over, even if it required riding in the rain. But that was not an option with her sister.

Meriel's riding had improved—it was almost impossible for it not to—but she would not be able to handle her horse in the dark, and certainly not if the ground was slick and muddy. That left the original plan in place. They would have to find somewhere to stay.

Crevan was focused on the problem of just where they should camp when Conor appeared beside him, startling him out of his mental workout. "I'm going to ride ahead and see if old Shaun has room."

They both knew Shaun would always have room for their laird. He was one of the few clansmen who lived on the outskirts of McTiernay lands raising not crops, but kyloe. The woolly cattle, with their long wavy coats, were not easy to round up, but they were hardy and could withstand the harsh Highland weather. Such farming required several hands. As a result, Shaun and his wife had a fairly large family. If asked, Shaun would have made room for not just Conor, but all of them between his home and the stables, but the women posed a problem. Shaun's wife and their children would feel obligated to give up their beds for Raelynd and Meriel. As far as Crevan was concerned,

Shaun's family needed a good night's sleep far more than Schellden's spoiled daughters.

"Hamish and Loman going with you?" Crevan asked, already knowing the answer. Both men were tough soldiers, but neither was a fool. If they could avoid the weather and the sour company of their small group, they would.

"Aye."

Crevan sent a sideways smirk to his elder brother. "Think that w-w-wise?"

Conor scoffed at the indirect attempt to say he or someone should sacrifice himself to play the role of chaperone. "The tension between you four is not of a passionate nature." Conor paused and licked his lips, contemplating if he should give unwanted advice. "You may not care, but it is going to be a long month if you intend to keep it in angry silence."

Crevan knew Conor was specifically referring to his treatment of not just Meriel, but Raelynd, who had also elected to ride somewhat apart and without uttering a word. Her choice to do so had plagued Crevan and he suspected that she did it because she knew it would bother him. It would be just like her. "It is going to be a long month regardless."

"Aye," Conor sighed. "Well, the clouds are dark, but they are moving. Hopefully, it won't rain. Regardless, I will be riding on ahead in the morning."

Crevan sent Conor a knowing grin. "You're going to prepare Laurel."

"If I thought that were possible, I would have left the second you two agreed to Schellden's plan."

"Still . . ."

"Aye," Conor sighed. "Consider yourself fortunate that in a month's time, you will not have anyone but yourself to please."

Crevan did not say anything and a few minutes later, Conor urged his horse into a gallop and disappeared ahead. His eldest brother was wrong about him being fortunate. Laurel was Conor's life. Though they fought, loudly and often, his brother was never happier than when his wife and his children were nearby.

Crevan wished the strong bonds of love that had found his three eldest brothers would also find him. But in his twenty-six years, Crevan had come to realize the likelihood of finding someone to share his life, whom he adored and also adored him, was extremely doubtful.

The kind of woman he wanted would never want him.

Somewhere northeast of them, the lands were being drenched, but thankfully, the brewing storm had passed by without a single drop falling on them. Both brothers elected to stop early near some cliffs to provide additional shelter in case the weather shifted again, and not in their favor. The river they were following fed into the small loch near the McTiernay Castle. The path was not the straightest route, but the least difficult, and also provided the most protection—but only because it was still fall. In the spring, the dry riverbed would be underwater and in a few months, the snow overhanging the jutting rock faces would make it potentially lethal.

Dinner had been quickly procured, prepared and cooked over a fire. In general, the gathering had been calm and un-eventful. Craig and Meriel chatted about everything and nothing, and to the relief of them both, Raelynd and Crevan remained as they had been all afternoon—warily quiet, speaking only when asked a direct question or when necessary. After dinner, no one argued when Craig suggested they settle down for the night and evidence of his own lethargic state was soon heard vibrating in the humid night air.

"Lyndee?" Meriel whispered, just loud enough for her sister to hear, who was lying close by.

"What?" Raelynd mumbled. She was not asleep, nor did she think any semblance of a restful state would be upon her soon despite her being awake most of the previous night.

"What happened between you and Crevan?" Meriel asked, feeling terrible that she had in many ways abandoned her sister for almost the entire day. Craig had taken it upon himself to teach her how to ride a horse. But after hours of patient instruction, he had come to the same conclusion she had the previous day—her even staying on top of the animal was a miracle.

When Raelynd did not respond, Meriel added, "Well, I'm sorry."

"For what?" Raelynd finally responded, with a bit more bite than she had intended.

"For leaving you alone today, especially when you and Crevan do not like each other."

"I was fine."

Meriel did not believe her sister even a little bit. "Well, I promise from now on to do what I can to help you with Craig's brother."

"Don't worry about it, Meriel."

"But, Lyndee, how are you and Crevan going to pretend to get along once we reach the McTiernay home?"

"Thankfully, I don't have to."

Meriel stifled a yawn. "What about when the four of us socialize?"

Raelynd rose up on her elbows and peered in the direction of her sister. "Socialize? I only have to exchange pleasantries with the man. *You* are engaged to him. It is I who should be pitying you."

Raelynd heard Meriel's quick intake of breath and winced at the harshness of her tone. Meriel had no idea that it stemmed from a place of jealousy, and until now, neither had Raelynd. "Listen, Meriel, Crevan and I will be fine. I just didn't sleep well last night. But I am glad that you and Craig are getting . . . along."

Meriel heard the question buried in understated observation and she realized that the friendship growing between her and Craig was being misconstrued. "We are getting along," she admitted. "We're . . . friends and I respect him, but it is nothing more than that, Lyndee. And when it comes to Crevan, I'm going to talk to him tomorrow about how he treats you."

"Please do not do that."

"Well, I'm going to, starting with him calling you Lyndee. He knows you don't like your full name."

Raelynd shrugged and lay back down. "He can call me whatever he wants. Now let's go to sleep."

Meriel yawned an agreement, rolled over, and in minutes, her breathing became deep and rhythmic, confirming she had joined Craig in slumber. Crevan must have thought Raelynd was asleep as well, because he quietly rose and slipped off in the direction of the river. Raelynd watched his silhouette disappear, hoping that he had not heard her and Meriel whisper on the other side of the fire.

She reclosed her eyes, but like last night, her mind would not let her rest. She had no idea how to explain to Meriel or anyone else the nearly palpable tension between her and Crevan. More importantly, she did not want Meriel to interfere. She wanted Crevan to treat her differently because he *saw* her differently. Unfortunately, all Crevan could see was a little girl when he looked at her, not a

woman. He certainly did not think of her sister as young
and immature. Then again, he had kissed Meriel. Maybe
that made the difference.

Raelynd sat up as the idea fully formed. That had to
be it! Crevan thought of Meriel as a woman *because* of
that kiss.

Raelynd threw off her plaid and quickly donned her
slippers. Finally, she had a plan when it came to dealing
with Crevan McTiernay. By the time they parted ways
tonight, the man was going to know she was every bit as
much of a woman as her sister.

Crevan approached the banks of the river, listening to
the strong current as it splashed over its rocky bed. Unfortunately, a swim was not an option. Compared to last
night's campsite, the river had considerably narrowed.
Still, Crevan hoped the waist-deep water might provide a
temporary reprieve for the turmoil he was feeling inside.
He did not blame Meriel, but hearing the whispered exchange between her and her sister had not helped.

Yanking his leine free from his waist, Crevan pulled the
shirt over his head and tossed it aside where it would
remain dry. He cursed Craig for being blissfully asleep as
well as his constant bad timing. Last night, Crevan had
almost succumbed to the desire to kiss Raelynd. And he
would have, if Craig and Meriel had delayed their return
one minute longer. And that minute had plagued him all
day with one question. If he had kissed Raelynd, would
she have kissed him back?

It was almost too easy to believe she would have. Her
hazel eyes expressed her every emotion as she felt it and
what had been reflecting in those dark green pools was
passion and entreaty. But, each time he mentally played

out the idea of kissing Raelynd, he could hear her chilling words, declaring him to be the kind of man women did not want. And yet, he believed her when she had told him that his speech was not among his flaws. But if not that, then what could they be?

Women had never flocked to him like they frequently did with Craig and his younger brother, Conan. But that didn't mean he was ignorant of their charms. Just because he was not constantly accosted by single women did not mean that he was ignored by the fairer sex. More than that, when he wanted to, he knew how to be and could be exceedingly charismatic. He just rarely felt the compulsion.

On the topic of character flaws, his brothers had a lot more faults than he. The McTiernay anger was just one example. Of the seven brothers, he was the calmest and least likely to lose his composure. Crevan prided himself on his control and ability to handle the most difficult situations and people. To his recollection, only one person had been able to push him beyond his patience level— Raelynd Schellden.

Cursing under his breath, Crevan scolded himself for musing over a woman whom he should not care about and reached down to unhook his dagger from his leather belt. He was just about to toss it onto his shirt when a branch snapped and caught his attention. He immediately pivoted and prepared to throw the dagger at the creature that was approaching. But the moonlight revealed no animal, or at least not a mortally lethal one.

Spinning the blade handle in his hand, he tossed it effortlessly on his shirt before placing his fists on his hips. He waited for what felt like several minutes for Raelynd to explain why she had come after him again. They had barely exchanged a few dozen words that day, and while the indefinable strain between them had not diminished, at least it had not risen. Her coming to meet him, alone, now, was about to change that, and not for the better. Especially with her openly staring at him. He wanted to rid himself of his thoughts about her; something he could not possibly do with her around.

"Stop staring and go back to camp."

Raelynd's reaction to the brusque order was instinctive. "You're engaged to Meriel, not me. I can stay if I want."

"Fine," Crevan yielded, and leaned down to splash water in his face, hoping it would help cool his rising temper.

Raelynd continued to stare at Crevan, unable to stop herself. She knew she was openly ogling him and wanted very much to stop. Looking away, however, was impossible. Never had she seen Crevan without a leine before, and she had not been prepared.

Over the years, especially when she had been young, she had ridden out to spy on the soldiers who were training under her father. As a result, she had seen many men half naked, and a couple of times, she had innocently witnessed them fully unclothed. Being soldiers, they were in shape and muscular, but her memory could conjure nothing like what she was seeing now in the partial moonlight. Crevan was something magnificent.

Not only was he significantly broader and more powerfully built, his torso was tan from the summer sun, hinting that he often did not wear a leine when he trained. Regret filled Raelynd for not riding out to the training fields more often this past summer.

"What do you want, Raelynd?"

Raelynd gave herself a mental shake at the reminder of just why she was there—to teach him a lesson. But before Crevan would agree to kiss her, she needed to end hostilities between them. "I came out here to tell you that I don't want to argue anymore. I would like us to be friends."

Her offer was met with silence as he kept his back to her. Deciding the man was impossible and to just accept defeat, she added, "Well it is obvious that everything I say or do makes you angry or at the very least further irritates you. So my only other option is to just stay away and hope you do the same.".

Still crouched from splashing water on his face, Crevan studied the fast-running stream rolling over and sometimes colliding with the terrain. It was interesting, even invigorating—far more so than the calm river it would become before it merged with the loch. Meriel was like those boring waters ahead and for the next month, her uninspiring personality would be his companion. "You can be aggravating, Raelynd, but you don't need to stay away."

Just about to turn around and go back to camp, Raelynd halted before taking a single step. "I don't?"

"Aye," Crevan murmured, throwing a rock into the turbulent water. "You don't try to make excuses for me."

"Why would I do that?" she asked, clearly puzzled by his explanation.

Crevan sent her a quick telling look. "Exactly my point."

For a brief second, Raelynd remained confused and then his meaning dawned on her. To her, Crevan's speech was just a part of who he was. To excuse it would be just as ridiculous as pardoning his blue eyes. Still, Crevan had just practically admitted there were some out there who had trouble accepting him because of how he spoke.

Raelynd was unsure of what to say or do with Crevan's semiconfession. She was tempted to go to his side, kneel down and comfort him, but part of her also wanted to reproach him. His pitiable belief that people judged him for

how he spoke was repellent. Her plan for proving to him
that she was a woman was going to have to wait.

"The only person I have ever heard make excuses or
even mention your speech is you."

"You wouldn't understand, growing up as you did with
only a sister and a doting father, but my whole life, people
have judged me or thought I was less of a McTiernay because of the way I talk."

Raelynd let go a gentle scoff of disbelief. "Even if that
were true, why not confront them? Prove them wrong?"

Crevan rose and turned to face her. "I decided long ago
to not fight people's mistaken opinions of me." And
before she could counter, he added, "But that does *not*
make me a coward."

"Coward? No," Raelynd agreed as she leaned back
against a large boulder. "But you *assume* people are judging you and therefore, you look for anything to prove you
are right. I always heard you McTiernays were confident
to the point of arrogance—you see yourself as a victim."

Every muscle in Crevan's body froze while Raelynd
was speaking. The restrained fury in his now blackish blue
eyes was unmistakable. Crevan took a step forward, narrowing the space between him and his accuser. "You have
no idea what you are talking about. You have never been
on the receiving end of looks of disappointment or pity."

Raelynd let go a denigrating scoff and pushed herself
off the rock. "*I* have no idea? Of all people, I know exactly
what you mean. But at least I try to defend myself and
gain their respect."

"And yet you still have none."

Raelynd paled and stumbled back as if she had been
physically assaulted. The simple statement had verified
her deepest fears. No longer would she be able to dismiss
her feelings of inadequacy as being just her imagination.

Her servants acquiesced because of her father and all those times she suspected people were yielding to her just to get rid of her were true. People did not admire her—or even like her. Letting go a small cry, Raelynd pivoted and ran back toward the campsite.

Crevan uttered a curse directed at himself and snatched his leine and dagger off the ground before going after her. He called out, but she refused to stop. By the time he caught up with her, she was nearly back to the group.

Grasping her arm, he immediately pulled her to his chest and buried his hands in her hair. "I didn't mean it, Raelynd. I was just upset."

Raelynd shook her head, crying, but did not pull away. "You are right. I've always known people didn't like me. Not even the men Father wanted me to marry."

Desire spiraled low in Crevan's belly, licking every nerve in his body. Raelynd's hair was soft and thick and even after two days of travel, it smelled of flowers and the tantalizing scent of woman. He caught himself wanting to pull her back and kiss the smooth white skin of her throat, so he could take a big, deep breath of her. It had been far too long since he had been this close to a woman and unfortunately, Raelynd Schellden was completely unavailable.

"Well, then those men were fools," he finally managed to say.

"Thank you." She sniffled and tilted her head back. "Besides my sister, you are probably my only true friend."

Her green eyes were misty with tears and he felt his throat tighten. Hair messed and cheeks streaked, she looked more desirable than ever and he could not stop himself from wondering how she would taste if she were to open her mouth beneath his. His unease drove him to chuckle and he let her go. "Friend? We fight all the time," he said, reminding himself of that fact.

Unaware of his growing desire, Raelynd nodded, licked her lips and started wringing her hands. Crevan watched in fascination, imagining how they would feel massaging his naked flesh. "You actually see me. Hear me," Raelynd began. "You know me better than anyone . . . maybe even better than my father. Meriel knows me in some ways, but she is oblivious to so much that takes place around the castle. She doesn't want to know. But you do—and you listen to me."

Swallowing, Crevan took a token step back, hoping the distance would help him maintain control. "But you don't listen to me."

Newly formed tears began to burn the back of Raelynd's eyes. She gazed up at him through a swimming blur. Instinctively, Crevan reached out to her and pulled her close, stroking her spine until her stiff, resisting body relaxed against his hard frame. He closed his eyes, for not a single battle wound compared to the torment of holding her in his arms. Had he really forgotten how wonderful a woman's touch could feel?

Crevan splayed his hands wide against the sides of her face. Tangling his fingers in her glorious hair, he made her look up at him. "Kiss me," she whispered.

Crevan longed for much more than a kiss. He wanted to learn all her secrets, to satisfy himself deep inside her. Realizing the dangerous direction of his thoughts, Crevan abruptly let her go and took a step back. "Practice on your arm," he said tersely, waving a finger at her bicep.

Raelynd blinked. She had wanted Crevan to kiss her, to feel his mouth on hers, but the absurdity of his advice snapped her back to reality. "My arm? Really?" She stepped forward so that once again she was looking directly up at him, this time, challenging him and his suggestion. "Is that how you learned? Or are you just as inexperienced as I and just don't want me to know."

His square jaw tensed visibly. "Goading me will not work."

Raelynd opened her mouth to argue, remembering just in time her main reason for running after him. Taking a deep breath, she said calmly, "Then I'm asking you as my friend. I intend to learn how to kiss. So if you refuse to teach me, then I will just ask someone else."

The only someone else she could mean was Craig and the last person he wanted seducing Raelynd was his charismatic, overly charming twin brother. Then out of the blue, it struck Crevan that the act of kissing Raelynd was probably the fastest way to end his inexplicable growing desire for her. Especially since she had practically admitted she didn't know how.

"Fine," he muttered, and drew his thumb across the soft bow of her lip, successfully rendering her silent. And before she could speak again, his mouth came down on hers.

Raelynd heard a moan and realized it had come from her. Crevan's kiss was far different than the one she had shared with Craig. That kiss had been what she had expected, the feeling of his lips against hers and the slight hope that he might teach her something to make her realize why people would want to embrace each other repeatedly. This kiss, however, reached down to the depths of her soul, paralyzing her with its intensity. A foreign feeling surged through her, driven by her heavily pounding heartbeat.

Her lips were soft and welcoming under the pressure and her soft moan did nothing to quell his desire. Pulling her tightly to him, his kisses became more demanding, as Crevan let his need for her be known. He began to nibble at her lips, encouraging her to open them with his thumb, but Raelynd instinctively just squeezed her mouth even tighter.

Breaking away, his breath fanned her cheek and the heat of his sapphire gaze burned her up from the inside out. With his lips almost touching hers, he asked, "Do you or do you not want to learn how to kiss?"

Raelynd could do nothing more than nod.

"Then open your mouth to me, oh feisty one," Crevan demanded huskily.

As her lips parted, his tongue entered her mouth and after her initial surprise, Raelynd tasted him back, hesitantly at first, then deeper. And she knew she had finally discovered the burning desire women spoke of when talking about their men. She also knew that she should retreat, but it was too late, even if she had wanted to do so. Her whole being had at last come alive and Raelynd knew she was not going to back away from the fire Crevan was creating within her. Instinctively, she coiled against him and buried her fingers in the softness of his hair, holding his mouth to hers, hoping the kiss would never end.

Crevan drew in a deep breath as her fingers massaged his scalp and then began to explore his back—stroking, testing, teasing. But when she drew them in and her hands began to roam his chest, he could bear it no longer and yanked her hands away. His mind told him to break free, but Crevan was consumed by his need for her. A piece of him had slipped away and without choice or question, wrapped itself around her.

She gave a low, throaty moan, unconsciously fitting her body sinuously against his. Her mouth was like dripping honey and his tongue glided in and out, drawing the sweetness from her into himself. Raelynd might have shared a peck or two with a man, but this was the first time she had ever been kissed.

Raelynd felt completely claimed, as if his tongue had the power to sear her soul permanently into his. Never in her life had she met a man who had made her this alive. In his arms, she felt truly beautiful. Crevan had awakened a sense of awareness that had lay deep within her, hidden and unknown. She also knew there was more. She wanted to discover such pleasures, experience the decadent sensations her body hinted at, and she said as much.

Crevan groaned. He knew he had to stop this passionate assault she was having upon his senses for he was very close to ignoring his inner voice to break off the embrace and search for some privacy where he could show her just how desirable she was as a woman. Forcing himself to end the heavenly experience, he let go and created significant space between them.

Raelynd looked at him, her eyes pleading for an explanation he did not have—or one that he certainly did not want to give. Unaware she was doing so, Raelynd reached up with her hand and touched her swollen, thoroughly kissed lips. Crevan had no idea what to say, but he knew what he needed—for Raelynd to leave . . . *now*.

"Lesson over," he managed to get out.

Hurt sprang into Raelynd's eyes and her hand immediately dropped to her side as pride quickly masked the pain he had inflicted. "So I now know how to kiss."

Crevan's mouth went dry with the understatement. Raelynd was a natural. She fit him like no other, but he certainly was not going to tell her that. "Good enough that you won't embarrass yourself. And as a friend that is *all* I will teach you," he finished, hoping that she understood that what just happened was never going to be repeated.

It wasn't like being with a woman was new to him. But

kissing Raelynd had been more than just good. Even allowing for the fact he had been without physical affection for a long time, holding her in his arms was unlike anything he had ever known. She had made him feel so alive. He was getting hard just thinking about it.

He and Raelynd needed to remember that for the next month she was Craig's intended. After the month was over, she would leave and Crevan would make sure they would not see each other again until she was safely ensconced in marriage—*to someone else*.

Taking a step forward, Raelynd reached up and gave him a soft, petal-like kiss on his cheek. "Thank you," she whispered with sincerity, and turned to leave.

When Crevan had first denied her request, the thought that maybe he was not very experienced had crossed her mind. With the exception of her sister, Raelynd could not remember seeing him in the company of a woman. *Dar Dia!* Had she been wrong. Crevan McTiernay may have been obstinate and the most aggravating of all the male species, but the one thing he could definitely do was kiss. Craig was the one who needed lessons. Thank goodness her engagement to him was a farce. After kissing Crevan, the idea of sharing anything physical with his brother turned Raelynd's stomach. Crevan, however . . . She would kiss him again right now if he asked her.

Raelynd entered the campsite. Her sister and Craig were still asleep, unaware of anyone's absence. She was about to lie down when she glimpsed Crevan's empty plaid and a frisson of panic went up her spine. She had a burning desire, an aching need, for not just another kiss, but to be with Crevan. Talk to him and have him talk to her. She had called him a friend but what she was feeling was much more than that.

She could not actually *like* him . . . could she?

Chapter 7

Raelynd signaled her horse to move up in between
Crevan and Craig to get a better look at her host and hostess
for the next month. The morning had been quiet since
Meriel had paired up with Crevan and she with Craig.
Raelynd had been wondering how the month would be
living in the McTiernay Castle. She had briefly met Lady
McTiernay a few times, and knew only that the woman
was very beautiful and that her father thought highly of
her. As a result, Raelynd had assumed Laurel would be
mild mannered, for her father disliked women who did
not respect him or refused to acquiesce to his being in
charge. So when the four of them passed through the Mc-
Tiernay Castle gatehouse, Raelynd had not expected the
lively scene taking place in the middle of the courtyard.

"Make your choice, my love," Laurel demanded, uncaring if her voice carried very far or what such a threat
might sound like to those who could hear her. Her long
wavy pale gold hair hung loose down her back, elongat-
ing her already tall, slender frame. "You either talk right
now, here in this bailey, or in an hour in our chambers. But
you will explain to me what is *really* going on."

Both Raelynd's and Meriel's eyes popped wide open. Neither of them doubted the honesty behind the threat. If the laird did not arrive in their chambers in an hour, Lady McTiernay was undoubtedly going to find him. They glanced around to the clansmen entering and exiting various buildings. All continued to work as if the spectacle of the laird and his lady publicly butting heads was commonplace.

Raelynd leaned toward Crevan and in a hushed tone asked, "Are they actually *fighting*?"

"Aye."

"Shouldn't we do something?" Raelynd asked, clearly concerned for the welfare of Laurel after speaking such a way to not just the laird, but a man far bigger than her.

"Na. Only Conor is fool enough to tangle with Laurel."

"Are you frightened of her?" Raelynd challenged, testing to see if Crevan was really serious.

"Sometimes," he admitted.

"Do they even know we are here?" Meriel asked, clearly as mystified as her sister.

"Certainly," Crevan replied, completely relaxed and unmoved by the scene.

Raelynd forced herself to stop staring at the arguing couple and looked at Craig and then Crevan. Neither seemed bothered by the heated argument taking place across the courtyard, which only confused her further, for the fierce love between Laird and Lady McTiernay was known throughout the western Highlands. "This cannot be good. Maybe we should leave."

Crevan shook his head and explained, "What you are seeing is far from strange. If they *weren't* fighting, then Craig and I would be concerned."

Meriel, who had finally gotten her mare to stop beside Craig's horse, gave voice to the other question on Raelynd's mind. "What could they be arguing about? I mean the laird only arrived this morning."

"Most likely it is about us," Craig answered nonchalantly.

Seeing that Craig's explanation only further puzzled Raelynd, Crevan added, "Craig is probably right. My guess is that Laurel doesn't believe w-w-we f-fell in love and w-w-wants to know w-what really is happening."

"She isn't the only one," Raelynd whispered.

"But why would Lady McTiernay not believe the news before even meeting with us?" Meriel innocently posed.

"Lots of reasons," Craig answered. "Including the one that just a few weeks ago Crevan and I came back for a short visit and neither of us mentioned you or your sister. Laurel is not going to be easily convinced that anyone— in particular you two, whom we have been in company with for months—suddenly caught our attention. Especially after we have stated for years that marriage was not in either of our near futures."

"W-w-watch," Crevan said, pointing his finger at the still quarreling couple. "See how Conor just tucked his hands underneath his arms?" Raelynd nodded. "That means it is almost over. Laurel w-w-will attempt to get the truth from o-one of us next."

Meriel leaned forward so that she could see her three companions and asked, "Should we tell her? I mean, if she already suspects the truth, how are we going to convince her and everyone else otherwise?"

"No, absolutely not," Craig quickly countered, knowing that neither Meriel nor Raelynd knew the real risk they faced. "Promise me, Meriel, that you won't say a word."

Meriel looked at Craig intensely, eventually nodding in agreement.

Crevan, still concerned because he knew how crafty his

sister-in-law could be, said, "Laurel can be quite tricky w-w-when she w-wants something, so be careful."

Somehow, they needed to convince Laurel that there was going to be a wedding. Almost victim to an arranged marriage herself, everyone knew Lady McTiernay's feelings about nuptials that were not based on love. If Laurel discovered their wedding was a farce, there was a good chance she would explode, spreading the truth way beyond the McTiernay borders.

Hearing the almost ominous tone in Crevan's voice, Raelynd was now absolutely convinced the situation she and her sister were in was far more serious than she had been told. "We will," Raelynd assured Crevan. "All will believe our nuptials are going to take place."

I also vow that at the first opportunity I have, I am going to find you, Crevan McTiernay, and demand to know what is going on. Crevan was going to explain just why she and her sister were at risk and how pretending to get married was the only solution—for though it sounded preposterous, Raelynd was sure there were no other options. For if there were, she doubted either McTiernay would pretend he was willing to relinquish his freedom.

The four of them slipped off their horses and began to make their way to the stables. They did not get very far before Laurel glared one last time at her husband, clearly frustrated, and then pasted on a bright smile before going to welcome her guests. Such sudden cheeriness made Craig and Crevan uneasy, mostly because it seemed sincere. Laurel's earnest smile meant she had a plan, but before they could warn either Raelynd or Meriel, they were both being hugged warmly. At the same time, Laurel's blue gray eyes were issuing Crevan and Craig an unmistakable message to stay quiet.

"I must admit to being surprised by Conor's news of

your upcoming nuptials, but I am also very excited at the prospect of adding two more sisters to our family," Laurel said almost too gleefully, clasping Raelynd's and Meriel's hands in hers. "We never did truly have a chance to talk during one of my short visits to your home. But now, with a month to prepare, we will finally have the opportunity to get to know each other better."

Craig took a deep breath and exhaled, knowing that any control he had had concerning his future during the next month had ended the moment they entered the court-yard. Whatever Laurel was planning could no longer be stopped. He started backing up slowly in an effort to slip away unnoticed, but Laurel quickly snatched his arm, halting his departure.

Turning toward him, she issued Craig and then Crevan a radiant smile, sending chills up both men's spines. Too many times had they been on the receiving end of such cheerfulness, and it was never to their benefit. "Before you both leave, please gather your intended's belongings and put them in your own bedchambers."

Crevan felt his jaw drop and was fairly positive that Craig was in a similar state of shock.

Laurel cocked her head, feigning surprise by their reac-tion. "I was not prepared for guests and I am reluctant to rearrange the children's bedchambers. But since you will be sharing much more than a room in less than a month, it only makes sense for Meriel to sleep in your bed, Crevan, and for Raelynd to stay in Craig's."

"But where are we to sleep?" Craig blurted out.

"Why, in the Warden's Tower with the guards or in the fields with the rest of the bachelor soldiers."

A picture of neat and tidy Raelynd cleaning his comfort-able, well lived-in room leaped into Craig's mind. "What about Clyde's room?" he immediately suggested, knowing his youngest brother was in the Lowlands training with Colin. "It might be more appropriate and they could stay together!"

A loud, grating cackle silenced the group. Conor, who had been listening as his younger brothers became more and more intertwined in one of Laurel's creative plans, did nothing to suppress his laughter. It was not a very brotherly or supportive reaction, but he could not help himself. He absolutely loved it when someone besides him experienced his wife's conniving ways.

Conor, knowing that Laurel was only just getting started, was not about to get entangled into her plan by the sheer folly of being present. He pivoted toward the Lower Hall and was starting to walk away when she called out to him, "I remind you, my love, that we have a meeting to finish our discussion in one hour and you better be armed with better explanations."

Conor, still heading to the Hall where he hoped to find some food and drink, waved his hand and let go another cackle. "I just hope you can be happy when you find only me, because, oh lovely wife, my answers shall be the same."

Laurel exhaled, indicating her exasperation, but quickly turned to address Craig's question. Before she could, however, Crevan issued her a stern look and said, "No o-o-one, especially my *intended,* is going to step foot in my room, let alone sleep in it. My things are in order, just the w-w-way I like them, and I w-want them to stay that w-way."

Craig immediately echoed his brother's sentiments. "Trust me, Raelynd doesn't *want* to stay in my room. That is *if* you kept your promise."

Soon after Laurel had arrived at McTiernay Castle, she had begun ensuring things ran properly. One of those responsibilities was the upkeep of the laird's and his family's bedchambers. Upon seeing Craig's room, she had issued him an ultimatum—help keep his room clean or live with the consequences. No longer were the servants going to spend hours picking up his stuff. Naive to her habit of mischievous means to gain her way, Craig had shrugged and quipped back, "Order is Crevan's thing, not mine. I don't care if anyone picks up after me. My room is messy, not filthy, and I like it that way. Everything is where I can see it." Over time, they had developed a compromise. Servants were allowed to clean just enough to prevent rodents from cohabitating with him, he was to bring his dirty clothes to the laundress once a week, and she would never attempt to straighten his room.

Laurel stared directly at Craig. "I assure you, everything is as you last left it." She then shifted her steady gaze to Crevan.

Raelynd felt ridiculous being talked about as she stood there and was about to agree to Craig's suggestion of Clyde's room, when Laurel raised her hand and Raelynd found herself closing her mouth without uttering a word. Crevan had been right. Laurel held herself with confidence, not letting the large size of her brothers and husband intimidate her.

"If you really feel strongly about your rooms," Laurel continued, "then I suggest you both go and find some *men* to marry and act like ladies of the castle somewhere else. There is already a lady of this castle, and *I* determine who stays where."

"I'm going to get Conor!" Craig bellowed, forgetting that Laurel had many ways of making someone see reason.

"Are you sure you want to involve your brother?" Laurel posed, crossing her arms loosely.

Crevan narrowed his eyes, clearly angry over the situation for apparently he knew Laurel had the upper hand.

If either he or Craig asked Conor to intervene, regret would immediately follow. Based on experience, Conor would intercede, but in a way that was not in their favor just to teach them a lesson about ever asking him to interfere with Laurel's decisions on such petty matters.

Craig closed his mouth and shook his head. He had only crossed Laurel once and he had no idea how she did it, but he had suddenly found himself with exceedingly uncomfortable bedding and his clothes had mysteriously caused him to itch, among several other clever and very unnerving things. All of them were deviously petty, preventing him from complaining to Conor without coming off as weak and soft. The day his bedding returned to its comfortable state and his skin no longer burned from constant scratching, he had thanked God and sworn never to cross Laurel again.

Looking at both Crevan and Craig and seeing their acquiescence, Laurel smiled and said, "Now that we have that settled, why don't you both join Conor and your nieces and nephew in the Lower Hall once you have finished dropping off your soon-to-be-brides' things in your rooms."

Both men grunted hearing her say *soon-to-be-bride* in an overly happy tone. Crevan just wanted to end the torture. He snatched a last glimpse of Raelynd and grabbed his and her belongings while Craig went to get Meriel's heavy bags from both her and Raelynd's horses.

Laurel watched them leave and wondered just who was supposed to be marrying whom. Neither man seemed aware that he was carrying the items of his brother's future spouse.

Still pondering what she had witnessed, Laurel pointed to the Great Hall. "Come, let us go sit down. Over refreshments and food you can tell me just what is really going on."

Raelynd heard Laurel, but her mind was still reeling

from what she had just witnessed. "How did you do that?" she finally managed to get out.

Laurel looked at her and blinked innocently. "Do what?"

"That!" Raelynd repeated, pointing at the two figures entering the large tower to the right. "No one ever gets Crevan . . . I mean Craig, to change his mind."

Meriel nodded her head in agreement. "I was sure you were going to lose that battle."

Laurel sighed, realizing another one of her instincts had been right. Not only was something highly suspicious about the supposed upcoming wedding, but both girls had much to learn. They had been sheltered not just by their father, but by circumstances. Laurel was painfully aware of not just what happened, but what *didn't* happen, when one lost a mother. These girls needed more than help preparing for a wedding, they desperately needed guidance. For a beautiful body did not make a woman and it especially did not prepare someone to be a wife.

Laurel gave Raelynd a mischievous smile and shrugged. "I did it with practice, of course. Don't worry. You both have a full month to learn the art of dealing with men . . . or should I say dealing with *husbands*."

Seeing Raelynd's and Meriel's faces blanch confirmed Laurel's doubts. Neither of them really wanted to be married or more importantly, *thought* they were getting married in a month.

So why was Conor so emphatic for her to do whatever she could to prepare for a wedding?

All three women gathered around the end of the Great Hall table where Laurel asked a nearby servant to bring out a small tray of food. The noon meal had already been served, but Laurel knew that after traveling, she was always ravenous, wanting anything to eat and drink besides water and bread.

"This is wonderful," Meriel said, licking her fingertips as the last of the meat was devoured.

"Aye," Raelynd concurred. "Could you please ask them to bring some more?"

"I can only offer you some more bread," Laurel answered, pointing at the half-eaten mound still on the tray. "We are having a celebratory feast for dinner this evening—a small one since I received such late notice—but even so, the cooks are busy and unable to prepare anything else."

Meriel sat back, slightly slumped, satisfied by the meager fare. "That sounds wonderful! I love festivities. I hope we have one every night," she exclaimed, uncaring of the work and time that went into such affairs.

Raelynd, however, believed as guests, they should have been treated better and given more food when asked. "At Caireoch, a visitor's comfort is more important than that of a few servants," she mumbled.

Laurel pasted on a friendly smile and said quietly, without any perceived animosity, "Well, I hope for your sake that you might feel differently someday."

Meriel, an innate peacemaker, tried to veer the conversation to happy topics. "Thank you so much for helping us prepare for our wedding. I cannot wait to begin working on my dress."

Laurel heard the subtle plea to change subjects but refused to be easily manipulated. "I love Craig and Crevan very much. They are my family and nothing is more important than those close to me. And I am not about to let them enter a marriage I think they might be miserable in."

Meriel squirmed and sank lower in her chair. Raelynd's only response was a stiffening of her back, but both reactions were enough to confirm that much more was going on. Laurel began to drum her fingers on the table.

Walking into the Hall, her goal had been to get both women to admit the truth—that the wedding was a farce. But after listening to them, Laurel was no longer sure she should coerce them into such a confession.

She had always liked the Schellden twins. Both were incredibly beautiful and usually very sweet natured. Unfortunately for them, they also had an overly doting father who had cocooned them away for most of their lives. As a result, their bodies had matured, but not their understanding of people.

After sequestering his daughters for so many years, marriage was about the only reason Laird Schellden could plausibly give for letting them go somewhere else and for such an extended period of time. So Crevan and Craig were helping Schellden protect his daughters. But from what? Or was it from whom? Laurel could ask them, but she suspected neither Crevan nor Craig knew the full scope of their circumstances. Asking Conor would be pointless, but then . . . he had to have known she would see through the situation. In a way, he was practically begging for her to meddle, because if it *was* a real wedding, Conor would have forbidden her from interfering. It was a leap in logic, but based on years of living with the devious, lovable man, it was a pretty solid one.

A grin crossed Laurel's face. *Thank you, Conor . . . I accept,* she said to herself, hoping Raelynd's and Meriel's resolve was strong enough to see their plan through to the end. Because they were on McTiernay lands now and no one was going to believe Craig and Crevan were actually marrying the two women sitting in front of her.

Conor was right. They did need her help. And she was probably the only one who could provide it.

* * *

Laurel opened the door to Craig's bedchambers and waved her hand at the mess, sighing with genuine exasperation. "This will be your room, Raelynd. I would apologize for the mess, but I am sure you were expecting it, knowing Craig as well as you do."

Raelynd gulped and looked inside, her eyes wide with horror. Items were strewn everywhere. Forcing herself to enter, she nudged aside several straps of leather to clear a place for her to stand.

Meriel, now able to see inside, yelped with elation when she spotted the large window showering the room in sunlight. With the grace of someone who had significant amount of practice living in chaos, Meriel quickly stepped around the odds and ends to sit on the bench and look down at the courtyard below. "You are *so* lucky!" she giggled with excitement. "To have this bench here with all this light."

Raelynd shuddered. Her sister would overlook all the disorder and see only how the room could be used for sewing and weaving. The bed was not made, nor from the way the blankets were lying atop the lumpy mattress, did it look like it had ever been made. Clothes—*men's* clothes— were strewn about, and several types of weapons were lying haphazardly on the floor. Most of the candles had burned down to their nubs with wax pools around them. A few had fallen to the floor or on the settee where they had been snuffed out. The mess could have been Meriel's if Raelynd had ever let their room get that bad.

"I had someone start a fire in both rooms and I will have someone come in and change the bedding and remove the armaments," Laurel said, "though Craig really does not like people to touch his things. But I am sure you know that. I hope you are prepared to constantly clean up after the mess yourself, though with Craig, you most likely had better just get used to it."

Watching Raelynd's repulsion as she studied the exceptionally cluttered room, Laurel felt a small pang of guilt. Deciding to give her a temporary reprieve, she corralled both women back into the hall. Raelynd impulsively headed to the other room sharing that floor.

Not stopping her, Laurel opened the door, letting them both peek inside the wall-to-wall filled room. "This used to be Cole's bedchambers," she said, referring to the third McTiernay brother, who had married and was now laird of a nomadic clan up north. "In a few years, I'll have the servants clean it out and give it to my son, Braeden, when he is older. But for now it is used only for storage."

After closing the door, she went back to the tower staircase and up a single flight. Similar to the second floor, the third held two rooms. "Those bedchambers belong to Clyde," she said, pointing to the locked door. "He has gone south to train with his elder brother Colin. Here is Crevan's room—which will be yours, Meriel."

Meriel eagerly peered inside and immediately felt her heart sink. Instead of a large window facing the courtyard with enormous amounts of sunlight, the room had only one small window and several narrow arrow slits facing the ravine and hills outside the castle walls. Seeing her things on the bed's very smooth coverlet, she felt her pulse start to thump wildly. Working on her tapestries would not be possible in the dim light.

Ignoring her sister, Raelynd strolled into the well-arranged room with a smile. The dimmer firelight produced a warm feeling she far preferred over the glaring afternoon light and everything seemed to have a place. Raelynd moved to the bed and caught herself just in time before she sat down. It had felt natural, like something she would have done in her own room.

Raelynd wondered if Crevan had similar instincts when he came in after a long day. What if she were already there? There was only one chair—would they both sit on the bed?

A soft sob interrupted her stream of thoughts and Raelynd realized Meriel was crying. Pulling her sister into her arms, she explained to Laurel, "I don't think my sister wants to be alone. Maybe we should share a room."

Meriel immediately nodded and pulled away. "If it's not a problem," she sniffled, wiping the tears from her eyes. "We have always slept together."

In many ways, Laurel felt for both sisters, but she also knew that continuing to treat them as their father had would not be fair to them or their future spouses. Letting go a critical chuckle, she asked, "Are you going to sleep with your sister on your wedding night as well?"

The comment had been directed at Meriel, but Raelynd felt its full impact. Not wanting Laurel to tell Crevan about the request, lest he think her incapable of acting like an adult, Raelynd clasped her hands together and said to her sister, "Meriel, this is how a room should look." Then to Laurel, she asserted, "For years I have been trying to get my sister to put things where they belong. A room should have order and be organized, which is how I run my father's castle."

Laurel listened as Raelynd rattled off all the things she oversaw. The self-aggrandizing list surprised Laurel, for it proved that Raelynd did know an enormous amount about running a castle. Unfortunately, she had never actually experienced all the work she supervised—only directed it.

"Before I leave you to get ready for tonight, there is

one more place and someone I would like to introduce you to."

Raelynd followed Laurel and then Meriel up one more flight of stairs to the top floor. There were seven McTiernay brothers, and even in her sheltered existence, Raelynd had heard about all of them. Conor, Laurel's husband, had assumed the weighty responsibility of becoming laird of the McTiernay clan upon his father's death. The second eldest had married into a Lowland clan and the third in line had accomplished what many had thought impossible—uniting the northern nomadic tribes. And since she and her sister were engaged to the twins, that left only the two younger brothers. One was gone and the other one was supposed to be awful.

Just before they arrived at the door, Raelynd licked her lips apprehensively. "Who is it we are going to meet?"

Laurel stopped in midstride. "Conan, of course," she said, and seeing the blood drain out of Raelynd's face, bit the inside of her cheek to keep from smiling. "Remember, he is about to become your brother as well."

Laurel gave the door a firm knock and upon hearing a deep grunt from the other side, opened the door and entered. "Hello, Conan. We have guests."

Across the cluttered, scroll- and paper-filled room was a man who was propping his forehead on his palm while he studied something on the table. "Tell her to go away. I am not in the mood. If she is lucky, I'll say hello tonight at dinner."

Ignoring his condescending remarks, Laurel prompted, "And how do you know it is a she?"

Without looking up, Conan jotted something down on the map he was staring at and asked patronizingly, "When have you ever tried to introduce me to someone who was *not* a woman?"

"This time you are wrong. I have not come to introduce you to a woman." That got Conan's attention. He looked up and immediately grimaced as he realized his mistake. "I would like to introduce you to Raelynd and Meriel Schellden."

"I know them."

"Did you also know they are engaged to your brothers, Crevan and Craig?"

Conan tossed the quill pen on the table. "I don't believe you." He shifted his gaze from Laurel to Raelynd and then Meriel before coming back to his sister-in-law. "They're more attractive than when I last saw them, but still not pretty enough to entice anyone into marriage."

"Well, then it is a good thing you aren't the one marrying one of us," Raelynd snapped. The rejoinder should have gained her an apology or he should have at least shown some type of remorse, but the man just raised an eyebrow, clearly unimpressed.

When Conan McTiernay had trained with her father as all the McTiernay brothers did at one point or another, he had avoided Caireoch Castle, much like Craig had done these past several months. Nonetheless, Raelynd had heard about Conan and how he belittled women. She had assumed he was like her father's more rough-mannered men, but never, *never* had anyone talked that way about her. And certainly not when she was standing right in front of them. After all, she was not just anyone; she was Laird Schellden's daughter!

Laurel saw Raelynd visibly bristle and was sure Conan had caught the reaction as well. Raelynd didn't realize that chastising him would not convince Conan to cease his ridicule, it would only encourage him. The second-to-youngest brother was undoubtedly the most brilliant of the

McTiernay clan, and as a result, he had little patience for anyone not as smart as he was.

Since few women had the unusual opportunity to learn at an abbey as Laurel had, Conan truly believed females were good for only pleasure and creating families. As far as Laurel knew, he had only made two exceptions to that belief—her and her good friend Ellenor, who studied with her at the abbey. It was unfortunate that neither Raelynd nor Meriel would be able to put him in his place like Ellenor had.

Still, encounters with Conan would be an excellent way for them to learn how to handle difficult people. Raelynd would not be able to order him to behave and Meriel's female wiles would do her little good. Both would have to devise other means to control his conduct toward them. Laurel also knew that unless provoked, he would successfully avoid them.

"Well, we will leave you alone, but we are having a small welcoming celebration in the Lower Hall and you *will* stop whatever you are doing and attend."

With a showy wave of his hand, he nodded in agreement.

"And I suggest you spend the afternoon packing, for the next month Raelynd and Meriel will be living on the second and third floors and you are to stay out of this tower."

Conan's jaw went immediately slack and his shoulders slightly slumped. "For them?!" he argued. "My brothers *are not* marrying the Schellden twins. I can promise you that. McTiernays only marry women who possess some degree of intelligence as well as a modicum of nerve." He paused briefly to point at Meriel. "You, if memory serves, like to sew, and you," he said, shifting his attention to Raelynd, "like to order people around and pretend you are all grown up. No way in hell a brother of mine is going to marry either one of you!"

Fury enveloped Raelynd. She opened her mouth to say something, anything to get him to retract his words, but nothing came out. Meriel, however, was not so easily silenced. "Well, at least I'm not an ass."

The unusually harsh words of her sweet-natured sister had no effect, but it occurred to Raelynd just what might with such an impossible personality. The same tactics Laurel had used on her. "Oh, but we *are* marrying your brothers," she cooed. "Ask anyone. Ask Conor and he will tell you that in one little month, I will be your *sister*. Other than Laurel, we will be your closest female relatives and no doubt we will be seeing each other often."

Raelynd smiled as she saw the blood drain out of Conan's face.

Laurel, deciding that enough groundwork had been laid, suggested, "I think it is time for you to return to your rooms and prepare for the night." Just after she closed the door to Conan's study, she added, "I will send someone up shortly with a bath for you both to share and to remove Craig's weapons. I will try to come back and see you again before dinner, but Conor and I have some unfinished business to discuss, so it may be the evening meal when we meet again. Which reminds me, dinner will begin promptly at sundown in the Lower Hall. Do not be late."

Laurel then turned and vanished as she went down the winding staircase, leaving both Raelynd and Meriel standing there alone.

Meriel let go a long sigh. "I guess we have to return to our rooms and unpack," she said miserably.

Raelynd reached out and grabbed Meriel's arm. "We might not be able to share a room, but remember how we used to switch places when mother tried to teach me how to weave?" Meriel nodded. "I think you should stay in Craig's room with all the light, and I should take Crevan's."

Meriel's head began to bob excitedly up and down. "We *are* identical," she whispered.

Relieved, Laurel softly let go a long breath she had been holding and continued down the staircase to exit the tower. She had no idea whose brilliant idea it was to pair up Meriel with Crevan and Raelynd with Craig, but their coupling had been based on obvious personality traits, not on the person beneath.

Thank the Lord, there was not going to be a real wedding. Otherwise, the situation would be a colossal mess.

Chapter 8

Though the castle was not yet in sight, Cyric knew that at any moment Caireoch would come into view. Both his guides had noticeably perked up, unable to hide their joy at the thought of ending their escort duty. Cyric was well aware that both of them blamed him for the journey taking so long, but he did not care. Such extended and arduous travel was new to him. Delays should have been expected.

"Do you intend to stay for any length of time after we arrive?" Cyric asked.

"None," came the short reply.

Cyric was relieved. Both men belonged to a neighboring clan and since neither had intentions of staying, they would not be poisoning any Schellden clansmen against him. This left him the ability to start anew, gaining respect and assuming the role of chieftain.

Cyric had started outlining ideas for achieving both goals when a large stone castle appeared in the distance. Soon he would be inside Caireoch's walls, being warmly welcomed by all who met him. Myriad questions began to swirl in Cyric's mind. Should he stay on his horse and ride in? Or should he get down and meet everyone face to face? Would Laird Schellden want to give him responsibilities immediately? If so, which ones should he assume first?

Cyric was almost giddy with excitement. His dreams and aspirations were finally coming to fruition. Too long had he yearned for a way to prove his worth to his father. Finally, he was going to have his chance.

As they rode closer, the size and makeup of the castle became clearer. Rather than a square shape with multiple towers, Caireoch had only two, both enormous. The gatehouse was also sizable, defended with a portcullis, a heavy gate, and most likely several murder holes. Together, the structures formed the shape of a triangular shield. Only the keep, which was attached to the gatehouse, was visible over the unusually tall curtain wall that connected the three anchors.

Predictably, the majority of the servants lived in cottages just outside the castle walls and not within. The small community was inhabited, but far from lively. Of the few people who were outside working, only a handful paused for a moment to look at him and his guides. Most of the clansmen and women were busy doing whatever had to be done before the end of the day.

Cyric had heard Highland women dressed differently, but he had not expected such a divergence between Lowland and Highland culture. In Ayr, Scottish women dressed like those of northern England, wearing bliauts, kirtles, or some kind of long, flowing gown. But from what he could see in the village, the women of his clan wore something far different. Their chemise served as a leine and gathered at the waist was the Schellden plaid. The bold material reached from the neck to the ankles, fastened with a leather belt and secured above the breast by a large brooch to form a loose shawl. By the various pockets created, the warm-looking garment looked serviceable, but bulky.

By the time they were at the gatehouse, Cyric had come to the conclusion that most everyone had to be inside, lined up, and waiting for his arrival. He was about to ask his guides to enter and announce him when, without a single farewell, they turned their horses and urged them into a gallop. Cyric would have to introduce himself.

Taking a deep breath, he sat for several seconds on his horse, alone in front of the massive gatehouse feeling more and more nervous. Once he went through that opening, his life would change. His uncle along with the steward, the top commanders, and whoever else was important would be there to welcome him, looking to him for guidance and approval.

Taking a deep breath, Cyric reminded himself that he had eaten and mingled with the top nobles in their kingdom, including Robert I, and urged his mount forward.

To Cyric's surprise, the activity inside the castle walls and the people's reaction to his appearance were no different than that of the village. The courtyard was larger than he had expected given the castle's triangular shape. As he assumed, the keep on his left was adjacent to the gatehouse and along that same wall were several smaller buildings, one of which he could see from the smoke, was the kitchen. On his right were more storage buildings and the Great Hall, which he was glad to see was impressive in size. The chapel was nestled between the Hall, one of the towers anchoring the far curtain wall, which held the stables, and the smithies.

He stared for several minutes, sitting and waiting, but not a single person stopped to greet him or even asked who he was. Incredulously, it was almost as if they *had* been told of his arrival, and to ignore him! Coupled with the fact that his uncle had not appeared, Cyric was even more disconcerted. For days he had been visualizing just

how his future father-in-law was going to receive him—
with appreciation and admiration. Whatever the reason
behind the hollow welcome, Cyric decided to at least get
off his horse.

Feeling more like an intruder than the next Schellden
chieftain, he urged his animal forward toward the stables.
He handed the reins to the young dirty stable hand, who
cocked his head and asked, "Just who are you?"

"I'm Cyric Schellden," Cyric announced loudly, but
still no one seemed to recognize the name. Not even the
boy, who just shrugged his shoulders and waited for Cyric
to unhook his bundle from the saddle before taking his
horse inside. *Someday,* Cyric vowed to himself, *they will
stop and acknowledge my presence and feel rewarded if I
felt inclined to do the same.*

"Welcome to Caireoch." The booming voice of his
uncle startled Cyric but was also a welcome relief, because he had no idea what he had been going to do next.

Schellden patted the young man on the back. Cyric had
the size, even the bulk, of a Highlander, but his amber
eyes contained the panicked look of a teenager on his first
hunt. "I hope you enjoy your visit. I am sorry that no one
was here to welcome you, but I had to finish up a meeting
with my commanders and wanted to be the first to greet
you." Schellden gestured toward the double doors of the
Hall where several armed men were exiting. "Come. I am
sure you are hungry and have many questions."

Cyric followed for he did have several questions, but
the nature of them had abruptly changed from what duties
he was going to take over first to . . . *enjoy his visit?*
Robert I had implied something far different. A visit did
not include a wife and a lairdship to his own prestigious
clan. Not once had he imagined Laird Schellden would
not be of the same mind as his king. It suddenly occurred

to Cyric that maybe coming here was not all he had believed it to be.

Schellden entered the hall and waved for Cyric to follow. "We actually expected you earlier."

Cyric glanced around at the few remaining men who were gathering their things. It was not respect he saw, but accusation, as if they knew without even being there that he was the cause of the delay.

"There is no meat left, but there is plenty of bread and ale," Schellden said before sitting down at the head of the table.

The way his uncle had arranged the room, there was no sharing of authority. Only one chair was at the table's end, forcing Cyric to take one of the six perpendicular seats. He suspected he should be glad that he wasn't being offered a bench, which served as the majority of the room's seating.

Cyric pulled a piece of bread free from the large loaf and chewed the soft, tasty morsel before swallowing some ale, hoping that both would give him fortitude. His questions were numerous, but he decided to stay away from the confrontational ones for now. Maybe his uncle was just testing him.

"Where is everyone?"

Schellden picked up a mug and swirled the contents. "Most are in the fields. We held games here for several days. The horses from the race ruined some of the lands and crops so everyone is helping to clean up and restore things to order."

The answer was complete, but Cyric still felt as if he were being censored, and he was not sure why.

"Would you like anything else while you and the laird talk?"

Cyric twisted around to see a pretty girl with dark

auburn hair and unusually large brown eyes hold up a nearly empty platter that still held a few pieces of meat and cheese. "I would," he answered. "Build me a plate of whatever meat is left and bring it to me."

Her dark eyes sprang open wide and flashed to the laird. Her warm smile disappeared, and she gave Cyric a terse nod before she left to do his bidding.

Cyric, once again mystified, turned back toward his uncle. "I had hoped to meet my cousins this afternoon as well. But perhaps it is a good thing they are not here to greet me. I should bathe and prepare myself to make a good impression," he quickly added, hoping diplomacy might lessen the perceived tension he felt.

Schellden leaned over, and keeping his face expressionless, said, "I am sure they would have liked to say hello, but unfortunately I doubt you will have the opportunity to meet them while you are here. Since their mother is dead and I did not remarry, both are at a neighboring clan preparing for their wedding."

Cyric nearly choked on the piece of cheese he was eating. His mouth had instantly gone dry and he picked up the mug and began downing its contents. "Did you say *both* of my cousins are getting married?"

"Aye, in less than a month. I am fortunate that the men they have chosen are well known throughout these parts and belong to a nearby clan, enabling us to see each other often."

"But . . . but . . ." Cyric sputtered as the few items his uncle had so far divulged sank into full meaning. King Robert might have led him to believe he would be the next Schellden laird, but his uncle obviously intended something quite different. "But the king told me that—"

Schellden cut him off as he stood up and scooted his chair back to make room for his departure. "Robert relayed to me that he wants to secure the future of this clan. My daughters are marrying able, strong men of whom I am sure the king will approve. The union will help eliminate the potential of clan rivalries and thereby protect the strength of the Highland armies."

Cyric stared at the piece of bread still in his hand. All the discomfort, all the pain, the cold, the exclusion he had felt for the past several days had been for nothing. He had arrived too late. Once again, he had been appraised by an elder and judged to be a disappointment. This time, however, Cyric was not going to just meekly accept the decision.

"Since the king told you of his desire to secure this clan, he must have also relayed how he intended for it to happen. I journeyed this very long distance based upon those expectations. I had been told that *I* would be marrying one of your daughters and would become the next laird of this clan."

Schellden was vaguely impressed and slightly disappointed. His nephew had spoken calmly but with a surprising amount of determination. Schellden had half expected, half hoped Cyric would whine and beg to be sent home, bringing an immediate end to this part of the plan. But, his nephew's departure would only resolve one of his problems, not all of them.

"Raelynd and Meriel are to marry Craig and Crevan McTiernay." Schellden paused, thankful to see by Cyric's expression that his nephew was well aware of the enormous power that Highland clan held. "If you desire, we can ride over and you can fight them for your rights to marry one of my daughters. I would, however, not expect any support from the king or any of your kin. The McTiernays have too many loyal allies and the king's intent is to stabilize the future of the Schellden clan, not destroy alliances."

Cyric studied his unreadable uncle. After years of

acting as a negotiator between some crafty and devious leaders, Cyric wondered if Laird Schellden might be playing him for the fool. But such a claim could easily be found false, so it had to be true. The heavy burden Cyric had been carrying suddenly became nearly intolerable as he realized his father's respect, which he so desired, might never be within his reach.

Schellden walked around to the other side of the table, clearly intent on leaving. But he halted so that he was directly opposite Cyric and faced him. "You are the only male Schellden heir. I will not relinquish the safety and the future well-being of my people based on blood alone. But you are welcome to stay and prove to me that you are ready and able to lead your clansmen."

Cyric rose to his feet and looked his uncle in the eye. "I accept. And if I do prove that I have the skills and the aptitude to rule this clan?"

Schellden scoffed. "First, you must learn only the king has the authority to rule. A laird does his best to manage and address his people's needs."

"I understand. I watched my grandfather perform for years as laird of my mother's clan. I am sure I am ready and you will see that as well when you charge me with clan decision-making and—"

Hearing how Cyric intended to prove his worth, Schellden's deadened face cracked into a large grin and he began to laugh, loudly. Trying to overcome his mirth, he turned to the pretty dark-haired servant and gave her a kiss on the cheek. "If you would get the steward to show my nephew where he is to stay when he is finished eating, I would appreciate it, my dear." Then his uncle disappeared, leaving only Cyric and the woman, who had served him his plate of food, in the cavernous room.

"Why so glum?" she asked as he slumped back into the chair despondently.

"This was not how it was supposed to be," Cyric muttered, resting his forehead in his hand.

"And how did you imagine Caireoch to be?"

"Busy, filled with people, ready and wanting to meet me." *Ready to adore me, admire me, at the very least respect me,* he added silently to himself.

"There were more clansmen here to receive you yesterday, but you did not arrive and there is much to do," she explained, sitting on the bench closest to him. "To survive in the Highlands all must do what we can. You will have to do the same if the laird is to determine you are fit to stay."

"You don't understand. I came here expecting to be welcomed . . . not put on *trial*," Cyric moaned.

The woman stood up and Cyric dropped his hand from his forehead so that he could look at her. She was not a striking beauty, but her waist was thin and her full figure was just the kind that he desired when he sought out a woman. Her rich brown eyes were also kind and gentle despite his treatment of her, for she obviously was *not* a servant. He wasn't sure what her relationship was to his uncle, but he was certain that the Schellden laird did not go around kissing just any young woman on the cheek.

She pointed at the pitcher at the end of the table. "I will fetch the steward. Until he arrives, if you want more to drink, you will have to pour it yourself. Consider that your first lesson in Highland survival."

"Wait, what is your name?"

"Rowena," she said with a wink.

"I'm sorry about before. I thought you were a servant," Cyric said rapidly, wishing he were acting more like his smooth charming self. "My name is—"

"I know your name," she interrupted, and bestowed

upon him a stunning smile that transformed her from a pretty woman into something quite breathtaking. "Good luck, Cyric. I think you will need it even more than I had originally believed."

Then she pivoted gracefully and glided out the door, leaving him completely alone. He had known she was mocking him, but he was not at all put off by it. It was not a cruel ridicule like the kinds he had experienced from his guides, but more like a tease one received from a friend. Cyric hoped he would see her again.

Chapter 9

Meriel watched expectantly as the two men placed the oval wooden bathtub on the floor near the hearth. She waited until the last person hauling hot water dumped the contents of two buckets and left the room before falling stomach down on Crevan's—now Raelynd's—bed. She raised herself on her elbows and rested her chin on her hand to watch with amusement the slow methodical way her sister was still unpacking. "It's so dark in here, Lyndee. You won't be able to find a home for each and every item," Meriel teased.

"Then I suggest you stop bothering me, go down to your room and finish unpacking."

"I'm already done," Meriel divulged, stifling a yawn.

Raelynd stood straight up and stared at her sister. "You can't be," she murmured, knowing Meriel had brought more than twice the amount of stuff she had. "Not with everything."

"If I unpacked the way you do, it would have taken me a week."

"What did you do? Just shove Craig's stuff out of the way to make room for your things?"

Meriel shrugged, indicating Raelynd's guess had been

accurate, and then rolled onto her back to play with her braid. "Your way may be cleaner, but it is also a whole lot slower."

Fact was, she *had* just pushed all of Craig's things to a corner and then proceeded to dump her belongings, spreading them around to create various piles on the floor. Her more precious materials she had draped on the furniture. It did not make sense to find a place for everything as Raelynd was doing if they were only going to stay a few weeks. She would spend unnecessary time searching for whatever she needed. Now she just had to look around. In Meriel's mind, not only was her way faster, it was far more efficient.

Raelynd, almost done, pulled out the gown she intended to wear that night. The deep rose bliaut had small pearls sewn around the neckline and the hem of each sleeve, perfectly matching the semisheer, cream-colored chemise she always wore beneath it. Digging in the bag, she pulled out her brush and the matching pearl hairpin. She rummaged around in it some more before hurrying to the other bag, which she had already emptied, to verify she had indeed gotten everything out of it.

"Meriel," she began, clearly uneasy. "Please tell me that you packed slippers."

Meriel went still, letting the braid she was holding fall to her chest. She had been so busy packing sewing materials, trying to squeeze everything she could into only four bags, she had not considered the odds and ends that went with dressing. She sat up. "I don't think I packed any. Didn't you?"

Raelynd shook her head. "I was so mad I wasn't thinking about shoes. The only ones I have are there."

She looked toward the two pairs of sopping leather double-soled turn-shoes sitting in front of the hearth. They were so filthy after two days of travel, washing them had been one of the first things they did. If lucky, the shoes would be dry by morning. They certainly would not be ready for that evening.

"Maybe Lady McTiernay will have some we can borrow," Meriel muttered, hoping she would not have to go barefoot. Many Highland women did but their father had been afraid of them getting cold and sick. After years of wearing shoes, their feet were not accustomed to walking around without protection.

The sound of someone on the other side of the door caught their attention. Meriel, hoping that it was Laurel, jumped off the bed and rushed to the door. Opening it, she was surprised to see Conan, descending the staircase. He stretched his neck to see around her figure and grunted when he saw Raelynd reinspecting what even he could see was an empty bag.

Meriel was about to close the door when she heard him say, "My elder brothers must have gotten the last three clever women in Scotland. The only ones left are pretty little girls."

Meriel fumed at the insult and was half tempted to chase after him, but taking one step onto the hard stone floor outside the room, she quickly jumped back onto the soft woven rushes that covered the bedchamber floor. "I wish he would try and woo me one time just so I could refuse. That man needs a good no."

"With his kind, it would be pointless. He would just think you were too dense to realize how lucky and fortunate you almost were," Raelynd said acerbically, dropping the bag onto the floor.

The sound of running feet was again outside the door, but both decided to ignore it. If Conan wanted to spend his time and energy jogging up and down stairs that was his choice. Meriel began to shimmy out of her bliaut. "I think the water is ready. Can you hand me the soap?"

Raelynd put her hands on her hips. "I told you to bring some."

"And I told you I didn't have any room!" Meriel barked.

"And I said to make some. You had more than twice as many bags as I did," Raelynd replied, her voice growing icy.

Meriel opened her mouth to give a strong retort when more running was heard, this time followed by a knock. Raelynd called out, "Who is it?"

"Me," came the soft, high-pitched reply.

Curious, Raelynd unlatched the door and opened it. Standing almost waist high was a little girl who looked to be around the age of seven. Thin with thick pale gold curly hair, she was the spitting image of her mother with the exception of her eyes. Instead of Laurel's blue storm-colored eyes, they were gray, with silver glints that sparkled with impishness. "Who are you?"

Not waiting to be asked in, the young girl flashed Raelynd a grin. "I'm Brenna," she answered, and walked toward Meriel, who was holding her bliaut up to her chest for she had on only her chemise. "Here."

Meriel reached out and took the light gray speckled mound being offered. "Thank you," she murmured, un-knowing just what it was she received. "What is it?"

Brenna puckered her eyebrows in confusion. "You don't know?"

Raelynd felt her jaw slacken. This was one of Laurel's twins. She had heard of Brenna and Braeden. In the same way Raelynd's father protected her and her sister, the Mc-Tiernay twins' father had never allowed them to venture away from the safety of their home. "That was you running back and forth?"

Brenna nodded. "I heard everything." Brenna beamed with pride. "Only Mommy's extra soap was in the storage room, but I'll try to help and get you shoes."

Raelynd hoped Brenna had only *thought* she heard everything, for if she let it slip that she and Meriel had switched rooms, it might cause some ill will to develop between them and their hostess. "I am Meriel," Raelynd said, testing the little girl, "and this is my sister, Lyndee."

Brenna bobbed her head and Raelynd stifled a sigh of relief and took the gray mound from Meriel's hand. It was soft and someone had taken the time to carve it into a rose. "Is this soap?"

Brenna again nodded enthusiastically and climbed up onto Crevan's bed. "Clyde likes to carve them when he's bored. But he's gone so that's the last pretty one."

Raelynd rotated the mound, studying it. Her soap looked much darker because of the ash. "I wonder where these flecks came from," she said, handing the rose-shaped lump back to her sister.

Brenna's mouth hung open with candid shock. "What do you put in your soap?" she finally asked.

Meriel shrugged. She had never once helped with the soap-making and had no idea what was involved. Raelynd crossed her arms and looked smugly down and listed the items. "Ash, tallow, lime, and some oil."

Brenna shook her head this time, letting her curls bounce all around her face. "What do you use to make it smell good?"

Raelynd blinked. The idea of putting something else into the soap had never occurred to her. "Nothing."

Brenna curled up into a ball on the bed and started giggling. "You use *boy's* soap."

Meriel smelled the gray mound. "It's lavender, Raelynd. It is wonderful."

Just then they heard Laurel's voice call out. "Brenna? Are you in there?"

The little girl bounced off the bed and went to the door. "Yes, Mama."

"Sweetheart, you need to leave our guests alone. You will have time to meet with them later, I promise."

"She's fine," Raelynd said, enjoying the little girl's company. With her sister being a twin, she always had a playmate growing up, but not a little sister whom she could teach things.

Laurel frowned, but finally acquiesced. "Just remember that dinner is at sundown, which is in only a couple of hours. It will be served in the Lower Hall with the soldiers to give Craig and Crevan a chance to introduce you both to all their friends and family."

Raelynd stepped forward, not realizing there was an alarmed expression on her face. "We have never eaten with the men. Our father never liked us talking with them, especially at mealtime."

"Well, I assure you that after being married for a few months, it will seem quite natural to be eating and talking with a bunch of rowdy soldiers. I have much to do, so I will see you at dinner."

As soon as the door closed, Meriel moaned and Raelynd issued her a look to remain silent for Brenna was in the room. "We made a promise."

Meriel nodded and finished undressing to bathe.

"What promise?" little Brenna prompted.

Raelynd grabbed her around the waist and swung her around. "Why, a promise to look our very best and make every McTiernay clansman and soldier wish he was the one betrothed to us."

Brenna squealed with delight. "Can I help?"

Raelynd, getting dizzy, put her gently onto the floor. "Absolutely."

Laurel smiled to herself and quietly exited the tower. As expected, trying to get Conor to admit there was no wedding had been a waste of time. The man had obviously made a promise to his friend and ally Laird Schellden, and short of it causing harm to someone in his family, Conor would not break it. In the end, the talk with her husband had accomplished only one thing. He had her convinced that she needed to at least act as if there was going to be a wedding, even though it was clear to her that not one of the four truly wanted or desired the event. She suggested as much to Conor and he had ordered her to do nothing more. She was to leave things alone. To Laurel that meant use more devious means.

Intentionally talking within her eldest daughter's hearing, she mentioned they had two guests staying in Crevan's and Craig's old rooms, knowing Brenna would not be able to stop herself from running over there and meeting them. Of course Laurel had followed, keeping out of sight, and while she felt that it slightly involved subterfuge, it was worth it. In those few short minutes, Laurel had discovered more than she had bickering with Conor for nearly an hour.

Tonight, she would confirm her guess.

Meriel grabbed her knees and rocked back, laughing heartily as Brenna attempted another strange coil with Raelynd's hair, pinning it in a less than appealing fashion. After they had both taken their baths, Meriel had been first to receive the delightful result of Brenna's care and attention. The resulting hairstyle was quite uneven, messy, and overall very amusing.

Now it was Raelynd's turn to have parts of her hair twisted into crazy knots they both knew would be a nightmare to brush out. But they didn't care. Without a younger sibling, they had missed out on such pastimes. It was pleasant to have some fun with the little girl as they waited for a maid to come help them prepare for dinner.

Two strong knocks were heard on the door. Raelynd stopped Brenna with a mock sad face. "Go open the door and tell them we are ready."

Brenna's shoulders visibly slumped, for she too was having fun, and she went to the door as she was told. Opening it and seeing Laurel, she cheered up and said with pride, "Mama, they are ready!"

Laurel stepped inside, looking beautiful. Dressed in a kirtle made of a brilliant shade of deep blue, she had draped the McTiernay plaid so that it loosely crossed her bodice and was pinned to her shoulder. Everything about her was perfect, except for her stunned expression. She had suspected that neither Raelynd nor Meriel would be ready after agreeing to let Brenna stay with them, but she had not expected them to be so *not* ready. Raelynd at least had her bliaut on, but Meriel was still only in her shift.

"You, Brenna, go downstairs. Bonny and Braeden are waiting for you to go eat dinner with Gideon tonight."

Brenna moaned. "Why can't I eat with Papa in the Hall? Tonight is going to be fun with Lyndee and Meriel."

Laurel shushed her and gave Brenna a little nudge. Her best friend, Aileen, had agreed to watch her own two children and Laurel's three during the dinner. But Laurel had to make a promise in return. That not only did she have to chronicle the night's events in detail, but also let her be part of whatever scheme Laurel concocted to deal with the two spoiled guests. Laurel had sworn she had no plan, but Aileen was not fooled. Her friend might not have had a defined plot in mind, but she would. Laurel was unable to help herself from getting involved if she thought her input was needed and, based on how Laurel described the Schellden twins, they definitely required help.

"Well, there is nothing to be done, I guess," Laurel said, and went to the bed. She picked up the pale blue bliaut laid out on the coverlet and tossed it to Meriel. "Dress as you walk and come with me."

Meriel knew she must have heard wrong and stuck the garment out in front of her. "But it is wrinkled and still needs to be prepared."

Laurel nodded in agreement. "It is regrettable to introduce you both like you are, but fortunately both Crevan and Craig have seen you perfected. Hopefully in the future you will manage your time better when you prepare yourselves for dinner."

Meriel stared at Raelynd, who was looking more and more uneasy by the second. At home, they had two maids to help them dress and do their hair. Though Laurel had never mentioned it, they had just assumed the same conveniences would be available to them at the McTiernay Castle. But it was becoming very evident that Laurel was not going to cater to their accustomed lifestyles. When their hostess had said dinner at sundown—she had meant it.

Raelynd swallowed. "Tell them we are sorry for not being prepared on time and will be down as soon as we are ready."

"I will make no such apologies," Laurel said simply.

Raelynd gasped, widening her eyes to saucer size for she had fully expected Laurel to comply with such an offer. After all, she had apologized. "Why can you not make our excuses while we prepare ourselves?"

"Because, while I could make excuses or even delay dinner, it would be rude," Laurel started to explain. Her voice was patient, but held no possibility of yielding. "I cannot expect to receive respect if I do not give it. Now come with me."

Meriel, busy cinching up the sides to her crumpled bliaut, said, "But what about our slippers?"

Laurel looked down and shrugged. "Be thankful it is warm enough to go without."

Minutes later, Laurel entered the Lower Hall with Rae-lynd and Meriel shuffling in behind her. The large room was completely full of men, all soldiers who were looking very anxious to eat. But instead of eating they were standing, and Raelynd realized it was because they were waiting for Laurel.

Feeling the unhidden looks of amusement, Raelynd pulled her shoulders back and stiffened her spine at the humiliation she was being forced to endure. With half her hair up and half of it down, she heard more than one chuckle directed at her comical state.

Meriel only wanted to hide. Her frightful dark gold locks were not quite as humorous as Raelynd's after Brenna's handiwork, but wearing only an extremely wrinkled bliaut with a shift underneath—no belt, no tartan, and no shoes—she not only felt half dressed, she looked it.

Laurel, giving no pity to their self-made situation, stopped every few feet to introduce them to a different group of soldiers. Each time Raelynd heard "these are Laird Schellden's daughters, who are betrothed to Craig and Crevan" she stole a glance across the room to where their supposed future husbands stood waiting. Both were staring inscrutably at them. Raelynd felt awful, and though she knew it was Craig she should be feeling embarrassed for, her focus kept shifting back to Crevan. Nothing, not even the looks of shame her father had infrequently given her when she sniped at a servant, hurt as much as his blank expression.

At last, they arrived at their seats and the very moment Laurel sank down onto her chair next to an already sitting Conor, the soldiers sat down and commenced eating. Raelynd gulped and took a quick look around the room. Not one soldier was upset at being forced to wait to eat. Many of them were stealing glances at Lady McTiernay and nodding their heads. They had waited to eat not just as a gesture of respect for their laird; it had been something they had actually *wanted* to do for their lady. These men really did honor Laurel.

Feeling the sleeve of her arm being pulled, Raelynd turned toward her sister. Meriel had inched closer and was now practically pasted against her side. She was cowering, causing several of the men—most notably the obnoxious Conan—to openly stare at her. Raelynd couldn't blame them as understanding dawned on her. The reason why people oftentimes did not treat either of them like an adult was because neither she nor Meriel acted like one.

Taking her elbow, she compelled Meriel to sit up. *Never again,* Raelynd promised herself. *Next time I enter this room or any other I will be given respect, not because Lady McTiernay demanded it, but because I earned it.* Leaning over, she whispered in Meriel's ear, "Sit with pride. We are Laird Schellden's daughters despite what we look like or what they think."

Hearing those words, Meriel immediately sat straight up in her chair and both women started to eat as if nothing were out of the ordinary. They pasted on smiles and met blatant stares with lovely expressions, pretending they had not a care in the world. When Crevan finally looked at Raelynd, she only nodded regally to acknowledge his attention. Meriel mouthed the words "I'm sorry" to Craig.

He gave her a semihidden half smile and with a sigh, said, "Well, at least you two aren't boring."

Seeing their sudden change in disposition, Conan, who had been sitting catty-cornered from them, issued a loud hoot, getting the room's attention. Crevan, sitting on Conan's left, swiftly punched his younger brother in the arm as a warning.

Conor, at the head of the table, leaned over to his wife and whispered with obvious sarcasm, "Is this your revenge for me remaining silent?"

Laurel smiled coyly and swallowed some of her drink before answering. "Why, Conor my love, you know that I don't believe in revenge. But I would continue to watch. I am sure there will be more to come."

Almost as if on cue, Conan started to wave a finger at both Raelynd and Meriel. Then with an exaggerated wink aimed at his brothers, he declared, "Gorgeous women you have found there. I now see how they captured your attention. They certainly have gotten mine."

Crevan dropped the leg bone he had been eating. "Conan, I'll w-w-warn you only o-once, do not speak *to* them or *about* them in such a manner again."

Coupled with a demeaning shrug, Conan grinned, leaving no doubt that was not the last word he was going to utter on the subject.

Minutes rolled by and people continued to eat as the tension in the air increased. All those near or about the main table waited for the explosion, for no one was wondering if Conan was going to ignore his brother's warning, just when.

Intentionally tapping a spoon on his plate, Conan

pondered out loud, "I have been sitting here wondering, as I am sure many others have been, just what it was that made my two devoted bachelor brothers suddenly want to propose and give up their freedom." Dropping the utensil so that it clattered to get even more attention, Conan continued, mockingly. "I guess it is their undying beauty."

Raelynd could not remember even seeing Crevan rise, and neither had Conan, for he was still in midsentence when Crevan's fist cracked his jaw. Conan went flying, falling into the men sitting to his right. Ale spilled everywhere and the affected soldiers began to pummel whoever had caused them to spill their beverages all over themselves. As more food and drink continued to be disturbed, others joined the commotion. Trestles and benches were now in danger of being damaged.

"Enough!" Conor boomed. Instantly, the entire room quieted in compliance.

Except Conan.

Pulling himself off the floor, he brushed some of the food off his leine and then pointed at Meriel. "Of course, whichever one of you marries her is the luckiest. Won't be hard to convince her to undress at night."

Craig moved to stand right in front of his brother, his fist flexing. Raelynd could see, however, that Conan was unfazed. Her green and gold eyes flashed around the room. Conan was the one speaking, but he was not uttering a single word the men weren't thinking. Craig and Crevan could beat their brother and every other man present, but it would not deter their remarks. And it certainly would not change their opinions.

Slowly, with her back straight and with the regal air of someone who was important and esteemed by all, Raelynd rose to her feet and looked at Laurel. "I want to apologize to you, Lady McTiernay, and you as well, Laird, for my and my sister's appearance. I assure you that we will not be unprepared for dinner again." Pausing, Raelynd turned toward Conan and issued him a fierce look that even those across the room could not miss. The soldiers went silent, and all eyes flickered between her and Conan. Unconcerned, Conan simply crossed his arms and smirked.

Never once wavering from Conan's gaze, Raelynd expressed to the room at large, "I regret for having to leave early due to a headache. I rarely get them unless in the presence of small-minded people. And to those who think I am being overly judgmental of my betrothed's brother when it is obvious he is still very young and immature, I ask your forgiveness." Then, curving her lips into a malicious smile, Raelynd leaned over the table and in a much lower voice so only those close could hear, said, "I would like to remind you, Conan, that we are going to be related very soon. You are certainly a nice-looking boy but you have a long way to go before becoming a man. I can change my looks in an hour. To change you into a presentable, desirable person would take a lifetime."

Their eyes remained locked, but no longer was a mocking, arrogant humor flickering in Conan's blue depths. Too late, he realized that all eyes were no longer glued to her, but him. Irate that she had not only requited herself, but did so memorably, he broke their stare, pivoted, and stomped across the Hall to exit in the back via the kitchens.

Once Conan had left, Crevan calmly stood up and moved over to Raelynd's side. Feeling his hand on her back, she forced herself to walk proudly toward the exit and into the cool night air.

Meriel had been just as stunned as the rest of the group, but she quickly recovered and rose to her feet. "I, too, would like to say good night to everyone present. I look forward to meeting everyone under more pleasant circumstances. Craig, would you escort me back to the North Tower?"

Craig practically leaped over the table and offered Meriel his arm. Giving him a genuine smile, she took it and sashayed by the rows of men who had once thought to ridicule her.

Once all four were no longer in sight, Laurel relaxed into the back of her chair and popped a piece of lamb into her mouth, with a look of immense satisfaction. Tonight's events could not have gone any better.

Conor, seeing her smug expression, muttered just loud enough so she could hear, "I cannot believe you actually *wanted* that fight."

"But look how informative it was. Besides, was it not exactly what you had asked me to do?" Laurel asked innocently. Conor's jaw went rock hard and Laurel did not fight the urge to lean over and kiss him. "Before tonight, no one would have believed Craig or Crevan was going to be married, especially to Laird Schellden's daughters. Both women needed something to shatter people's impressions of them and allow their true character to be revealed for all to see."

Grimacing, Conor shoved his plate with food away from him. Grabbing his mug of ale, he told her, "Next time find another way. I was hungry until I was forced to watch Conan act like an ass and have my younger brothers' honor be saved by two silly girls."

Laurel shrugged, still very satisfied. Raelynd and Meriel had looked foolish but in the end it had only worked in their favor. She would not have changed a single thing, including how they came to Craig and Crevan's rescue, and Laurel's demeanor clearly said so.

Conor huffed, wondering at the nightmare he had created. He had told Laurel to help plan a wedding—not work on people's characters! Worse, he knew his wife had only just begun! *Damn you, Rae Schellden,* he silently cursed. *I didn't want to be involved, and yet here I am, getting tangled in this mess just as you knew I would be.*

Conor looked down at his very happy wife. "Stop. I mean it. Stop every plan you have and leave everything and everyone alone. You're right," he whispered, "there is no wedding. There never was."

Laurel waved her hand to shoo him away. "This afternoon I just might have agreed. Now, I am not so sure."

Conor slunk down into his chair, intertwined his fingers and stared at the ceiling. Most people had calm marriages with only bouts of excitement. With six brothers and an enterprising wife, peace bestowed itself rarely. He had no idea what was in store in the coming month, but he knew it was too late to stop it. Unfortunately, Laurel enjoyed developing and implementing a good strategy as much as he did.

At least this time her plans are for Craig and Crevan, he told himself. And it was their decision to agree to Schellden's crazy scheme. *It is only fair that they should have to pay the price.*

Chapter 10

Raelynd stood motionless under the night sky, still somewhat stunned by everything that had happened. Yes, she had defended herself surprisingly well against Conan, but her shock was stemming from what occurred just before. Never in her life had she needed a hero more than when Conan first disparaged her in front of everyone, and when Crevan defended her, she could not have imagined a better one. Never had any man ever looked more attractive than Crevan when he punched his brother in the face because of what Conan had said about her.

She moved her eyes toward Crevan, who was looking across the courtyard, but she knew his mind was elsewhere. His dark brown hair gleamed in the firelight. Like his brother's, his hair fell just past his shoulders, but where Craig almost always had his pulled back, Crevan let his flow free. Remembering how it felt the night he kissed her, Raelynd resisted the urge to dive both her hands in the soft, thick mass.

Without warning, Crevan shifted his gaze to meet hers. No longer did his expression reflect shame, but approval. The McTiernays were known for their brilliant blue eyes, but Crevan's were different. They were a deeper shade, reminding her of sapphires. And tonight, it was not humor sparkling in them, but something else. Crevan's eyes were filled with admiration, which rattled Raelynd to her very core.

"Crevan," she said softly, "thank you."

"I didn't do anything. You were the one who made him stop," he said firmly.

Not wanting to argue, Raelynd glanced down and spied his knuckles, which were scraped and bleeding. Instinctively she reached out and lifted his right hand to take a better look.

"It's nothing," he assured her, and halfheartedly attempted to reclaim his hand.

Her touch was both reassuring and alarming. When Raelynd had entered the Lower Hall in a state of disarray, he had been appalled. He should have known that Laurel would have quickly recognized the same self-regarding tendencies in Schellden's daughters he had witnessed. But instead of looking the other way or lecturing her, his sister-in-law simply made both Raelynd and Meriel live with the consequences of their decisions. As a result, in a mere half hour, Raelynd had revealed the strong woman he had always suspected lurked underneath. What he had not imagined was that when this side of Raelynd finally did emerge, how he would feel. Escorting her from the Hall with her on his arm, he had not only felt satisfaction, but deep honor at being the one to do so.

All that emotion, her touch, plus the memory of their kiss were about to obliterate the little self-control Crevan could maintain around her. A surge of self-preservation took over and unconsciously knowing it would make her pull away, he said, "If that is how you are going to appear at dinner each night, it is going to make my brother's job that much more difficult getting people to believe he would want to marry you."

Before Raelynd could even react, Meriel bounded out of the doors, laughing alongside Craig. "That was fantastic, Lyndee. Only problem was you did it before we ate. I'm starving!"

Craig, oblivious to the tears welling up in Raelynd's eyes, captured her by the waist and swung her around. "You were amazing!" he shouted. "Never has Conan been publicly trounced by a woman like that!" Then he set her down on her feet and pointed at Meriel. "And you . . . Lord, woman, what did you *do* to your hair?!"

Meriel tried to frown at him, but she was unable to hold it for very long before breaking out into laughter again. "It wasn't me! It was your sweet little niece Brenna."

"Bad idea! Never let her touch either of your heads again!" Craig commanded good-naturedly.

Meriel playfully swatted him. "Not all our ideas are bad. Just think about how much easier your conquests with women will be once word spreads about tonight and how you will literally fight for their honor no matter *what* they look like."

Craig rolled his eyes. "That was the first and last time that will happen."

"Well, then at least applaud Raelynd's idea to put our physical similarities to work," Meriel said with mirth. "For the next month, it will not be your overly tidy betrothed sleeping in your room *and* cleaning up all your stuff. It will be me, and I just shoved it all to one side of the room so you can easily spread it all back out when I am gone."

Craig beamed. "*Finally,* a woman who understands me!" Turning back to Raelynd, he gave her a wink and bent over to plant a kiss upon her cheek. "Thank you," he whispered with detectable sincerity.

"Now," Craig said, looking back at Meriel before grabbing her hand, "I believe you said you were starving. I'm famished as well. So I say let's get some meat into our bellies before we make any more ill-fated decisions!"

Giggling, Meriel craned her head back as she was being half dragged to a building situated between the Great and Lower Halls with doorways providing access to each. "Don't worry, Lyndee! I promise to get you something too!" A second later, both figures disappeared as they entered the kitchens.

Raelynd, still feeding off Craig's gaiety, smiled and waved. Then, without thought, she glanced back at Crevan. Seeing his dark, brooding expression, instantly her cheerful one disappeared.

Crevan knew he was overreacting. He had told himself to just leave the courtyard multiple times, but he could not bring himself to depart, giving his brother even more opportunities to charm Raelynd. She had been upset upon Craig's arrival and he had hugged her, teased her, made her smile, even kissed her . . . all things he wanted but would not allow himself to do with her. If he did, he would do far more.

Her grave eyes drew him in. Last night he had kissed her to end his swelling primal needs but now the memory only served as a tormenting reminder of what was in reach.

Raelynd licked her lips and Crevan, unable to take his gaze away from her mouth, reached out and pulled her gently against him. Though her body was stiff and unyielding, she was trembling and he knew what would happen if he kissed her. Powerless to stop himself, Crevan slowly, inevitably, lowered his mouth to hers, smothering any possibility of her protesting. And like before, she melted into him, clinging to him in confusion and desire.

Catching her face between his hands, his mouth ravished hers and in return her tongue was wild and thoroughly undisciplined. Soft and inviting, she was creating a desire inside him to unite deeply with her, to lose himself in the harbor of her depths.

Raelynd closed her eyes and let herself fall into his embrace, sinking into the one pair of strong arms in which she would ever feel comfortable. His mouth slanted over hers and his tongue penetrated and stroked until she was breathless. Raelynd's arms wrapped themselves around his neck, and she twisted her fingers into his hair, holding on for dear life. Her response to his touch shocked her and Raelynd was sure she was on fire, that every fiber of her was being aroused into a hot burning flame for nothing in her life had prepared her for the sensations Crevan was inspiring.

Crevan could feel pieces of his soul slipping from his grasp. It was the most incredible kiss he had ever experienced. How long had it been since someone had kissed him like this? The answer was not *too long,* it was *never*.

Feeling her begin to tremble, Crevan broke off the kiss, lifted his head, and sucked in air. Raelynd fell against him, her chest heaving with the effort it took to breathe. Suddenly, the doors to the Lower Hall opened and two soldiers exited, followed by others. Dinner was over.

Raelynd quickly withdrew from his side before one of the men sauntered up to her, smiling. "You can come to dinner any way you want, my lady, if you'll do that to Conan again."

He was barely finished and on his way when another shouted out at her, "Mighty impressive, my lady!"

Then one of them walked up directly to Raelynd and

kissed her hand, saying, "Run away with me instead. I like a woman who can look good with her hair tousled." Crevan waited for Raelynd to reclaim her hand and order him away, but she had no idea what the soldier had meant. She just stood, rapidly blinking her saucer-sized green eyes. Unlike her sister, Raelynd had not practiced how to flirt and be coy with men, but these soldiers—many of them he knew personally to be quite shameless in their pursuits—didn't know that.

A sense of overwhelming possession seized Crevan and he roughly shoved Raelynd behind his back. "Don't say another w-w-word."

Raelynd, unaware of the silent challenge taking place, was furious. Men were complimenting her, even kissing her hand as a gesture of respect, and instead of applauding how she was handling the situation, Crevan was once again treating her like a child. Raelynd tried to shake off the grip he was maintaining on her arm and step back around. "I—" she began, but got no further as his grip on her forearm tightened.

If the soldier was aware of Crevan's hold on her, he said nothing as he stared Crevan directly in the eye. After several seconds, the soldier nodded, gave a slight shrug and headed across the courtyard to catch up with his friends. Both he and Crevan knew that if he had not walked away, he would have received far more than a punch.

Once the wayward soldier was out of earshot and the Lower Hall had been emptied of men, Crevan eased his grip. "Just why did you feel it necessary to bruise my arm?" Raelynd demanded, yanking free.

Raw possessive emotion still coursed through Crevan and her naivete caused him to snap. "I wouldn't have to if you were a mature woman who knew when she was playing with fire."

152 *Michele Sinclair*

Raw, cutting pain flashed in Raelynd's hazel eyes. "And just who are you protecting me from? Because the only man I am in danger of being near is you!"

The doors to the kitchens opened, lighting up the northern section of the courtyard. Raelynd could feel the weight of her sister's troubled eyes upon her, but could not muster the ability to say anything reassuring. Instead, she spun on her heel and marched across the bailey, entering the North Tower.

Crevan watched as Raelynd disappeared into the large drum tower. His face was unreadable, a graveyard to the emotions spinning inside him. Standing quietly in shock, both his brother and betrothed were staring at him. It would not be long before Craig would be seeking answers. *"Mo Chreach!"* Crevan cursed, and then headed out the main gate.

Craig swallowed the bite he had stopped chewing and looked at Meriel. Her smile had disappeared and her infectious laughter had ended the second Crevan barked uncharacteristically at Raelynd. Both heard the departing insults, but neither could discern just why they were spoken.

"Maybe we should just keep the two apart," Craig finally suggested.

Meriel nodded. "Far, far, far apart."

Crevan vigorously shook his head as he emerged from the water, scattering droplets around him. Despite the time of year and the months of summer sun, the loch was still cold as the rivers feeding it originated from even higher in the Torridon Hills, just north of McTiernay lands. And yet the noticeable chill of the water had done nothing to ease the tension coursing through him.

Grabbing his leine he threw by the shoreline, he donned

the garment and then started to pleat his plaid when he heard a crunching sound of feet approaching the semi-secluded portion of the shoreline. Only one person would guess he would have come here. A second later, Craig emerged from the woods and without a word, walked up to where Crevan had placed his blanket and began to spread out his own.

Crevan frowned, but said nothing as he picked up his things and sauntered up to his blanket. He had intention-ally not joined the men, either in the Warden's Tower or those in the training fields. He wanted to be alone, but he should have known that was not going to happen after Craig witnessed his grotesque lack of control back at the castle. Tossing his sword and dagger on the soft grass beside the dark material, Crevan lay down, propped his arm so that he could use it as a pillow, and braced himself for a well-deserved condemnation of his cruelty to Craig's betrothed.

Craig took a deep breath. Realizing his brother was not going to say a word—neither an apology nor a justifica-tion, he exhaled deeply and sank down on the blanket. Letting his arms rest on his bent knees, Craig mentally wondered again just why Crevan and Raelynd disliked each other so much. The answer eluded him, but after the latest fight he just observed, the two had to stay apart.

It was difficult enough to convince any Highlander to do anything or not to do anything, but one of his brothers? And Crevan, due to years of being ridiculed, had a stronger sense of pride than all seven of them together. He also had learned to ignore anything said which he did not want to hear.

Suddenly Craig was struck with an idea. Only one person could convince Crevan to change his methods when dealing with Raelynd. Somehow, Craig needed to get Crevan to have a little chat with himself.

"I was wrong," Craig began, smiling internally as he knew those three words would be the best ones to get his brother at least to hear what he was saying. "I should be the one dealing with Raelynd, not you."

Craig paused. Crevan still said nothing, but he knew his brother was listening. If he wasn't, he would have turned over to his side. But he hadn't. Craig picked up a stick and began drawing in the dirt. "Raelynd is pretty, prettier than most, but she is stubborn and often immature. I realize that she can be grating to someone who prefers quiet, demure women not so vocal with their opinions."

Craig stopped again and gave his brother an opportunity to say something, but Crevan remained silent. Still he had not rolled over. Taking that as a positive sign, Craig continued. "I guess it is lucky that I, and not you, am her betrothed, because after what you said tonight, Raelynd probably never wants to see you again." Craig let go a soft chuckle and twisted around to face Crevan. "But that was what you intended . . . right? For her to leave you completely alone and just ignore you?"

Nothing.

With a shrug, Craig turned back around. "I mean what does it matter if you and Raelynd get along? In less than a month, she will be back home, free to marry someone who either appreciates her independent ways or is wise enough to not change them. Until then, maybe you and she should just refrain from being around each other. And when that is not possible, I promise to do a better job of running interference."

Craig inhaled and stretched his back, hoping he sounded supportive enough that his brother might latch on to the suggestion. Standing up, he looked back at Crevan, who still was lying prone but his eyes were now closed. He had not moved a muscle, and though his breathing was steady, Craig deep down knew his brother was far from asleep and had heard every word.

Deciding he could do no more, Craig grabbed his plaid. "I'm going to go and sleep with the men in the fields. The humid air is more oppressive here than in the open. Talk to you tomorrow."

Alone with only his thoughts, Crevan listened as the soft echoes of snapping branches turned into the light sound of Craig's mount riding off into the distance.

Crevan knew his brother had been trying to dissipate his anger toward Raelynd. Craig had even admitted to being in error, which meant that he was near desperate to end hostilities. Problem was that Crevan was not angry with Raelynd, but himself.

The effect she was having on him was baffling, for Craig was right, Raelynd *wasn't* the type of woman he typically sought for company. Plus, when he spent time with her, it was not long before all his years of practiced self-control disappeared. It shouldn't take a lecture from his brother to stay away from Raelynd, he should be *wanting* to keep his distance. But for months now, he had done just the opposite.

Raelynd was ignorant to the effective ways of running a castle, but at least she had undertaken the responsibility and Caireoch's size made it an onerous task. At first, Crevan had only felt a slight admiration of her courage to keep trying, to rally in defense when criticized. But in the last couple of days his thoughts had been consumed with her. This just wasn't like him! Blaming the kiss was too easy. He had kissed lots of women, many of whom—unlike Raelynd—actually knew how to kiss. In the past, he had been able to easily compartmentalize such experiences and effectively ignore them. His reactions had been rational not emotional, and Crevan longed for them to be so again.

It was imperative he regain control over his emotions and behavior. To do that, Raelynd needed to be absent from his thoughts, and for that to happen, they needed to meet. Together, they would calmly discuss their relationship and the two kisses they had shared. After agreeing how it meant nothing and how it would never happen again, the tension between them would dissipate, to everyone's relief.

That was the solution. They just needed to talk.

The sooner the better. For both of them.

"Come in," Raelynd said just loud enough for Meriel to hear, hoping she would not have to get off the bed.

She had suspected her sister would be venturing up to her room if enough time passed. For as long as Raelynd could remember, she and Meriel spoke before retiring, discussing their day, their frustrations, new revelations, and making plans for the morrow. Tonight, however, Raelynd was not in the mood to talk, and certainly not with Meriel.

"I should have known you weren't going to come down and see me," Meriel stated as she closed the door behind her. Like Raelynd, she had finishing dressing and combed the knots out of her hair.

Raelynd flopped down on her back. How could she explain that what she wanted, more than anything, was just to be alone . . . in Crevan's room . . . with her thoughts. She did not need Meriel to tell her she had overreacted. Even as she marched across the bailey to return to her bedchambers, she had known that Crevan was both wrong and right. He thought her immature, and Raelynd refused to accept that condemnation, but if she were being honest, she had to admit to being somewhat self-centered. What was truly irritating was that it had been *Conan* who had made her realize it. And now that she had, Raelynd did not know what to do about it.

Meriel walked into the room and sank into the only chair. "I'm sorry you and Crevan don't get along better, but do not blame yourself. You two are just very different. His calm demeanor causes you to erupt and it is clear you can pull out the worst in him."

Raelynd did not want to talk about Crevan. She did not want to hear how she was bad for him and he for her. "You and Craig seem to get along quite well."

Meriel shrugged and stared at her intertwined fingers as her thumbs rotated around each other in circles. "I, too, am surprised by our friendship."

"Friendship?"

Meriel knew why her sister doubted the term. To the general public, Craig was outspoken and full of energy, but he had a far different side to him than she would ever have guessed. Craig was strong and smart, and despite his outgoing personality, he held an inner self-control she always thought a real man should possess. And for a second, she had wondered what it might be like to be more than just his friend. But that second had passed quickly. They both prized their freedom too much to give it away.

"Aye. That is all it is. I don't think Craig has had very many female friends and though I believed myself to have had a few male ones, Craig is different. Neither of us is wondering if we have another motive when we say or do anything. It's nice."

Raelynd listened to the admiration in her sister's voice when she spoke about Craig and was about to contradict her claim of mere friendship when Meriel said, "I'm glad you are betrothed to him. Together you make a good couple."

Raelynd's heart plummeted. Until now, she had not realized just how much she had been hoping her sister liked Craig not just as a friend, but something more. It would somehow excuse the perplexing feelings she had whenever she was around Crevan.

Once again the topic of conversation was too close to the one subject she wanted to avoid. "Do you think Conan will try again to provoke us?"

Meriel took the bait. Her head snapped up and she looked at Raelynd, her eyes narrowing. "Do you doubt it? I mean I had heard how Conan could be rude, but his remarks were unbelievable!" She pointed to the floor above and continued. "Especially after seeing his precious room. It was more cluttered than Craig's stuff and mine put together! Next time that man says a single nasty word to us, you should go upstairs and clean up his work area. That would teach him a lesson," Meriel ended, nodding with satisfaction at the thought.

The idea had appeal and Raelynd was glad to have a reason to laugh. "Good idea, but it would have to be you. I never intend on going near that man's door. Did you see the look on his face this afternoon at the thought of leaving his study? That place is sacred to him. I don't think I want to even be *around* if someone messed with his things, let alone be the one to have done it."

Meriel exhaled, letting her lips trill, and rose to her feet. "You are right, but he is still insufferable. Tonight, when Laurel compelled us into the Hall and I saw all those men waiting, I realized I *can* be a little self-absorbed. But *Conan*? He is far worse. He is completely indifferent to the pain he inflicts on others."

Raelynd sat up, surprised to hear her sister had come to the same revelation she had. "I was thinking the same thing. I mean, sometimes I don't consider others, but at least I am not unkind to them."

"Well, good night. I'll see you tomorrow. Hopefully it will not be nearly as eventful as the past few days have been. I need a day off before I can start thinking about others and their needs," Meriel said teasingly.

"Good night," Raelynd said, and watched the door swing close behind her sister.

Forcing herself to stand up, she loosened the ties on her bliaut and pulled it over her head. She then removed the woolen overtunic, leaving on her shift. Moving back to the bed, she just stared at the coverlet. It was one thing to flop down on top of the mattress, but it was far more intimate to nestle her body within the same sheets in which Crevan had once slept.

Raelynd glanced around the room. The dim light from the small fire bounced off the walls. The cozy feeling it gave still remained, but now it also emanated something else—loneliness. And it was not her sister's company for whom she longed. Despite their arguments, their raised voices, and even the harsh words they had exchanged, it was Crevan she wished to see.

Raelynd pulled back the coverlet. It only took two days to become accustomed to seeing him before she fell asleep; hopefully it would take no more to end the desire.

Crevan curled his knuckles and touched the door, hesitating. Just moments before, he had run into Meriel on the stairwell, who had not refrained from making it clear that he was to cease hurting her sister. Gone was the shy and retiring woman he had barely gotten to know that day in

the stables. Meriel had a semifierce side to her personality
and she had made it clear that she did not care if Crevan
did blame Raelynd for everything. He, too, was the cause
of their constant bickering. Crevan doubted he would have
been allowed up to his room if he hadn't assured Meriel
multiple times that he agreed with her and was going to
apologize. He almost half expected Meriel to follow him
and listen outside the door, but he had been standing there
for nearly five minutes and he had yet to hear her come up
the stairs.

Drawing in a deep breath, he bolstered his resolve and
knocked.

"Come in," Raelynd muttered, clearly unhappy about
being bothered. Crevan almost turned back around and
left, but he needed whatever it was between Raelynd and
him to be over.

Raelynd had yet to get in the bed when she heard
Meriel knock on the door. She thought about ordering her
sister to just go away, but with Meriel, that would only
stiffen her desire to come in and talk. Castle servants
might have believed Raelynd was the most stubborn twin,
but she was overly accommodating compared to her sister
when Meriel was on a mission.

Seeing Crevan enter, Raelynd felt her mouth drop
open. "Why are you here?" she finally asked in a
choked voice.

Crevan swallowed. Gone was the chaotic, unkempt
look from earlier. Raelynd was wearing only a white chemise with a scooped neck that revealed all too well the
swell of her breasts. Brushed until her hair shone like
strands of lustrous glass, the dark golden locks tumbled
carelessly down her back. He looked straight into her
eyes, swirls of green and gold held within a face only
equaled in dreams.

Mentally, Crevan gave himself a shake. Aye, she was alluring. What woman wouldn't be standing nearly naked in his room? Swallowing, he avoided answering his own question by asking her, "How is the room? Uh, are you comfortable?"

His nervousness disarmed Raelynd. Forgetting about her state of dress, she rolled her eyes and sighed. "It depends. With the exception of your *family,* I think most people are going to believe our story. But Lady McTiernay? She knows something is not right."

"What did you say to her?"

"Nothing," Raelynd answered truthfully, shaking her head. "Meriel and I never strayed from the story, but she asked questions. It would help us a lot if we knew the whole reason we need to not just be away from our home, but to have the world think the four of us are engaged."

Unconsciously, Crevan walked up to Raelynd and placed his hands on her shoulders. "I agree that you should know, but I swore an oath to your father that I would not say anything to you. Promise me that you will not pursue this further."

Raelynd tilted her head and studied his earnest expression. "I will do as you ask if you agree when this is over to tell me the truth, even if my father refuses."

Crevan grimaced, but nodded his head. Raelynd knew he was yielding to her demands, but thought the request a justified one. His leine was untied and in the opening she could see his dark chest hair that the material usually hid. Of its own accord, her hand rose and settled onto the opening, feeling the warmth and strength of his chest. "Thank you," she whispered.

Crevan looked down and got lost in the large hazel depths staring back at him. Her eyes told him everything he needed to know. There was no pretense there. He may not have wanted it to happen, but he could no longer deny that he desired her. Raelynd, however, was young, inexperienced, and ignorant of what it was like to feel passion. For her, what they were sharing was just something new and exciting.

Knowing that and desiring her anyway made him a fool.

Raelynd's stubbornness and self-centeredness were qualities he disliked in a woman, but she also possessed passion, independence, and most of all, a belief in him. Raelynd did not see an incomplete man or a person with defects. She also did not see him as a McTiernay, the younger brother of one of the most powerful lairds in the western Highlands. All she saw was him and it was the most powerful, alluring thing he had ever encountered. He did not possess the control to be alone in her presence, for the desire to kiss her, touch her, *know* her was growing, not ebbing, and next time he would not be able to walk away. And walk away he must, for if he ever saw shame in her eyes because of something he did, it would possibly kill him. His only option was space and time. These feelings arose quickly and only with physical distance and absence could they disappear.

Crevan took a step back. "I also wanted to say something about what happened . . . between us . . . outside." He paused to cough and clear his throat. "I cannot explain why I did that, other than it was a natural thing to do. You and I would probably have embraced any person in the same circumstances. But for the sake of our friendship, I think we should agree that it won't happen again."

Raelynd stood shocked. Crevan had done everything possible to avoid even the word kiss. And what they had shared *was* a kiss. But he was trying to say that the incredible experience that left her and him breathless—meant nothing. And until just now, she would have agreed for she had been trying to convince herself of the same thing. Now she was not so sure.

Raelynd closed the distance between them intending to test his conclusion and see just how indifferent he would remain if she pulled him into an embrace similar to the one they had shared after exiting the Lower Hall. But before she could even initiate her plan, there was a knock on the door.

"Raelynd? It's me, Meriel."

Crevan hastened to the section of the wall next to the hearth. As he moved a tapestry aside, she could see a small door. Without saying another word, Crevan pushed it ajar and disappeared down the secret passageway, letting the weaving swing back into place, once again hiding the opening. A second later, Meriel entered, not waiting for her sister to beckon her in.

"I thought Crevan was up here," Meriel murmured, looking around the obviously empty room.

"He was here, and we talked. I think we are both going to try to be friendlier in the future," Raelynd said, slowly edging her way to one of the arrow slits. Her sister was talking but she was not paying attention. Instead, she scanned the scene below until Crevan finally came into view and then disappeared into the blackness of night.

The man was exasperating and frustrating and many, many other things, but Raelynd knew that her feelings for Crevan had grown significantly in the past few days. At times, she had thought of him both as an enemy and as a friend, but he had grown to be much more than either. She was confident that if she had kissed him when he was in her room he would have succumbed to his physical desires and kissed her back. However, it would not have made his wishes for them to stay apart less real. Crevan wanted to limit their relationship. At most, he would allow them to be friends, like Craig and her sister.

Raelynd knew she should feel relieved. The last thing she had ever wanted was any type of entanglement, especially an emotional one. And yet, it was not relief that filled her. It was a far more disturbing emotion. One she didn't recognize and was afraid to name.

Meanwhile, Crevan headed back to his blanket he'd left by the loch's shoreline. He lectured himself that his meeting with Raelynd was a successful one. He had met with her—in her shift no less—looking beautiful and *nothing had happened*. Finally, he was making progress.

Deep down though, Crevan was well aware that his control was only borrowed. "*Aireamh na h-Aoine ort,* Cyric," Crevan cursed out loud. Everything was that man's fault. The faster he was out of the Highlands the better.

Chapter 11

"Tog às a' rathad!" came a sharp heckle.

Raelynd let go a small high-pitched shout. It was not quite a scream, but it was enough to make the little boy cackle with satisfied joy.

"That's just Gideon," Brenna said, wrinkling her nose at the proud interloper. Another little boy ran up and collided with him so that they both fell to the ground laughing, supremely pleased with themselves. "He is almost as *baoth* as Braeden."

"Just whom does he belong to?" Raelynd asked, not even attempting to hide her irritation, and stepped around both wriggling bodies. She had only been there for two days, but Brenna's brother seemed to be constantly underfoot every time she ventured out of the tower. Having a friend to encourage his teasing behavior and reward its success was going to make this month even longer.

Brenna pointed to a large cottage not far away. "He's the son of Mama's best friend. Miss Aileen's really nice, but her *son*," she said with a sneer, looking back at Gideon to give him one last glare, "is not. I cannot wait until Bonny is old enough to help me get back at them. It's not fair there are two of them and only one of me," Brenna huffed.

Then seeing a woman emerge from another cottage, Brenna instantly got over her anger and ran toward the plump lady, giving her a large hug. Raelynd found it hard to believe just how many people Laurel's little girl knew. When she had agreed to let Brenna introduce her to some of the clansmen and women, Raelynd had never dreamed she would be introduced to any more than a handful of people. And yet, every few steps they were forced to stop. Raelynd was beginning to wonder if little Brenna was unusual for knowing so many of her people, where they lived, what they did, and what was going on, including the good and bad in their daily lives—or if she herself, being Laird Schellden's daughter, was atypical for knowing so little about any of her clansmen who lived outside the castle. Raelynd had a sinking feeling that it was the latter, not the former.

"Ceud mìle fàilte!" came a melodious shout from the cottage Brenna had just pointed to. A woman with light amber-colored hair appeared and was walking briskly toward them. Tall and broad shouldered, her features were strong and yet held a delicate, refined quality that made her very attractive. "You must either be Lyndee or Meriel Schellden. I'm Aileen, Gideon's mother."

Raelynd blinked at the name Lyndee. Somehow, coming from this woman, the nickname she had given herself seemed silly and immature. "You can call me Raelynd."

Aileen's brown eyes softened. "Then Raelynd it shall be. My husband is the commander for Laird McTiernay and—"

A small hand tugged Raelynd's dress. "—and she's Mama's best friend."

Aileen smiled. "That is right. I am," she said to Brenna. "And I hope we can become friends as well. And just where is your little sister? I thought you were to play with Bonny today."

Brenna smiled. "She's taking a nap. I'm too old for naps and Lyndee said I could play with her."

Aileen shook her head and then looked back at Raelynd. "Well, if all is well I must go, but I am really looking forward to meeting you more formally this evening."

Raelynd's brows furrowed. "This evening . . . ?" she repeated softly, drawing the word out.

"Tha mi duilich," Brenna whispered, biting her bottom lip. "Mama sent me to tell you this morning about the party," she said in a voice barely perceptible. "I forgot."

Raelynd's heart skipped a beat. *Another* party? "When?"

Aileen interjected to Brenna's relief. "Tonight at sundown in the Great Hall. Laurel assured me it is supposed to be a very small guest list."

The mention of the guest list size did not do anything to calm Raelynd's racing pulse. She and her sister had taken their meals in their rooms since last evening. Only little Brenna had been able to coerce Raelynd from her chambers to go visiting. The little girl was about to put her and Meriel in danger of repeating their first mistake of not being ready for dinner. Though this time it would not be their fault, Raelynd doubted Laurel would understand or even care.

Grabbing Brenna's hand, Raelynd sent a quick smile to Aileen. "I look forward to seeing you tonight, but we must return now. I need to tell my sister and ensure we are ready in time."

Aileen's brows shot up and there was a twinkle in her eyes to match her knowing smile. Raelynd knew instantly that the woman was fully aware of what had transpired the night before, and in a way, she felt judged. But what Aileen's conclusion was about her, Raelynd could not discern. And at the moment, it did not matter.

Brenna almost had to run beside Raelynd to keep up with her long, hurried strides back to the castle. "What's wrong, Lyndee?"

"Nothing," Raelynd answered quickly. "I just don't want to be late tonight."

Brenna stopped short, yanking Raelynd's arm, forcing her to halt as well. "Let's go back to the village! We have lots of time and I wanted to show you the training fields. I promise Mama won't come get us for hours."

"No," Raelynd said, her voice somber. She had almost replied, *I won't ever be humiliated like that again,* but she stopped herself just in time. "It is important that I tell my sister and that we are not late. We can see the fields another day. Besides, I need to ask your mother to make sure your uncle Conan is invited this evening."

Brenna's silver-specked eyes widened to saucer size. "Uncle *Conan*? No one ever wants him to be at dinner—at least not girls."

Raelynd fought to hide her mischievous smile. Brenna was young, but the little girl was exceptionally perceptive. "Well, I assure you that I am not like everyone else and that I most certainly *do* want your uncle to be there. We have much to discuss. So I need to go."

Blond ringlets bounced as Brenna dramatically slumped her shoulders and rolled her smoke-colored eyes. Raelynd took pity. "But just because I have to return does not mean you cannot stay and play with your brother."

The little girl crinkled her brow at the thought, but a second later let go a long sigh. "Well, someone should look after him. I can't wait until Meghan gets back."

Raelynd watched the little girl scamper off. She had

never met Meghan, nor was she likely to, as she was
visiting Ellenor and Crevan's brother, Cole, until the birth
of their second child. But whoever she was, Brenna and
Braeden loved her. They talked about her continuously
and Raelynd found herself often wishing she had someone saying such flattering, admiring things about her
when she was not around.

Ignoring any distractions, Raelynd went directly to
where the weavers worked and waved at Meriel to stop
and meet with her. Where Raelynd had felt nearly tortured
with boredom for most of the day, Meriel had been perfectly happy and content. She had found and been welcomed into the small group of people who made much of
the materials used not just by the castle, but by many
clansmen and women. Meriel, of course, had no desire to
make plaids, blankets, or rugs. She preferred to design
and create intricate tapestries that were generally ac-
claimed to be some of the most beautiful in the Highlands.

Meriel quickly packed up her things and met Raelynd
in her chambers on the third floor of the North Tower. She
wasn't in the room more than a few minutes when random
thumping and scraping could be heard. "What is that?"

"Better question is *who*," Raelynd answered, "but that
is another discussion. First, I just learned that Lady Mc-
Tiernay is having a small gathering of selected people
from the clan to dine at the Great Hall. And our presence
is required."

Meriel instantly paled. "When?"

"When else do the McTiernays do anything? Sundown."

Meriel sank into the nearby chair as Raelynd began to
rummage through her things to find the black velvet gown
she was going to wear that evening. "What is it about sundown the McTiernays like so much?"

"I have no idea." Raelynd grunted with satisfaction at

finding the garment. She was glad she had decided to bring the somewhat striking gown. It fit her impeccably. The intricate gold embroidery along the hems coupled with the sheer, light cream chemise she wore underneath, made the ensemble both simple and elegant.

The night had hardly begun and Crevan could already feel his skin crawling. Raelynd was acting far too confident, knowing the merciless intent of Conan's desire to embarrass her once again. And his disagreeable brother seemed oblivious to the trap she was setting. Who was going to win this battle was hard to determine, but Crevan was finding it difficult to listen to their insincere exchanges of flattery and do nothing. Everyone present at the small dinner group knew an explosion was imminent, and yet with the exception of him, all—including Craig and Meriel—were blithely conversing.

"I heard that you especially wanted me to be present," Conan drawled with mocking charm.

Raelynd gave him a side glance accompanied with a small disingenuous smile. "I did. I did you a disservice the other night. Men prefer women to enhance their meals, not make them unsightly."

"Well, tonight, you, Lady Lyndee, could enhance even Crevan's solemn night skies."

Crevan gritted his teeth at the star-gazing reference. He wondered if Raelynd remembered the first time they had met on top of the tower. But based on her lack of reaction, it was unlikely. It rankled that she had forgotten and he suddenly wanted to get her attention. *"Raelynd,"* he began, emphasizing her Christian name and not the silly one she had conjured, "I should caution you about becoming f-friends w-w-with my brother."

"Why, isn't he capable of being friends with a female?" she asked, her eyes wide with false innocence, but Crevan knew that look. It was far from harmless.

Crevan was about to answer, when Conan took advantage of the brief silence. "No, my brother doesn't think I can be friends with a woman. But then neither do I. Women are for . . ." He paused to look back at Laurel at the other end of the table and when he saw her engaged in conversation, he dropped his voice and continued, "Producing babes and taking care of the home."

Crevan glanced at Meriel, waiting for her to say something, but Meriel and Craig were too busy talking to each other and ignoring the rest of the party to be even vaguely aware of the discussion taking place.

Meanwhile, an undeterred Raelynd smiled and placed her elbows on the table to rest her chin on interlaced fingers. "What about pleasure? Aren't women necessary for that? Even for you?" she asked loud enough for the entire table to hear. As intended, it got the interest of all.

Crevan choked, but Conan just narrowed his gaze. Their little game had shifted unexpectedly and once again his brother relished the attention. "Aye, women are needed for that and other things. Including taking care of themselves. I'm glad to see that you and your sister can look decent, that is, when you try *real* hard."

Crevan could feel his blood begin to boil but one glance at Raelynd told him that while last night his interference was appreciated, tonight it could result in serious damage to his well-being.

Raelynd raised her brows and let go a deep exaggerated sigh. Crevan noticed that Conan suddenly saw what he had known for some time now—that Raelynd was quite intelligent and surprisingly cunning. Aye, she was immature in some areas, but those were limited to few. Only a fool would believe her lack of management skills meant all her social abilities were just as weak.

"I wanted to ask you, Conan, about all those items you store in the North Tower, but maybe I should just tell Lady McTiernay instead about the pests that I think have moved onto the fourth floor since you have vacated your room. Perhaps I should even suggest that everything get cleared out and cleaned. Maybe I'll even volunteer to help," Raelynd said smugly, and then reached over to plop a piece of cheese in her mouth.

Raelynd had made the remark only loud enough for those at their end of the table to hear, but the look in her eye made it clear that she had no qualms about restating it so that all in the room could learn of Conan's secret trips back to his study. *"'Se peasan a th'annad."*

"'Se bleigeard a th'annad," Raelynd returned, glad to see that her calling him a brat was far more painful than him calling her a pest. Conan would never truly respect her. It was unlikely he would ever even like her, but he would no longer underestimate her either.

"Céard atà uait?" Conan grumbled.

"An apology," Raelynd said simply. Conan's angry blue eyes pierced the distance between them, but he remained silent. She did not say when, but they both knew she didn't intend to let anyone leave until Conan uttered the words.

Instantly, Crevan was on guard. He knew his brother, and Conan would not so easily admit defeat, especially not with an apology as Raelynd had just demanded. Just as Raelynd believed she had a trump card against his brother, Conan most likely held one against her. Laurel must have also recognized Conan's dark look and concluded that she needed to become engaged with the other end of the table.

"Lyndee, Meriel," Laurel called out, "what do you both plan on doing to entertain yourselves for the next month?"

Both women looked at each other for the answer, and then to Crevan and Craig. But they, too, were just as baffled as to what to say.

Laurel sat back and gave a nod to Aileen, which was not missed by any of the four. "I know that you intend to spend a *lot* of time with your betroths. . . ." she said, drawing out the one word, watching with hidden mirth at the squeamish reaction it received.

"You are right," Craig interrupted, "but unfortunately, being gone for so long, we have much to do. So while we will come spend time—"

"—w-w-when we can—" Crevan added.

"—our work will take us away from the castle sometimes for days. . . ."

Crevan suppressed the urge to say *weeks,* but he knew from how Craig was rattling with excuses that his brother agreed fully with his sentiments.

Laurel shrugged with reluctant acceptance. "So what will you both do in the meantime?"

Aileen, Laurel's best friend, sat forward and said, "You both are to get married in a month, correct?" After seeing two slightly bobbing heads, she added, "Then why don't you make your wedding dresses?"

Laurel nodded. "I'll even supply the material." That made Conor slump farther down into his chair with his lips pursed even more in irritation. He had bought those beautiful materials for his wife, not for two dresses that were not going to be worn any time soon or by someone related to him by blood or marriage.

Sensing her husband's tension, Laurel reached over and clasped his hand, but continued to study the other end of the table. "And if you wouldn't mind helping out with

Brenna. I have to address some responsibilities and will be in and out of the castle for the next few days. Braeden will spend most of his time with his friend Gideon or his father. Glynis, our head housekeeper, has agreed to look after Bonny, but having Brenna as well is just too much for her."

Meriel nodded her head; Raelynd bobbed hers more enthusiastically. Taking care of Brenna was a gift. Meriel would be thrilled to make a dress, but to Raelynd, the chore would be sheer torture. Besides, looking after the little girl would be easy for Brenna could practically take care of herself.

Conan opened his mouth to make a sharp retort, but Raelynd's gaze swiftly descended upon him and she pointed up to the imaginary floor above them. "Meriel and I are ready for our apology. And just be glad we are not demanding it to be even more public."

With a great show, Conan rose slowly to his feet and coughed several times into his fist. Pasting on a fake smile, he said to the group at large, "I would like to humbly apologize for my behavior at the arrival of Lady Raelynd and her sister, Lady Meriel. It was my intention to provoke my brothers as I had not seen them in several months, rather than inflict pain on either of them."

"Why, I almost believe you," Raelynd whispered teasingly.

Conan produced an earnest grin and with his chin, he gestured to the group on the other end of the table. "If I had known such a statement would cause the looks on Hamish's, Finn's and Aileen's faces down there, I would have done so much earlier. Thank you."

Raelynd fluttered her eyelids and sighed. "Ah, Conan, I will always be available to help you become a better man and brother."

"Lucky me."

Crevan was about to choke. The insincere flirting between Raelynd and his brother had transformed to one of a different nature, and if possible, one that was significantly worse. Their banter's tone had transitioned from caustic to affable. Too many times had Crevan witnessed Conan woo women, and even those who knew of his brief attention span fell prey to his charms. Unfortunately, at the moment, all of his brother's charisma was focused on Raelynd, and it was working.

"Stop it," Crevan heard himself hiss.

The angry pitch seized Raelynd's attention. "What?"

"Stop encouraging my brother," Crevan answered, his voice barely above a soft whisper.

Straightening her back, Raelynd stared Crevan directly in the eye. "At least your brother goes after what he wants and doesn't suppress his feelings by calling them friendship."

Conan, picking the worst possible time to physically intrude, leaned over and stuck his head close to theirs. "Can I listen? Or are you afraid, brother, that I just might steal her away from you?"

Furious, Crevan pulled back, his eyes cold and proud. "From me?" he scoffed. "O-once again, you are mistaken. Raelynd thankfully is not my problem, she's Craig's." Then he stood up and with a small nod to Laurel and his eldest brother, left the Great Hall.

Later that night, Meriel leaned back in the big chair situated in Raelynd's room to stretch her arms and release a long yawn. "I cannot believe how little Crevan spoke this evening. Do you think it was because of how he talks?"

The comment momentarily stunned Raelynd. Aye, Crevan was not as talkative as his brother Craig, but in her mind, he was far from silent. And even when Crevan was more quiet than usual, to believe his speech was behind the reason was absurd. "I doubt it. Crevan seeks approval from no one."

Meriel shrugged her shoulders and yawned again. "I guess you are right, but I would think his speech would seriously annoy you."

"Me? No. Why?"

"I don't know. You just always demand perfection from everyone regardless of who they are or what faults they have."

Raelynd turned to argue, but closed her mouth slowly without saying a word as memories of life at Caireoch Castle came to mind. Too many of them were of her being highly critical of those around her. "I'm tired," she lied, "and you keep yawning."

Meriel rolled her eyes, but pushed herself out of the padded chair and headed to the door. "I know when I am no longer wanted."

The door closed and Raelynd went to sit down and think in the chair her sister had just occupied when she heard a soft single knock. Letting go a deep, perturbed sigh, she called out, "What did you forget?"

Raelynd had hoped her sister would just pop in, grab whatever item she had left behind, and quickly retreat back to the second floor, but only silence filled the room until another single knock was heard. Meriel would not be going away. Rising, Raelynd strolled to the door hoping her slow speed would irritate her sister as much as being forced to get up and answer the door did her.

Grabbing the rope, Raelynd gave it a yank. Nobody was there. Raelynd narrowed her gaze and stuck her head out into the corridor just in time to spy Conan sneaking up the staircase. "Was that you knocking on my door?"

The disappearing foot halted in midair and then stepped back down, followed by its mate. A second later, Conan was in view, sauntering up to her door. "First, it's not *your* room, and secondly, your question makes it seem like I was pounding desperately to get your attention."

Raelynd crossed her arms and leaned against the door frame, refusing to let him think he could intimidate her with his swagger, his close presence, or his words. "Normally I would agree that two knocks are hardly the sounds of desperation . . . unless of course they were made by you and upon *my* door." She paused and then looked down the empty corridor once more. "How did you get in here? Lady McTiernay has ordered at least two soldiers to guard this tower to prevent *those not allowed* from coming in," she finished, pointing a finger toward his chest.

Conan smiled and deep dimples appeared. On most men they would have come across somewhat feminine, but not on him. Strangely, they caused his cheeks and chin to appear more angular and therefore more rugged. The man was devastatingly good looking, maybe the best looking of all the McTiernay brothers, but he lacked qualities that Crevan had, which kept him from being anything other than nice to look at—if he weren't such a *burraidh*.

"I doubt Laurel posted them to guard you from me," Conan countered.

Raelynd blinked once. "We finally agree. Nevertheless, how did you get in?" The question was more than just mild interest. If he could sneak in, then she could slip out.

"I have my ways."

Raelynd rolled her eyes. She was not in the mood for his games and stepped back to close the door. But before she could do so, Conan whipped out his hand and stopped her. She gave him what she hoped was a withering glance. "I'm sorry, Conan. If you are looking for a good night kiss, you'll have to go elsewhere."

"Raelynd, you don't need—"

Raelynd held up her hand and interrupted, "I'm Meriel."

Conan opened his mouth and Raelynd readied herself for a caustic remark. But instead, his face transformed from the normal confident one filled with arrogance and self-conceit to one of weariness. "Let's call a truce, shall we? I know you are not Meriel and it is obvious that no matter how quiet I try to be, you are going to know when I'm in my study. So I won't tell Laurel about you and your sister's little act of defiance—and believe me when I tell you that I am doing you a great favor in that regard—and you don't tell her I'm still staying upstairs."

With a small shake of her head in disbelief that she was about to agree to anything Conan put forth, Raelynd shrugged her shoulders in acquiescence. "First tell me how studying maps creates all that noise."

Just the mention of his favorite subject changed Conan's demeanor yet again, this time into one of an eager youth. "Whenever I'm trying to work out a problem, I walk. Helps me think and nobody does that better than me," he finished with a wink, and turned to saunter back to his room.

Raelynd just shook her head. "Good night, *a bragadair na mblat is na mbreth*."

Conan pivoted back around at the satirical compliment but instead of issuing an insult he just studied her. "You, Lady Schellden, I just might have underestimated."

"Oh, surely if you did it was only by a little."

Conan licked his lips in a poor effort to hide his smile at the clever rejoinder. "I'll admit you are not nearly the insipid, dumb creature I originally thought you to be, but that doesn't mean I like you."

Raelynd laughed at the concept. "And I doubt that I will ever truly like you. But I have good reason behind my contempt."

"As do I," Conan stated with complete seriousness. "You would be no good for Craig. You do not have true feelings for him."

"Do not worry about Craig. He is aware that I do not love him, just as I know he does not love me."

"And yet supposedly you are to be married."

Raelynd locked her jaw and with an unwavering stare, answered, "Aye."

Conan quickly marched back to where she stood and, moving in very close, he whispered, "Why? Why *marriage*? Just who are the four of you protecting? Your father?"

Conan just asked her the one question she wanted answers to herself. But as she had none to give, Raelynd merely shrugged, trying as hard as she could to maintain a blasé persona. "What was it you just said? You have your ways? Well, we have our reasons. Your brothers know what they are doing." *They better,* she added to herself.

"Well, if they do, then it will be the first time—at least for Craig," Conan rejoined.

"Unlike you, who always knows what he is doing and never makes a rash or unwise decision."

Conan arched a brow at the sarcastic, but fierce defense of his brothers and openly assessed her. Raelynd forced herself to remain motionless and act unfazed by the candid scrutiny. "I think I just might have been wrong to think you weren't pretty enough to marry. If you ever need anything, I am only a floor away."

Raelynd could not help but let her jaw drop in shock as he left her side and disappeared up the stairs. The man was incorrigible, but at least they were no longer trying to verbally flay the other alive . . . at least for now. But his singling out Craig about not knowing what he was doing had her perplexed. What did he mean? And why had he not included Crevan?

Crevan snuck into the North Tower through the murder hole located in a hidden spot on the external side of the tower's plinth. His anger still simmered inside and he knew it would not dissipate until he spoke with Raelynd and made sure she understood the dangers of flirting with Conan.

The man was notorious for treating women poorly and then seducing them. The illogicality of it still confounded him, but he had accepted the fact that, with very few exceptions, his little brother could charm almost any woman into doing anything. And after tonight, it was clear that Raelynd was not among those impervious few.

"Good night, *a bragadair, na mblat is na mbreth.*"

Hearing Raelynd, Crevan stopped abruptly in the stairwell, remaining hidden. *Good night, oh boaster of might and knowledge?* And he did not need to wait long before his guess of whom she was talking to was confirmed.

"You, Lady Schellden, I just might have underestimated."

The *gaduiche*! Crevan felt his insides turn. It was one thing for Conan to charm women, but it was another when he himself was beguiled.

As Crevan continued to listen to both of them claim to dislike the other with obvious joy, his usually well-controlled temper started to rear. What was Raelynd thinking? First Craig, then him, now Conan? Did she intend to seek out every McTiernay brother? *Good thing you aren't around, Clyde, or you would be mincemeat in this woman's hands.*

The sound of Conan's footsteps continuing up to the fourth floor reclaimed his attention and the image of Raelynd going upstairs with him suddenly flitted through Crevan's mind. Unable to shake the unthinkable idea, Crevan ascended the last few stairs to the third floor. He did not know what he expected to find, but he was not prepared for Raelynd to still be out in the hall, lost in thought. That was until he came into view.

"What are you doing here?"

The cold welcome in contrast to her demeanor toward Conan left him feeling empty with only anger to fill the void.

"Maybe I should be asking what *Conan* was doing here," Crevan snapped.

The jolt of seeing Crevan just as she was thinking about him instantly disappeared, leaving only a wintry feeling in its wake. How the man got along with anyone was beyond her. Even Conan was easier to handle for he was always contemptuous; one just had to be ready and refuse to respond to his barbs. But Crevan was another matter. The friction between them was personal and it was not in her power to keep his words from hurting.

"What do you think he wanted?" she asked sarcastically. Crevan had been right there at the dinner listening to her threaten his brother with her knowledge of his being upstairs.

Crevan took a deep breath and sought to get a firm grip on his resolve. One of them had to stay calm and rational and he was determined it was going to be him.

Refusing to have an argument in the hallway where his brother and her sister could hear, he marched down the hall and, catching Raelynd's arm in a light grip, brought her into his room and closed the door. Instantly, he knew he was in trouble.

Just last night he had stood in this room with her and nothing had happened between them. He had truly believed he could do it again. But unlike Raelynd, who was just learning what it was to be a woman, he was fully aware of his needs and desires and what it would take to alleviate them. And while a cold swim was far from what he wanted, when it came to Raelynd, it was his only option.

Raelynd watched as Crevan silently pivoted and grabbed the rope handle to open the door. She could not believe it. He just dragged her inside and intended to leave without a word? "Where are you going?"

Crevan didn't turn around. "Away from here."

"You mean away from me."

"Aye."

Raelynd crossed her arms in frustration. "So, you came to look at me, snap a few words in my direction, and disappear. What kind of man are you?"

Hearing that final question, Crevan's spine went rigid and he moved in close to look down at her. "I'm the kind of man who knows when to leave."

"I think you want to stay."

She was right and they both knew it. So when she went up on her tiptoes and pressed her open lips to his, he did not refuse. At first her kiss was tentative and Crevan struggled to keep from responding. However, Raelynd, stubborn about everything, refused to stop and the kiss gradually turned possessive and sensuous, tantalizing his very core. Crevan knew she would only continue her pursuit until he caved and returned the embrace.

Gathering her in his arms, Crevan pressed his lips softly against hers intending to break away almost immediately. But when Raelynd's arms went around his neck, her tongue took advantage, mating with his. Gone was any remaining willpower as they teased and tasted the other.

He kissed her, hard and deliberately, letting her feel the frustration and temper she had aroused in him, letting her know that he was now in command.

Raelynd moaned with sheer pleasure. When Crevan remained resistant for so long, she almost had given up hope. Maybe she was wrong and he did not have feelings for her, but the pressure against her mouth was deep and persuasive and undeniable. Crevan desired her just as she did him. Something primitive and utterly feminine deep inside compelled her to press her body against his and she felt him begin to shake.

Cold air hit her face and her eyes sprang open. She was no longer in Crevan's arms and she struggled to remain standing as her numbed senses came back to life. Raelynd knew she was to blame for the abrupt ending. There had been no thought behind her actions, only desire. Her body had craved to experience the same passion and attention her mouth was receiving. It had been unexpected and her reaction had been instinctive. And yet, it somehow had caused Crevan pain. "I . . . I'm sorry. I just wanted to prove that you and I—"

"Don't worry about it," Crevan said, interrupting. He gave a slight shrug in an effort to appear unaffected by the embrace. "You're just discovering things and wanting to kiss men is not unusual, but uh, you shouldn't with me. Everyone thinks you belong to my brother."

"For only three more weeks."

Three long weeks, Crevan thought to himself, and raked his hand through his hair, glad he had moved to the other side of the room. "Well, I don't need any more practice so you'll have to find someone else to have fun with."

Raelynd swallowed, unwilling to comprehend what Crevan was saying. It was as if he was telling her that she only wanted to be kissed, that she would have thrown herself at anyone. And what was that "find someone else to have fun with" comment? Didn't he understand that she had met a lot of men, mostly not by choice, including him. But he was the one who made her heart race and her skin tingle. He was the last thing she thought about before she fell asleep and the first thing when she opened her eyes. And the way he just kissed her, Raelynd couldn't believe that Crevan didn't feel the same.

"I don't believe you. What just happened proves you are attracted to me."

Crevan took a deep breath and exhaled. With a small shrug, he said, "Aye. I'm attracted to you. What man wouldn't be? And this casual flirtation needs to stop, because you, my lady, are not ready for more."

My lady, Raelynd huffed internally. *You, Crevan Mc-Tiernay, are the one who is running away.* "I believe I am."

"Really? Because 'more' is a relationship. More is marriage. And for those to thrive takes hard work. You avoid anything that is not easy or done for you. That makes us wrong for each other."

Raelynd felt the full impact of his assessment and the honesty that went behind it. It hurt, deeply, but pain had been his goal. Her work ethic was not behind Crevan's fragile desire to put not just physical, but emotional distance between them. And though hard to imagine, she knew of only one thing that would cause Crevan to shrink away from something that he wanted. Fear. Not for himself. But for her.

"Look at me," Raelynd quietly ordered. And when his blue eyes finally locked on to hers, she saw stark need etched into every line of his face. She also saw the control and self-discipline that governed that need, and was once again reminded that with him, she would always be safe.

"Can you ever remember a single time that I was unsure of what I wanted or of myself?"

Crevan swallowed. Raelynd was many things, but indecisive was not one of them. It was a character trait he admired. Hesitation caused from self-doubt put one at a disadvantage of being easily manipulated. "I cannot."

Without releasing her gaze, Raelynd moved toward him until once again she was in arm's length. "Until you, I never desired to be kissed, touched, or even to have a man in my presence."

Crevan's jaw clenched and his eyes slightly narrowed with cynicism. "If you recall, it was what? Only a few days ago you were chasing my brother . . ."

Raelynd threw her hand up in the air, cutting him off. "I was not chasing your brother, if I was chasing anything . . . it was . . . well, I don't know how to put it . . . but it was knowledge! How was I supposed to know that he had no idea how to kiss someone? I thought if anyone knew how it would be a McTiernay and Craig was *leaving*. I never wanted him. I never wanted any man until you."

"Raelynd," Crevan said with the patient tone one used with a child, and reached out to grip her shoulders, "you just learned what it means to want someone."

Raelynd licked her dry lips, noting his set face, clamped mouth, and fixed eyes. Crevan was both right and wrong. While she was inexperienced, he needed to understand that what made her desire him was not simply a good kiss, but something far more powerful and rare.

Reaching up, she put her hands on his in the hopes that it would keep him from moving away from her once again. "Of all the men whom I have ever met, I rely on your judgment the most. Aye, even more than that of my father. I love my father, but to him I need to be coddled, even protected, from the truth. You"—Raelynd paused as

she blinked back the tears starting to well in her eyes—
"have always been honest with me, but only in the past
few days have I understood what a gift that is. Please,
please don't treat me as a child. Stop protecting me. I need
to understand my feelings and I only become more confused when you push me away."

Raelynd waited for Crevan to do something, say anything. She had tried kissing him into admission and knew
she could do so again, but that was not how she wanted to
gain his affection. She choked on a sob as tears she had
been trying desperately to hold back scalded her eyes,
flooding them until her sight disappeared.

Crevan gathered her up in his arms and buried his
face in her hair to hold her. He had only meant to protect
himself, not hurt her. All his life he had been sure of
his actions—of what was right and wrong. Problems, regardless of size or nature, had clear solutions . . . just not
always easy ones. But with Raelynd, Crevan was finding
it difficult to even define the problem. In his mind, there
were many and for each one there was a different, and
often conflicting, resolution. He was in a battle for his
sanity and whichever way he chose—leave or stay, he was
going to lose.

Raelynd lifted her head, her eyes still filled with tears.
Crevan's heart clenched in his chest, knowing what they
both wanted and what it would mean.

Tenderly, Crevan stroked her face, brushing back her
hair. "If I kiss you . . ." he whispered.

"I know and I don't care."

And no longer did Crevan. *Right and wrong be damned,*
he thought as he placed a hand on the back of her neck and
laid a kiss on her mouth that was so soft, so beautiful, they
both trembled. Slowly, he parted her lips and drew her in
to him, seeking all the passion that she had to offer. Her

body pressed against him, snuggling against his chest. A deep groan of satisfaction escaped his throat.

When his lips finally had touched hers in a soft, deep kiss, every nerve in her body sprang to life. She could feel the power of his restraint and it only excited her more. The feel of his tongue in her mouth, touching every corner, tasting her, reached down to the very depth of her soul, paralyzing in its intensity.

He pulled her even tighter against his torso, straddling her legs over his powerful thighs as he untied the laces to her gown. She could feel the throbbing mass of his erection, and her lower body instantly responded to the intimate contact of his male arousal. Raelynd bit her lip upon the onslaught of wet desire and a small whimper escaped her lips. The growing need to touch and be touched by him was one unlike she had ever known. And in that moment, Raelynd knew he was the only man she would ever give herself to.

Raelynd's soft cry did nothing to restrain Crevan's intentions, it only motivated them. His questing hands roamed all over her body as he maneuvered her bliaut over her head, swooping down to hungrily recapture her mouth lest she protest. He delved deep inside until she was once again under his spell, meeting his driving tongue, thrust for thrust, taking and giving back in turn. Her honest response ignited an unquenchable desire for more.

Knowing she would not protest, Crevan edged aside her chemise to expose the curve of her shoulders, and shifted his attentions lower. Delicate kisses soon turned passionate as he found the sensitive vein on her neck pulsating with the rhythm of her heart. He nuzzled it and gently sucked, delighting in her quiet gasps, while she buried her head in his chest and clung to him tightly.

Before he could leave evidence, Crevan made his way

to her chest in a line of searing kisses. His right thumb brushed over a nipple, and began to tease the already taut nubs. His heart pounded. Crevan thought he would go out of his mind with the craving he felt.

"Ah, love, tell me to stop," he begged, knowing only Raelynd's plea would give him the ability him to end this growing need.

The palms of his hands were cupping her breasts fully, kneading them, making her unable to speak. And yet a distant part of Raelynd heard Crevan's plea and answered him the only way she could. Arching against him, seeking the excruciatingly sweet pleasure, Raelynd laced her fingers into his wavy hair and offered her breasts to his hungry mouth.

Her impassioned response caused Crevan to lose restraint and he lowered his mouth to encompass a pink bud. It was firm and ripe and the taste of it sent a shudder of excitement through him. "You're so beautiful," he told her as his tongue left a trail of fire as he moved to the slope of her other breast. "You take my breath away."

Raelynd's body began to throb and she could no longer hold back her moans as again and again, he stroked her hardened peaks while gently rasping his teeth against them. But when Crevan knelt down and began to rain hot, wet kisses over the thin chemise, down the length of her belly, the added stimulus became too much. Raelynd could no longer stand up. Her legs crumpled but instead of falling she was in the air, being carried to the single big chair in the room.

Nuzzling his ear, Raelynd whispered, "I bet you never had so much fun in this chair."

"Not as much fun as you are about to have," Crevan chuckled. He knew she was still riding the sensual high he had created. And while a lone voice was murmuring about the hazards of what he was about to do, a much louder one was reminding him that Raelynd wanted this just as much as he did. She wanted to feel desired, learn what passion meant, and experience physical pleasure. And he wanted to be the one who introduced her to such ecstasy.

Finding the opening to his leine, her hand dove in and her fingers began to stroke the dark, silky chest hairs they found. Sexual tension seized his insides and he grasped her wrist, stilling the burning touch. Tonight had to be just about her, not him. His gift would be the memory of her responsiveness to him. Otherwise, they would be tied to each other forever. Something Crevan knew she did not want, even if she didn't realize it.

When Crevan halted her hand, the amorous fog that had surrounded her began to lift. Raelynd tensed and was about to protest when his mouth reclaimed hers in a kiss that was much deeper than before. It was as if all their previous kisses were a mere prelude to what was about to follow.

She had hoped he would return his attentions back to her breasts when his hand moved to her leg and began to caress her silky skin. With each stroke, he lifted her chemise higher and higher. Her heart pounded as her body burned and trembled with anticipation, instinctively seeking what was to come. She had the wildest urge to jump back as he edged closer to her core while depositing kisses over her cheek, then earlobe, and finally her lips.

Blood pounded in her veins, her knees trembled. Her entire body began to shake as his hands drifted lower, finally tangling his fingers into the intricate twists of her honey-colored curls. She arched against him. "Oh, God," she moaned, and began to writhe in his lap.

Soon the pressure of his palm wasn't enough and her hips begin to rock against his hand. Crevan needed no further encouragement and eased one finger into her damp heat. She was burning for him and that heat belonged to him. With a low, husky groan, he began to stroke and caress until Raelynd was twisting in his arms.

Raelynd cried out when he slid into the most secret of places with a touch so gentle she couldn't believe the pleasure streaking through her. Stunned, all she could do was cling to him helplessly, letting the pleasing sensations take over her mind and soul. No one had ever touched her like that, but he had only begun. Adding another finger, he drew lower finding all the previously unknown places of pleasure until her lower body tingled with tremendous need. And yet, she craved even more of him inside her.

"Crevan. Oh, please, Crevan. Please." Raelynd writhed against his hand, clinging to him, pleading for more. She thought she would go mad. Then she felt the delicious twisting sensation build swiftly inside her. With a soft, choked exclamation, she surrendered to the glittering storm that swept over her.

As she parted her lips to cry out, Crevan clamped his mouth tightly down over hers, swallowing the soft sounds. He groaned, forgetting his own need, lost in the innocent beauty of her response, feeling as if this inevitable moment had been written in the stars and nothing could have prevented it.

Crevan took several deep breaths in an effort to regain his composure. Raelynd's breasts were still pressed against him, and he could feel the rapid pulse in her neck pounding against his shoulder. He had never experienced ecstasy by just giving someone else pleasure. There was only one explanation and he was a fool to have denied the truth until now.

He was in love with Raelynd Schellden.

If it had not had happened to him, he would not have believed it possible, but in the period of a few days, his feelings for Raelynd had grown beyond interest, admiration, and friendship. It was far from intentional, and in many ways unwanted. Somehow, though, he would have to fall out of love with her. For Raelynd Schellden was not his to have, nor would she ever be. Consequently, he needed to stay away from her because next time he was not sure he could stop himself from claiming her as his. As much as he wanted Raelynd, forcing her to be with him would be worse.

Women, especially feisty spirited ones like Raelynd, never had and never would seek him as a partner in life. And despite Raelynd's genuine response, that fact had not changed.

Crevan felt a finger slide down his cheek in a soft caress. He looked into her velvety green eyes. "I'm sorry."

Raelynd smiled. "Why? I don't remember complaining. And don't tell me that you were not enjoying yourself."

Crevan grasped her stroking fingers in his hand. "I did, but it cannot happen again."

The seriousness of his tone captured Raelynd's full attention and she sat up, yanking her chemise back onto her shoulders. "You mean until we are married."

Picking her up, he stood and then placed her back in the chair. Raking his hands through his hair, he said, "I'm not going to marry you."

The cold, sober words were like buckets of ice water raining down upon her head. "Because of Craig?" she asked, her voice faint, knowing the answer.

"No . . . I mean yes, you belong to him. But that's not the only reason." He turned to look her directly in the eye.

"Raelynd, I am the first man you have ever kissed. You are experiencing things until now you had no idea existed."

Hurt pride caused Raelynd to respond. "I had an idea."

"Love, I may have been fooling myself, but you weren't deceiving me. You wanted to learn what it was to feel like a woman. The reason you wanted *me* to be the one to teach you is because of all the men you know, you probably thought I to be your biggest challenge. I only wish that I lived up to that image." Crevan let go a sigh and walked over to the door. Before swinging it open, he turned and said, "You have the potential to be a great wife, Raelynd. You deserve someone better than me and someday you will realize I'm right."

Raelynd watched as Crevan disappeared through the door, shutting it behind him. *Oh stubborn man, I may have been fooling myself, but I promise you, you cannot deceive me,* she said out loud to herself, paraphrasing his words.

His comment about her belonging to Craig was ridiculous. She and his brother barely exchanged a dozen words even when they sat right in front of each other. She would have to keep her distance from Craig just to keep people from realizing just how much she *wasn't* his. She was Crevan's and was hers, and if he was honest with himself, he would agree. One did not need to be old and have multiple experiences with passion to know the difference between liking someone, seeing them as a challenge, and being in love. . . .

The thought stilled Raelynd. She did know the difference and though at one time Crevan was a challenge, then someone she liked, he had grown far beyond that in the past few days. She loved him. Passionately, wildly, and it was not a crush that would eventually die due to absence. Though she could not prove it, she knew Crevan felt the same. So why didn't he want to marry her?

You have the potential to make a great wife, he had said. *Potential.* Raelynd mulled over the word and all the conversations they'd had during the past few months. What she needed to do was make him proud of her. Then, she would be irresistible.

Chapter 12

Cyric reached over and grabbed the once full pitcher of ale and poured the last of its contents into his mug. He grimaced for a moment and then smiled as he realized there was plenty more all around him. He downed the drink and reminded himself of how brilliant he was to come to the buttery. It was the perfect place to hide away from everyone and everything. Servants came back here only during mealtimes and the butler just ignored him when he added a couple of fresh drums to the already large stack of barrels sitting against both sides of the narrow room.

The benchlike table he was sitting on wobbled as he leaned over to refill his drink from one of the buckets, hanging off a nearby barrel spigot. He plunged his mug into the golden heaven and pulled it out with pride, deciding such a method was much easier than trying to pour himself more. This way less went onto the table and the floor and more went into him.

Cyric let go a loud belch and smiled. "Good one," he said, complimenting himself.

"Who's in there?"

The soft, musical voice startled him and he nearly fell

off the narrow table. "Rowena," he mumbled, praying his speech only sounded slurred in his head.

He had thought about her often the past couple of days for she had been the only person who had been kind to him. Everywhere he went his eyes searched for her, hoping to get a glimpse and if possible find a way to talk with her again. Now here she was. And just like everything else here at Caireoch, now that he got his chance, he was going to mess things up.

Rowena popped her head into the room and her eyes grew wide as she saw Cyric on the preparation table at the other end of the room. "Why are you sitting there and just what are you doing?"

Cyric produced a large grin. "No chairs. Had to use the table." Waving his mug at all the barrels, he added, "I think my uncle has too much of this stuff. It will go bad in a few days if he doesn't drink it up. I'm just trying to help."

Rowena stepped into the room and crossed her arms, shaking her head. "This buttery stores ale for all who live and support the castle. The butler is one of the busiest men who work for the steward, making sure there is enough for all to have."

Cyric grimaced and his shoulders fell. "Another thing I did wrong," he muttered.

Rowena bit her bottom lip at the pitiful man in front of her. He was incredibly good looking, but to her, he was much more attractive in this state than when he tried to be impressive. "Move over," she said gently, and after he complied, she hopped onto the table beside him.

Cyric nudged her with his shoulder. "I've decided this room is my favorite place in Caireoch."

Rowena smiled in understanding. "The bakery used to be mine. It was always warm and smelled wonderful."

Cyric bobbed his head, his golden eyes wide. "I like

bread, but it doesn't get you drunk, like this stuff." He paused and moved closer to her ear and whispered, "And there are people around a bakery."

"You don't want to see anyone?"

Cyric shrugged his shoulders. "They don't like me. I keep messing things up."

Rowena reached over and took the almost empty mug out of his hands and put it on the other side of her. "Well, I don't thinking drinking yourself into unconsciousness is going to help."

"Nothing will," Cyric sighed, letting his head fall against the wall behind him. "I don't even like to get drunk, I just thought it would be better than going out there."

"And what is out there that is so awful?"

"Failure. Ridicule. Humiliation. And something even worse," he mumbled.

Rowena tilted her head and her brown eyes looked steadily into his. "What?"

"I don't even want to be a laird. Never did. I want to work with the king. You know, solving clan problems, responding to attacks. Stuff that I understand." Cyric watched as Rowena bit her bottom lip at the idea of him giving advice to the king. It bothered him. "I'm good at it. Really. I'm better than *anyone* at finding peaceful solutions when given a chance. But it doesn't matter anymore. Once Uncle tells my father what happened today, I'll never be allowed near the king, let alone become a laird."

Rowena studied Cyric and almost told him that indulging in self-pity was not going to help. She had been out assisting her mother in the village and had not heard of any rumors, so whatever happened could not have been that bad, but maybe it was. The man felt like all of the Schellden clan was against him and soon they would be if he kept acting pompous or dejected. Maybe he just needed a friend. "I doubt you could have done something so terrible in one day that would result in such loss."

Cyric reached out and fingered a loose brown curl that was framing her face. The light smattering of freckles on her nose and cheeks was endearing and he wished he could kiss every one of them. "You really are pretty."

"Ah, the ale is talking."

"Aye, the ale and me. Pretty and smart and nice. I wish I was worthy of kissing you."

Rowena drew his hand from her hair and gave it a soft kiss. "Maybe someday you will be."

Cyric shook his head. "Not after today. Not if you knew."

Rowena released his hand and placed it in his lap. "Let me decide. Tell me what happened."

Cyric rolled his eyes to glance at her and seeing she was serious, said, "First, I was forced to wear my bedcovers to the laundry to recover my clothes."

Rowena's hand flew to her mouth to hide her amusement at the conjured image of him walking across the courtyard wrapped in a sheet.

Cyric rolled his eyes at her response. "Well, at least you are not laughing. It was either that or some awful gown that was left in my room."

"Gown? You mean a lady's dress?" Rowena asked incredulously. Only she and her cousins wore bliauts. Most of the clanswomen wore arisaids, which were far more functional and sturdier garments in which to work.

Cyric nodded. "I called out but no one was around and after an hour I gave up and went to find my clothes. I was told by the steward that they had been the first to be gathered and laundered. And do you know why? He said it was in deference to who I am. Ha! Like that was the reason."

"And what did you say?"

Cyric glanced sideways at her and said, "I told him that I'd rather be like everyone else and dress in something dry in the morning."

Rowena pursed her lips in an effort not to smile. She wondered how surprised the steward had been to find Cyric wandering around in his bed sheets. No doubt the steward believed stealing Cyric's clothes was the easiest way to keep him in his room until he was ready to deal with him. Rowena considered telling Cyric that he didn't fail, but actually passed the most likely prearranged test, but decided against it. "Well, I can understand how that might be a little embarrassing, but the laird will understand."

"He didn't with the chickens."

Rowena's dark eyebrows shot up inquiringly. "Chickens?"

"Aye," Cyric said, and exhaled, trilling his lips as the memory took over. "After I was dressed I found my uncle, who wasn't happy because I was late."

"Late to what?"

"I dunno," Cyric replied, shrugging his shoulders. "But I know that look he had. It's the same one my father gives me. And it is not a good one."

Rowena could not decide if the ale was helping the conversation or hindering it. It was making Cyric more approachable as well as incredibly honest, but also harder to understand. "I thought you said chickens. What was the laird doing with chickens?"

Cyric crinkled his brow. "Nothing. We were going to the training fields where he was going to introduce me to his men. We were walking across the courtyard and he was pointing to one of the towers talking about something when somehow I ran right into a bunch of crates full of chickens and ground corn. They fell over and broke and chickens went everywhere. Their food was stuck to my shirt still wet from the laundress and they started pecking at me. It hurt."

Unable to stop herself, Rowena started to laugh. Oh, how she wished she could have been there to enjoy the scene. Accidents were common around the castle, but rarely were they so amusing. Rowena wondered if it was truly an accident or something the laird had masterminded to judge Cyric's reaction.

"Go ahead, laugh." Cyric's voice was resigned to the idea. "My uncle just gave me another 'look' and told me to help clean the mess up and that I would have to meet the men another time."

Rowena took a deep breath and suppressed her mirth. "Both events I agree are not flattering, but they are not anything that would keep you from becoming a laird or working with the king."

"That's what I thought," Cyric agreed, bobbing his head. "So as soon as my uncle returned I went to meet him to talk about how I could help him. I know weapons. So I thought, start there."

"That sounds like a good idea."

Cyric gave an exaggerated shake to his head and waved his finger. "Bad idea. He let me go on and on about my skills and when I was done, did he ask me to lead the soldiers? Train them, demonstrate what I can do? No. He asked me why I wanted to be a laird."

He stopped and Rowena sensed his disquiet. The answer must not have been a good one. "And you said . . ."

"The truth. That I wanted people to respect me. If I was laird everyone would have to listen and give value to my ideas. I am guessing that was not what I should have said."

Rowena rolled her eyes at the obviousness of his last

comment. She glanced at him, but he was studying his interlaced fingers, unaware of her critical reaction. She was distantly related to the laird and his daughters through her great grandmother, the sister of Laird Schellden's grandfather. As such, she had been treated like family, though her mother made sure she understood the limitations of their connection. Being near the same age as Lyndee and Meriel, she had grown up playing with them and was very aware of the effects from their father's overindulgence. She also knew they were good and wonderful people deep down. Rowena guessed that Cyric was not nearly as arrogant or self-centered as he seemed. He was just a victim of similar coddling.

"Of course I realized immediately that I gave the wrong answer," Cyric continued. "But when my uncle next asked just how I planned on proving to him that I could be a good laird to the clan, my mind went blank. I certainly couldn't tell him that I didn't think I had to prove anything. I thought all I had to do was pick one of his daughters and marry them."

Rowena pulled physically back at the idea. She knew that arranged marriages were common and that the king supported them if it strengthened clans and alliances, but the concept had not been practiced in the Schellden clan for several generations.

Cyric grimaced and raked his fingers through his black hair. "I don't like the idea any more than you, but I thought that was what I was to do. Anyway, believe me, I am fully aware that 'blood alone' is not going to get me anywhere up here, especially a lairdship. So, my uncle asks again, how do I plan on becoming laird. This time I have an answer."

"Which was . . ."

"That with my knowledge and skills I could lead the army and that alone would earn me the right."

Rowena produced a low whistle. "That is one way," she murmured.

"Aye, exactly what my uncle said," Cyric replied, his voice vacant. He did not even want to tell Rowena what happened next. His uncle had pummeled him with questions. How many soldiers does a clan need full time? When do they get to farm? What was the cost of having an army, fitting them with weapons and feeding them as they trained? How does one support such men with housing and what do you do if they become married and have children? Could he, as laird, be responsible for taking care of the well-being of multiple soldiers' families who would need clothing, shelter, and food? If so, how? If not, then where would his soldiers come from when attacked and how did he expect to protect the clan?

Cyric had no other option but to admit that he did not know the answer to any of those questions. And then came the moment that made him relook at his whole future.

Rae Schellden had risen to his feet and stared him in the eye. "You are surprisingly arrogant for someone who knows so little about being a Highlander, let alone a Highland chieftain. I wonder what King Robert would say if he knew how little you comprehend about the workings of a clan and its armies. But I can tell you how my neighbors would react when they learned such weakness reigned at the head of the Schellden clan. My people would exist no more."

Cyric had swallowed in disbelief. "I cannot believe our close allies would raise weapons, especially if the king had—"

"Not *our* allies, *mine*," Schellden corrected. "And understand this, you are no longer in the Lowlands where the

English have infected your customs and ways. *I and I alone* make the rules and decisions for this clan—no one else. I am loyal to King Robert and out of my respect for him I will give you until my daughters' wedding to prove yourself as a *potential* heir."

Cyric let his head fall back against the wall once more as his uncle's words repeated themselves over and over again. Cyric's headache returned and he went to search for his mug. Seeing it on the other side of Rowena, he hunched over and rubbed his temples.

"What are you good at?" she asked

The unforeseen question surprised him and he sat up. "What do you mean?"

Rowena spread out her hands and shrugged her shoulders. "Just that. What can you do well, maybe better than well?"

"I know a lot about weapons."

Rowena sighed. Every Highlander knew how to fight. "Anything else?"

Cyric scratched his chin. "I can help people with their problems. My grandfather tells me that I have a way with finding out what people want and getting them to get along."

"Then start there. Show my uncle you can solve problems, not just cause them."

"How?"

Rowena smiled and hopped off the table, grabbing the mug before he could. "I don't know. You just said that you did. But I would start by getting sober."

Cyric waved his hand at her. "I'm always sober. Not really good at drinking too much. Besides, I don't like drunks."

Rowena was relieved though not surprised. Men who did drink often learned quickly how to keep from sharing their thoughts—especially self-denigrating ones—when drunk. Cyric was unlike any Highlander she'd ever known. Physically he was the size of one, and if his muscles were a sign, Cyric was not lying about being able to use a sword. But he was far more refined and handsome than most swordsmen she had met.

When she had first encountered him, she had thought him useless due to years of being pampered. And while he had definitely been coddled, she suspected that was only one layer of him. The insecure need to gain his father's respect was another. But if one looked hard enough beyond those two impressions, they would realize there was far more to Cyric. In actuality, he was a very complex man, full of intelligence, wit, and a desire to improve. He was learning lessons he should have been taught years ago, but he was learning them.

Cyric Schellden was indeed more than she had originally believed and she suspected the laird would think so too if he gave his nephew a chance. She just hoped Cyric would find a way to earn it.

"Just remember," she said as she moved to the doorway, "one cannot prove himself with things he knows nothing about. Don't try to be a Highlander. Just be yourself."

Chapter 13

Meriel poked her head into the last place she could think her sister would be—the kitchens. Built between the Great and Lower Halls with doorways giving access to each, the kitchens were actually a set of smaller rooms merged together. The vaulted ceilings and large central hearth made the rooms appear larger and airier than they really were. Only a handful of servants were inside working; all but one turned to look at her and smile.

Almost everyone they had met at McTiernay Castle was nice and supportive, with two exceptions. The steward and the cook.

"Fiona?" Meriel asked timidly. "Do you know where—" But before she could finish the sentence the gray-haired, stoutly built woman pointed her stubby finger to the back. Meriel sighed in relief. The woman could cook but she was also incredibly difficult and could berate one with her tongue just as well as someone else could with a stick.

Meriel angled her head and behind the kitchen she could see fragments of the scullery, a place she preferred to avoid. Grimacing, she walked through the kitchens and stopped at the open door that led into the enclosed grassy area. In the middle were two figures, one large and one small, hunched over an indeterminable object. "Well, that is one way to look after Brenna," Meriel commented, gaining their attentions.

"Come over here!" Raelynd called out eagerly. "Brenna is showing me how to make scented soap."

Meriel's eyebrows rose questioningly. How her sister could be interested in such an endeavor was a mystery to her, but then Raelynd had always needed to understand how things were done. "It helps me run things smoothly," Raelynd would say. Meriel often thought things ran smoothly in spite of her sister, not because of her. There was the steward after all. Besides, nothing ever went wrong, so how hard could running a castle be?

Even here with Lady McTiernay gone north for the day to visit a friend, things were in order and working as they should. Of course, if they didn't, Fallon, the Mc-Tiernay's steward, would be right there, demanding to know why. After the past three days, Meriel learned how thankful she was that their steward was nice. Fallon's temperament matched that of his frizzy gray and red hair. A judgmental soul, he constantly stroked his wild beard and chided her for always being where she shouldn't, before ordering her back to her room. Brenna had tried to excuse the man, saying he was crusty around people with whom he wasn't familiar and it took a while to get to know him. Meriel had opted to stay out of his way as in a month she would be home and back to her old routines.

Raelynd picked up the gray speckled mass. "Come smell!"

Meriel refused and so Raelynd came to her, placing the nondescript lump under her nose. The mass smelled of roses. "Nice."

"I know it's roses and you like camellias, but they don't

really have the fragrance needed for soap. Begonias also do not—"

A deep booming voice took over the conversation. "How you two women manage to be where you shouldn't all the time is a mystery. Unless you intend to help prepare the meals, leave these kitchens. And do not venture into the inner bailey until it is time for dinner. Some of the men are going to train in the courtyard and I will not be responsible for your safety. It might be safer if you just stay in your rooms."

Meriel joined her sister in giving the man a scathing stare, but the burly steward was unfazed. Knowing they could do nothing else, Raelynd and Meriel brushed past him with Brenna in tow, grabbing some food as they exited the kitchens. Such thievery would put Fiona in a foul mood, but that was Fallon's problem. He could deal with the cranky woman.

As they entered the North Tower, they saw Fallon gesture to the guards and knew that he was ordering them to prevent their exit. "It's like we are prisoners!" Raelynd exclaimed, marching up the stairs to Meriel's room. The untidy bedchambers had become their daytime haven with all the light and nights were shared in Raelynd's room by the fire.

Meriel followed Raelynd and Brenna up the stairs and into her room. Slipping off her shoes, she walked across the odds and ends to the windowsill where her latest incomplete masterpiece lay waiting for attention. "I spoke to Craig about the guards and he refused to do anything! He didn't understand why I would care about them wanting to make sure we are safe!"

"Safe!" Raelynd huffed, and fell onto the bed, landing on her stomach beside little Brenna. It was the one place in the chaos Meriel called a room anyone could sit or, in her case, lie down. Raelynd watched as her sister immediately picked up the garment that had received her nearly undivided focus for the past three days. "Aren't you done yet?" Raelynd moaned.

Knowing Raelynd was only bored, Meriel spread the light gold bliaut out. "Look what I've done so far. I'll make a chemise from this," she said, holding up a piece of sheer linen, "and then I will embroider the hems in gold and pearls. Isn't it lovely?"

Raelynd looked toward the windowsill and nodded in agreement. The gown was going to be beautiful, just as everything Meriel did with a needle and thread was. "It is too bad that it shall never be worn."

"That is where you are wrong. It will be worn, by you, on your wedding day."

That comment got Raelynd's attention. "I'm not going to—"

Meriel bristled and pointed to Brenna. "Of course you are going to wear this dress, Lyndee. Even if you weren't getting married to Craig, you would have to eventually marry for the sake of the clan."

Raelynd grimaced. "I don't think you should call me Lyndee anymore."

Almost dropping her needle from shock after years of her sister refusing to respond to anything else, Meriel looked up and asked, "Why?"

"I don't know," Raelynd said with a shrug. "To make Father happy."

Meriel did not believe her but she knew better than to press Raelynd for the truth. Her sister had been acting odd since this trip began and probably would not be back to normal until it was over. What she needed was her freedom.

"I need to get out of here," Raelynd exhaled, echoing her sister's thoughts.

"Why don't you go riding?" Brenna suggested, picking up a brush, hoping to play with Raelynd's long hair. "That's what Mama always does. She says getting away to go riding not only helps her, but me, Papa, Bonny, and probably has saved Braeden's life."

Raelynd chuckled, wishing she could. But the one time she had gone near the stables, Fallon had intercepted her. She and Meriel would be allowed to ride if their future husbands accompanied them. Everyone else, however, was busy and it was too dangerous to allow them to venture out alone.

"What did Craig have to say this morning?" Raelynd asked, knowing that he usually stopped by briefly to say hello to Meriel before he left for the fields. But according to Brenna, Crevan had yet to make an appearance anywhere near the castle.

The little girl knew almost everything that was going on inside the curtain walls. Brenna couldn't be deemed a gossip as she usually did not share what she learned, but she was a master eavesdropper and no conversation was safe from her ears if she was running around. And according to her, Crevan had not set foot inside the castle walls since the dinner party three nights ago.

Crevan was staying away just as he promised, only Raelynd never dreamed he actually could. Not if he truly felt about her the way she believed.

Meriel plunged a needle into the gold cloth. "Craig really did not talk about much today. I think news came from Father and before you ask, I didn't learn anything. Craig would only say that plans were going just as they should be and in a month we would be going home."

Raelynd coughed and when Meriel looked, she pointed to Brenna. The little girl had just unplaited Raelynd's hair and was busy brushing but she was also listening.

"Ouch!" Meriel cried, and then sucked her finger. "Oh, no, it's ruined!" She picked up the broken needle so that all in the room could see. "This! This is why I should be with the seamstresses and weavers. There I could sew with others who understood what I was doing, appreciated its difficulty, and I could *replace broken needles*!"

Raelynd's and Brenna's eyes popped open. It was rare to hear Meriel raise her voice and both knew who she was yelling at—Fallon, who claimed she could not join the seamstresses as they were too busy to entertain her.

"Is this right?" Brenna asked as she completed the intricate braid Raelynd had taught her.

Raelynd pulled the woven hair in front of her and inspected the overly loose braid. Seeing the apprehensive gray eyes, she sent Brenna a glowing smile. "It's wonderful! I can't believe how much you have improved. Now you can help me fix this bed."

"Don't you dare!" Meriel shouted. This time her anger was directed at those in the room.

"What?"

"Start cleaning. First the bed, then you will be straightening around the bed and before I can stop you everything will be put up and impossible to find. Sit back down and don't try it again."

"Then what else are we all to do? You cannot sew and I'm tired of doing nothing."

"We could go swimming," Brenna offered.

Raelynd mopped her brow. "I would, but we are stuck in this hot tower."

"I'm not stuck," Brenna countered.

Meriel leaned forward and in her typical soft mellow voice said, "Unfortunately, sweetheart, you are. Those guards won't let us leave and I doubt they will let you go anywhere either while training is going on."

"No one ever watches the back way."

Raelynd's and Meriel's spines both went rigid. "Back way?" they repeated simultaneously.

"It opens on the other side of the wall. It's how I sneak into the village." Brenna's grin grew until it took over her whole face. "Even Braeden doesn't know about it. He thinks he knows everything. But he's wrong. He just knows boy stuff."

"Brenna," Raelynd hollered, picking the little girl up and swinging her around. "You are my new, most favorite friend. Let's grab some food and go on a picnic followed by some swimming!"

Brenna was the first out of the murder hole, followed by Raelynd and then Meriel. Just as promised, the secret exit hidden by a broken cart that held a large stack of freshly chopped wood had led to the other side of the castle walls.

Walking on the outskirts of the village, all three kept quiet, hoping not to catch anyone's attention. As they maneuvered past the last set of cottages, Brenna started to giggle. Raelynd scanned the scene and spotted Aileen's son, Gideon, and Braeden playing swords with sticks. "They are going to be so jealous when I tell him what we did. Teach him for thinking girls can't have any fun."

Meriel licked her lips. "Do you think we should be doing this? I don't want to get Brenna in trouble."

Brenna tried to glower, but her pale blond hair and gray eyes set in an angelic face completely countered the attempt. Her voice, however, conveyed the stubbornness she felt. "I'm not a little girl like Bonny. I'm big enough to know how *not* to get into trouble."

Raelynd pulled Brenna back behind a cottage and out of sight. "Are you now?"

"Aye," Brenna confirmed, bobbing her head up and down. "I'm as old as my brother and he's *always* in trouble. Papa took him to see the training fields and Braeden almost got chopped up while everyone was training. I would have known to wait. But I didn't get to go."

"Just how far are the training fields?" Raelynd asked, wondering if Crevan had been spending time there.

"Not far from the loch. They are close to where Crevan sleeps at night."

"How do you know where Crevan is sleeping?"

Brenna shrugged. "He told me the other night when I asked where he was going. He said he likes to look at the stars by the water near the rock where I learned how to dive. Do you want me to show you?"

Raelynd's green and gold eyes twinkled with anticipation. "I would love for you to show me. I'm guessing it is a perfect spot for a picnic."

The area Brenna took them to *was* perfect for a picnic. Trees crowded most of the loch's shoreline, but they were enjoying one of the few places that had a wide clearing with the forest to the left and rolling hills leading back to the castle on the right. In the far distance the majestic gray giants of the Torridon Hills could be seen.

Meriel licked her fingers after swallowing the last piece of bread and lay down to stare at the cloudless sky. "Fiona really is a good cook."

Raelynd nodded and stretched. "Think she would let us live if we sneaked some more food out tomorrow?"

"Probably not, but I say we try," Meriel said, laughing.

Brenna, not understanding, stood up and declared, "I'm hot. I thought we were going swimming."

Raelynd grinned and got to her feet. "You are correct and I say we tarry no longer. So strip off—"

A ghastly scream like a woman in terror engulfed the clearing, blocking out all other sounds. It was followed by a moaning sound and Raelynd was instantly chilled to the bone. "Where is it?" she whispered to Meriel, who was also busy searching the scene.

"It can't be," Meriel murmured to herself. "It's not night. We didn't do anything."

Brenna began to shake and huddled close to Raelynd as another, even louder shriek filled the air. "What is it?"

"A wildcat," Raelynd answered as she stroked the little girl's back while trying to find out where the danger was coming from. She had never seen one live, but she had witnessed the damage a wildcat could cause when hostile. And by the sound of the cries, this particular animal was very unhappy and aggressive.

"There," Meriel said, and pointed directly to the edge where the forest met the grassy hills, making it equidistant from either direction the three of them chose to run. They could move into the loch, but unlike other felines, wildcats were not afraid of water and even liked to fish.

Raelynd, finally spotting the animal, let go a soft curse. Well-defined with brown and black stripes that matched a thick ringed tail ending in a blunt black tip, it was just as she feared. A wildcat—one of the most treacherous predators in the Highlands. It could grip its prey, climb trees, fall unharmed from great heights, and sprint with blinding speed.

Hissing, the large cat's hackles were raised and it was staring at the three of them, constantly inching closer. They were its prey. The only thing Raelynd could think of was that its cubs were nearby and it considered them a threat. And if that were the case, simply leaving the area was not an option. The cat would chase them and attack until it was assured they posed no further danger.

The cat snarled again and Raelynd knew they had very little time before it charged. "Meriel, take Brenna and when I say run, you two head as fast as you can back to the castle and get help."

Meriel's eyes grew large. "What are you planning?"

Raelynd reached down and picked up a large, partially eaten leg bone, hoping the scent would be enough. "I'm going to distract the cat by climbing that tree and throwing it this bone for food."

Brenna squeezed Raelynd's waist, burying her head. "Mama would kill it."

Laurel's ability with a bow and arrow was well known among the western Highland clans. Until now, it was never a skill Raelynd had any interest in learning. "Everything will be fine, Brenna. Just reach out to Meriel and . . . now! Run!"

The moment Meriel had Brenna's hand clasped in her own, Raelynd had given the signal and they started running in the direction of the castle. As they had walked to the loch it had not seemed that far, but now the distance felt massive. She wanted to look back and see Raelynd and know where the cat was, but it would only slow them down. If Raelynd's plan worked, they needed to get help as fast as possible. If it did not, then she and Brenna had no time to look around. Their only hope was encountering someone before the wildcat reached them.

Raelynd launched herself toward the trees, heading for the closest one she could climb. The pounding of the cat as it closed the distance confirmed she had been right to divide their small group. Reaching the tree, Raelynd hauled herself up on the first branch and was about to climb to the next one when the cat caught up to her. Raelynd dropped the meat bone, but the animal ignored it. Instead it contracted its muscular body and then leaped, snagging Raelynd's dress as it came back down.

Pain seared through Raelynd's leg and she could feel warm blood streaming out of the wound, but fear for her life kept her moving upward. By the third branch, she turned to assess her situation and upon seeing the extended claws, realized her plan had been flawed. The cat was going to climb.

Panic engulfed her as Raelynd watched the wild animal jump high into the air and reach out to seize the tree's bark. Then, just before it grabbed hold, it suddenly yelped and convulsed, falling back to the ground.

Down below the animal twitched and Raelynd saw the arrow embedded deep in its side. Hearing the sound of pounding horse hooves, Raelynd looked up and saw the angry face of Laurel with her bow prepped and ready to fire another shot. Raelynd's jaw went lax and she nearly fell out of the tree.

"Are you hurt?" Laurel demanded, sliding off her horse. "Can you get down?"

"My leg," Raelynd answered, and immediately started to descend as another rider joined the scene.

The large man had shoulder-length auburn hair, braided on the sides and pulled back allowing her to see dark green eyes that flashed disapproval. "She's fine," he said, answering Laurel's unspoken question about her daughter, "but calling for you. I had one of the men escort them back to the castle."

"Thank you, Hamish. Please help her," Laurel ordered.

Raelynd was about to argue and tell them both that she needed no help, when the pain in her calf became unbearable and her injured leg gave out. She fell right into Hamish's arms. He proceeded back to his horse, hauling both her and him onto his mount. Then he and Laurel aimed their horses back to the castle, leaving behind the picnic blanket and sack.

Guilt plagued Raelynd and she slunk down into Hamish's arms as the three of them rode back in silence. She knew Laurel was furious and could not blame her. Brenna could have been seriously injured or even died, and Raelynd's own wound did not help dispel Laurel's anger. And Crevan . . . Raelynd cringed to think about his reaction.

"Doesn't she belong to you?" Obe inquired.

The question startled Crevan and he almost dropped the dagger he was holding. The smithy was one of the few places little Brenna avoided that also provided a view into the comings and goings of the castle. So until he wanted others to know he was around, Crevan had insinuated himself into the small area.

Ironically, for years Crevan had believed the old silversmith did not like him. Obe rarely spoke and avoided contact with people as much as possible. But sharing the same space with him for a few hours each afternoon during the past several days, Crevan had discovered the smithy was distant with everyone. The man was not taciturn; he was shy.

Crevan went to the opening and looked out at the commotion near the gatehouse. Laurel slid off Borrail and handed her horse's reins to the stable boy. She did not look happy. Behind her were Brenna and Meriel, but it could have been Raelynd. The two looked identical so it was hard to tell just who it was at a distance, but he guessed

Meriel due to the overly pensive look. "I wonder what has Laurel so upset," Crevan murmured to himself.

"Probably that," Obe replied, using the misshapen sword in his hand to point toward the other side of the bailey.

It was then Crevan understood the root of the court-yard's disquiet. One of Conor's guards, Hamish, was carrying an injured person into the Star Tower. Crevan was half tempted to seek out Meriel and chance encountering Raelynd just to inquire as to who his friend was carrying and what had happened. But before he could decide, the guard moved out of Hamish's way so that he could enter the tower and for a brief moment, Crevan was able to see who was in his friend's arms. Raelynd.

From so far away, Crevan could not discern the extent of her injuries, but that she was being carried into the Star Tower spoke volumes. Primarily the private chambers of the laird, his wife, and family, the unusually tall tower saw few visitors. But it was also where Laurel sent anyone who was seriously hurt. The light in her dayroom was one of the brightest in the castle and it made inspecting and stitching up wounds easier.

Without thought, Crevan headed to the front gate and confronted Meriel. "W-w-was that your sister I just saw?"

Meriel blinked in surprise and then again at seeing how dark Crevan's blue eyes had turned. The storm brewing in them matched the hard line of his mouth. It frightened her. "I . . . I . . ."

"Oh, Crevan," Brenna bawled, and buried her head in his stomach, latching her arms around his waist. "It was so awful. We were out on a picnic and a wildcat came, but Raelynd got it to chase her so we could get away. She would have *died* if Mama hadn't come and killed it."

"But she didn't, right?" he asked, holding his breath.

Brenna nodded, but Meriel answered. "It got her leg. That's all I know."

A frisson of fear coursed through Crevan at the thought of something happening to Raelynd. He hated fear and he most especially hated reacting to it. Crevan took a grip on his nerves and pivoted. He had to see her, make sure she truly would recover, and then he would give her a lecture that she would remember for life. It was time she started thinking of others!

Crevan rounded the last set of stairs that led to the fourth floor and Laurel's sitting room. Three arched windows let in the sun's rays, illuminating the room decorated in gold and green. Two empty chairs were in front of the crackling hearth, which was already warming the spacious room. Several chests of various sizes were positioned along the walls for easy access and under one of the windows was an overly stuffed settee, upon which a large, busty woman sat ripping cloth into strips.

Hagatha, the clan's midwife and one of Laurel's closest confidants, was one of only three souls Laurel would have ever left alone in her room. But when one first looked upon her, just the opposite impression came to mind. Hagatha had bright red untamable hair and wore a crimson chemise with a plaid arisaid secured by a man's leather belt. The woman was outspoken and at times irreverent, but she was fiercely loyal to Laurel, who returned the sentiment.

Hagatha gestured with her chin toward the bed. Pale and unmoving, Raelynd lay prone with her wounded leg exposed. Several deep scratches were overshadowed by one long gash that went nearly down the full length of her calf. Anguish ripped through Crevan knowing the pain she was in.

Hearing someone enter, and knowing what was to

come, fear knotted inside Raelynd. She had never been
stitched with a needle and the pain already emanating
from her leg was excruciating. Turning her head, she saw
Crevan. Her heart jumped, thinking he had come to be
there with her, and then plunged as his face revealed
barely controlled anger. It triggered her own. She was in
pain and guilt flooded her. What she didn't need now was
a sermon. "Leave me."

The unexpected order shook Crevan into movement.
He walked over to the bed and stared into the ripped flesh
where the softest of skin used to be. "Of all the reckless,
thoughtless things, Raelynd. Did you tell anyone before
you went out? Did you even bother to ask for an escort?"
He shook his head, answering his own question. "And
why? Because you didn't want to hear the word no. When
are you going to learn?"

"I told you to leave," Raelynd repeated.

Hagatha, done ripping the cloth to tie the wound once
stitched, stood up and said, "The girl made a mistake."

"She could have died."

Hagatha arched an inquisitive brow at Crevan's lack of
concern for the others who had also been in danger.
"Well, so could have Brenna and Meriel if it wasn't for
her bravery."

"W-what you call bravery, I call f-foolish."

Hagatha scoffed disrespectfully as she did to anyone,
including the laird, when she found them worthy of it.
"You are a harsh and judgmental fool, lad, which in my
experience, is unlike you. Might want to ask yourself why.
Meanwhile, I think the girl is right. You should leave, especially before Laurel gets back with the medicines. I
get the feeling she somehow thinks you and Craig are partially to blame for ignoring women you supposedly intend
to marry."

Crevan stared inscrutably at the audacious woman and then glanced back at Raelynd. She refused to look at him, but her pallor was getting worse and he knew he was partially to blame. He came in here demanding from her what he had not been able to do himself—consider the consequences of his actions.

He so wanted to see her as the girl Hagatha referred to, but she wasn't. Raelynd was a woman and no matter how frustrating she was, he would continue to desire her and that was a problem. Until the end of the month, she was Craig's. But after that, she belonged to her clan. She was born to be a chieftain's wife and a laird was something he was never destined to be.

"She's out," Hagatha said, confirming Laurel's presumption that Raelynd would not remain conscious beyond the first stitch.

Relieved, Laurel quickly finished sewing up the gash. "It looks bad, but the wound is not as deep as I thought. She should be up and walking in the next day or two if she doesn't fever."

"You're still angry."

"Somewhat," Laurel lied, tying off the string. Truth was she was furious. She had yelled at Brenna, whom Meriel stood up for when they returned. In a better mood, Laurel would have admired the fact that both women had risked themselves to protect her daughter. "I'm mostly riled with myself. I should have known that boredom was not the way to get them to admit the truth and ask to return home."

Hagatha pointed to Raelynd, lying on the bed. "This one won't ever admit to anything. She's stubborn. Maybe just as stubborn as you."

"But far more foolish."

"Her man Crevan feels the same."

Laurel's head shot up and she halted, stirring the paste she was making for the poultice. "Crevan was here?" she asked with a mischievous smile.

"Aye. Mad and afraid and mean."

Laurel licked her lips with constrained eagerness. That meant she wasn't wrong. His avoidance for the past three days made her hesitate in her earlier guesses about where his true feelings lay, but not anymore. "Crevan is not her man. She is to marry Craig."

It was not often Laurel had the opportunity to shock her dear friend, but that simple statement did. Hagatha's jaw dropped. "Can't be. Crevan loves her and she him. It's obvious."

"I know."

"Then why is she to marry . . . ?"

Laurel shrugged her shoulders. "I've tried every way I know to get Conor to tell me and the four of them refuse to budge from their story."

"Maybe they don't know the reason why."

"Crevan and Craig certainly do."

"Maybe. Or maybe they just think so."

Laurel exhaled, smearing the medicinal mixture on Raelynd's leg as Hagatha bound it. For many, the eccentric midwife was far too forward with her opinions, and rarely applied tact to even the most uncomfortable situations. That's why Laurel loved her so. She never had to wonder if Hagatha was tempering or embellishing her viewpoint. Besides, her knowledge of the McTiernay brothers was extensive and she had incredible intuition. So, Laurel listened when her friend spoke. "Hmmm, would explain some things. But there has to be another way I can help these two—not just for Craig's and Crevan's sake, but their own."

Hagatha watched Laurel work with pride. The laird's wife had skills before they met, but she now was just as proficient, if not better, as she herself was at tending the sick. "You know, if boredom is what set them off, then that could be fixed."

Laurel tied off the last of the bandages and stood up. "Devious you are, Hagatha, but I like it, especially since time is not on our side. I just need to shake loose the wisdom they already possess. Give it a chance to breathe."

Hagatha's eyes began to twinkle. "Well, English, I wish I could stick around and see how things go, but babes are about to be born."

Laurel smiled and winked at her friend. "It will be interesting. Think I should invite Aileen into the plan?"

"Aye," the midwife laughed boisterously. "If you don't, she'll scold you for meddling."

"Beside myself, she has the perfect solution for the monotony of a noble's life."

"Aye, that you two most certainly do," Hagatha grinned.

Chapter 14

Fathomless black eyes held Cyric's golden gaze for several silent moments before the man gave a signal to his horse toward the gatehouse. Once through, the old farmer urged his mount into a lope and was soon out of sight. The situation was bad.

Cyric shook his head and headed toward the Great Hall. He had almost been convinced that he was once again naive to Highland customs and relationships. But his uncle had decided not to meet with the unwelcomed visitor, and though Schellden's decision was intentional and based on previous interactions, it had been the wrong one. Soon, someone was going to be dead and clans would be at war. The thought of the impending and yet unnecessary blood about to be shed made Cyric shudder with anger.

Pushing open the two large doors, Cyric quickly scanned the room. Only servants who were finishing collapsing the trestle tables after the evening meal remained. His uncle and his men had left.

"Out!" he shouted to all in the room, doing nothing to hide his frustration.

Surprised, all work stopped as eyes shifted to him.

Cyric had never been unpleasant or outright discourteous, which allowed most of them to ignore some of his more obvious Lowland mannerisms. Tonight, however, his demeanor was anything but friendly and everyone silently decided that enough work had been accomplished for the night and it was time to leave.

Finally alone, Cyric sat down in one of the hearth chairs and buried his face in his hands. Caireoch was well maintained and the servants who supported the castle were disciplined and hard working. Still, they stared at him with an unwavering eye as if they were assessing him. Rowena had claimed it was his imagination when he had commented one night that it was more than a little unsettling to be judged and found lacking by a servant.

Tonight, though, he did not care. He didn't care what anyone in this clan thought of him or his ideas.

The door creaked and, hearing footsteps, Cyric didn't even look up when he shouted, "I said out."

"Well, at least you can bark like a laird."

Cyric's gaze immediately shifted to the curvaceous figure walking toward him. "Maybe that's all I can do. Tonight I learned that to be a Schellden chieftain requires one to be overly confident and intolerant of other opinions, and I want no part of it."

Rowena arched a single dark eyebrow and said playfully in an effort to yank Cyric out of his dark mood, "So, then why don't you just leave? If you don't want to be laird, then—"

"Not now, Rowena. I'm not in the mood to be cajoled, placated, or scolded."

Rowena paused in midstride at the seriousness in Cyric's tone. He raked a hand through his hair and settled back in the chair to stare pointedly at the dying fire in the hearth. Whatever was bothering him was not just a trivial matter of wounded Schellden pride. Previously, fear of disappointment had been behind his stress. Tonight, however, genuine anger was the cause.

"Should I leave?"

Several seconds passed before Cyric finally spoke. "I admit to being a fool. Not because I had believed my uncle would be eagerly waiting for me, ready and willing to have me marry one of his daughters and quickly assume a leadership role in this clan. I put to you that almost anyone when told such news by the king would have believed the same. My foolishness was in that I had attempted to prove my value in areas I knew nothing about. But that does not justify my uncle's current unreasonableness."

Rowena resumed her walk, but slower. "Ah, the famous Schellden obstinacy. It runs in all of our clansmen—including those who grew up far away."

Cyric scoffed at the insinuation and rose to his feet. "Obstinate?" he repeated while looking her dead in the eye. "At least I listen. I listened to my grandfather, my instructor, my king . . . *even you.*"

Rowena licked her lips and nodded, acknowledging that he had been receptive to what she had said. Upon seeing her admission, Cyric began to pace. His face was dark, almost haunted, as if he knew something he wished he did not. In many ways, he reminded her of her late father, who was also a thinker, prone to pacing as he worked through a problem.

Until now, Rowena had no interest in him as a man, despite his unquestionable good looks. If anything, she had taken pity on Cyric. But like his uncle, she had again misjudged the Lowland relative. Cyric was ignorant of much, but that did not mean he was weak willed. Far from.

"What happened?"

Cyric halted briefly to look at Rowena as she took a seat. His first impulse was to refuse to tell her. She was a woman and to frighten her with only suppositions was both ungentlemanly and dishonorable. And yet, Rowena might be the one person who was in a position to prevent the impending clash. She had influence with his uncle where he had none.

"Do you know of the McHenrys?"

"Aye," Rowena answered as she furrowed her brow, clearly puzzled by the question. In her father's youth, one of the smaller McHenry clans had settled on the northern Schellden border. From time to time, they would steal a cow, and a Schellden clansman, in retaliation, would see to it that some of their sheep would go missing.

"Ian McHenry arrived today to talk to the Schellden laird and yet my uncle refused without explanation."

Rowena let go a long sigh of relief. "I wouldn't worry about it. The rivalry between the Schellden border farms and the McHenrys has been going on for years, but it never gets too bad."

Cyric grimaced and shook his head before resuming his strides back and forth in front of the large stone hearth. "I know all about clan border skirmishes of that sort. Ian McHenry was not here to discuss the pinching of animal stock."

Rowena opened her hands, palms up and gave a shrug. "But with Ian McHenry it is always about the theft of his sheep."

"Not today it wasn't."

"How could you know?" Rowena pressed defensively. "You don't know him. Ian McHenry always looks like he's upset about something."

Cyric paused and crossed his arms before looking directly into her puzzled brown eyes. "Highlanders aren't the only ones who deal with raids, Rowena. I know men and I know when they are angry over a few stolen animals and this was not one of those times. This was personal."

Rowena stood up and walked over to place a hand lightly on his forearm. "You make it sound like McHenry is going to do something awful."

"He is."

Rowena stared up at him incredulously. Skepticism was etched in her wrinkled forehead.

"Rowena, I admit that I tried to prove myself with expertise that I didn't have, but that does not mean I am completely without some skills. My grandfather had me sit with him while he handled clan affairs since I was ten. In that time I learned many things, including what a man looked like before he was about to attack. And Ian McHenry intends to be heard—one way or another."

Rowena recoiled. "Attack? He wouldn't! While pockets of McHenrys are littered throughout the Highlands, the majority of their clan is located far to the west. I've heard they are fierce fighters, but Ian McHenry is without an army. Going against our laird's men would mean his and his family's death."

"By the time my uncle attacks, it will be too late."

Rowena took another step back as the gravity of what Cyric meant registered on her face. "Too late for what?"

Cyric took a deep breath. Rowena's face had paled considerably, indicating she believed him. That fact alone was reassuring. Unfortunately, it did not change anything. "Rowena, I don't know what Ian McHenry is planning, but he came here in an effort to avoid bloodshed. Only you can convince my uncle to ride out and meet with him."

Rowena's already large eyes grew even wider. "Me?"

"Reason with my uncle. Plead. Do whatever you have to. You two are close. Don't deny it."

"Aye, we are family, and he has been like a father to me since mine passed, but I cannot talk to the laird about clan affairs. Nobody could now that he's made a decision." Rowena took a deep breath and crossed her arms to think for a moment. Then with a small shake of her head, she said, "If you truly believe that you are right, then you are going to have to find a way to stop things."

"I would, but McHenry knows I don't speak as the Schellden chieftain."

Rowena grimaced for it did seem impossible. "You once claimed that you were better than anyone at finding peaceful solutions."

"Only if both parties are willing to—"

Rowena's lips thinned at the excuse. "Then you are not what you claimed," she retorted in cold sarcasm.

Cyric's deep golden eyes took on a black layered look and he crossed his arms, causing his already large muscles to appear even bigger. Once again, he transformed from a mere man to a fearsome Highlander.

Rowena stretched out and put her hand on his arm as she had before. The feel of the heat coming from the sinewy tissue made her stomach tingle and she had to let go. "How often do two disputing clans come *willingly* to discussions?"

Cyric blinked as the undeniable truth of what she was hinting washed over him.

Biting her bottom lip, Rowena waited for Cyric to say something, to agree, to disagree, but he said nothing. "You worry so much about what this clan thinks. You need to find the confidence I believe you have when not among those who, I admit, are constantly judging you. If you are genuinely good at resolving clan troubles, then you need to apply those skills now. Prove what you can do. Sometimes in the Highlands, you have to seize what you want.

And no matter what anyone says or how the laird treats you, you *are* a Highlander."

Cyric felt his whole body tighten and his heart begin to pound. He had been listening, but when Rowena touched his arm, he had quivered with desire. As she spoke, he watched her lips, soft and pink, and he wanted so badly to kiss her he couldn't think straight. For days now he had wanted her more than he had ever thought it possible to desire any woman. But he refused to allow himself to chase after her. He didn't want to charm her or seduce her. He wanted her to see him and like him as he truly was. Until now, he did not realize what that was.

In the Lowlands, his size and coloring caused him to stand out. His use of weaponry and the diversity of his abilities also were uncommon. And it wasn't unusual for him to use his height and muscular bulk to intimidate those who thought to cross him. But as a Scotsman in the Highlands, he felt even more out of place . . . until now. Rowena was the first to recognize who he was. He was a Highlander by blood and had the chance to be one in action.

Rowena believed in him.

The realization hit Cyric full force and suddenly his need for her was all-consuming. A great shudder wracked him and he became intensely aware of the sensual hunger in his guts. Luminous auburn pools studied him and Cyric reminded himself to refrain from starting something he couldn't finish. And yet, all he could think about was kissing her.

Rowena stared into the golden eyes that were boring holes into her soul. There was no mistaking their dark look. Never had she been the reason behind such blatant desire in a man and her every nerve ending immediately responded to his unspoken message. Her mind urged her to step back and maintain a respectable distance, but her body would not obey.

Unable to deny himself any longer, Cyric bent his head and brushed his mouth lightly across Rowena's startled lips. He had intended to end the embrace with just that simple kiss, but the velvet warmth of her skin invited him to have one more. This time she leaned in and welcomed him.

Her hands slowly moved up his chest until her arms stole around his neck. Encouraged, Cyric kissed Rowena slowly, with a deep, tender possessiveness. The moment her lips parted, he swept his tongue inside, delighting in the taste of her before he expected her to pull away. But she didn't.

As soon as their tongues made contact, the connection between them ran like a bolt of lightning through his body, awakening every nerve. And based on her response, Rowena had experienced the same. Cyric had kissed women before. Many women, many times. But not like this. Never like this. With a groan, he drew her closer to him until he could feel the softness of her breasts and her body pressing against his own desperate yearning.

Rowena was not inexperienced when it came to kissing men. Encouraged by Meriel, she had experimented and discovered it to be an engaging pastime, but nothing more. Cyric's kiss, however, was like nothing of previous encounters.

His lips had only touched hers like a whisper, but she had been completely unprepared for the flood of sensations the simple contact would create. Her mind instantly blocked out everything except him. All she knew was she wanted to be closer to him and in fear that he might prematurely end the embrace, her hands curved around his neck and moved in closer. When his tongue claimed her mouth, she clung to him kissing him back, relishing his warmth, wondering how she was unquestionably drawn to his embrace, and why it felt so right.

Desire coiled tightly inside her body, causing her to moan softly and her head to spin. A second later, Cyric finally ended the long kiss and Rowena did not ask why. She knew. Thankfully, Cyric had maintained his power of self-control. She certainly had not felt any inclination to stop it herself.

Cyric reached out and swept a dark strand of hair away from her temple, touching her as he would a rare and precious flower. His body could still feel her all soft and vulnerable pressed up against him and he wanted more than anything to lose himself within her. But not yet. The next time he held Rowena in his arms, he would be worthy of doing so. She would know her belief in him had not been unwise.

"Would you do me a favor, beautiful?" he whispered tenderly, and waited for her to nod. "Wait for an hour, then go tell my uncle that you saw me leave to go after McHenry."

"But he—"

Unable to resist, Cyric tipped her chin up with his fingertips and lightly kissed her again. "One hour," he repeated. Then he walked over to where he had tossed his sword and departed the Great Hall.

Rowena stood transfixed for what felt like a long time. Her mind was reeling and her emotions were swirling like a powerful whirlpool. What had just happened? Cyric had appealed to her compassionate side. He was nice and misunderstood, but not someone she was interested in romantically. Until now.

Cyric Schellden was a rarity among men and she had fallen into the trap of believing him to be weak because he cared about what others thought of him. That because he desired respect he couldn't command it. That a man needed

to be unemotional to be a man. She had been wrong. Cyric
was much more. And he thought she was pretty.

No, he had called her beautiful. *Did he mean it?* she
asked herself. Her heart began to pound at the thought that
he had not. Good Lord, had she fallen in love with the one
Schellden every one of her clansmen wished would leave?
Even as she asked herself the question, she knew its
answer. She had. Rapidly and hard.

Rae Schellden spied the campfire and the two silhouet-
ted figures sitting on either side. He could not make out
either of their features, but he knew who they were and
urged his horse to close the distance. He had been seething
since leaving Caireoch and was not even close to becoming calm. Never before had anyone so openly defied his
wishes and in a few moments he would know why.

Stopping his mount almost directly in front of the two
squatters, Rae slid off his horse, glaring at Ian McHenry.
He then shifted his gaze to his nephew. Cyric's arms were
stretched out toward the fire, trying to get warm. He was
shivering and it wasn't even cold. Bloody scratches were
all along his legs as a result of riding through prickly thistle bushes instead of around them. Cyric's riding skills
were not in question. He could handle a horse, but did
Lowlanders never ride at night?

Rae stepped out of the shadows and into the circle of
light cast by the campfire. As if that was his cue, Cyric
rose to his feet and sent him a beaming smile. "See,
McHenry? Laird Schellden has come, as I promised."

Rae clenched his jaw and said nothing.

Cyric was unfazed at the cool reception and walked
over to his side. "I was explaining, Uncle, how you recognized that McHenry's visit was not just about border raids,

but something far more personal. Therefore, you wanted to handle it privately."

Rae fixed his hazel eyes on Cyric's golden ones, his expression unreadable. No one had ever dared to speak for him. And he would not be trapped into accepting a decision that he most clearly did not make. And yet his nephew continued to hold his gaze, unwavering. Cyric knew such actions were not just inexcusable but potentially deadly. But he refused to succumb to Rae's intimidating glare. Cyric was making it clear that he had no regrets.

Breaking the gaze, Rae glanced at the man still sitting by the fire. The old man should have been entertained by the clash of wills. Conor McTiernay would have been on the ground laughing at the fact Rae's nephew had dared to intercede in a clan decision. But Ian McHenry just stared into the fire.

"Speak your mind, McHenry."

Black eyes swiveled to meet Rae's. They were empty, angry, and in pain. Missing sheep were not behind this man's suffering. Cyric had been right. Whatever trouble plagued Ian McHenry was personal in nature. Rae walked over and sat down. He would address Cyric's methods later, but now was not the time. His focus turned solely on McHenry.

The old man, seeing that Schellden was finally ready to listen, wasted no time. "Your man Farlon has a son."

Rae nodded once. "Tevus."

Ian's face became wooden with contempt. "Aye, Tevus," he repeated coldly. "He got my daughter with child but Farlon refuses to let the boy do what he must."

Damn. Tevus was barely fifteen and nothing close to a man. Not the choice a father would have for his daughter and certainly not one McHenry would have welcomed.

Rae leaned on his elbows and raked his hands through his hair. Cyric had been right to force this meeting. Being turned away as he had been, Ian McHenry would have resorted to violence to remedy his daughter's honor. If what he claimed was true.

Rae looked up. "How do you know a Schellden is to blame for your daughter's condition?"

The air became instantly still. "Are you calling my daughter a liar?" The tone of the simple question, though barely audible, held an ominous quality.

Rae didn't flinch. "I'm asking if it is true."

"Both she and Tevus claim it is his."

Rae took in a deep breath. McHenry clearly hated the situation and did not consider a connection with a larger and powerful clan as advantageous. The man was fiercely independent. Farlon, if anything, was worse.

A farmer most of the time, Farlon was also a good fighter and one Rae depended upon when going into battle. For years, Farlon had despised Ian McHenry for pinching his cattle. Moreover, he had plans for Tevus to begin training this coming winter after the boy had finished helping prepare the land for winter barley.

Rae glanced to his left. Cyric was still shivering and most likely thirsty. No water bag was beside him or hanging off his horse just a few feet away. Rae suspected food and provisions to sleep outside had also been thoughtlessly left behind. Rae shook his head. "It's hard to believe you're a Highlander," he muttered.

The harsh assessment got a reaction from McHenry, whose head shot up with surprise. The action clearly made it clear that Ian had been thinking the same thing.

Tired of being judged for not falling into a stereotypical description of what a Highlander was supposed to behave like and pretend to enjoy enduring, Cyric opened his mouth to defend himself.

Rae cut him off. "But at least you act on your convictions.

When you rode out here and committed me into following you, it was to prove you understood the situation better than I. Let's see if you can be as persuasive with Farlon. Tomorrow you get to finish what you started."

Rae waited for Cyric to back out or make excuses as to why he had to return to the comforts of Caireoch, but no such pleas came.

"Don't look discouraged, Uncle," Cyric instead answered, with a hint of anticipation. "I just might surprise you."

Three days later while journeying back to Caireoch Castle, Rae Schellden was more than surprised. He was still in a state of shock. Farlon had let Tevus marry Ian McHenry's daughter and even gave the new couple the old cottage he had first built for him and his wife. Plus he and Ian had finally reached an agreement about stopping the raids upon one another's stock. The solution was unconventional, but both parties benefited and it meant an end to the bickering.

And it was all because of Cyric.

When it came to negotiating, the man commanded authority. He was fair, courteous, and digested the complaints of both sides so that he understood the real reasons behind their pain. And when he did speak, people listened. Including him.

Cyric might have been far more capable than Rae had believed him to be. Maybe it was time to see how Cyric responded to some more difficult leadership situations. He said he was a master with a sword. Could he train men who already considered themselves skilled?

Chapter 15

After two days of being forced to remain in bed, Raelynd was eager to be released from confinement to do anything. So when Laurel mentioned that she would be gone for a few days and would require her and Meriel's help, Raelynd leaped at the opportunity.

"Hurry, Meriel. Lady McTiernay is waiting for us," Raelynd said impatiently as she watched her sister hunt for her missing shoe. "I thought being messy was supposed to help you find things faster."

"Ah-ha!" Meriel called out as she unearthed the wayward item. "It does. Just imagine how long it would have taken me in a room like yours. I would have had to search everywhere versus just the floor."

Raelynd shook her head, knowing this battle was unwinnable. "You would only have to look where it belonged."

Meriel quickly slipped on the shoe and followed Raelynd down the stairwell and out of the tower. As they both walked the short distance to the Great Hall, Meriel noticed her sister's gait was surprisingly fast for someone seriously injured just two days prior. "Doesn't your leg hurt when you walk?"

"Just a little, but I don't want Lady McTiernay to think

I am incapable of helping. Besides, it is actually better when I move. It keeps it from becoming stiff."

Meriel took a deep breath and let it out. "You seem very sure about what we are going to do."

"Of course I'm sure. You are going to join the weavers and I am going to assist the steward in overseeing the castle. What else do we know how to do?"

Meriel shrugged, acknowledging the point. If they were to actually be of help, it would be in an area of their expertise. Still . . .

Meriel stopped just before tugging on the Hall's door handle. "Have you noticed how every time we make assumptions with Lady McTiernay, we turn out to be wrong?"

Raelynd bit her bottom lip. Her sister had a good point, but it was too late now. "Well, whatever it is, it has to be better than lying in bed."

Meriel opened the door and both women entered the large open room. Usually, it gave those who entered a warm feeling of welcome. Similar to Caireoch, the high ceiling was decorated with stone vault ribs. The room, which could be divided into smaller areas, each with its own hearth, was currently organized as a single meeting space. The spacious setting for only a few people made Raelynd uncomfortable. As if she was being led into a trap.

The feeling was only compounded when she saw Lady McTiernay's guest. At the far end of the room, near the main canopy, sat Laurel and her best friend, Aileen. During the second dinner party held in this very room, Raelynd watched as the two conversed. They did not talk as most friends do. They liked to plan and did so mischievously. Raelynd knew, for she, Meriel and Rowena often conversed in the very same manner.

"Come! Come sit down and join us!" Laurel offered

with surprising warmth. Such happiness compounded Raelynd's anxiety. Meriel was right. Not all was as it appeared.

Raelynd slid onto the bench located at the end of the table and Meriel sat down right beside her. "You asked for our help, Lady McTiernay?"

Laurel smiled smoothly. "We are soon to be *family*," she reminded them, hinting again of her skepticism. "So call me Laurel. And as far as help, it is much needed. Conor and I are going to be away for a few days and there is much to be done around the castle in our absence. Aileen will be watching my three along with her children, so she, too, will need assistance. It should keep you both fairly occupied and help prevent things from becoming too dull."

Raelynd almost physically deflated with relief at the mention of supporting the castle. Meriel, however, thought both responsibilities sounded dreadful. "I'll watch over the children," she offered, hoping it might be an option.

Laurel shook her head. "You each have your strengths, but like everyone else, you have weaknesses as well. And as your guardian for the remaining two weeks of your engagement, it is my responsibility to prepare you as best as I am able for the role of wife."

Meriel swallowed. *Wife?* She didn't want to become a wife or knowledgeable on domestic matters. She preferred focusing her time on more enjoyable activities such as weaving and embroidery. "While I appreciate your concern, I don't think it is really necessary."

Laurel clicked her tongue and furrowed her brow disapprovingly. "Meriel, trust me when I say that it is. As a married woman, you will be responsible for maintaining a home. You told me yourself that you left such chores to Raelynd and I have noticed myself how you lock yourself in your room, completely unaware of all that must be done for you to eat and sleep, let alone weave."

Meriel glanced at Aileen. The woman possessed small feminine features but she was not remotely petite. Unlike Laurel, she preferred an arisaid over a bliaut, wearing the colorful plaid like a shawl, with a large silver brooch fastened at her breast. Her arms were muscular from manual labor and her hair, just a shade darker than Raelynd's, was tied with a large square linen kertch. This woman might have been a friend to Lady McTiernay, but she worked hard.

Meriel licked her lips nervously and said to Aileen, "I hope you don't expect much."

Laurel sat back and shook her head, pretending to be puzzled. "Meriel, I think you misunderstood. *You* are to assist Fallon in my stead. Raelynd will be with Aileen, handling her responsibilities while she watches over the children."

Meriel felt her jaw drop as her heart began to pound hard, as if she had just run several miles. *Please,* she thought, *please change your mind.* She knew almost nothing of running a castle and had remained ignorant intentionally. The few aspects she was aware of seemed dreadful. Managing people, making decisions, fixing problems, dealing with sour personalities—there was never an end. Raelynd thrived on such authority. She should be the one taking Laurel's place.

Raelynd agreed. "I don't understand," she gritted out, unable to hide her anger. Finally, there was an opportunity to cast off the cloak of pampered daughter and demonstrate her management skills, but she was not going to be allowed to take it. "I think I would be far more useful in the castle. I know what Fallon expects much better than Meriel and he is not going to want to train someone in the ways of running a castle."

Laurel nodded her head and produced a slight grimace. "True. Fallon is not going to be pleased, but my decision still stands. It is unfair Meriel is completely unaware of all the work you do running Caireoch Castle for your father." Then Laurel leaned closer so that Raelynd could see the seriousness swirling in her storm-colored eyes. "Experience of living another person's life, even temporarily, can be invaluable, Raelynd. I won't let anyone—including you—rob you of it."

Less than an hour later, Raelynd was reiterating those words to herself repeatedly. Laurel had been completely inflexible and unwilling to listen to either her or Meriel about modifying the assignments. Not only were they to perform *all* the daily chores that she and Aileen were responsible for, their duties were to start right then.

Fallon had come in and announced that Laird McTiernay was ready to leave and that Laurel's horse Borrail had been prepared and was waiting for her just outside the stables. Immediately, Laurel made her good-byes and departed, leaving Meriel in Fallon's hands and Raelynd in Aileen's.

Aileen had asked if she wanted to change into something more durable than her kirtle, but Raelynd already considered herself dressed for laborlike activities, opting for a simple velvety overtunic instead of a bliaut. Besides, Raelynd had nothing more durable than her kirtle to put on. And the option of wearing an arisaid was unacceptable. Such garments were for village clanswomen who worked for a living, not for the daughter of a powerful laird.

So without any further delay, Raelynd felt as if she had been conscripted as Aileen's personal servant. If Laurel hoped to humiliate her with such a dictate, she was going

to be disappointed. Raelynd refused to let her win. And if
Laurel's point was for Raelynd to learn a new skill, she
would still be wrong for there was not one chore Aileen
mentioned that she didn't already know how to perform.
No, for the next few days, she would do as requested and
when she learned nothing from the *invaluable experience
of living another's life,* she would demand an apology.
And she had better receive one or this farce was over.
There was only so much her father could expect her to
endure and she was hovering at that limit.

   Fallon pointed his finger at the scullery and Meriel recoiled. A few days ago she had watched from the kitchens,
which were only just bearable, as her sister and little
Brenna made soap. She squeezed through the tight entrance and into the open, surprised that the outdoor space
was far bigger than she had believed. To her right was a
small area where buckets filled with water waited for
either clothes or utensils. To the left was a long narrow
garden ensconced between what had to be the Lower Hall
and the outer curtain wall. A dirt path wound its way
through various bushes, fruit and nut trees, and vegetable
patches, enabling someone to come and pick what was desired for that day's meal.
   Fallon stayed inside the kitchen, refusing to attempt to
squeeze through the unusually small opening. "Find Myrna.
She's Glynis's daughter. Tell her that you are acting in
Lady McTiernay's stead." Then, just as abruptly, he turned
around and left, leaving Meriel to wonder how she was
to know what to do and for how long.
   Meriel stretched her neck, but she could not see the
garden's end nor someone who might be named Myrna.
With a grimace, she began to meander down the twisting

pathway when a very sharp thornbush caught the opening to her long sleeve. *No wonder Lyndee prefers kirtles,* Meriel thought to herself as she tried to free the delicate material from its captor.

"Here, let me help you," came a high-pitched, but not piercing voice from behind.

Meriel looked back to see a very petite but busty young female hurrying to her side. Her dark brown hair was hanging in a single braid down her back, but its curly nature was evident despite its being tightly plaited. "There," she said as she liberated Meriel's sleeve. "I'm Myrna and you must be Meriel."

Meriel stood with her mouth open for a few seconds before replying, "How did you know?"

Myrna's laughter had a musical quality to it and instead of coming across derisive it invited one to join in. "Your sister was back here one time and I asked how to tell you and her apart. Her answer was to just look at your faces. The one who looks completely lost and uncomfortable would be her sister, Meriel, or well . . . you."

The answer made complete sense and it would be something Raelynd would have told someone who spent their time in scullery gardens. "I . . . I am here to help. Or to find you. Or to order you to do something. Or . . ." Meriel said rapidly, stumbling over the words. "Myrna, I have no idea what I am here for. Lady McTiernay wants me to be her while she is gone and I have not a hint at what that means or entails."

The surprised expression on Myrna's face made it clear that none of the servants had been told of Laurel's decree. Thankfully, Myrna recovered quickly. "I shall pretend you are Lady McTiernay . . . and that you cannot remember anything about our normal routine. Would that work?"

Meriel nodded in relief and began to weave her way

through what she learned were onions and beets, discovering how to decide which vegetables were ready to be picked. In the end, it was the Lady of the Castle's decision as to what was to be eaten that day. But before the meals could be prepared, Meriel would have to find out which crops had been harvested from the larger fields and what meats were available from the morning's hunt. Never did Meriel realize how much went into preparing a simple meal for so many. But she had been given little time to dwell on the concept before being ordered to oversee another chore.

"Lady Meriel?"

Meriel immediately stood up, embarrassed to have been caught sticking her rear in the air as she inspected the rushes in the Lower Hall. Food and drink had spilled everywhere their first night due to the fight between Conan and his brothers. Fallon had left her there with the charge of deciding just which rushes should be replaced. Meriel's first response—to just replace them all—had been met with a withering glare and a lecture about wasting time and money required for necessary things. Yet when she asked why replace them at all then, Fallon's contempt more than doubled and he gave another sermon on the perils of inviting unwanted creatures.

Meriel wiped her hands on her dress, no longer caring if her bliaut remained clean. She had always thought the Lady of the Castle directed activities from afar, not in person. No wonder she rarely saw Raelynd during the day. "I am Lady Meriel."

The older clansman took a step closer and nodded with relief. "I'm Jaime Darag."

Meriel looked up, understanding why he was named after an oak tree. The man stood nearly seven feet tall, hunched. "Aye, Jaime, how can I help you?"

"I am the main candle maker for the McTiernays, my

lady, and it being Monday, I am to make the candles for the stairwells, hallways, and servants' quarters."

Meriel stared at him, wondering why he was talking to her. He obviously knew what needed to be done. "Do you need to know how many to make?" she guessed.

Jaime chuckled. "No, my lady. I know the number, but there is no tallow in the storehouse and without it I cannot make the candles."

"Oh, you need to find Fallon, Jaime. I'm sure he knows where the tallow has been moved."

The old man looked at her strangely and said, "The steward told me that you were seeing to such matters."

Meriel grimaced, remembering the candles in the North Tower stairwell and how most of them had already been consumed and needed immediate replacement. She had no idea what tallow even looked like let alone if Lady McTiernay had any. "Is there nothing else you can make candles out of?"

"I could make them with beeswax, my lady. But I need permission."

The door opened and another man came in, but this one was far younger, shorter, and more portly. He was also agitated and was doing nothing to hide his frustration.

Returning her focus to the candle maker, Meriel asked, "Do you know where some beeswax is? I mean do we even have any?"

"Oh, aye, my lady. Lady McTiernay always ensures there is beeswax available for candle making."

Meriel smiled and clapped her hands together. Problem averted. "Then I give you my permission to make today's candles with beeswax, Jaime Darag." She had scarcely finished the sentence when Jaime turned to leave and the angrier man stepped forward. "Let me guess, Fallon sent you to me."

"Aye," the man replied, crossing his arms. "You need to do something about those dogs!"

Meriel blinked. Dogs? "What . . . dogs?"

"Clyde's dogs. He left them here and with Meghan visiting Lady Ellenor up north they are running loose and this morning they broke in and snatched most of the bread before I could chase them out again. Now there's not enough to feed everyone tonight. You need to decide just who is going without."

Meriel felt her mouth drop open. This could not be a typical day. And if it were, she had been right to loathe the job of Lady of the Castle. It was a nightmare without measure. She would rather be Myrna, who had to cut the vegetables, clean the pots, skin the meat, and deal with Fiona—the most disagreeable cook ever to be born.

With a sigh, she pointed to the door and followed the baker to the scene of the crime. She was no more than fifteen feet into the courtyard, when a scream was heard just as several of the livestock broke free from their pens. Within minutes the stable hands had the animals back under control, but not before three carts full of goods were turned over and several people got knocked down, some of whom were slow to rise on their feet again.

"My lady!"

Meriel shivered and glanced at the boy racing across the courtyard, ignoring the mess and the chaos around him. "The steward wants to know your decision about the Lower Hall's rushes."

Meriel closed her eyes. The next time the priest gave a sermon on hell, she would know just what he meant. She needed to last through today. For tomorrow, she was going to convince her identical twin sister to take her place.

* * *

Raelynd turned the village well's handle and stared incredulously at the empty rope. Someone had removed the bucket, making it impossible for anyone to get any water. She was already angry for being made to do servants' work, which had been compounded upon learning that the water she needed to clean everything with needed to be obtained by her.

Grabbing the two empty buckets, Raelynd marched back to Aileen's cottage, located not far from the well, but certainly not close either. Inside, Aileen was playing with Bonny, teaching her how to stack wooden blocks high without them falling over. The boys were jumping around using blankets from the beds as capes and sticks for swords. Raelynd felt her frustration rise again at seeing the woman do nothing but entertain herself and several children.

"Aileen?" No response. "Aileen, there is no bucket in the village well. We are going to have to get one of the servants to bring us water from the castle's water supply."

Aileen grinned at the little blond girl in front of her and shook her head. "No, no, no," she cooed. "One of the boys must have taken it again. Just tie one of ours on the rope."

Raelynd opened her mouth to protest. Tying one bucket to the rope meant she would only have one to carry water, doubling her labor and her trips. Saying so would be pointless as it had obviously happened before and this had been Aileen's solution. Forcing herself to remain silent, Raelynd took both buckets back to the well and did as suggested.

During the third trip, Raelynd felt her fingers begin to ache as the metal handle pinched her skin. She switched back to her right hand, but it had not recovered from carrying it previously. Carrying two buckets would not have been possible. They were incredibly heavy and the weight of the water only seemed to grow with each trip.

"There," she said, nearly out of breath as she almost dropped the bucket onto the table.

Aileen looked down at the damp wood from where the water had sloshed over. "Well, I guess you can begin with the table. Today is cleaning day and everything in this cottage must be scoured and rinsed." Seeing Raelynd's appalled expression, Aileen waved her hand and smiled as if she understood the horror she was asking. "Finn hates his home to be soiled in any way and it wasn't until I had Gideon that I could convince him to reduce the chore to once a week! Anyway, there's a cloth on the chair behind you. Just dip it in the water and start here at the table and work your way through this room and into the bedrooms. Oh, and before it gets much later, you should think about supper. Finn will be coming home in an hour or so and will want something to eat as will the children, myself . . . and you of course."

The simply stated request vexed Raelynd enormously. "I'm supposed to cook supper? Am I also to prepare tonight's dinner?" Raelynd gasped.

"No, no. Just this afternoon's meal. Because Finn is the commander of the laird's elite guard, we are invited to the castle to dine at night."

"But I can't . . ." Raelynd whispered as terror twisted in her stomach. She had overseen the preparation of food and meals many times, but to cook it herself? She didn't know where to begin.

"I do it every day. Be glad you don't have to manage the young ones at the same time." Aileen chuckled with supposed encouragement. "I'll talk you through the steps and you will realize it is not that difficult a task. The meat can wait until tomorrow to be skinned. Finn won't like it but he can survive until dinner on just vegetables, fruits, and bread."

Raelynd felt as if her chest had collapsed and all the air in her lungs had escaped. Was Aileen serious? *Skin the meat?* Raelynd was more than familiar with the onerous chore and had yelled at many a scullery maid for wasting meat by skinning it poorly. But physically doing the chore itself? Never.

"Tomorrow you will need to make a trip either to the castle or one of the nearby farms for more vegetables, but I am fairly certain we have enough to feed everyone today," Aileen said as she continued looking around. "You'll need more water for cooking the vegetables and of course you'll need to start the fire. Oh, I didn't clean the hearth this morning, so that must be done first. At least the outside woodpile has been replenished."

Raelynd stood transfixed, unable to speak or move. Aileen sighed with compassion. She bent down and picked up Bonny and cradled the young girl on her hip. "I realize you may not be aware of all that must take place to keep a home running—"

The comment snapped Raelynd back into the present. If Aileen thought managing a single cottage home difficult, she had no idea the effort it took to oversee a castle and the needs of multiple families, not just one. "I am more than aware, Aileen."

Laurel's friend reached up and yanked off the kertch from her head to reveal the lovely tawny mass it had been concealing. "Then I guess I should leave you to do what you know must be done. Children! Come! Let's go play in the meadow and give Lady Raelynd some room." A minute later, Aileen was gone and Raelynd was left alone to prepare for Finn and his afternoon supper.

Raelynd collapsed on her bed. She should be dressing and preparing for dinner—something she not only had been looking forward to all day, but needed. Her body, however, was not cooperating. Every muscle was exhausted and aching with pain. But that throbbing in her limbs was nothing compared to the sharp pounding in her head. She had lived nearly twenty-two years and in that time, never had she been scolded and admonished as she had been today.

Oh, Aileen had used a pleasant tone with each and every nitpicking thing she found to be corrected, but Raelynd knew it was not genuine. For it was the exact tone she herself used with her servants when giving them instruction. The difference was that Aileen *knew* the effort it took to perform all the chores. Finn, however, did not care and in his home, it did not matter whose daughter you were or to whom you were engaged. When Aileen stated that the man did not like his home to be soiled, Raelynd had thought she meant obvious grime, not a thin layer of dust on the mantel no one was using! The man was insufferable!

He complained at the lack of meat and asked why the newly harvested crops were not being served. He bemoaned the vegetables he was given, claiming them to be poorly cooked and bland. Both assessments she inwardly agreed with, but it bothered her that neither he nor Aileen cared that she had never cooked before and was just learning how to manage all that she needed to do in the short amount of time she had. An encouraging word was what she had needed. Not a tedious account of all she failed to do well.

Raelynd closed her eyes, recounting Aileen's routine.

Clean on Monday
Wash on Tuesday
Mend on Wednesday
Churn on Thursday

Bake on Friday
Visit the sick on Saturday
Rest on Sunday

Sunday was a very very long time away.

She had survived Monday, but Tuesday was laundry—the one chore for which she demanded near perfection from her servants. Would Aileen be just as critical? Maybe she could convince Meriel to change places with her. But before she could plan out how and when, Raelynd was asleep, still dressed in her soiled kirtle and with slippers on her feet.

"You are still doing it wrong. Didn't your mother teach you anything?" Brenna asked candidly, as only a young child could without fear of retribution.

The young boys in the room began to giggle and Meriel closed her eyes and counted to five, wishing again that she had risen in time to talk with Raelynd about switching roles. Unfortunately she had fallen asleep and only awakened when Fallon started pounding on her door. "My mother died when I was twelve," Meriel finally answered.

Brenna was not sympathetic. "I'm only seven and I know all the dances. How are you supposed to teach what you don't know?"

Meriel bristled, praying someone would come in and ask for the little girl. Brenna's question was a legitimate one, but it rankled that it came from someone so young. Raelynd probably did know everything Brenna did at the same age. She had received such instruction like a dry cloth absorbed water. Meriel had resisted against such teachings and her mother acquiesced to her rebellion. She never knew the Lady of the Castle also was responsible for educating a handful of selected young boys on the topics of religion, music, dancing, and hunting before they grew old enough to begin weapon training.

"Ah-hem." Meriel twisted to look who was clearing his throat in an effort to gain her attention. No surprise, it was Fallon.

She didn't know whether to be relieved at the possibility that she was going to have to end this week's lessons prematurely or fearful at what new problem he was going to pass on for her to handle. Didn't he remember yesterday? She could still hear Fallon's booming voice ringing in her ears about how no one who grew up in a castle could be so inept as to how to run one.

"Fallon," she acknowledged.

"You are needed, my lady, in the buttery."

Meriel rose to her feet and followed Fallon to the corridor that linked directly to the buttery and the kitchens. Meriel scanned the small room and could find nothing wrong. The bakery had been complete mayhem, but here the barrels lined up against the back wall appeared to be intact, no leaks were visible, and nothing seemed to be amiss. "Everything looks fine, Fallon."

The burly steward's face turned bright red so that it nearly matched the scarlet streaks in his gray beard. "Count the barrels, my lady."

Meriel did as asked. "I see five."

"On average, my lady, do you know how many people drink the castle's ale on a given day?"

A heaviness centered in Meriel's chest as another lecture was about to begin.

"There are typically between seventy and eighty people who depend on this buttery for their drink. Half of those are soldiers either coming in from the training fields eager for their turn at a warm meal and a mug of ale or are standing guard, protecting this place through day and night. The other half are people who serve this place with little acknowledgment of their efforts. But the one thing they are assured of is four to five large mugs of ale each day," Fallon finished, swinging a large mug that was more the size of a small pitcher than a drinking cup.

Meriel swallowed and remained mum for she knew Fallon was not yet done. "A single barrel holds thirty-two gallons, enough for just over two dozen men. And with four unopened barrels and one already being drained, the buttery does *not* look fine, my lady. It looks empty. The ale will be gone before tomorrow's end and all will be looking to you to decide who will go without."

Meriel stared at him in astonishment. *"Me?"* she asked incredulously. "Why me?"

"You are the Lady of the Castle."

A frisson of anger went up Meriel's spine. "I'll tell you right now that I will not be making that decision. I had nothing to do with the stores getting so low and I will not be involved in angering those to be affected by someone's poor performance," she huffed.

"As of yesterday you were in charge of those stores and the laird *will* hold you accountable."

Meriel's green eyes widened with fear of what was to come. "What can I do about it, though?"

Fallon just stared at the young woman for several seconds, dumbfounded. He knew Lady McTiernay was unusually gifted in the ways of running a castle, but he had not realized how truly blessed he was that she had not arrived to McTiernay Castle naive and clueless to castle life.

Fallon took pity on Meriel and lowered his voice to what he hoped was an amiable level. "The bottler, my lady. You need to find the butler and tell him to bring up more barrels and how many to retrieve."

The simple answer irked Meriel enormously. Why didn't he just state that in the first place? Why couldn't Fallon have come into the Great Hall and said that she needed to find the bottler and have a dozen barrels added to the buttery? The man intentionally made things difficult just so he could give a lecture. He obviously thrived on them. No doubt he even tried to critique Lady McTiernay on the methods of running a castle on more than one occasion. There was no way he could help himself. "And what if I cannot find the bottler? It is obvious he has not been attending the buttery for several days. Perhaps he is sick."

"Then, my lady, I suggest you find someone who can restock this room."

Meriel glared at the back of Fallon's head as he disappeared into the corridor. She was not prone to violence, but someday she was going to physically attack that man. He, too, had some lessons to learn, but a long lecture was not going to be her method of delivery.

Raelynd stifled a yawn as she threw the dripping wet leine over the bush for it to dry.

"Ah, Aileen's finery looks clean, my lady. What you are doing for her is a mighty fine thing. I did not know that another noblewoman besides our own lady would help with such work."

Raelynd put her hands on her hips and surveyed the meadow, which was littered with linens and clothes from the castle village. Every Tuesday, the women got together if the weather was favorable to do the wash by the riverside. Not everything got washed each week so by the time most items made it to the river, they were filthy. Work started at dawn to allow the sun most of the day to bleach and dry the laundry. Raelynd had seen the sunrise before, but only after staying up all night enjoying some festivity, certainly not because she was at work. And yet, she felt good.

"Aye," Raelynd finally replied to the clanswoman who had laid her stuff to dry nearby. "It does look clean. I thought I would never finish. Aileen has so much more than everyone else. I wonder how a single family can accumulate so much laundry."

The woman laughed, but it held no ridicule. "Aye, they are privileged to have so much laundry, aren't they? I wish my man had some more undershirts and I had the bed linens to wash that you did. To live in a cottage of the commander's size may need more tending, but it's worth it, don't you agree? To have all that room?" Then before Raelynd could answer, the woman waved her hand and added, "But then why am I telling you, my lady? You live in a *castle*. The small amount of wash we did this morn doesn't compare to Thursdays when the laundress comes out with the castle linens. I'm sure it is the same where you're from."

The fields they had covered this morning were quite large and to think the castle laundry's needs were even greater was hard to envision. She had never actually spoken to her laundress about where the clothes were washed or dried.

"Well, it was a pleasure to have you join us this morning, but I best get back and work on supper," said the woman, who immediately turned to leave.

Raelynd went over to where she had stashed the wooden board, lye, and animal fat soap Aileen had given her this morning. She headed back looking forward to eating some bread and fruit after such an arduous morning.

"You have finally returned," Aileen stated. She had

made the comment in a friendly tone and with a smile, but it did not matter to Raelynd. It was rude. Aileen knew what she had been doing and the hard work was completely unappreciated.

Deciding to ignore the barb, Raelynd went over to the table and lifted the linen cloth covering the loaf of bread and pulled a piece off. She was just about to sit down and pour herself some water when Aileen asked, "What are you doing?"

Raelynd stared at her incredulously. Was Aileen's question serious? "I'm hungry and thirsty and I was going to sit for a while. I've been up since dawn."

Aileen's eyes met Raelynd's disparagingly as she watched Raelynd chew the bread. "I am fully aware that you have been up for a few hours, and while your efforts are appreciated, food still must be prepared and yesterday not all the cleaning was completed. The chamber pots must be washed out today."

Raelynd was sure she had not understood correctly. She was Laird Rae Schellden's daughter. She was Lady of Caireoch Castle. Chamber pots, garderobes, wash basins . . . these were for chambermaids. Not her. There was a limit. "I'm not cleaning a chamber pot."

Aileen ignored the comment. "And as for the bread, I put that out for the children to nibble on once I realized you would be serving supper late today, so please do not have any more."

Raelynd swallowed the single bite and went to pour herself a drink only to find the pitcher empty. Aileen nodded as if Raelynd was confirming there was no water, not actually desiring some. "Aye, I normally fetch some water before I leave for the river, but you can get it now. Be sure to get enough to prepare supper. Once you are done, if you are still hungry, go to the castle kitchens. I'm sure they have plenty they can give you there."

Raelynd glared at Aileen, who appeared oblivious to the tension building in the room. She was half tempted to explain that critical comments voiced in a pleasant tone did nothing to lessen their impact; if anything it only made them worse. Instead, Raelynd rose to her feet and grabbed the bucket to head out the door. If she stayed any longer, all the negative emotions boiling inside would explode and that was about the only thing that could make this day any worse. Or so she thought.

That night Raelynd heard a tapping on the door and considered ignoring it. She was completely out of patience to talk to anyone, including her sister. Too much had happened and very little of it had been good.

The tapping continued and Raelynd stifled a groan. Meriel, when she chose to be, could be far more stubborn than anyone in their family. Rising to her feet, Raelynd went and unlatched the door to open it.

Meriel walked in and wrinkled her nose. "Lord, Lyndee, you really should bathe. You stink."

"I may stink, but taking a bath is a waste of energy and time for tomorrow I shall only grow to smell foul again. Besides, I'm too tired to wash and dry my hair."

Meriel made another face but then gave a shrug and went to sit down in the chair. "I understand. I have never been so tired in my life. You would not dream of everything they want me to believe Lady McTiernay does on a daily basis."

Raelynd took a deep breath and slowly exhaled. Meriel was in the mood to talk and in truth, she was not the only one. Maybe they could lean on each other to get through the next couple of days until Laurel returned. "What are they having you do?"

"Meet with the scullery maid and help select vegetables and then seek out the butcher to learn what meat is available before talking with the cook to decide on the meals."

"It gets easier," Raelynd said, pulling off a slipper. "I no longer even think of it as a chore. Kind of like brushing my hair."

Meriel huffed and intertwined her fingers. "Well, that is not all. Fallon has forced me to be in charge of *everything*. He just leaves all the problems to me to solve while he handles other things. I try to meet with the various staff and give instructions, but I am constantly interrupted with problems."

Raelynd nodded and covered her mouth in an attempt to hide her yawn. "Aye, there is always something. Just make the decision and hope it is the right one."

Meriel twisted in the chair and gaped openly at her sister when she saw that Raelynd was serious. "*That* is the problem! *Our* chambermaids never fight or just refuse to finish their responsibilities because they feel it is unfair they have to do more work because one of them is sick."

Raelynd wanted to ask at what castle did her sister live in, for it certainly wasn't Caireoch. "It's not exactly uncommon."

"It isn't?" Meriel asked in disbelief. "Well, what about moles? Do you have to chase those nasty little burrowing creatures in our garden? Do we even have a garden?"

Raelynd couldn't believe Meriel's questions. Had her sister truly never ventured into any of the working areas of Caireoch? "Aye, we have a garden. A large one. Remember you complaining about the bees earlier this year and I said it was because the fruit trees were blooming? Where did you think those trees were?"

Meriel crinkled her forehead and then shrugged. "I thought they were out in the fields, with the farms, where they grew the food."

Raelynd began to undo her long braid and massaged her scalp, not knowing how to respond. "Did you get to meet with the weavers?" she asked, hoping for a more positive topic.

"Not once!" Meriel moaned. "The candle maker ran out of what he needed and told me he could make the candles from beeswax. I thought that was a splendid idea, but—"

Raelynd gasped. "You didn't give him permission, did you?"

"I did. What else was I supposed to do?"

"Either find some tallow or have some made. The candle maker should have been keeping track of what was in storage, warning you or the steward when he was low."

Upset with Raelynd's tone, Meriel furrowed her brow and said through gritted teeth, "Well, he didn't. So he used beeswax and now Fallon says Laird McTiernay will be furious with me."

Raelynd bent over to slip off her other shoe, mumbling, "I bet he will be." Beeswax burned much cleaner than tallow, but animal fat was much easier and far cheaper to use, especially in large quantities. Raelynd had standing instructions to use beeswax in select areas at select times.

"But that will be nothing compared to when he learns that I approved of Father Lanaghly's request to use the extra material I saw in the storage rooms to remake all the cushions in the chapel. You won't believe me, but Fallon's face turned almost a deep purple. I truly thought he was going to pass out."

Raelynd collapsed on the bed. "If I could trade your day for mine, I would, but you would hate me, for what I am doing is far harder than anything I have ever done before."

"Just what are you doing?"

Everything, Raelynd thought. "Cooking, cleaning, washing. I even have to get the water."

"Ugh."

Meriel's response was appropriate, but if she had been clueless about castle responsibilities, there was no way she could imagine the work and the effort Raelynd was expending. "The work is awful and hard, but that is not what truly bothers me. It's Aileen."

"She seems so nice."

"And that's just how she relays every criticism—nicely. Not once has she said thank you or good job or I appreciate all that you are doing. She just says 'Please don't eat the bread, it is for others,'" Raelynd said, sarcastically mimicking the sweet tone. "Or 'You missed a spot, please redo the table.' Or 'You are finally back' after hours of me bending over a board in the river to clean *her* family's clothes!"

Meriel chuckled and leaned back in the chair. The sound infuriated Raelynd, who sprang back up to a sitting position. "Just what is so funny about how I am being treated?" she demanded. "I at least tried to sympathize with you, though not a single thing you mentioned isn't something that I deal with almost on a daily basis!"

"I was *laughing* at you because I have heard you say *those very same things* to our servants!" Meriel shouted back, feeling no need to spare her sister's feelings after Raelynd had shown no mercy. "*And* you also use that same fake cheerful voice, thinking that it will make what you are saying so much better. I'm sure our servants feel the same way about it as you do."

Both sisters stared at each other in horror. They rarely fought and when they did it was over something minor. The last time they had attacked each other's character with such honesty had been prior to their mother's death. Such loss brought out their protective natures and both intentionally insulated the other when and where possible to keep them from getting hurt.

Meriel bit her bottom lip in mortification. "Oh, Lyndee, I'm so sorry. I just never knew your job was so hard, so . . . exhausting. I've never been so miserable."

Raelynd brushed away a tear. "I'm sorry too. I know how hard it is to do what you are being asked. I still make mistakes, so don't worry about it too much. I think we both just need some sleep."

Meriel sniffled and then nodded in agreement. After a quick but reassuring hug, she left, leaving Raelynd to play over and over again Meriel's accusation.

You say those very same things to our servants.

Raelynd found it hard to believe she had not connected Aileen's behavior to her own. Meriel had been mad, and her intent had been to lash out, not be instructive, but her sister was right. She spoke to those in the castle just as Aileen did to her. She had no idea how completely infuriating it was. Crevan had mentioned it many times, but in all honesty, she had not believed him, even though she had always felt the undercurrent of disrespect from the servants. No one ever did anything outright, just as she had not openly defied Aileen, but acquiescence was not agreement and certainly not the equivalent of respect.

Crevan had tried so many times to explain how her sweet tone may have been better than a nasty one, but it was no substitute for sincerity. That genuine appreciation could win even the hardest of personalities. *Sincerity and appreciation,* Raelynd thought to herself as she unlaced her kirtle before removing it.

Leaving on her chemise, she blew out the candle and then fell onto the bed. Fatigue affected every aspect of her body, but her mind would not stop churning. Something was niggling at her.

And then it struck her what it was.

Nooooo, Raelynd shouted inside her head. But it was too late. She could not pretend that Laurel had not orchestrated the last few days just for this very reason.

"Experience of living another person's life, even temporarily, can be invaluable, Raelynd. I won't let anyone rob you of it."

Laurel had been right. The experience had been invaluable and life changing.

But Raelynd vowed to never admit it, least of all to Laurel.

Chapter 16

Cyric sat and listened as four of the western Highlands'
most powerful men spoke their minds about the king's
brother's progress in Ireland. When first invited to the
meeting this morning, Cyric thought he had misunderstood. His clansmen's general treatment of him had improved in the past few days. The outright rejection of his
presence was gone as well as the verbal slights within his
hearing, but Cyric was fairly confident that they were still
made when he wasn't around. And these days, that was
quite often.

Unlike before, when he was always lurking somewhere
within Caireoch's curtain walls, he now could be found
there only during the day's last meal. Most times he was
at the training fields mingling with the men, providing
support whenever he was asked. His uncle knew he went
to the fields and never said a word—either of encouragement or dissuasion. And while no one ever asked him to
leave, there was an underlying current from the handful of
men in charge conveying that if his presence was tolerated, his interference would not be. But Cyric no longer
cared as he once had.

Rowena had remarked on his change during one of

their recent nightly talks. She had great insight into others and their emotional states, more than he thought anyone realized—including his uncle. So when she made even the simplest of statements, he listened.

Rowena had refused to explain what she meant by his change, only that it had nothing to do with those around him. At first, her opinion puzzled him as he believed himself to be the very same man who arrived a few weeks ago. But when he went to stable his horse after a particularly long ride, Cyric realized she was right. His uncle had introduced him to a few local families and Cyric decided to see what he could of Schellden lands within a half-day's ride. Upon his return, a stable boy asked a simple question. Should he go and find the laird, the steward, or one of the commanders for Cyric to relate all that he did that day?

The question was initially baffling. What would be the purpose? Who would care? And then, at that very moment, Cyric finally understood. He had asked the stable boy to do that very thing the few first times he had ventured out of the castle walls. And he had not even gone very far or done anything really to remark about. In the Lowlands, he had been secure, with no need to prove himself to others for they knew of his skills, from fighting to riding to resolving issues. Here, though, no one did and in seeking their approval, he tried to tell them. If he had been able to stand outside himself and look objectively at his behavior, he would have called himself a fool. Rowena had been a judge of character for him, but she had been much nicer and prettier in delivering her assessments. Still, she was right. He had changed.

No longer was his confidence something he sought from others. Previously, it was only when people he respected thought well of him that he could then believe in himself. When they did not, he found himself adrift, mastering a series of skills with only one goal—to get them to respect him. As a result, insecurity had been a constant companion.

He would leave the Highlands a different person. For now, he believed in himself. He knew what he was capable of and that was now sufficient. For the first time in his life, he felt like the man he had always wanted his father to see him as. The difference was he no longer needed his father's validation. He wanted it, but it was no longer necessary. But these changes were internal. Nobody—except Rowena—could be aware of them.

So yesterday, when four notable men from neighboring clans arrived for an impromptu meeting, Cyric had not been prepared for his uncle to invite him to attend. Not briefed about who and what they were to talk about, Cyric assumed it was something minor or local. Perhaps the gathering for some games, or the upcoming wedding of his cousins. But it was far more serious and it wasn't long before his attention was completely focused on the subject at hand.

The invasion of Ireland.

"But it does not matter, I tell you," said Gilbert Grant. "Ireland has no true High King. Hasn't for years and so it is not an invasion. We were asked to come."

Cyric leaned back and said nothing. In many ways, Grant was correct. Ireland had no High King. But invited? More like an agreement was made between Robert I and Ó Néill along with some of his allies, who ruled a significant portion of northern Ireland.

"You want us to send men, when you have no authority to send any of your own," challenged William Camirun.

Cyric found the accusation slightly amusing as William Camirun had no authority either. Like Gilbert Grant, William was not a laird. Both men had strong connections to Robert I, Grant through Robert de Grant and Laurin

Lovat, and he was here as an envoy to help find support for the king's brother. But unlike Grant, William Camirun was a close cousin of Angus Og, who just received the grant of Lochaber from the king, and he did have men.

"There is not one enemy to battle, but two," stated John Fraser, who was laird of a clan that was allied through blood and marriage to Sir Alexander Fraser, a noted strong supporter of Bruce. "Most of the Irish are going to align themselves with England."

"The English have done nothing to join the fight," Grant stated.

"Edward the second is a fool, but he will eventually send his men. He will have no choice but to convene a Parliament in Dublin soon," Rae Schellden finally interjected. "And if there are not enough Scots backing Edward, the king's brother will be defeated when England does send support."

Gilbert Grant's fist slammed the table. "Exactly! Which is why Moray needs men now. He sets sail as soon as he is able to return with supplies and men. He did bring back the means to finance our support."

"Not that we will see any of it," William Camirun mumbled.

Conor McTiernay, who had been listening, sat back and asked, "What bothers you, Fraser? Losing men?"

John Fraser stared at the mug on the table long and hard. "I understand Edward's pursuit, but the massacre of whole villages, of women and children, this is the behavior of English soldiers. Not Highlanders. And what about you, Schellden? Do you intend to support the king?"

Rae Schellden shook his head. "Not with men. I lost too many achieving the victory at Bannockburn. I'm still replenishing and training forces. Supplies may be possible, but not in significant quantities. Too many of those men who died were farmers. Several crops have gone untended. Their wives are only just starting to remarry men who will man the farms."

John Fraser turned to Conor. "And you, McTiernay?"

Conor sighed. "I agree the carnage rumored to have happened should not be ignored. But aye, I will be sending men. My youngest brother, Clyde, will be going along with three-dozen men. Twelve each from me, Colin, and Cole."

"That's all?" questioned Camirun, surprised.

Conor glanced at Schellden and then back at the young man. "I'm not convinced that our good king will not be calling for men."

The simple statement silenced the group. What was Robert I's plan? His brother Edward Bruce was in Ireland fighting for control, but anyone who met Robert I knew the new king was not likely to just leave the English alone.

Schellden turned his gaze toward Cyric. "You have been quiet, Cyric."

Cyric blinked but with a shrug said, "I can only listen. I have neither authority nor men."

"True, but you have a better understanding of our king and his ambitions. What do you know of Robert's true plan?"

Cyric leaned back and considered the answer. He had been told directly very little and it would be easy to evade answering based on that truth, but it would not help these men. And yet, he was not inclined to persuade them to a particular path. "I've not been told directly, but I did discern much via other ways when I was with the king before I journeyed here." There, they now knew that his opinion was conjecture.

"And?" came the simultaneous question from both Grant and Camirun.

"And Robert's primary plan with Ireland is to drain

England of its resources, deviating Edward's focus from Scotland to that of Ireland where it will be harder to recall his men . . . if needed."

Conor leaned back and rubbed his chin. "So King Robert does intend to attack."

"I cannot say for certain, but aye, I believe so. And as you suspect, the king will be calling for men to support *him* and not his brother to fight the southern borders in the near future. But that doesn't mean he is not interested in what his brother is trying to do. Like Scotland, Ireland is populated by Gaels, who also despise England and its oppressive rulers. With Edward as King of Ireland and Robert King of Scotland, their alliance would enable them to attack England on multiple fronts. Edward could go after Wales while our king could attack England from the north."

John Fraser took a deep breath. "We will support King Robert when the time comes," he stated simply, without the need to explain his reasoning.

"Then I will talk to my cousin about sending men to Edward," William Camirun asserted, surprising all as he seemed the most reticent about doing so. "If England conquers Ireland, the Isle of Man would once again be in danger of English rule."

"Then it is settled," Schellden said, rising to his feet. "Grant, you have your answer. Camirun, Fraser, thank you for coming and I shall not delay your return with unnecessary festivities. My steward will see that you are well stocked with food and provisions." The three men looked relieved as they rose, said good-byes and left the Hall, for each one was eager to begin his journey home while there were still several hours of light.

"McTiernay, I believe your wife needed to speak to me," Schellden said with a grin, which only made Conor's grimace grow.

"Aye," Conor returned, and then glanced pointedly at Cyric.

Cyric felt the level stare and returned it out of curiosity. Why did the man feel the need to assess him? He was not a threat with his brothers' upcoming marriages to his cousins.

"I shall get her," Conor said eventually, and then added, "Shall we meet in your dayroom?"

Schellden raised a single brow and then nodded. Both men exited the room, leaving Cyric alone. His uncle had given him little attention during the meeting, which was understandable considering the topic. But right after Cyric had given his opinion about what he concluded to be the king's goal, his uncle had issued him a blank stare, the kind one gave when making a determination. Cyric was unsure of his uncle's verdict, but he was satisfied with his own contribution that afternoon. It was asked for, not volunteered, and he spoke the truth without giving unsolicited advice. If his uncle thought otherwise, then next time he wouldn't ask him to sit in, let alone speak.

Cyric wished Rowena would seek him out and join him. He could ask her what she thought of the situation. Since their kiss, she had only sought him out at night, after the last meal of the day had been served and while servants were still cleaning. He knew it was a tactic to protect herself and wanted to tell her that she did not have to fear he would kiss her again. He wanted to, very much, but the risk of losing her advice, her friendship—her sheer *company*—was just too high.

"So the rumors were correct. You were invited to the talks," he heard a soft voice say from behind. He twisted his head to see Rowena, winding around the tables being erected for the next meal, approaching him. He smiled. "And I also see that they went well."

"Very well," Cyric confirmed. "Or I am a fool. And I doubt my uncle would have asked me to join in on a discussion of importance to the king if he felt that way. My opinion was even requested."

"I am not surprised."

Cyric raised a brow as he watched her near. "I am," he confessed. "I'm just fortunate that I knew something of the topic."

"You are intentionally downplaying the incredible diplomacy skills you possess," Rowena chided as she sat in the chair next to him.

"I am?"

The question was innocently posed, but far from ingenuous. Rowena leaned over the arm of her chair and teasingly cooed, "You should consider becoming an advisor to the king."

"Only if you come with me."

Rowena tried unsuccessfully not to chuckle. "And just what would I do when you disappeared to solve the problems of Scotland and its people."

"You?" Cyric asked, arching an eyebrow mischievously. "You would charm everyone around you. Your compassion and your wit—"

"Don't forget my great beauty," she inserted.

"*And* your exquisite beauty would enrapture everyone."

Rowena pulled back slightly and bit her lip to stifle a grin in an effort to look serious. "Then I best not go. You would have to spend so much time fighting off my admirers you no doubt would get in trouble with the king."

Her brown eyes were sparkling with laughter and Cyric was mesmerized. He loved how she played with her bottom lip when contemplating something. Rowena was not beautiful in the traditional sense, but every time he looked at her, his pulse would begin to race. The woman was smart, sensitive, and all things he ever wanted. He trusted her with his heart and soul, and he knew the feeling would not go away anytime soon. Probably never.

He reached up, cupped her chin with his hands and then kissed her slowly, taking his time, letting her feel the endless need and love inside him. "I think I'm falling for you, Rowena," he said as they finally parted.

Rowena swallowed. Her eyes locked with his, asking questions—questions she did not dare ask aloud. "Don't . . . say that. Not that."

Cyric stilled as he assimilated her answer to his near declaration. He felt his heart turn to stone and the sweat caused from the heat building between them instantly chilled. She did not love him. Their relationship was to be one of only friendship. Of all the blunders he had committed in his lifetime, this one was the worst of all.

"You have my apologies, my lady. It shall not happen again," he said, his manner cool and aloof as he shifted to the right side of his chair, opposite where she sat.

Rowena stiffened as though he had struck her. "I . . . I . . . I will see you later," she offered noncommittally, and as her form receded from view, a heavy weight seemed to overtake his limbs. He did not move.

His mind urged him to run after her, challenge her to admit her own feelings, and prove his own, but his limbs remained paralyzed. His month was nearly over and he would return to where he belonged. Until then, Cyric intended not to see Rowena again if he could prevent it.

Chapter 17

Raelynd stirred from her sleep. Something woke her up.

Another faint tap. "Lyndee?"

Raelynd closed her eyes and stretched. After she had finished for the day, she had taken a long bath and washed her hair. The removal of the grime and the warm water had relaxed her sore muscles so much that she decided to have a small dinner in her room and then go straight to bed. Work had not been as grueling now that she knew how to organize her time better to manage everything, but it was no less physically tiring.

"Lyndee?"

"Coming," Raelynd growled, and dangled her feet off the side of the bed to stretch again before going to open the door.

Meriel walked in, still dressed. "What time is it?"

"Late, but not that late. Servants are only just now finishing their work and going home or to their rooms."

"Oh," Raelynd uttered while yawning. She hoped her sister would take the hint and realize that tonight was not a good time to chat. Meriel, however, remained oblivious. She sat down, kicked off her slippers, and pulled her knees up to hug them. Whenever she sat that way, Raelynd knew something serious was on her sister's mind.

"Didn't you hear that Laurel returns tomorrow tonight? After tomorrow we are reprieved. I thought you would be happy."

"I am," Meriel said, frowning.

Raelynd closed the door and sighed. "Your happy face usually includes a smile. What's wrong?"

"Nothing," Meriel answered too quickly.

Raelynd flopped down on the bed since there was no spare chair. "I don't believe you."

"Would you make me a promise? One that you swear to uphold regardless of situation or circumstance?"

Raelynd turned her head to study her sister. Meriel knew she usually wasn't receptive to such strong requests. "If I can," Raelynd answered hesitantly.

"Promise that you will do everything in your power to maintain the responsibilities of Lady of Caireoch Castle."

"You do not need a promise about that. When we return, everything will go back as it was."

"I'm not sure that it will."

Raelynd again studied her sister. "What do you mean?"

"Promise me? Everything in your power?"

The promise seemed unnecessary so Raelynd nodded. "I promise. But what has you so concerned otherwise?"

"Nothing I can say specifically. It's just that Craig and I were talking tonight—"

Raelynd bolted upright. While she was longing for Crevan, Meriel had been sneaking out to meet Craig! "What are you thinking, Meriel? What if someone sees you and Craig kissing each other?"

Meriel reared her head back and crinkled her brow. "Kiss Craig? Is that what you think? I've told you, we are only just friends."

"Friends," Raelynd repeated. "Are you not the same person who claimed not even two months ago that men were good for only passing the time?"

Meriel's eyes grew large at the memory. "Aye, and I still feel that way. Craig, however, is an exception," she said emphatically. "I never thought I could be friends with a man, let alone someone like him, but we really do get along. I can tell him anything and he listens to me."

"I thought you could tell me anything," Raelynd said, somewhat hurt.

"I can," Meriel assured her, "but lately, you have been so tired and grumpy and I really needed a friend. Craig has been standing in as temporary chieftain while his oldest brother is away and so we've been talking at night about our awful days."

"Awful?" Raelynd asked, puzzled. Her days had been full, but not as horrible as they had been. She had just assumed things had also improved for her sister. "Are you not finding the responsibilities easing now that you are more familiar with what needs to be done?"

Meriel physically bristled. "No. Not at all. Beyond preparing for the day's meal, it is something new every day. I would have to be here a year before I would become even familiar with everything, let alone comfortable. That is why I know I can never be the Lady of the Castle for our clan. I would go mad."

"Well, calm yourself." Raelynd sighed and lay back down. Her sister might be right. So much was involved in running a castle. Spending a few days in the position gave someone an appreciation of the magnitude as to what needed to be done, but not the experience. "Is that what you wanted to talk about? What you have been doing?"

Meriel shook her head. "No. Craig has been having similar struggles being in charge with Laird McTiernay away, so we've kind of grumbled to each other. It was something else he said tonight that has me thinking you have been right all along. Our pretending to marry is not only to justify our departure and our long absence, but for our protection. Father is trying to shield us from something and I get the feeling from Craig that it is not working."

The need to go back to sleep suddenly disappeared. Raelynd felt her body tense. "Why? What did Craig say?"

"It wasn't what he said, but what he asked. He wanted to know if I would agree to handfast with Crevan. Not to continue pretending, but to actually agree to a handfast ceremony next week. I thought he was teasing, but he became very serious and said that it was important." Meriel lifted her head and stared right at Raelynd. "He was scared for me."

Raelynd swallowed. To marry for a year and a day was not uncommon for there were many reasons to advocate a temporary pledge through handfasting. But Meriel and Crevan? Everything in Raelynd wanted to shout and scream no. "Then why not handfast with Craig?" Raelynd proposed, sitting back up. "You and he get along so well. If you must handfast with someone, let it be him."

"I suggested that very thing—"

"Then what is—"

"Unless I want to be Lady of Caireoch Castle, he is to handfast with you!"

"Me!" Raelynd huffed, jumping to her feet. "Is your mind gone? Is his?"

"I asked him to explain, but he refused. Craig only repeated that I needed to persuade you to handfast with him for your own protection."

Raelynd began to pace. "But it makes no sense. He doesn't want to get married any more than we do. He would be miserable. . . ." she mumbled to herself, knowing how different their personal habits were.

"Lyndee?"

Meriel spoke her name in genuine fear and Raelynd paused to look at her sister. "Go on to bed and give me time."

"Remember your promise."

Raelynd walked her sister to the door. "I will. I just need a little bit of time to think."

And to get some long-needed answers.

And this time, Crevan McTiernay, I am not taking no for an answer.

Raelynd waited until she heard the faint sound of Meriel closing her door before she went back in and quickly dressed. Her deep blue bliaut was somewhat elegant for what she had in mind, but it was the only clean gown she had until after tomorrow's wash. Last week, she would have asked the laundress to wash her clothes uncaring of the castle's schedule and priorities. Now, having been on the other side of such duties, such special requests would be reserved for true necessities and not whims.

Taking a brush to her long hair, Raelynd briefly considered braiding it before discarding the idea. It would take a significant amount of time and while it was nearly dry, in places it was still damp. She next slipped on her shoes and then exited the tower via means of Brenna's murder hole.

Having worked so much in the village this past week, Raelynd was confident she could have found her way around the cottages even if the night was filled with thick fog. But once outside the village, she was glad the night was cloudless and a nearly full moon was out to help light up the way. Cooler air had come in, eliminating the oppressive humidity, giving the light breeze a crisp feel, but it was still plenty warm if one was moving.

Heading toward the loch, Raelynd began to look for where they had enjoyed their picnic, hoping Crevan had not chosen to sleep somewhere else after the wildcat incident. She entered the small clearing and let go a sigh of relief. A small fire was burning and she could see the silhouette of Crevan's large body extended beside it with his arm tucked under his head.

She took another step and the sound of the leaves and small twigs cracking under her weight echoed across the clearing.

Crevan's head snapped in her direction. "Who is there?" he barked at the shadows.

He knew it was not Craig or any other person of any bulk—the footsteps sounded too hesitant and too light. No woman knew he was out here and Laurel had not yet returned. It could be Obe or even Neal the stable master, but both men were older and went to sleep early. Crevan was still mentally crossing out names when Raelynd finally came into view. For a second, he thought he was imagining her. He had done so many times, picturing her coming to him in the middle of the night with open arms, but none of those visions had seemed this real. Also, she had been smiling and eager. The expression heading toward him was not anger, nor was it friendly. There were so many emotions tied to the taught lips and pursed brows— fear, concern, apprehension, distress—he could not choose, but together they announced she was dealing with a problem. He only hoped that it was not the very same dilemma he had been mulling on since he and Craig got a very cryptic description of the changes taking place in the Schellden clan.

The Schellden farmer who had come to trade knew

very little about the happenings of Caireoch Castle or the laird's nephew, who was visiting from the Lowlands. He just said that while some did not like Cyric in the beginning, many were changing their minds, including the laird. The one outcome Crevan had believed to be least likely, but feared the most.

If Cyric did somehow prove to possess the abilities to lead the Highland clan, then Rae Schellden would probably support the king's idea of him marrying either Raelynd or Meriel. The most likely choice would be Raelynd as she was best positioned in the clan to be the next laird's wife. This was unacceptable and Crevan said as much to Craig. Craig pointed out that Raelynd would most likely make herself so obnoxious she would dissuade Cyric's attentions, causing him to choose Meriel. And if this were to happen, Craig made it clear that he would not allow her to spend a life miserably married.

One possibility remained—the very one all four of them swore at the onset of this awkward situation never to choose—marriage. Crevan had sworn if this very problem did arise, then it would belong to Rae Schellden and only to him. That Crevan would not be forced into marriage. But that was before. Now he had been analyzing the situation from all angles to discover another possibility. But he had not come up with an alternative.

As Raelynd got closer, Crevan jumped to his feet. Her hair was down and the gown she had on left nothing to the imagination. His body defied his will and instantly reacted to the sight, making him infinitely glad he had not yet undressed.

Raelynd stopped right in front of him. "I'm sorry to bother you, but I need to talk with you about something Craig said to my sister."

Crevan felt his stomach suddenly twist in a knot. If she had the news, then that would explain her unhappy expression. Reaching out, he collected one of her hands in his. Instinctively, he began to massage the palm and noticed the hardened, calloused skin where it had once been soft and smooth. His insides clenched.

Raelynd saw the anger flicker briefly in Crevan's eyes before he could suppress it and was puzzled. She looked down to where his gaze was focused and realized just what had upset him. She took back her hand. "I'm fine. Truly I am. I'm not sure that I ever want to wash linens in the river again or cook dinner or clean the floors—"

"Laurel had you doing what?" Crevan barked.

"But in the process I learned much," Raelynd deflected, arching a tawny brow mischievously. "Some of the very things you had tried many times to explain."

Crevan looked long into Raelynd's green and gold eyes and saw her bright, unstoppable spirit and an indomitable force—but it was now tempered. Somehow in the matter of a few days, Raelynd had finally come to understand the missing ingredient she needed to become not only respected, but beloved by those around her. A frisson of jealously rippled through him. He had always believed Raelynd could be an incredible woman, and now that she was on the verge of becoming just that, he was going to lose her forever.

"I'm proud of you, Raelynd," he said quietly. "More than you will ever know."

Their eyes locked, and her heart began to beat more rapidly. She had vowed to herself to never fall for a man who did not love her for herself. It had been an easy promise for she did not believe it possible, but here Crevan was. He knew her and she could see his love for her in the depths of his deep blue gaze. "I will love you forever, Crevan McTiernay."

"Don't," he choked. The simple declaration took Crevan

by surprise. He needed to hear those words so much and yet, Raelynd was meant to be the next Schellden chieftain's wife. She was not for him.

"You love me too," Raelynd stated, no qualms reflected in her tone of voice or her eyes.

"Raelynd—"

"I think a part of me has loved you for a very long time." She continued taking a step back so that she did not have to look up to meet his gaze. "Why else would I subject myself to your lectures? I knew when you were in the Great Hall. I could have avoided you but chose not to. So you, who believes so strongly in self honesty, were you also seeking me out?"

Crevan opened his mouth to answer, but she did not give him the chance to deny the charge. "I mean if I really had been an irritant to you, you would have just stayed away. Your brother did, not because of me, but he rarely ventured inside Caireoch so it was possible. You, however, did not avoid the castle or the places you knew I frequented."

"I never wanted to avoid you, Raelynd," Crevan finally managed to say.

"I know that," Raelynd said, and started to pace. "I think you enjoyed our debates. I know I did. You never would just agree with me and I knew that whatever you said, even if I thoroughly disliked it, was the truth as you saw it. Am I not correct?"

"Aye, but—"

Raelynd interjected, "You have always been honest with me. Promise never to stop."

She paused and looked him in the eye. She was laying a trap. No effort had been made to conceal her objective and any man could have avoided becoming ensnared, but Crevan opted to do what he had always done. She knew the truth anyway. "Aye, I promise."

Hearing those three words, Raelynd moved in close once again. "You know me better than anyone. Even better than my father because he refuses to acknowledge my faults. Meriel wants to be honest, but we are too close and her nature won't allow her to see me as anything but her sister. But not you. You have always seen me as I am. Look at me. I see you. All of you. And I love everything that I see. You cannot refuse my heart for I have already given it to you."

Crevan swallowed and studied how the moonlight was playing against her. Waves of gold tumbled over her shoulders and he remembered how her softly rounded breasts felt in his hands and tasted in his mouth. Every muscle in his body tensed and he forced his eyes to close in an effort to block out her beauty. His memory, however, could not be ceased so easily. His self-control was at its breaking point. He could no longer deny that her feelings for him ran just as deep, just as strong as his did for her. But it changed nothing.

Crevan's jaw tightened and his gaze swept over her in one swift, heated glance. "You need to leave, Raelynd. Now."

"I'm not going anywhere. I came here to talk to you. I want the truth."

"Fine, here is the truth. You should not be here and you know that. Hasn't sneaking out like this already put you in enough danger? Why aren't you in bed?"

Raelynd ignored his bark and without warning leaned against him, resting her hands on his chest. "I beg you do not treat me as a child. I know that something happened today and tomorrow everything might change, but here, right now, I need you and you need me."

Her innocently whispered plea ended the internal battle Crevan had been waging with himself. No longer did he possess the will to resist. Giving in to his primal desires, he whispered her name and taking her face into his hands, closed his mouth roughly over hers, searing her lips to his. Raelynd did not resist. With a muffled cry, she threw her arms around his neck and returned the feverish embrace.

Holding her face gently between his hands, he refused to let her go long after the time the kiss should have come to an end. Instead, he lingered against her lips, kissing them soft and deep, capturing her tongue and drawing it into his own mouth. She was offering the essence of her vibrant spirit and he accepted fully, completely knowing that it would forever consume his soul. Never would there be another woman for him.

Raelynd sucked in a quivering breath when he finally released her lips. But he was not letting her go. Hot, intense, dangerously compelling sexual desire blazed in his eyes. There were so many questions still between them, but she could not remember what they were. All she knew was that she loved Crevan with every bit of her heart and that he felt the same about her. That was all that mattered.

Urging Raelynd to her tiptoes, Crevan curved his hand around the nape of her neck and bent his head to kiss her again, softer this time. Breathing in her scent, he moved to bury his face in her neck, delighting in the softness of her skin. She moaned and it sent sparks flying through his body. He began to stroke her back, keeping her body pressed to his, half hoping, half fearing that his evident desire would make her stop him. But she didn't pull away. Instead, her fingers clenched around his shoulders and he knew then that he was not going to be able to stop. His want for Raelynd was too great. She was his and tonight he would stake his claim. No one else would ever know her like him.

Moving from her neck, his lips traveled lower, as his

fingers caught the edge of her gown and began to slide it off her shoulder. Crevan pulled her close to him and he heard her gasp as he cradled one of her breasts in his hand. Slowly he kneaded the soft mound through the velvet barrier as he continued to assault her shoulder and neck with kisses. He waited until she was quivering so violently she could no longer stand before he scooped her up in his arms.

Taken by surprise, Raelynd instinctively clutched Crevan's shoulders as he carried her to the soft grass where he had placed his plaid. His strength belied the fact that while she was not large, she was tall and far from being considered lightweight. And yet he moved as though she were weightless. In a handful of steps, they were by the fire and she felt her slippered feet once again touch ground. Apprehensive he might change his mind and try to send her away again, Raelynd threw her arms around him and kissed him with renewed eagerness, relieved when he returned the embrace.

Crevan had no intention of sending Raelynd away. Short of her ordering him to stop he doubted he could end what he had started. He was clinging to the fleeting remnants of his self-control just enough to keep things slow lest he frighten her away. Burying his head once again in her nape, he reassured himself that Raelynd really was in his arms, wanting him, desiring him just as much as he did her.

Returning to her lips, he kissed her, lingering, savoring every moment as he began to untie the laces of her bliaut. Once loose, he drugged her with a mind-numbing kiss and then quickly pulled the heavy gown over her head. Then, not daring to raise his mouth from hers for fear that he might somehow lose her, he pushed the chemise off her shoulders and finished undressing her. Naked in his arms, she was

perfection and Crevan knew he would never again see another to compare. Gently, he picked her up again and settled
her on his soft, worn plaid. A moment later, he reclaimed her
mouth as he lowered himself along the length of her.

Raelynd moaned with partial comprehension of her undressed state. Crevan was kissing her with an intimate ag-
gression that seared her senses, making her think only of
what her body was telling her and that it wanted more, not
less. Whenever he started to stop and pull away, her fingers
clenched around his shoulders and kept him from leaving.

Wanting to touch and caress him, Raelynd reached and
tried to pull free his leine. Need, not experience, caused
her to release his buckle, freeing his belted plaid from his
waist. With a groan, Crevan tore his mouth free from hers
and sat up, causing the cool night air to tease her over-
heated skin. Quickly he stripped off his leine and carelessly tossed it aside. For an instant, he stood naked in the
moonlight and black hair formed a triangle on his chest,
accentuating the muscled breadth of his torso. Her eyes
scanned downward to rest on his lean hips, long powerful legs, and what was between them. Raelynd's pulse increased, running hotter and faster. She wanted him. God,
she wanted him. She closed her eyes, afraid he might see
her blatant lust for his body.

The feel of his weight let her know that he had rejoined
her side. When his fingertips lightly stroked her cheeks,
her eyes fluttered open and were captured by the intensity
of his gaze. Her heart raced. Blue pools burrowed deep
into her, communicating directly to her soul. *I know you.
I know you as no one ever has. I want you. I will have you.*
And offering no resistance, she pulled his mouth down to
hers. His kiss held so much tenderness she thought her
heart would swell in her chest and choke her.

Crevan slowly lavished kisses over every inch of her

face. As he did so, his thick mat of hair rubbed against her nipples, causing her to moan with true pleasure. He had intended to be gentle and slow, knowing Raelynd was riding on a river of emotions and sensations that he had created, but her jutting breasts and narrow waist were playing havoc with his remaining self-control.

His eyes became shadowed with excitement as his mouth trailed down her throat and his hand found her breast, cupping it gently, almost reverently. Sexual tension seized his insides and he allowed his thumb to slide over the hardened nub. Slowly he made his way down to her breasts.

"You're so beautiful . . . so incredibly beautiful," Crevan whispered, just before he took the nipple into his mouth. The taste of it sent a shudder of excitement through him and he thought he would go out of his mind with the steadily growing craving to know every morsel of her delectable body.

At first, Raelynd thought she was in heaven as Crevan held her between his lips, flicking his tongue over her sensitive flesh, but then he began to suckle. The added stimulus was too much, and Raelynd lost restraint and began to writhe beneath him. A wanting so intense pulsed throughout her body causing her most secret place to dew. But he was not done. Turning his attention to the other breast, his tongue was velvet torture. She twisted and moaned while her hands clung to his shoulders as Crevan transported her to a realm where torture and delight were one.

He kissed the curve of her breast and she felt his hands encircle her slender form, clinching her, and then slowly slide downward. Lost in a liquid fire, Raelynd held her breath as Crevan began an intimate caress of her thighs. Remembering what he had done before, she found that it was exactly the relief she had been wishing for and arched her back in eagerness for his touch.

Up and down, closer, closer, his fingertips teased her until the blood pounded in her veins and she felt her knees tremble. Her entire body began to shake as his hands finally drifted over her mound and his fingers laced through the soft thatch of hair between her legs. They stilled and soon the pressure of his palm was not enough for her. Raelynd crushed his plaid in her grip as her hips lifted involuntarily off the ground in demand of more.

"Crevan, please," she pleaded.

"Shhhh . . ." he whispered in her ear, but complied with her demand and touched her in that most intimate of places.

Raelynd sucked in her breath. Desire scorched through her, igniting sensations he had only just begun to introduce to her and she longed to experience them again. Slowly he parted her with one finger, then another, opening her as she rocked against his hand.

Crevan smiled, letting his finger tease the rim of her melting wet core. Her uninhibited response was more than he could have ever dreamed. He languidly explored her with a deliberate possessiveness, finding all the secret, hidden places and making them tingle with need. She was hot, wet, and more than ready. And it all belonged to him.

Her female scent filled his senses, making Crevan only desire her even more. He continued to tease, touch, and play, stroking the flames of her heat until she was writhing, crying out in demand for more. The overwhelming invitation was one he could no longer deny. With the increasing urgency of her body's unconscious demands, he was at last close to the prospect of his own satisfaction.

Settling himself between her legs, he continued his attentions until she cried out in a desperate plea, "Please . . . please, Crevan."

Crevan grinned and began to move his hips, allowing his arousal to rub against her. Cupping her breast with his hand, he kissed her deeply. "There is nothing to be afraid of," he whispered in her ear. "Trust me, love. Never doubt me again."

Raelynd was drowning in a world of sensations, her mouth, her breasts, everything was competing with her lower body, and they were losing. She heard him talking, making promises, but all she could say was please. She was on the brink of something and Crevan was the only one who could give it to her. Without it, she was sure she would perish.

She felt his hand on her thighs, urging them to part as he slowly lifted her hips and began to penetrate. Then he stopped. "Raelynd . . . open your eyes."

The tip of his manhood was just touching her sex and yet he refused to continue. "Raelynd . . . look at me."

The request finally penetrated her passion-filled senses and she did as requested. At the same time, instinct took over and she twisted, forcing Crevan to drive forward and slide into her in one swift thrust. Sharp pain enveloped her. Raelynd closed her eyes and she cried out in astonishment, despite being foretold years earlier by her chambermaid of what to expect. But what her maid had failed to account for was Crevan's size. He was big. Very big. He was opening her, stretching her, making a place for himself in the very heart of her.

Crevan gathered every scrap of his remaining self-control and paused, allowing her to adjust before going any further. The pain, so evident on her face when he entered her, soon disappeared and Crevan could refrain no longer.

Making love to Raelynd was like entering the gates of heaven. She was so warm and soft, the throbbing in his loins was near unbearable. He could not stop himself and tried to slow his pace, but with each thrust she greeted him more eagerly.

"Put your legs around me." Crevan groaned the barely

audible instruction. His face fell against her neck. When he felt her legs gather to obey him, he began to move, with each thrust growing in need and force.

Crevan rose to see her face. He was close, but Raelynd was even closer. Her eyes were wide open, iridescent-gold-ringed peridots brimming with love. Then with a loud cry, she began to shake with pleasure as it engulfed her body. With each shudder, her velvety tightness gripped him. Exquisite, intense, primal pleasure—it was so much more than he had imagined.

Delirious, she lay beneath him, her body still quivering from pure sensation and yet she refused to let him go. He could not recall a single time he had been with someone who held on to him the way she was and he knew why. Raelynd would never let him go.

With that knowledge, Crevan drove into her one last time, filling her completely, and in that instant his entire body suddenly became rigid. He felt himself disassembling as his passion raged beyond his control. He buried his face in the pillow of her hair to filter the savagery of his cry. Ecstasy met sensation in a way he had not thought possible.

Long minutes passed and gradually Raelynd came back to earth. Crevan had done the impossible. He had gained her trust, so completely that she let go of every bit of control and gave herself completely. She was now his. He had taken her, possessed her, claimed her, in ways she had never dreamed. She had not thought it possible to love him more, but she did.

Crevan didn't have the strength left in him to roll away and he was unfazed by the prospect of staying right where he was forever. Raelynd was the perfect lover. She was natural, unself-conscious, and incredibly seductive. Just then, Raelynd pulled away and fear struck his heart in that half second before she moved to curl into the curve of his body. Safe in his arms, she gazed up and traced a finger along his jawline.

He gazed down and his arm stole protectively around her. Need tore through him, ripping away all of his carefully constructed defenses. Raelynd had become the fire in his blood; she was now as necessary to life as the air he breathed. Which made the agony of knowing she could never be more to him than she was at this moment all the more painful.

Crevan lightly kissed her and in that small touch Raelynd knew something was wrong. Once again, he was withdrawing from her. "Don't," she ordered in hushed tones against his chest. "Don't you dare tell me to leave, that you don't love me and that this meant nothing. You've never lied to me. Do not start now."

Crevan's arm squeezed her as his free hand raked his hair. "I won't."

Raelynd lifted herself onto her elbows and looked down at him. "I love you."

Crevan tucked back the thick strands of her hair behind her ear before tenderly caressing her cheek. "And I love you. I didn't know it was possible to love someone this much."

Raelynd swallowed and closed her eyes. Crevan had just uttered the very words she had longed to hear and yet something was wrong. "But . . ." she added for him.

"But there are things you do not know. Things that cannot be changed by what we shared or admitted tonight."

Then the reasons she had snuck out to see him came rushing back to the surface of her thoughts. "Craig spoke with Meriel. What he said, what he asked didn't make sense."

Crevan's brow wrinkled. "Craig came to you?"

"No, he saw Meriel. He wants me to handfast with him and my sister with you."

Crevan lay completely still with the only exception of his hand absentmindedly stroking her arm. He had not considered handfasting. It was not permanent like marriage, but Craig's idea had merit as for at least one year both women would be protected.

"Tell me," Raelynd pleaded.

"I promised that if ever you needed to know I would no longer keep the truth to myself. Everything you suspected was correct. There was another reason behind your father sending you away and it was tied to why your departure had to be under the umbrella of impending marriage and not visiting neighbors."

Feeling the need to hear this without distraction, Raelynd sat up. The breeze was light but without Crevan's warmth, it chilled her skin and she reached for her chemise and quickly pulled the item over her head.

Crevan knew why she was taking such action but the thin material did very little to hide her form as the firelight lit her up from behind.

"What was the reason?" she asked.

Startled, Crevan realized it was the third time she had asked the question. He grabbed his leine and yanked the shirt on, needing any type of barrier to prevent him from ignoring her request and taking her again. "Your cousin Cyric."

"Cyric?" Raelynd echoed, clearly unable to place the name.

"Your uncle's only son, who until nearly a month ago lived in the Lowlands. He is now with your father, who is discerning whether or not he is a fit leader for the Schellden clan and a potential husband for either you or Meriel."

Raelynd's jaw dropped. She shook her head with increasing vehemence. "No," she murmured. "My father would never do that. He would never make us marry. . . ."

"He might not, but the king would and there is not many a man who would defy King Robert, especially as your father happens to agree with him."

"But . . . but . . . you . . . I want you . . ."

"Craig is right. The solution is for you and he to handfast and I with Meriel."

Raelynd lifted her hand to stop Crevan from continuing. "Why is *that* the solution? Why can we not continue as we are for another month until my cousin leaves? Then we can do as we please."

"If Cyric learns you are not married, he will come demanding his rights. Especially now."

"What do you mean? Why now? Why not before?" Raelynd demanded.

"Because your father was trying to prove him to be unfit to lead a clan the size of his. Rumors arrived this morning that the outsider who at one time was ridiculed is now being reconsidered by all those in the castle, as well as the soldiers in the field."

"What does that mean?"

"It means that if Cyric wins over the people, which it sounds like he is close to doing, he will be positioned to be the next Schellden chieftain."

Raelynd's shoulders sank. "And my father expects me to wed the chieftain. But why Meriel then? Why do you have to handfast with Meriel and not me?"

"If you were not available, who would Cyric choose to solidify his rights to the title?"

Raelynd's mouth slackened. "Oh." He would choose her sister and then she would be in jeopardy of becoming mistress of Caireoch.

"If Meriel was willing to take on your responsibilities, then handfasting with Craig would be a possi—"

Raelynd waved a hand. "It is not. She made me swear to do whatever is possible to keep her from such a fate." Silence filled the small area as Crevan gave her the time to digest what she had learned. "I understand that if Craig and I handfast, he would be positioned to be laird. I would retain my position as Lady of Caireoch and Meriel would be protected, but what about you? You gain nothing from this plan. Why would you agree to something you do not want?"

Crevan leaned forward and held her chin gently in his hand so that she could not look away. "For you. To ensure your happiness or the closest thing to it. You are destined to be Lady of Caireoch and my brother desires the title of laird. I will not take that dream away from him nor deprive you of what you do so well. Could you be happy if your sister is miserable? Could I if Craig was?"

Raelynd began to breathe heavily as full comprehension of her potential future became clear. Then fear took over. "Is it for certain then? Do we have no choice? Is Cyric truly a threat as was told to you?"

"I do not know," Crevan replied, pulling her into his arms, regretting that they were in such an unwinnable situation. "But I will find out."

Raelynd held on to him. "Maybe you heard wrong. Maybe Father found my cousin incapable of leading anyone and forced him to return to his home."

Crevan held her and said nothing. For even if Cyric did leave, he knew he could not seize the title his brother had craved for so many years.

Chapter 18

Crevan watched as Craig urged his horse ahead, quickening their already fast pace. The sky had turned cloudy once more and the way was poorly lit, forcing their already tired mounts to work even harder. Soon they would have to stop for the night.

After Raelynd and Crevan had left the loch to tell Meriel about Cyric, the three of them found Craig to discuss the situation. Coming to no other solutions, both men left just before dawn for Schellden lands to determine if the rumors about Cyric were true. Raelynd and Meriel had never met their cousin and the few stories they had heard were not flattering. Regardless, both women were vehemently against the idea of being coerced into a lifetime commitment with someone they did not know, let alone love.

That left the options of marriage or handfasting.

Crevan knew that if Craig agreed to handfast with either of the Schellden twins, Rae would put his brother in the role of becoming the next Schellden laird. So did Craig. And while he loathed the idea, he absolutely refused to force Crevan, quiet and reserved, who refrained from speaking unless necessary, into such a role. He also could not leave Meriel vulnerable to Cyric if at all possible, despite his vow against relationships that lasted any enduring amount of time. So when Raelynd again suggested her sister handfast with him, Craig rejected the possibility before Meriel could.

Meriel had her own reasons for refusing to handfast with her friend. First, her father would expect her to assume at least part of the role as Lady of the Castle and the prospect of doing even some of Raelynd's responsibilities for a year filled Meriel with abject horror. But that paled to knowing that by being with Crevan, Raelynd would be tied to someone with whom she fought so often. The only possible, *survival,* arrangement for all four of them was the one Craig had proposed earlier. He would handfast with Raelynd and she would agree to do the same with Crevan.

Hearing Meriel talk before setting out on the journey, Crevan had inwardly cringed. He liked her, she was nice, but a future with her as his wife, even in name only for a year, was not one he was ready to accept. "Before we decide anything, Craig and I will ride out to your father's and confirm the rumors, one way or another."

With a look of relief, Craig had quickly agreed. "We will leave immediately and return with news."

"And if what you learn is bad?" Meriel had prompted.

"Then we will do what we have to," Raelynd had answered simply while staring unflinchingly into Crevan's dark gaze. "We are strong and a year is not that long."

Crevan knew that she was wrong. It would feel like an eternity. As he rode he considered all the possibilities and not a one that resulted in her with someone else was palatable for any length of time.

He knew Craig was thinking about the possibility of handfasting with Raelynd. His silence proved that. Normally one to fill the air with conversation, his brother had been unusually silent throughout the morning, lunch, and afternoon. Craig was only quiet for that long when in deep thought. It made Crevan wonder what he thought about. Was his brother eager to be positioned to become the next Schellden laird? He and Raelynd were cordial, even amicable, but Crevan knew that his brother did not love her. Did that weigh on Craig's mind at all? Was he still attracted to Raelynd? He had been just a few weeks ago when this whole nightmare started.

The thoughts and questions kept racing through Crevan's mind, tumbling out of control. It was unlike him, but he was not able to summon his normal emotional detachment to problem solving. "Are you sure?" he asked Craig without warning.

The cryptic question normally would have needed clarification, but as there was only one topic on either of their minds, explanation was not required. "Aye," Craig answered.

"Becoming Schellden laird . . . is that w-what you w-want?" Crevan pressed.

Craig held his breath. He did not want to lie, but he refused to shift the weight of that responsibility to his brother. Furthermore, the expectation of his family to seize such an opportunity was enormous. To turn down the chance of becoming a laird—a privilege a fourth son was unlikely to ever have—would disappoint everyone. And to Craig, failure in the eyes of his brothers was a much heavier burden to carry. "It would be a great honor to lead such a powerful and well-respected clan," he finally answered, hoping the half answer was enough to satisfy his brother.

Crevan said nothing and kept moving. "Stop up ahead?"

Craig nodded, knowing the clearing to which Crevan was referring. It was one they used often when journeying between the two clan headquarters. "The horses can drink their fill and I know I need some sleep," Craig said somberly, hinting that his normal jubilant thoughts had been replaced with darker ones.

A flash of silver was all the warning they received before a heavy blade was being swung in their direction. Another quickly joined it and instinct took over as the brothers unsheathed their broadswords to deflect the unexpected attack.

"Halt!" came a piercing bark. "It's the McTiernays."

Crevan waited for the opposing blades to be resheathed before he slowly lowered his weapon. Only then did his eyes adjust enough to see that the attacker was one of Rae Schellden's guards. "Callum, I didn't know someone w-w-was on guard in this area."

"There's been a lot of company lately," the Highlander grunted, and gestured to his three companions to continue their watch duty. "The laird aware you are coming?"

"It was not a planned visit," Craig answered indirectly, sheathing his own sword. He was just about to dismount when Callum stopped him.

"I suggest riding on ahead for another half hour or so and making your camp down the river. There has been some animal activity here lately and it is not safe."

Crevan studied the man to see if he was earnest. This clearing had strong currents and the rocky shoreline kept it from becoming a favorite among larger, predatory animals. Still, Callum's desire for them to keep going was sincere.

"So what brings you both back so soon and without brides?" Callum asked, posing the one question Crevan hoped to avoid.

"Personal reasons," Craig muttered for both of them.

Callum chuckled. "Let me guess. You want to know about our visiting Lowlander."

The slight insult gave Crevan hope and he joined his brother on the ground, freeing his horse so it could wander to the water for a drink. "Aye."

"And just what is your opinion of Schellden's nephew?" Craig pushed.

Callum sighed and Crevan wished he could discern details of the guard's other body movements, but the moonlight was too dim. "The man is a Lowlander and knows nothing of our customs and ways."

Hope again began to rise within Crevan.

"But I will admit to being surprised by his skills with a blade," Callum added. "And he did prevent our clans from going into battle with the McHenrys north of us."

Crevan raised a brow, for the man he had briefly met did not seem capable of such a feat. "Cyric did that?"

"Aye. And gossip has that he also provided input about the war with Ireland and England. I was not there, but I understand his words were well received."

Craig exhaled and Crevan felt his insides collapse. Still, participating in a couple of meetings without embarrassment was not enough to warrant the position of laird of such a large clan. The weak point enabled Crevan to still cling to his hope. "W-we w-will ride f-for ourselves and see."

"I suggest you go to the training fields in the morning," Callum hinted, pulling the reins on his horse in preparation to leave. "Cyric is usually out there at dawn for drills. I will be interested in your thoughts on our southern relative. Will you be long at Caireoch?"

"W-w-will there be a need?" came Crevan's quick counter.

"I cannot say," Callum replied, and although Crevan

could not see the man smiling, his voice indicated that he
did find some humor in the situation. Another hint to be
prepared for the unexpected. "I'll send word you are
coming. And don't forget, move downstream to camp,"
Callum added, and then left without waiting for a reply.

Dawn peaked over the horizon and found both Craig
and Crevan on the outskirts of the Schellden training
fields. The area was wide open and there were few places
to hide within hearing. Consequently, the brothers opted
to remain farther back, where there was thick foliage to
block their presence. They could not hear everything, but
they would be able to see and remain out of sight.

They had risen hours previously after only a short nap,
but sleep no longer plagued them. Adrenaline surged
through their veins as they waited to see the man who held
their futures in his hands. It was not often Crevan prayed
for someone to perform poorly, especially if they were not
an enemy, but deep down that is exactly what he hoped to
see. A Lowlander fail miserably.

Pink clouds started to fill the horizon and Schellden's
men began to gather in the distant field in various groups.
"Do you see him?" Craig asked, knowing Crevan had met
him once before, though only briefly.

Crevan shook his head. But they did not have to wait
long. When Cyric arrived, Craig did not need to ask if it
was him. After spending recent months with Schellden
and helping his commanders train dozens of new recruits,
Craig recognized everyone on the field—except one.

Cyric looked like a Schellden. Tall and wide, the man
handled his mount effortlessly, which was a surprise.
Gossip had it that Cyric was unaccustomed to the prickly
bushes of the Highlands and it made him a timid rider.

But that was not an accurate description of the person who was joining the group practicing with broadswords and targes.

For a while, Cyric was content to just watch and Crevan was beginning to wonder if that was all he did, when Cyric stepped in to give instruction. The boy was young and was struggling with the switch between using the targe alone as a defensive shield and coupling it with the broadsword in an attack. Crevan was unsure of what Cyric said, but the short exchanged worked, for there was immediate improvement.

Cyric stayed there offering several more tips before moving to those practicing close combat. The *biodag* was the one weapon everyone carried, whether a farmer, carpenter, baker, or soldier. The long stabbing knife typically was hung round the waist or attached to the belt and most soldiers carried more than one.

It was dangerous training and often men got injured, but too often the knife was key to winning a battle. Broadswords broke or if an unlucky strike took one unaware, it could knock the larger blade right out of the hand, but not a dirk.

"Look, *sgian dubhs,*" Craig whispered, pointing to what Cyric was having the men do.

Crevan nodded and continued to watch, frowning. The men were returning the small killing knife to their holsters placed high on the sleeve near the armpit. The small knife was used not as often in battle, but in unexpected times of defense. Cyric was training the men on not just how to use the miniature blade, but on how to rapidly draw it, and then quickly turn it in their hand so that it was ready for attack. It was brilliant as those fractions of a second could be the most lethal. A man wary of a situation could fold his arms, placing one hand on the *sgian dubh* so that he could pull it out in a flash if needed.

For the next two hours, Crevan studied the Lowlander as he made his rounds in weapon after weapon. The halberd, a combination of spear and ax on a long handle, was a difficult and unwieldy weapon for some, but Cyric looked not only graceful but deadly as he demonstrated how a foot soldier could effectively cut and thrust with it, killing a horseman. The Lochaber ax with its rounded edge and waved ends was also of no challenge. And Cyric's ability to manipulate a spear with speed and accuracy was on par with old Olave's skill at his peak. The only weapon they did not see Cyric use was the longbow, but Crevan assumed the man was not only familiar at shooting an arrow but quite proficient at it.

The Lowlander was impressive with weapons, but training was the ultimate responsibility of the commander, not the chieftain.

"I've seen enough," Crevan muttered, and was about to leave when Craig grabbed his arm.

Crevan scanned the field to see what got Craig's attention. A fight had broken out where they were using claymores, the heavy two-handed sword. The stance of the men was no longer one of challenge and seeking ways to distract and defeat as part of a training exercise, but of true battle. Such situations had to be resolved quickly before someone got seriously injured or even worse—killed.

Crevan could feel Craig rising and was about to join him in racing out to the fields in hopes of reaching the men in time to stop them when they suddenly saw Cyric on the scene. Within seconds, both men dropped their swords and a minute later headed toward opposite training areas. For the first time, Crevan regretted not being able to hear what was said. But one thing was clear. Cyric had stopped the fight and somehow convinced both men to move on with relatively little argument.

All morning he had been watching the Lowlander, but it was only in the last handful of minutes that Crevan become truly concerned. What he just witnessed was not a skilled fighter, but a leader. Those men did not capitulate because of who Cyric was, but of what he said. If the soldiers respected Cyric, then the prospect of Cyric being proved an unfit leader was very unlikely.

Crevan moved away from his lookout spot to retrieve his horse.

Craig joined him and mounted. "To Caireoch?"

"Aye," Crevan said. "Schellden is probably w-waiting f-for us. I doubt Callum kept quiet about our arrival."

"The old man should have a lot to say."

Crevan grimaced. He was afraid of just the opposite— that Rae Schellden would have very little to say. For what they just witnessed was pretty self-explanatory. Cyric was obviously fit to lead or at least could be trained to do so. Question was, did Rae now want his nephew to inherit his title?

The doors to the Great Hall opened and two large, dark-haired Highlanders entered. Rae Schellden watched as the men walked toward him, both with stern, unhappy expressions. Normally, he found feigning emotion to achieve a strategic advantage to be fairly undemanding, but today the effort was quite difficult. It was also imperative that he was successful in giving the right impression, otherwise this month, his plans, and the future of his clan could be in jeopardy.

Conor and Laurel had only left the previous day to return and it was only fortune shining favorably down on Rae that made him send Callum out just in case the two brothers decided to make an impromptu visit. The young soldier did well in diverting attentions and reported that the two groups of McTiernays were unaware of the other as they passed each other in the night.

Rae waited until Craig and Crevan were within just a few steps before he said, "I assume you are here because of gossip about my nephew, Cyric."

"W-w-we are," Crevan answered impassively.

"I was going to send word today that circumstances have changed."

Craig crossed his arms. "How so?"

Schellden leaned back and sipped the golden liquid in his mug contentedly. "I assume you first went to the training fields."

"Aye."

"Then you saw my nephew helping with some of the training," Rae stated, gesturing to the bench and table in front of him.

Crevan narrowed his eyes and took the seat Rae pointed toward. "Quite impressive."

"Aye," Rae agreed, and waved his hand, getting the attention of Rowena, who he suspected was there less to help with preparing the Hall for the next meal and more to eavesdrop. He smothered a grin and signaled her to get two mugs and some ale, before continuing. "He is. Surprised me enormously. I don't think my brother is aware of even half of his son's talents. But then we fathers often find it difficult to see our children as they are."

Craig swung his leg over the bench and sat down. "We could not hear him, but from the little we saw your nephew did not appear to be incompetent."

"W-with w-weapons or as a leader," Crevan added, deciding to not avoid the topic, but plainly put it out there to be discussed.

Rae exhaled and then put his drink on the table so that he could lean on his elbows. "You are right. He is competent or will be with a little more guidance. So as soon as you both release your claim, I will support Cyric when he chooses one of my daughters for a bride. The king is right. One of them must get married to secure this clan's future."

"Is that f-for the best?" Crevan posed. "F-for your daughters or your people?"

"You know that I desired my daughters to marry someone who understands the responsibilities of running a large Highland clan and someone whom my neighbors would trust and could maintain established alliances with. But you also are aware of their refusal to do so. No more. They will marry and from what I have seen, my nephew is good enough to be a husband to one of them," Rae answered. "Besides, you both made it clear that if Cyric was found capable, he and my daughters would be my problem."

Crevan issued him a measured, cool and apprising look. "Who leads this clan af-f-fects all those around."

Rae studied the younger man appreciatively, but said nothing.

Craig reached up and grasped the liquid fortification Rowena was offering. He took several swallows. "What if someone else married or even handfasted with Raelynd or Meriel? Would you still name your nephew as the next Schellden laird?"

Rae leaned back and studied the table as if he were in deep thought. "Depending on whom, of course—no, probably not. My nephew is not familiar with our ways. He is often uncomfortable with Highland weather and mountainous lands, though I think he would grow comfortable with time. He is slowly gathering respect, but without being in a position of absolute authority through marriage to one of my daughters, I fear he may still be viewed as a Lowlander and not be accepted by all of the clan."

Hearing that answer, Crevan immediately rose to his feet. "I suggest you prepare to leave f-for McTiernay Castle f-for your daughters w-will be married in two days. I'm sure Raelynd w-w-will w-want you there."

Rowena snuck out the back of the Great Hall and into the corridor that led to the buttery and kitchens. Moving quickly, she ignored the looks of servants and dashed into the courtyard. Stopping, she looked around, trying to decide where she could find Cyric at this time of day.

Since their last encounter, she had not seen him, not even in passing. At first, she had been relieved for she was not sure her heart could withstand another encounter. Her mind, though, was constantly drifting back to him, wondering what he was doing or wishing she could tell him about something that happened, knowing he would find it just as amusing. She missed his smile, his easy manners, and his laughter. But mostly she yearned to have him near. Cyric was the only man who ever engaged her in conversation of value and solicited her viewpoint. He teased her and appreciated her own sense of humor.

But then he had teased her on the one topic with which she could not cope. He had not actually said the word "love," but in that instant, Rowena realized she feared him doing so.

Cyric had not been hers to love.

She had vowed to keep Raelynd and Meriel's secret about their fictitious engagement. In doing so, she had doomed her own future.

At first, Cyric had been new, different, and even humorous. Then he had begun to fill up places in her heart that she had not even known were empty. Raelynd and Meriel had not wanted love and marriage, but deep down, she had. It had not occurred to her that she was, in fact, lonely until Cyric had arrived and they had grown to be friends. And then he had kissed her. He was everything a woman might want in a man and more than she dared hope to ever find.

As days went by Cyric's abilities to be a leader became more evident to everyone—not just her. But she knew the truth. Raelynd and Meriel would be returning unmarried and Cyric would be asked to select one of them to be his wife. And he would. More than that, Rowena knew that he should. For his sake and for the clan's.

So she had reminded herself that he was a tremendously attractive man who had been fawned over by women all his life. He was accustomed to flirtation and no doubt had kissed many, many women. She was just one more and to assume she meant anything else was foolish.

It had almost worked.

Somehow she had found the strength to lock away her desires and carry on with their friendship platonically. Talking, teasing, even flirting she could handle. But declarations of love? Even almost ones?

He had kissed her with a low, inviting passion that took her breath away. She had seen the steady glow of happiness in his eyes when he looked at her. And her heart had crumbled knowing that in a few months, maybe even weeks, he would be gazing at Raelynd that way on their wedding night.

But all that had changed. Raelynd and Meriel *were* getting married to the McTiernays! Cyric was free! He was free to marry her and she him. It mattered not if he wanted to stay, or return to the Lowlands or even work for the king. She loved him and he needed to know that.

Seeing one of the chambermaids leave the tower that held Cyric's bedchamber, Rowena raced across the bailey and confronted the young woman. "Is Cyric, the laird's nephew, in his chambers?"

The girl's delicate pale features accentuated her thin lips and high cheekbones, giving her a grim countenance. "He came and he left."

Rowena stepped back into the girl's path as she tried to step around her. "When?"

Medium blue eyes flashed with impatience and she shifted the linens she was carrying to her other hip. "I cannot remember, and no, I don't know where he was going." The chambermaid started once again to proceed toward her destination when she suddenly stopped and turned back around. "I did hear him mumble something about needing to get clean."

Rowena inhaled deeply and bit her bottom lip as she exhaled. There were not many places to bathe around the castle, especially this time of day. The kitchen servants would be busy getting food prepared and the chambermaid would have known if he had called for a bath. That left the river. Its mouth was at the Beauty Firth so its waters were cold. A few weeks ago she doubted if Cyric could have tolerated anything less than room temperature, but the man had found his Highland roots.

After convincing the stable master to let her borrow a horse for a short while, she rode out without telling anyone where she was going. The river twisted and turned and thick trees lined both sides of its banks. It was not unheard of to bathe in the river—in fact it was quite common— but there was no single place along the river to which people gravitated. Rowena slowly made her way along the shoreline, hoping that she had not chosen the wrong direction. She was about to give up when she finally saw him. He was standing with his back to her, fastening his belt to secure his plaid. His hair was wet and his leine clung to his damp shoulders.

Distracted by the evidence of his muscular frame, Rowena was not prepared for him to grab his sword and whip around. "I give you one warning. Disarm yourself and dismount."

Rowena's brown eyes widened. Cyric had moved so fast and there was nothing welcoming about his stance. "I . . . I . . . am unarmed," she finally managed to get out.

"Rowena?" he asked, his golden eyes narrowed with disbelief.

"Aye, it is me," she exhaled, able to breathe again.

Cyric moved to her side and helped her down. "What are you doing here?"

"I came looking for you."

"I know that, but why?"

Rowena opened her mouth and closed it several times and rubbed her hands together nervously. "Craig and Crevan McTiernay were here."

"The McTiernays? The ones who are marrying my cousins? Why?"

"They heard about you and came to find out for themselves if the rumors to your skills were true."

"How do you know this?" Cyric asked as he crossed his arms.

Rowena felt herself shrink a little in shame. "I was in the room helping serve drinks."

Cyric closed his eyes and chuckled, knowing Rowena only performed the role of a servant if there was a personal reason. "So my uncle allowed you to eavesdrop," he surmised. "And just what did he tell them?"

"That you were skilled but he would support you as laird of this clan if you were married to Raelynd or Meriel, which cannot happen because they are to be hand-fasted in two days," she said, unable to hide the sheer joy of those words.

Cyric was taken aback by her jubilant demeanor. "I had surmised so much already. I was going to talk to my uncle about returning home before the week was out."

"So soon?" Rowena gasped. "But I thought, well, I thought you would want to stay in the Highlands for a little while longer before you went to see King Robert."

Cyric was mystified. Since their kiss, he had kept his distance and she had done nothing to seek him out, confirming that she desired his absence. "The possibility of getting such a position with the king is remote even if I had my father's support, which is something I doubt I will ever have. I plan on returning to Ayrshire. As for staying at Caireoch, I have only one reason to stay longer."

Rowena felt her heart begin to race. This time when he told her of his feelings she would not run away. This time, she would throw herself into his arms and kiss him so that he would never doubt the depth of her love for him. "And that reason is?"

Cyric leaned over and picked up his dirk and knife, sliding one into his belt and the other between his calf and the coiled leather straps of his shoe. "Well, it is as you just said. My uncle believes in me and more importantly, I now believe in myself. I think I would be a good laird and unlike these McTiernays, I am a Schellden."

Rowena could feel the blood drain out of her face. "What are you saying?"

"Simply that the laird is my uncle, he has no sons and I should be the next Schellden chieftain." Cyric shook his head and water droplets went everywhere. As soon as he stopped, he realized her face was splattered with tiny dots of moisture. Instinctively he reached out to brush her cheeks with his thumb. "Sorry."

Both reacted to his touch and sprang apart. "I'm not hurt," she murmured, and then realizing the insanity of the remark, quickly added, "It's fine. I mean I'm fine."

Cyric ran his hand through his wet hair, wishing he could make her disappear. She had been plaguing his thoughts and he refused to let her know how much her rejection had hurt him. "What do you think, Rowena?" he asked in what he hoped was a nonchalant tone of voice. "Should I confront the brothers who usurped both of my potential brides? Would they fight or do you think they might relinquish their claim? I mean you said handfasting, not marriage. Doesn't sound like they are fully committed and all I need is one brother to change his mind. Then I will be free to marry as the king originally wished and rightfully claim to be the Schellden heir."

He glanced at her prepared for her to laugh and return his banter, but her usually warm brown eyes held only an emptiness, and it was leveled at him. "I thought you did not want to be a clan chieftain."

"Aren't you always saying that I should not let others so easily dictate my life and my future? I would have thought you'd be the first to support the idea," he teased, hoping to revive the sparkle in her eyes she had had upon her arrival.

A flash of wild grief ripped through Rowena and it transformed into anger. Her fury at Cyric was genuine, but she was equally furious with herself. Humiliated at knowing how transparent she had made her feelings, riding up to see him, exultant over seeing him. Whatever she thought she had seen and felt from him—desire, longing, passion—she had been wrong. He felt none of those things.

Her spine went rigid as injured pride took over. "Your future is not of my making. I have no opinion."

She went to grab the reins to her horse, but missed. He stepped in and gathered them for her, placing them in her hands. He could not tell if Rowena was truly upset or not. Her conduct said yes, but he could not fathom why. She knew that he had no real interest in marrying his cousins or running a clan.

"I know I control my own destiny," he gritted out as he helped her onto her horse.

Rowena savored the feeling of his hands upon her waist as he placed her effortlessly on top of the large animal. Then they were gone and the pain of knowing she would never again feel his touch was overwhelming. He sent her a silly lopsided grin. She knew the smile was his way of trying to cheer her up and it was too much. Hurt and anger lashed out, looking for his company.

Icy laughter bubbled out of her chest. "You think you control your destiny? From the moment you arrived in these Highlands other people have decided your life. You came here with the *king's* decree and yet quickly conceded defeat. But the sad truth is there was nothing to challenge. That's right. The engagement was a ruse and as anticipated, you surrendered rather than confronted the two men who seized your fate. Now it is too late."

Rowena jerked the horse's reins and headed away from the river, fighting to maneuver through the trees as tears streamed down her face. She had broken her promise, and she had intentionally inflicted pain upon the man she loved. As a result, Rowena had just set into motion the one thing she had feared the most. For if Cyric had not planned to challenge Crevan and Craig McTiernay, he would now. Pride demanded it. Cyric was blessed with a calm, agreeable nature not common among his clansmen, but that did not mean Highland and Schellden blood did not run in his veins. They did and his dignity would require a response.

She had to do something. She had to warn Raelynd and Meriel about Cyric and she had no time to lose.

Rowena steered her horse west and urged it into a gallop. The stable master would be furious and no doubt would eventually seek out the laird and tell him that she had not come back. But by that time, it would be too late. For she intended to find the McTiernays and return with them.

Then, somehow, she was going to convince both brothers to fulfill their intentions as soon as possible. For if they didn't, Rowena knew she would lose Cyric forever.

Chapter 19

A shout, almost like a sharp scream, echoed all around Raelynd. Sounds in the forest at night were deceptive. Whatever was chasing her could be far away or very close. She had to keep running. Pain shot through her legs but she knew she could not stop. If she did, she would lose everything. Wind started to howl violently, causing the tree branches to whip uncontrollably. One snapped against her collarbone just as another cry filled the air.

Raelynd jerked and her eyes snapped open. She could feel her chest heaving and knew that she'd had another nightmare. What about, she could never remember, but for the past four nights, she had woken scared and breathing heavily. Rarely was she plagued with unpleasant dreams, but they always coincided with when she felt powerless and out of control. And they would not relinquish their hold until Crevan returned with news. Only then would she find peaceful slumber.

Forcing her legs to uncurl, she stretched her calves and endured the pain as blood rushed back into the semideadened limbs. She tried to glance across the room when a severe twinge in her neck prevented her. Raelynd rubbed the angry nerve, promising herself that this was the last night she was going to sleep in the hearth chair.

Able to move with a little less pain, she tried once again to peek at Meriel. She was still asleep on her bed, the place she had slept since Raelynd had returned to explain all that Crevan had told her about Cyric.

That was three nights ago.

Since then Raelynd had felt numb. A month ago she had been naive, unaware of the pure joy of love or the agony of its loss. But even if she could, she would not return to that state of innocence. She only wished she could talk to her sister about everything, but Meriel refused to even discuss the situation. The morning after the brothers had left, she had woke up, pasted on a smile and dedicated her days to sewing in Craig's room. She only left to eat and join Raelynd at night to supposedly visit. But she would only come in and sit on the bed, eventually falling asleep from exhaustion. It was the first time Raelynd had not been able to confide in her sister or her sister with her.

Outside she heard a faint shout and wished she had Meriel's view of the courtyard. Raelynd felt her eyelids starting to slip back down when the thought that Crevan had returned sent a jolt of adrenaline through her. Springing out of her chair, she grabbed her bliaut, threw it over her chemise, and laced it as quickly as she could.

Meriel stirred just as Raelynd grabbed her slippers and was putting them on. She glanced at the dark arrow slits in the wall and confirmed it was still night. "Where are you going?"

Startled, Raelynd yelped and her hand flew to her chest. "Don't *do* that!"

Meriel sat up and rubbed her eyes. "Why are you getting dressed?"

"I think Crevan and Craig are back."

Meriel's eyes flew open and she threw off the coverlet Raelynd had placed on her after she had fallen asleep, still dressed. "Wait for me," Meriel mumbled, and leaned over the side of the bed to find her shoes where she had kicked them off. She was just slipping them on when there was a heavy knock at the door.

It was Crevan.

Raelynd could feel her heart pounding and suddenly she could not move. Meriel, however, did not have that problem and raced to the door to open it. Crevan entered and behind him was Craig. Without thought, Meriel threw her arms around his neck. "I'm so glad you are back."

He chuckled, but Meriel knew it held no true mirth. She let go and moved out of the way so that he could enter the room. She was about to close the door when she heard a familiar female voice.

"That's no way to treat a friend who just spent a most uncomfortable long day on a horse just to see you."

Craig's expression held no sympathy. "You were warned."

The shock of seeing Rowena yanked Raelynd out of her daze. "What are you doing here?"

Rowena walked over and gave her friend a warm hug. "I came to see you get married, of course."

"Handfasted!" Craig and Meriel chirped simultaneously.

Rowena's brown eyes moved rapidly between the two. "Raelynd, I thought you were to marry Craig."

"She is," Craig answered, moving to Raelynd's side. "Meriel and I are only friends."

Rowena did not argue, but she did nothing to hide her skepticism. Friends did not hug each other as Craig and

Meriel did after an absence of just a few days. "So when is this handfasting to take place?"

Crevan's jaw hardened for it was the only topic Rowena had focused on since she caught up with them. "Tomorrow afternoon."

Rowena issued him an icy glare. "I thought we agreed that was too late."

"That is because you weren't listening," Craig inserted, clearly frustrated.

Meriel was confused. "Why is tomorrow too late?"

"Because if you are not married by the time Cyric arrives, he is going to challenge Craig and kill him!" Rowena said.

Meriel started to shake her head vigorously. Rowena obviously had forgotten how good Craig was with a sword. Her father believed him the best commander he had ever had. Her hazel eyes bored holes into Craig's blue ones. "Could he?"

Craig shrugged. "He's good."

The simple answer was the equivalent of an affirmation and the conversation picked up speed as Meriel issued a stream of questions Craig and Rowena answered, too often simultaneously and in contradiction.

As the noise level rose, the normally spacious bedchambers grew cramped. Raelynd caught Crevan's eyes and then headed toward the door. She was not sure if the other three weren't interested in coming or whether Crevan made it clear they were not invited, but when he joined her outside on the curtain wall adjacent to the tower, she was relieved to see he was alone.

A recognizable large dark figure popped out from Brenna's murder hole and slinked off into the night. "I wish I had known that it only took a little noise to get rid of Conan," Raelynd said softly, trying unsuccessfully to hide the sheer panic she felt inside.

Crevan said nothing and only opened his arms, offering what she needed most.

Collapsing against his chest, she began to weep. Crevan had not needed to say a word. His deadpan expression had said it all. "So it is true. My father thinks my cousin capable of being laird."

"Aye," he whispered against her hair. "But he would only support Cyric if he married either you or Meriel."

"And did I understand correctly? Cyric knows the truth and he intends to stop the wedding?"

Crevan took a deep breath and exhaled. "Rowena told him and she believes that he will soon come here and challenge one of us as a result."

Raelynd could not help her growing sense of unease. "Will he?"

"Pride is a powerful thing."

Raelynd pulled back and for a long moment she just looked at Crevan. She did not need to repeat the question. "Then we must handfast immediately as Rowena suggested."

Crevan gathered her hands in his. "It is too late. The last time we spotted him, he was no more than an hour behind us. Besides, it is one thing for Craig and I to pledge ourselves for *your* protection, it is quite another to race into marriage to save ourselves."

He then escorted her along the wall to an opening that enabled them both to see the majority of the large inner courtyard, including the gatehouse entrance. There he held her and waited. Less than ten minutes passed before the doors were opened and two riders entered. One she recognized as her father, and she knew without being told the other tall dark blond-headed man was her cousin Cyric. And he was angry.

"I'm here and I know you are expecting me," he growled. The deep voice was clear and unmistakably serious. "I know the truth and I demand Craig and Crevan McTiernay come out and face me."

Raelynd felt Crevan's eyes upon her and she looked up at him, knowing what she would find. Crevan would not hide and neither would his brother. "I'm coming with you," she said.

Taking her hand, he went back to the tower and descended the staircase. By the time they reached the bottom, Craig, Meriel, and Rowena had joined them. They walked out into the courtyard and they were not alone. Cyric's bellowing had awoken all who had been sleeping in the castle, including Conor and Laurel.

Raelynd was the first to speak. "Hello, Father."

Rae caught the unhappy look from Conor. "I apologize for the hour of our arrival. It was . . . unavoidable." Then his hazel eyes softened as they moved to his daughters. "I missed you both this month."

"And we missed you," Meriel assured him.

"Craig and Crevan came to visit me and told me of your plans. Then Cyric came to me expressing his . . . um, displeasure upon learning the circumstances of the arrangement. He desires to marry one of you and I support his claim." Rae shifted his gaze to Crevan and then Craig. "I will not allow two men I admire and respect as much as I do you to postpone your own lives and marriages for unnecessary reasons. Cyric is capable of becoming the Schellden chieftain when I pass and it is my daughters' responsibility, not yours, to marry and secure their clan's future."

Conor yawned loudly and stretched his massive arms and chest, seizing everyone's attention. "Sounds good. Glad to hear it, Schellden. Craig, Crevan looks like you escaped."

Laurel jabbed her husband in the ribs. "What?!" he exclaimed.

Ignoring his older brother, Craig took a step toward Raelynd and circled an arm around her own waist. "Schell-den, I appreciate your candor, but I have no intention of withdrawing my offer of marriage."

Cyric had remained silent during the conversation. His attention had been solely on Rowena, who only met his stare with one of her own. After years of hearing and helping to resolve numerous disputes, Cyric was well aware of the destructive nature of pride. It drove men to act in ways contrary to their personality or even their true desires. Cyric had no interest in becoming the next Schellden chieftain, but pride dictated that he do whatever necessary to achieve that right. If he did not, no one would respect him and that was the one thing he could not, would not lose.

"Then I challenge you. Here and now," Cyric said without inflection.

"No!" Meriel shouted, and felt the resulting weight of all eyes upon her. Bolstering her courage, she moved so that she stood in front of Craig. "I am not worth it and I will not let you risk your life for me."

"Well, I'm not going to let you marry him," Craig huffed.

"No, it is I who is going to end this," Raelynd asserted, looking directly at Cyric. "I am familiar with running Caireoch Castle and am the most knowledgeable to support you as second in charge to my father. I am offering to handfast with you tomorrow afternoon and in return my sister gets to retain her quarters in the castle, and you agree to end hostilities with the McTiernays. Handfasting will give you time to develop your role in the clan and secure your claim to be the next laird. But after a year and a day, we agree to end the union. You can then marry someone else and she will assume my role, leaving me free to live where I please and marry whom I want. Do you agree?"

Cyric studied Raelynd. If he agreed, she and he would be together for at least one year and a day. She was strong willed, outspoken, and quite beautiful. Rumors had not done her justice. Normally, such a rare combination in a woman would have caught his attention, but Rowena had ruined his desire for anyone else. But Raelynd was not seeking passion from him, she was offering a compromise. She restored his pride by enabling him to become the next laird, and at the same time she would gain her freedom. A year of their life was the price.

"I agree."

Upon hearing those two words, Conor clapped his hands. "Good. Now can we get back to bed? Fallon," he said, finding the burly steward, who looked more than a little annoyed at being woken up in the middle of the night. "Find Laird Schellden and his nephew a bed in the Warden's Tower and get them better accommodations in the morning."

Rae Schellden congratulated Cyric and then followed the steward into the nearby tower. Conor placed an arm around his wife's shoulders and directed Laurel back to their bedchambers without any argument. With no fighting pending, the crowd lost its interest and began to disperse.

Crevan joined them, disappearing without a word. Raelynd knew that she did not need to explain her actions. He understood them. Their destinies were written by people they loved.

Raelynd offered the man she had just met and agreed to marry a quick nod. "Until tomorrow afternoon."

He returned the gesture. "Until then."

Raelynd turned and Meriel hastened to her sister's side. Craig issued one final glare at the man who had disrupted so many lives over the past month before pivoting and escorting the two women back to their rooms.

Only Rowena and Cyric remained in the courtyard and the tension between them was almost palpable. A year and a day he would be married and to Rowena it could have been until death. For it didn't change the fact that he chose being laird and Raelynd over her.

"Rowena," Cyric said, his eyes pleading with her to understand.

And she did.

Cyric did love her. But he was still caught up in this image his father had of him. The man would not rest until he had his father's respect. "Do you really intend to marry Raelynd?"

"I have no choice."

Rowena bristled. "No, you do. And what you so desperately want cannot be gained by marrying Raelynd. Tomorrow afternoon will be the demise of your dreams and when they are gone, do not come back to me for support or understanding. I have no intention of being around."

Then she was gone and Cyric found himself alone. He was not surprised. Pride had driven him there and by tomorrow afternoon, it would cost him the woman he loved.

Morning came early the next day, or at least it felt like it to almost everyone who was rudely awakened in the middle of the night. Only Father Lanaghly had been blissfully unaware of the commotion and able to get a good night's sleep.

Conor barked an order and Laurel decided to let it pass. He was tired and the midmorning meal had arrived almost at noon. Plus she had forced him out of the Star Tower, giving her dayroom to Raelynd so her sister and Rowena could help her prepare. She had even encouraged young Brenna to join them, which mollified the young girl enormously after being forced to stay in her room last night when it had been clear that something very interesting was taking place in the courtyard. But mostly Conor hated his home being used as an emotional battleground, for it was the one type of fight he knew not how to win. Laurel, however, was looking forward to sundown.

Standing at one of the Great Hall windows, she waited patiently as she cradled her youngest child on her hip. Neither she nor Bonny liked it when she was away from the castle visiting and it took several days before the little girl was willing to be away from her mother's side when she returned.

Soft wavy brunette curls lifted from Laurel's shoulder as Bonny pointed to the gatehouse. "Look, Mama. Crevan has come back home."

Laurel smiled and kissed the child on the temple. "That is good news, Bonny." Then, over her shoulder, she called out, "Come take a look."

Conor let go a "hrmph" and continued his conversation with his commander, Finn. Rae Schellden joined her. He watched as Crevan marched determinedly toward the Warden's Tower and disappeared inside. "Finally," Rae grumbled, but Laurel knew he was relieved.

"You had doubts?" she chuckled.

By the time she had met and confirmed her suspicions with Laird Schellden almost all the pieces were in place with the exception of Cyric. Unknowingly Rowena was the one who corrected that small bump. She had not been part of Rae's original plan, but a welcomed addition after watching the two bond. He considered her a third daughter and her happiness was of great importance to him.

"Aye," Rae admitted. "I had not planned for Cyric and

Rowena to fall in love. She tends to be overly guarded and I'm afraid too little time has passed to break down the barriers she has placed around her heart. And after last night . . ."

Bonny started to squirm and Laurel let her down. "True, but you heard her when she thought they were alone. Only when you love someone very deeply do you get that angry."

Rae chuckled. "She will need that spirit in Perth with all the people and pomp and circumstance at court. But I believe she will do well there."

"Aye," Laurel agreed. "The queen is not much older than Rowena and I suspect they will get along well."

Schellden waved a finger toward the Star Tower across the inner yard. "And while it looks like Crevan is coming to his senses, will Raelynd? I hate to admit it, but my daughter has my stubbornness."

"She also has your ability to correct mistakes before she makes them."

"Only if she sees them."

Laurel grinned mischievously and crossed her arms. "Don't worry about that. I made sure there was someone with them who will point out any mistakes she sees."

Schellden tilted a single brow and looked at her uncertainly. "Who?"

Laurel's smile broadened and her eyes danced. "The one person without whom your plan would have never come together. Brenna."

Brenna lay on her stomach on one of the window benches watching Meriel twist and curl her sister's hair. It had taken them forever to get dressed and when they finally started doing their hair—what Brenna had been pining to begin for hours—they wouldn't let her help. She hated being seven. Almost everything being discussed made no sense. But one thing was clear—no one was happy. And after a morning of tears and comments that a year wasn't so long, Brenna decided that she was never going to get married. It was obvious that the whole event was very painful and she was pretty sure that getting a husband was not worth the misery.

"Brenna, can you bring me that comb?" Meriel asked, pointing to the ivory object just out of Brenna's reach. The little girl got down and handed over the comb.

"Why is Rowena so mad?" she finally asked, hoping to at least clarify one mystery.

Meriel opened her mouth to refute the assumption, but closed it before she did so. "Raelynd, look at Rowena," she whispered. "Brenna is right. I thought she was just upset like I was at the situation, but she is not sad, she's . . . well, like Brenna said, she's mad."

Raelynd pivoted in her chair and considered her long-time friend. Rowena was sitting on the settee, knees pulled against her chest, and she was rocking slightly while staring into the fire. Her sister and Brenna were right. Rowena was mad.

Rowena had bathed and done her hair early that morning and Laurel had let her borrow a gold dress that accentuated her dark feminine features. Normally, such a dress and the prospect of a wedding would make her bubble with excitement. But Rowena was far from being even mildly pleased. She so rarely let anything visibly rile her, they had not recognized her anger.

Glad for any excuse to delay getting ready, Raelynd rose to her feet and walked over to her friend. "What is wrong? Last night you arrived and practically begged for a wedding to take place."

A tear escaped and Rowena quickly brushed it away. "Not this wedding. I did not want you to marry a man you do not love."

"But I did not love Craig either."

"This is different."

"How?"

Brenna went back over to her window seat and flopped back down on her stomach, propped up her elbows and rested her chin on her palms. "Because she loves Cyric like you love Crevan," she answered.

All three women's heads snapped to stare openmouthed at the little girl. Meriel was the first to speak. "I promise you, Brenna, my sister does not love your uncle Crevan. They fight all the time."

Brenna produced an unimpressed shrug. "So do Mama and Papa."

"*I* was the one who was going to handfast with Crevan," Meriel explained, thinking that their similar looks had confused the young girl.

A puzzled look took over Brenna's face and her silver eyes searched Raelynd's. "That's what I don't understand. Why would you do that if *you* love Crevan? And why did he agree?"

Raelynd swallowed. "Whoever I marry will become laird of Meriel's and my clan. So we did it to ensure the happiness of my sister and your uncle Craig," she answered, refusing to look at Meriel.

"*My* happiness," Meriel repeated, mystified as her mind quickly replayed recent conversations. How many times had she rejected Raelynd's idea that she and Craig join? And she had emotionally forced Raelynd into doing everything she could to keep her from possibly becoming responsible for Caireoch. "Raelynd, you should have said something."

Raelynd stared at her fingers. "I didn't even realize I loved Crevan until recently. He only admitted his feelings the night he and Craig left to see Father. When they came back and we all agreed to handfast, what choice did he have? Crevan was not about to steal the only opportunity Craig might have at becoming a laird."

Meriel started to pace. "Craig doesn't want to be a laird."

Raelynd scoffed, unable to comprehend such an absurd idea. "Every man, every soldier desires deep down to be in charge of a clan—especially one as powerful as ours."

"Not everyone," Rowena muttered. "Cyric dreads the idea."

Raelynd jumped off the settee as if it had pinched her. The tight knot already present in her stomach just doubled in size. "I'm confused."

Brenna giggled.

Meriel stopped her pacing and leveled a glare at the child. "This is not funny, Brenna."

Unfazed, Brenna tossed her pale gold curls over her shoulder and sat up. "It is to me. No one wants to marry the person they love!" Then her gray eyes turned serious and seemed to instantly age and fill with wisdom. "I'm bored. And *nothing* makes any sense. I'm going to find Mama. Maybe she can tell me why Crevan can't marry Lyndee when he is *the only one* who wants to be a laird."

With a childlike growl, she got down, shuffled across the room and left, leaving everyone in the room stunned.

Rowena raised her head and stared at her two friends, her eyes flickering between them. "Did I understand Brenna right?"

"Crevan *wants* to be a laird?" Meriel posed.

Raelynd stared at Rowena. "Cyric loves *you*?"

A tense silence enveloped the room as everyone digested what they had just learned. Assumptions had to be reversed, decisions had to be reconsidered, and most importantly, personal desires that had been suppressed had to be reexamined.

"Why am I just about to handfast with Cyric?" Raelynd finally asked aloud.

Meriel shook her head. "I have no idea."

Rowena huffed. "Because if you don't, Cyric will believe he was played a fool. All his life he has worked hard for the respect of his family and he doesn't believe he can get it any other way."

Raelynd stood motionless for several seconds. "Do you believe that, Rowena?"

Rowena paused and considered her answer. Spinning around in the settee, she sat up with her back straight and her eyes clear. "No I don't. And I don't believe your father does either."

Raelynd went back to the door and yanked it open, planning to call for Brenna. Instead two little boys fell inside. "Braeden. Gideon. How fortunate to find you here. Do me a favor and go find your mother and my father. You do know him, right? Laird Schellden?"

Dark heads silently bobbed up and down, fearing she was going to make them confess what they had been doing. "Please find them and tell them that there is going to be no wedding this afternoon."

Braeden was the first to get to his feet. "You mean no one is marrying anyone of you?"

Raelynd nodded. "Aye, that is *exactly* what I mean. We are tired of allowing our lives to be dictated by the desires of everyone else. So until that is understood, we are staying put."

Gideon's eyes became huge. "We can't remember all that."

"Just remember the part about us refusing to marry.

That should be enough," Raelynd directed, and then gave them both a slight push out into the corridor and closed the door.

"There," she said, feeling confident and hopeful for the first time in days. "I have been told twice now to never let anyone else determine my future. I think it is time I listened."

Crevan entered the stairwell to the second floor. The Warden's Tower was where the soldiers slept, as well as the steward and a few others. Only two rooms in the tower were suitable for guests. He, Craig, and Conan were supposed to be sharing them. Fortunately for Schellden and his nephew, the weather had not turned bitter and all three of them had opted for other sleeping arrangements.

As he took the last step, Crevan considered what he was about to do. He had not planned what he was going to say and he had no idea what reaction to expect from Cyric. Normally, either one of those factors would cause him to refrain from confronting the man, but today, no action was not an option.

As the first pink rays of dawn chased away the night, it had occurred to him he had not said a word. Cyric demanded his rights. Meriel tried to sacrifice herself, Craig had protected her, and Raelynd had offered to save them all. Rae had spoken and even Conor offered his opinion. But he had remained silent.

Never had Crevan felt so inadequate. He had been powerless to do what he wanted and had been ashamed of his weakness. Not until morning arrived did he realize that his feelings of helplessness were within his control. He had given his power away. It had not been taken from him. It was past time to reclaim what was rightfully his.

Never before had he avoided an enemy and Crevan had

every intention of facing this one. Today, he was going to stop living his life to please others at the expense of his own happiness.

He was not going to give up Raelynd for another day, let alone a year. If Craig really desired leadership, then he would have to seek another way to attain it. And if his brother did so, then he would also have to learn how to make decisions that did not involve a battle plan and weapons. Though he would never say it aloud, Crevan knew he would be a far better chieftain than his brother. Cyric, on the other hand, was another matter.

Before Crevan left Caireoch, he had spoken to a handful of men whose opinions he trusted and all of them had the same things to say. Cyric was a Lowlander and it was obvious, but he was also smart and brilliant with a sword. They did not know about him as a leader of the clan, but Cyric had proven himself capable of dealing with and gaining the respect of other clan leaders. Would they follow him? None of them could answer the question. But the fact that they didn't outright refuse said enough. With sufficient time, Crevan suspected they would. After all, Cyric was a Schellden.

But what did Cyric want? What had driven him to confront them last night and demand his rights? Why not a month ago? Pride? A sudden desire for power? And what were his plans once the year was complete?

The only way to learn the answers was to confront the one who had them.

Crevan stopped at the only door that was closed on the second floor and rapped hard three times on the wooden planks. He did not have to wait long before it swung open.

Golden eyes held Crevan's blue ones for several moments before Cyric stepped back. "Come in."

Though raised in the Lowlands, Cyric was unmistakably a Highlander. His height was almost that of Crevan's and his chest was slightly bulkier. His hair and facial structure were nearly identical to Rae's, but his eyes must have come from his mother's side. Surprisingly, the golden orbs held not the arrogant countenance of a man who felt victorious.

A deep crease was notched in the space between Cyric's brows and the set of his shoulders was tight. Stress lines bracketed his mouth. If anything, the man looked like he was preparing to sacrifice himself by assuming a heavy burden.

"W-w-we need to talk."

Cyric raked his hand through his hair and nodded. He then waved to one of the several folding chairs leaning against the wall as he sat down on one that was already open. "You want me to walk away, but you must know that I cannot do that."

Crevan grimaced and grabbed the uncomfortable item and popped it open. His grandfather had hated the folding chairs with a passion, stating that sitting on the floor and leaning against the wall was more comfortable. He had been ridiculed commissioning one of the local carpenters to build him several chairs like those he had seen used by royals with arm rests and high back supports. The result was twenty oversized, bulky chairs made from bog wood, which his grandfather placed in the Great Hall.

It was his father's idea to make them comfortable by padding them. Conor had been the first to steal one from the Great Hall and by the next night three more disappeared. Only then did his father notice the change in the Hall decor. Crevan could still remember his father's flushed face as he was about to threaten all those who had procured chairs without permission. He was stilled by his mother's gentle hand upon his arm. His older brothers,

Cole and Colin, had followed Conor's lead and taken the second and third chairs, but it was their mother who had taken the fourth.

After that nothing was said and he and Craig refused to be left out and stole one chair for each of their rooms. Within the first week after being padded, only seven chairs remained in the Hall and his father made it clear that none of them had better come up missing. In the end, each brother had at least one chair in their rooms, with Cole and Conor having two. His mother had somehow managed to get another into her dayroom without anyone noticing and it wasn't until their father's death did they discover where the other two had been hiding—his solar.

"Something wrong?" Cyric asked, seeing Crevan's hesitation.

"No," Crevan answered, and sat down on the stretched leather. "I just f-f-forgot that these chairs w-were stored here."

Cyric produced a half smile, half grimace. "I asked my uncle about his padded chairs and he blamed your father for the idea. Said it was too expensive but his vanity required it."

"Sounds like Rae," Crevan said, leaning his elbows on his knees. "W-w-we have a problem."

Cyric drew in a deep breath. "Well, at least you said 'we.' That gives me the impression that you don't have a desire to meet in the courtyard."

Crevan found himself smiling at the man's humor. "W-w-we could. But know that I've seen you f-fight. I'm better, but I'm tired of letting things and people decide my f-fate."

The simple honesty behind the comment caused Cyric to laugh and the infectious sound made Crevan join him.

The tension that had filled the room moments before had been lifted. But the situation remained unchanged.

"I cannot let you marry Raelynd. She's mine and I w-w-won't let you have her."

The statement could have been construed as a challenge or even as a threat, but Cyric's instincts said that either interpretation would have been wrong. Crevan had simply intended to communicate where he stood on the subject and was giving Cyric the opportunity to counter. "Do you not believe that a Schellden should be the next laird of the clan?"

"I think Rae Schellden is going to live many years and has no intention of releasing his authority any time soon. W-whoever marries Raelynd w-w-will not have a pulpit to prove themselves on f-for many years."

The point was valid and one that Cyric had not considered before. It added to the reasons he did not want to be the Schellden chieftain, but unfortunately, it did not negate any of the reasons he still sought the role. "Do you understand why I cannot just walk away?"

"And w-w-what about Row-wena?"

"Rowena?" Cyric scoffed and stood up, grimacing. The abrupt reaction to the question prevented him from disavowing his feelings, but neither did he feel the need to open up and discuss them either. "What about her?"

Crevan assessed the man in front of him. He had assumed Cyric craved the role of chieftain for other reasons than that of preserving his honor. But he could find nothing—not passion, eagerness, not even desire for power or prestige—to substantiate that assumption. "You don't actually w-w-want to become a laird, do you?"

Cyric's brows rose a fraction in surprise. His first instinct was to lie and swear that he did, but at the last second he refrained. The blunt question was not intended to insult, but was meant to uncover the truth. A tactic Cyric often applied during negotiations.

Like him, Crevan was also patient, disturbingly insightful, and incredibly candid, all of which made him stand apart from his clansmen. And yet something about Crevan made him unquestionably a Highlander. It was that indefinable quality that Cyric feared he would always be missing. "You are not anything I assumed you to be."

"And that w-was?"

Cyric sat down and decided to be just as open and honest. "I was told that you avoid conversations, but that's not true, is it?"

The accurate assessment caught Crevan by surprise, rendering him momentarily speechless. Even his brothers could not see Crevan as he was, only as they believed him to be. "People assume many things about me that are w-w-wrong. In truth, I just prefer to listen bef-fore I speak."

Understanding flashed in Cyric's eyes. "I sympathize. People decided long ago what I was and have never expended the effort to see who I really am. And before you ask, I will tell you because strangely, I think you might understand.

"I am a man without a home. I always have been. I'm a Highlander. I look like one and in the Lowlands I am told that I act like one, but as you are aware, in just the few minutes we have spoken, I am not a Highlander. At least not in the traditional sense. The only place I have ever felt comfortable was at court. There clansmen come from all over Scotland and because I belong in no one particular world I can relate to them all, without letting emotional ties sway my opinion."

"So w-w-why don't you go to court? Be an advisor? Too f-few have that ability and King Robert needs such men, especially w-w-with his plans for England."

The question was legitimate and Cyric was keenly aware of Crevan's scrutiny. "I want to prove to my father that I am a Schellden worthy of his respect," he spoke truthfully.

Crevan got up and went to the small window. It was dirty. The chambermaids had obviously not cleaned the room in a while. Then again, company had not been expected.

When he had walked into the room, he had no idea how to resolve the situation of Cyric marrying Raelynd without entering into physical combat. Crevan certainly had not expected to end up liking Cyric. Who would have thought he had more in common with this Lowlander, this supposed enemy, than he did with most of his own brothers?

Crevan had never bonded and developed lifelong friendships like his brothers had. His unique relationship with Craig was due to their being twins more than personality driven. Essentially, Crevan had always felt alone, mostly because people never saw him for who he was. It had not occurred to him that Cyric could be facing a similar problem. And if he was, then Crevan already knew the solution. The problem lay in that it was not a solution one could just tell someone. It had to be identified by the person themself.

"Do you know w-why I didn't say something last night and w-w-waited until today?"

Cyric shook his head and waited for the answer.

"Because it w-w-wasn't until today that I realized I have been a f-fool. For w-weeks, hell, f-for years, I let my brothers and other people dictate the direction of my life. To f-f-fight their misconceptions about me w-would have taken enormous effort and honestly, I didn't think it mattered. But I realized this morning that letting others decide my f-fate w-w-was about to cost me everything."

"And you tell me this because you think there are similarities in our situations?" Cyric asked, his voice defensive as he rose to his feet once again. "My father did not ask me to become a laird."

Crevan turned and looked the man directly in the eye. They were nearly the same height and of similar build. Physically, neither could intimidate the other. "And yet, he is still the reason you seek the title. Or did I misunderstand? Explain to me again w-w-why you are not marrying the w-w-woman you love. Isn't it so you can assume a lifelong responsibility you don't want in hopes of pleasing someone w-w-who isn't even here?"

White knuckles appeared on Cyric's tightening right hand and Crevan didn't even duck as the fist smashed into his jaw. Insults like the one he had just issued were not ones men walked away from unhurt. But Crevan did not have time for Cyric to come to the same realization he had come to only that morning. Brutal honesty was painful, but it was fast.

Crevan propped himself up on his elbow and stared up for what he was about to say would only cause him to be knocked back down again. "That might make you f-feel better and I don't deny that it was justified, but you and I both know it doesn't change the truth."

"Which is?"

"I w-want to be a laird. The next Schellden laird. I w-w-want to marry Raelynd and spend the rest of my life ensuring the Schellden clan continues f-for many generations. But not a single person thinks I can because of how I speak."

Cyric reached down and clasped Crevan's arm, helping him up. Anger still lurked in the golden depths, but Crevan could see that the man was at least considering what he had to say.

"And how are you going to prove to everyone they are wrong?" Cyric asked.

"By simply doing the job. It w-w-won't happen the day Raelynd and I marry, but in time, people w-will realize the truth. That I can be a good chieftain and a respected ally, even if I do not speak as w-w-well or as smoothly as everyo-o-one else."

"I'm supposed to believe it is that easy, am I?" Cyric scoffed. "Becoming an advisor to the king is far more complicated, not to mention highly unlikely."

"Convincing Rae that I—the last person he considered—should be the next Schellden laird is not going to be easy. May not even be possible. But only if I don't try, w-w-will I have f-f-failed."

Cyric's mouth formed a firm, unyielding line. "We have another problem."

"Row-wena," Crevan exhaled.

A muscle on Cyric's jaw flicked. "Aye. I guess I'm pretty pathetic and easy to read."

Crevan rubbed his aching jaw, recalling her constant chatter about Cyric and how he didn't deserve someone to love him. "No, she is. W-w-what I don't understand is w-why you don't want to marry her."

"I did. I do. She made it clear, however, I was not to ask her."

Crevan chuckled, clearly incredulous. "W-well, after spending a day riding w-w-with her, I'm pretty sure she has changed her mind."

"So what are you suggesting?

"I'm thinking you are about to be right by my side getting married, my f-f-friend."

Cyric grinned. He couldn't believe it. An hour ago he was in a state of deep misery over his fate. Now he was practically eager to live his life. "I believe your priest was expecting to marry two couples today, was he not? It would be a shame to disappoint him."

Before Crevan could respond a loud thump came from the other side of the door. Grabbing the handle, he yanked the door open and two boys fell into a room for the second time that day.

"W-what . . . Braeden . . . Gideon?"

Braeden jumped to his feet and, true to his personality, he pretended he did nothing wrong. "Mama told us to come see you."

Crevan looked at the two boys with skepticism. Neither of them flinched. Gideon wrinkled his nose as he examined a bloody scrape on his elbow. With a shrug, he dropped his arm and said, "I don't think those girls are going to agree to marry either of you."

Crevan pursed his lips to stifle a grin. "You don't?"

Gideon had known all the McTiernays since he was born. His father was the commander of the elite guard, his mother often spent time with Lady McTiernay, and Braeden was his best friend. That he shouldn't speak so bluntly to a member of a very powerful family did not even occur to him.

Braeden bobbed his head, backing his friend's assessment. "That's what we were supposed to tell you. They are really mad at you right now. I think they might stay in that tower forever."

Crevan leaned down as if he was going to divulge a secret. "Do you w-w-want to know o-one of the best things about being a man?" Seeing both heads nod vigorously, he answered, "W-we get to be strong enough to carry the w-w-women w-we love to w-where they need to be."

Cyric laughed in agreement and clapped Crevan on the back. "That's right. Maybe we should show them what we mean."

Braeden grimaced as he watched his uncle and the other man walk out of the room and head for the tower stairwell. "Being strong *never* works for Papa," he whispered to his friend, recalling the one time he had seen his father carry his mother into the Great Hall.

Gideon sighed. "Uh-huh. I don't think your uncle understands how mean girls can get when you try that kind of stuff. Remember when I dropped Brenna in the laundry barrel?" Braeden faked a huge shudder. His sister could not pick them up, but she could put dirt in their food, hide thistle thorns in their clothes, and dump fire ash on them when they weren't expecting. "I guess they never had sisters."

Epilogue

Cyric whirled Rowena around, entranced by her laughter. The Great Hall was filled with McTiernay soldiers and clansmen congratulating Crevan on his marriage. Hardly a soul knew Cyric and only a few more recognized Rowena—a fact that could not make Cyric happier. Crevan and Raelynd were at the center of attention and from what Cyric could see, they had little opportunity to enjoy their new status of husband and wife.

"Thank you, my love," he whispered in Rowena's ear.

"For what?"

"For agreeing to marry me. I'm not sure I could have handled knowing you might decide to disavow me in a year."

Rowena playfully punched his arm. "If you had asked me to handfast with you, you would not have had to wait a year. I would have disavowed you this afternoon!"

"You tried. It didn't work," Cyric reminded her.

"Well, you burst into the room and threw me over your shoulder. How was I supposed to react? Grateful?"

"Aye, my love. Otherwise I couldn't do this right now." Cyric captured her mouth in a deep kiss that left them both breathless.

"You know who should really be grateful—Raelynd and Crevan. If it wasn't for us, I doubt they would be married right now."

Cyric rested his forehead against hers and smiled. "Aye. You are right. Raelynd was most stubborn until we helped Father Lanaghly convince her otherwise."

Rowena pulled back and with a mischievous twinkle in her eye, said, "Well, maybe later tonight I can show you just how grateful I am that you did burst into that room."

Cyric swallowed and decided he could stand no more. He grabbed her hand and no one saw them again until late the next morning.

"I told you it would work," Rae said, his voice full of self-satisfaction.

"I must admit, you were correct . . . this time," Conor agreed grudgingly.

"I was right about your wife too. A month under her guidance and both my daughters have turned into women their mother would be proud of. I don't know how to thank her and you for letting them stay here. I know at times it had to be trying."

"You don't need to," Conor countered, offering a mug of ale to his friend. "What you did for Crevan is more than enough repayment. Not many would recognize the leadership qualities in Crevan with his brother around. You did."

Rae took the mug and watched the young man across the room. He was beaming and each time his eyes connected with Raelynd's his smile only grew. The days would not always be as blissful as they were now, but what the two of them had would form a foundation that would get them through anything.

"Craig is a natural commander of soldiers. In that arena

he is self-assured and an incredible asset to any clan. But I knew from the first time I met Crevan that he could be a great leader and that his greatest challenge in becoming one was himself. Until he realized what he wanted and believed in himself enough to fight for it, he would continue to capitulate to how others saw him."

"Lucky for you, Raelynd was what he wanted."

Rae swirled the ale in the mug and smiled. "Luck had nothing to do with it."

Braeden arched his back and puffed out his chest the way he saw his father do when he wanted to look more powerful. "You both should thank me," he said seriously.

Gideon and Brenna looked at each other and then at him. "And why should we thank you?" Brenna asked.

"Because if it wasn't for me, Crevan wouldn't have gotten married and there wouldn't be a party. It was my idea to listen at the doors. If it wasn't for that, we wouldn't know about them being mad and giving Crevan the idea to carry Raelynd to the chapel. I'm trying to think of the ways you could show your appreciation."

Brenna's jaw dropped open, but Gideon was the first to protest. "If *anyone* should show appreciation, it is you and your sister to *me*," he stated emphatically.

"And how is that?" Braeden challenged.

"You only listened at the door. *I* was the one who got Father Lanaghly to come to the room and convince Raelynd to marry your uncle. I told him that she was mad and that carrying a girl was a bad idea. And I was right. If I hadn't gotten the priest, *no one* would have gotten married today. And I know exactly how you can show me your appreciation. You can do my chores."

Brenna stomped her foot. She absolutely refused to do anyone's chores. Besides, Braeden and Gideon should be thanking *her*. "Neither one of you did *anything*. If it wasn't for me, Raelynd and Rowena would still not know who they loved! I was the one who told them. Until then, they were going to marry the wrong person. Everyone knows that love is more important than anything else."

Gideon started to make gagging noises. "You just proved, Brenna, that you know *nothing* about boys. We don't care about love."

"Then what *do* you care about?"

Braeden shrugged his shoulders and looked at her as if the answer were obvious. "Fighting. And now that Crevan is going to be laird of the Schellden clan, he can fight whoever he wants."

Brenna narrowed her gray eyes and pressed her lips together in anger. "You are *impossible*!"

Gideon watched her stomp off. "I guess it is something girls just don't understand about us until they get older."

Aileen licked her lips, unable to hide her grin. "If only Hagatha were here and not playing midwife," she said.

"Aye," Laurel agreed. "She should be enjoying this victory as well. It was her idea."

Aileen tilted her head in a nod and watched the couple across the room. "If it wasn't for us, I doubt they would have ever gotten together. It was under our guidance that Meriel and Raelynd truly blossomed into beautiful women."

Laurel popped an almond in her mouth. "In truth, my friend, Hagatha may have had the idea, I might have laid out the plan, but it was you who executed it brilliantly."

"Don't forget Fallon. He was the one who guided Meriel," Aileen pointed out.

Laurel waved her hand dismissively. "Fallon simply did the job he always did. He did not have to sit and watch as Raelynd slowly learned from her mistakes. I would have gone mad."

"My contribution was less than a week. You had to guide her the rest of the month."

"You are right. *We* truly pulled off a miracle," Laurel conceded. "If only Hagatha were here to enjoy our success," she sighed again.

"Do you think anyone appreciates us, Fallon?" Fiona posed.

The steward frowned. "Most days I would say no. I doubt anyone truly understands the effort you and I put in daily to see this castle runs as well as it does. But that happy couple over there? They are the exception. I have no doubt that Crevan and Raelynd recognize that it was our activities and support that enabled their union."

"I hope so," Fiona muttered. "I hope they know all the times I made that food just suddenly appear when they needed it, sent it to their rooms and helped Meriel not poison everyone with her meal selections. People forget how important food is to a situation, and not just any food. The right food. That takes time and preparation."

Fallon nodded in agreement. The old cook was by far the most cranky soul who worked at the castle, but he understood why. It was the same reason he was often classified as having a sour attitude. Taking care of everyone and anticipating their needs was extremely taxing.

Added to that, the responsibility of guiding and helping not just Meriel, but Raelynd was very difficult. One had to choose the lessons very carefully, knowing that Meriel would discuss them with her sister. It was through those chats that Raelynd and Meriel had grown as women, and now Raelynd possessed the skills to be a great lady.

The facts were inarguable. Without him and Fiona, Raelynd would not have turned into the woman with whom Crevan fell in love. This family once again was in his debt.

"Look at your father," Crevan instructed Raelynd when they got a moment alone.

Raelynd smiled. "He looks happy. I think he is glad I finally agreed to marry."

"Aye," Crevan said under his breath, "but he doesn't look surprised."

Raelynd took another look at her father. "What do you mean?"

"Simply, that he is strangely at ease with all that has happened. I have seen your father surprised before and trust me, that is *not* the expression he wears."

Raelynd grimaced, finally understanding what her husband was hinting at but finding it hard to believe. "Maybe he just has had enough time to get used to the idea or maybe he is just pretending so as not to alarm anyone into thinking he is unhappy with our union."

Crevan gave his wife a squeeze and said no more, letting her believe that her arguments explained her father's behavior. But he was far from convinced.

The man learned that Raelynd was not to join with Cyric, his nephew, but a fourth son of a neighboring clan. He agreed too quickly to Crevan being named as the

Schellden heir, and the fact that they had not handfasted but married had not fazed Rae in the slightest.

Crevan had never met a better strategist when it came to human interactions than Rae Schellden. A month ago, when Rae first persuaded them into the ruse, Crevan had been suspicious of his motives.

"You really think my father orchestrated this whole thing?" Raelynd teased.

Crevan frowned and nodded with a taut jerk of his head. "I do."

"But my father coupled you with Meriel and me with Craig," she reminded him. "Do you really believe he planned for us to switch partners and then for you and I to fall in love knowing how much we didn't care for each other? And what about Cyric and Rowena? Were they part of his grand scheme too?"

"Maybe you're right," he conceded. "That much planning would be too much even for a McTiernay. Besides, your father had no control over what happened while you were here. And that is when everything changed."

Raelynd rested her cheek on Crevan's chest so that he couldn't see her face. But while she didn't think it possible for anyone, including her father, to arrange all that happened that led to today's vows, she was not at all sure that none of it was planned.

From the very beginning Laurel had seemed to be aware of the true nature of their relationship. And she was behind much of what had happened to her and her sister. Crevan was wrong.

Raelynd lifted her head up and smiled. Plans to orchestrate events to lead up to their wedding might have been impossible for the male side of the McTiernay clan, but thank the good Lord, McTiernay women were more than capable of achieving such a mission.

* * *

"Look at them," Craig said, with mock disgust.

Meriel laughed and elbowed his side. "You are just jealous. You wish you could be that happy."

"I *am* that happy," Craig argued. "And it is precisely because I am *not* married."

"I thought all you men were eager to find wives who adored you and were willing to do anything you asked."

A deep chuckle bubbled in his chest. "Ahh, how mistaken you are. Besides, I am not sure that description fits your sister."

"She adores Crevan."

"And can you see her doing anything he asked?"

Meriel bit her bottom lip and flashes of her experiences with Raelynd ran through her mind. She loved her sister, and while Raelynd was much more appreciative and understanding, she was still the stubborn, opinionated person she always had been. And Crevan, he was never going to be the life of the party. He was steady and solid, but she could not see him matching Raelynd's excitement for life. "No," she finally answered. "I almost feel sorry for them now that I think of it."

Craig nodded and gave her a quick, platonic hug. "I'm glad we are just friends. We have everything they do without all the complications."

"I agree," Meriel said, leaning against his hard frame. Marriage meant change and compromise. Neither of which she could see herself desiring.

"Promise me we will never fall in love."

Meriel sighed and her mouth curved into an unconscious smile. "Don't worry. I am quite certain we are both smart enough to avoid that fate."

More by Bestselling Author
Hannah Howell

__Highland Angel	978-1-4201-0864-4	$6.99US/$8.99CAN
__If He's Sinful	978-1-4201-0461-5	$6.99US/$8.99CAN
__Wild Conquest	978-1-4201-0464-6	$6.99US/$8.99CAN
__If He's Wicked	978-1-4201-0460-8	$6.99US/$8.49CAN
__My Lady Captor	978-0-8217-7430-4	$6.99US/$8.49CAN
__Highland Sinner	978-0-8217-8001-5	$6.99US/$8.49CAN
__Highland Captive	978-0-8217-8003-9	$6.99US/$8.49CAN
__Nature of the Beast	978-1-4201-0435-6	$6.99US/$8.49CAN
__Highland Fire	978-0-8217-7429-8	$6.99US/$8.49CAN
__Silver Flame	978-1-4201-0107-2	$6.99US/$8.49CAN
__Highland Wolf	978-0-8217-8000-8	$6.99US/$9.99CAN
__Highland Wedding	978-0-8217-8002-2	$4.99US/$6.99CAN
__Highland Destiny	978-1-4201-0259-8	$4.99US/$6.99CAN
__Only for You	978-0-8217-8151-7	$6.99US/$8.99CAN
__Highland Promise	978-1-4201-0261-1	$4.99US/$6.99CAN
__Highland Vow	978-1-4201-0260-4	$4.99US/$6.99CAN
__Highland Savage	978-0-8217-7999-6	$6.99US/$9.99CAN
__Beauty and the Beast	978-0-8217-8004-6	$4.99US/$6.99CAN
__Unconquered	978-0-8217-8088-6	$4.99US/$6.99CAN
__Highland Barbarian	978-0-8217-7998-9	$6.99US/$9.99CAN
__Highland Conqueror	978-0-8217-8148-7	$6.99US/$9.99CAN
__Conqueror's Kiss	978-0-8217-8005-3	$4.99US/$6.99CAN
__A Stockingful of Joy	978-1-4201-0018-1	$4.99US/$6.99CAN
__Highland Bride	978-0-8217-7995-8	$4.99US/$6.99CAN
__Highland Lover	978-0-8217-7759-6	$6.99US/$9.99CAN

Available Wherever Books Are Sold!

Check out our website at
http://www.kensingtonbooks.com

More from Bestselling Author
JANET DAILEY

Calder Storm	0-8217-7543-X	$7.99US/$10.99CAN
Close to You	1-4201-1714-9	$5.99US/$6.99CAN
Crazy in Love	1-4201-0303-2	$4.99US/$5.99CAN
Dance With Me	1-4201-2213-4	$5.99US/$6.99CAN
Everything	1-4201-2214-2	$5.99US/$6.99CAN
Forever	1-4201-2215-0	$5.99US/$6.99CAN
Green Calder Grass	0-8217-7222-8	$7.99US/$10.99CAN
Heiress	1-4201-0002-5	$6.99US/$7.99CAN
Lone Calder Star	0-8217-7542-1	$7.99US/$10.99CAN
Lover Man	1-4201-0666-X	$4.99US/$5.99CAN
Masquerade	1-4201-0005-X	$6.99US/$8.99CAN
Mistletoe and Molly	1-4201-0041-6	$6.99US/$9.99CAN
Rivals	1-4201-0003-3	$6.99US/$7.99CAN
Santa in a Stetson	1-4201-0664-3	$6.99US/$9.99CAN
Santa in Montana	1-4201-1474-3	$7.99US/$9.99CAN
Searching for Santa	1-4201-0306-7	$6.99US/$9.99CAN
Something More	0-8217-7544-8	$7.99US/$9.99CAN
Stealing Kisses	1-4201-0304-0	$4.99US/$5.99CAN
Tangled Vines	1-4201-0004-1	$6.99US/$8.99CAN
Texas Kiss	1-4201-0665-1	$4.99US/$5.99CAN
That Loving Feeling	1-4201-1713-0	$5.99US/$6.99CAN
To Santa With Love	1-4201-2073-5	$6.99US/$7.99CAN
When You Kiss Me	1-4201-0667-8	$4.99US/$5.99CAN
Yes, I Do	1-4201-0305-9	$4.99US/$5.99CAN

Available Wherever Books Are Sold!

Check out our website at www.kensingtonbooks.com.